"I'm glad you came here for ⌐

Nola paused, taking in his words. It was probably the nicest thing he'd ever said to her...and also the most intimate. "I'm...I'm glad I did, too. Last night was fun. We haven't really hung out one-on-one before."

He flipped the last few pancakes onto the plate and then turned off the burner. He pushed the pan back on the stove top, making sure it wasn't next to the edge. Wiping his hands off on a towel, he deposited it back on the counter and stepped closer to her. His voice was low, almost husky, as he finally spoke. "I wonder if we didn't miss a lot of opportunities."

She swallowed hard, unable to find the words to respond. All she could think about was the way his eyes pierced through her and made her feel shaky, like her knees were going to wobble and give way at any moment. He reached forward and ran a hand down her arm, starting at her shoulder and ending at her fingers. Then his fingers were intertwined with hers and he was pulling her to him.

And she went.

Dreaming
of a Heart Lake
Christmas

Dreaming
of a Heart Lake
Christmas

SARAH ROBINSON

FOREVER

NEW YORK   BOSTON

Copyright © 2022 by Grand Central Publishing
The Christmas Wish copyright © 2019 by Melinda Wooten

Cover art and design by Daniela Medina. Cover photos © Shutterstock.
Cover copyright © 2022 by Hachette Book Group, Inc.

Forever
Hachette Book Group
1290 Avenue of the Americas, New York, NY 10104
read-forever.com
twitter.com/readforeverpub

First Edition: September 2022

Forever is an imprint of Grand Central Publishing. The Forever name and logo are trademarks of Hachette Book Group, Inc.

The publisher is not responsible for websites (or their content) that are not owned by the publisher.

The Hachette Speakers Bureau provides a wide range of authors for speaking events. To find out more, go to www.hachettespeakersbureau.com or call (866) 376-6591.

ISBNs: 9781538755082 (mass market), 9781538755075 (ebook)

Printed in the United States of America

OPM

10 9 8 7 6 5 4 3 2 1

To Norah Grace

Acknowledgments

To my husband and daughter, thanks for being such inspirations in my own happily-ever-after that I wanted to keep writing them for everyone else.

To Nicole Resciniti at The Seymour Agency, having you as my agent for almost the last decade has been an incredible journey in growth, friendship, and more. Thank you for all you do to support me every day.

To Lea and Emily at et al Creative, thank you for your kindness, understanding, and compassion toward me and my life circumstances while working on this book. You showed incredible kindness when my daughter was sick, and that isn't something I'll ever forget.

To the readers, I can't wait to get to know you more and for you to get to know me and my work more. Please feel free to find me online or join my Facebook group anytime: Facebook.com/groups/RobinsonsRamblings.

Dreaming of a Heart Lake Christmas

Prologue

Twenty Years Ago

Tanner Dean frowned as he stood in front of his parents' sprawling Victorian lake house, loosening his black tie. The somber drone of guests milling around the living room and reminiscing about his mother's life sounded like melancholic white noise from the driveway. He rolled his shoulders, his muscles straining against the too-tight formal jacket. He hadn't worn this suit since his baseball awards dinner last year, and it barely fit over his broadening teenage shoulders. Dozens of cars filled the wide tree-lined street and spilled over into his neat front yard.

He walked over to the red pickup truck that was half on the thick green grass and half on the driveway, glaring at the deep grooves the tires had left in the dirt. He'd only just gotten his license a year ago, but even at his age, he knew the damage a heavy truck could have on someone's yard.

That was the last thing he wanted his dad to have to deal with after today.

"Tanner?"

He turned around to see his younger sister's best friend approaching him.

"They are, um...they are about to start the slide show." Magnolia Bennett looked down at her hands, fidgeting with her dark red painted nails. "Your dad asked me to find you so you could join."

"Do you see all this, Nola?" He waved his hand toward the de facto parking lot that had sprung up. "It's a complete mess."

She looked around, her brows knitting. "What?"

"The grass." Tanner squatted down to survey the damage closer. "See what this guy's tires did? That's going to take a lot of landscaping work to fix."

Nola placed a hand on his shoulder and guided him back to a standing position. "We can figure out the yard tomorrow. Let's go inside."

His eyes found hers, and he paused for a moment as he registered the concern in her expression. He glanced behind her toward the house. Two women stood on the front porch dressed in black dresses, both crying as they spoke, their blond heads close together—one was his old third-grade teacher, the other the president of the PTA. His mother had been adored in Heart Lake, and her funeral this morning had certainly been an example of just how deep that love had run.

His stomach churned at the thought of walking back into that house—into that crowd. All the open feelings. The hugs and empty apologies. Sweat pooled against his collar as he imagined it.

"Not yet," he replied, his voice slightly above a whisper. He cleared his throat. "I'm just...just...Not yet. Okay?"

Nola nodded, her eyes soft. "Okay."

He looked around, unsure of what he wanted to do instead. He felt lost, and everything seemed so overwhelming that he couldn't seem to form a coherent thought in his head. Despite the fact that he'd known this was coming, he still felt surprised. His mother had been battling breast cancer for years, but the last six months had taken a dramatic turn that had been difficult for his entire family to watch.

"I have some poster board in the trunk of my car left-over from the career fair at school," Nola added after a quiet moment had passed between them. "What if we made some signs telling people where to park?"

Tanner hesitated, and the corner of her full lips curled in a soft smile.

"I won't make you talk, or ask how you're feeling," she added. "Deal?"

He nodded, grateful that she seemed to understand what he needed. He didn't want to say anything—he was too empty for that. But it would be good to have something to do with his hands, anything to be useful on this day when he felt so helpless. "Yeah. Let's do that."

She led him to her small coupe parked against the curb halfway down the block. Nola popped open her trunk and handed him a few pieces of poster board and a handful of markers. "I don't have any stakes to put them in the ground, but I have tape. We could tape one to the mailbox or something like that."

"I can get some stakes from the shed." Tanner placed the blank poster board on top of the hood of her car and began writing parking instructions in large, black letters. "And I think we have a staple gun in there, too."

"That's a good idea," Nola agreed, working beside him on an off-center red NO PARKING sign.

They worked quickly and quietly, finishing the signs and gathering a few wooden stakes and a staple gun. Nola helped him position each board as he stapled it into place and stuck it in the ground. When they were finished, Tanner felt a tension ease in his chest. He watched Nola as she straightened the last sign and stepped back. Ironically, this had been the

longest amount of time they'd spent around one another that
hadn't involved arguing. It wasn't that he didn't like her, but
Magnolia was younger than him and was his kid sister's
annoying friend. She tended to be a bit bratty and spoiled,
but right now he didn't see any of that. He'd seen her and
his cousin Amanda holding Rosie's hand during the service.
They seemed to keep his sister upright throughout the entire
funeral and that meant the world to him. He needed to know
Rosie was okay, but he didn't have the emotional bandwidth
to step in himself. It comforted him to know that she had
people who could do that for her.

"Ready to go inside?" he asked Nola, though he was really
asking himself.

She nodded but didn't speak. Instead, she slid her arm
around his and walked with him back toward the house. He
appreciated the gesture, even though she was much shorter
than he was and he had to bend sideways to accommodate
the height difference. Nola Bennett might just be his sister's
best friend, but he supposed she wasn't so bad overall.

Hell, she just might be the one good part of today.

Chapter One

It had been some time since Magnolia Bennett had seen the giant lit-up mechanical pine cone in the middle of the town square in Heart Lake, Michigan. A long-held holiday tradition, it perfectly encapsulated the whimsical nature of Nola's small hometown. A smile tilted the corners of her perfectly glossed lips as she drove past the reminder of childhood memories and turned off of Main Street to find herself pulling into the Hobbes Grocery Store parking lot.

Putting the car in park, Nola took a minute to stare out her windshield at the familiar storefront decorated with red-and-green wreaths and Christmas trees to celebrate the upcoming holiday. The last time she was here had been for her grandmother Gigi's funeral, and while that had been almost a year ago, she still wasn't sure she could bear all the old reminders of someone she had cherished so much. Which Hobbes would no doubt be chock-full of—both memories and people who would want a piece of her.

After taking a deep breath through her nose, Nola exhaled slowly out of her mouth. There was no escaping the errand tonight. After all, she needed to stock up on food—and wine, of course—before hunkering down for the next week or two at her grandmother's home, also known lovingly as "The Castle" by those around town. It was a historic site for the area, reminiscent of an era long gone, and Gigi had left the entire place to Nola in her will. She had been shocked when she'd found out, but there was no doubt Gigi would have done something so kind as her dying wish. It was the type of person she was. She had wanted Nola to succeed, and the money from the sale of the house would certainly help Nola launch her own consulting practice. Gigi had always supported Nola's dreams—so much, in fact, that she'd helped pay for her MBA at Northwestern and still found the time to send her a dozen of her famous snickerdoodles on the first of every month. Those were much appreciated given Nola's complete inability to cook, or bake, or do anything remotely domestic.

Thankfully, she already had a buyer for The Castle lined up—Craig, her former high school boyfriend, who now ran a very successful real estate development company in the area. His plans to turn the lot into an upscale waterfront condominium complex next spring was certainly going to benefit the town by bringing in new, wealthier residents that could finally put Heart Lake on the map. Western Michigan wasn't a bustling metropolis, and so modernizing the homey old towns seemed like a great way to help it catch up to the times.

At least, that was what Nola had decided to tell herself.

Grabbing her purse, she stepped out of her car and found herself sliding slightly on the icy ground as she made her way to the store's entrance. High heels might not have been the best choice for the current weather, but where she had come from, convenience was compromised for beauty. Chicago certainly wasn't New York or Los Angeles, but it had the Magnificent Mile, and a young woman in the business world was expected to look the part. With sharp heels, tight pencil skirts, and a blazer that reminded everyone she was there to make a statement, Nola had found herself quickly enveloped by the bustling city when she'd first gone there for college and then never left. Gigi had often gently remarked that Nola hadn't come home enough, but it had always been hard to find the time to visit because of her job as a senior manager at a business consulting firm. She'd like to say she had a thriving social life that kept her busy as well, but that wouldn't be honest. True, she had a great spin class worth rolling out of bed at 6:00 a.m. for five days a week and a gaggle of friendly coworkers to grab a coffee or cocktail with on the nights she didn't work late. But was it home?

No. It was work. Heck, she barely ever saw the inside of her Wrigleyville condo during daylight hours, let alone the nearby baseball stadium.

Still, she was happy—busy, yes, but she was going places. You don't get to rise up the ladder if you aren't willing to put in the effort.

"Can it be?" Nola lifted her eyes to see a woman standing just inside the doorway of the quaint grocery store. Adorned in a brightly colored knitted poncho, her grandmother's best friend, Marvel, stepped in for a hug. "My God, it *is* you! How long are you home for?" The tiny woman wrapped her arms around Nola and squeezed tightly before taking a step back and clapping her hands. "Good Lord, you smell lovely. What's that perfume you're wearing?"

"Chanel." A warmth crept up Nola's cheeks. "Gigi gave me my first bottle on my sixteenth birthday and I guess it's my signature now."

"It's perfectly Magnolia." Marvel inhaled deeply. "Classy yet sweet."

Few people still called her by her full name, but Nola didn't mind. Marvel had always been one of her favorite people—a local potter who was every bit the aged hippie, she had been close friends with Gigi for years. It was an unusual friendship in many ways, since Gigi had been at

least twenty years older than Marvel and every bit the sup-
porter of etiquette and sophistication that Marvel couldn't
care less for. Gigi was known for her high collars, pearls,
and ability to transport guests back to the Victorian age
when they would visit The Castle. Somehow, though, the
two women had become best friends despite having almost
nothing in common. Marvel owned a clay studio in town
and did unusual events like pot throwing and smash-the-art
nights. Gigi had always claimed throwing pots was the perfect cure for her arthritis, and admittedly, Nola had enjoyed
a few nights smashing clay sculptures herself.

"Well, I am actually back in town to do a little work. Just
here to grab some food and supplies for the week. I'm staying at Gigi's for the holidays." She tossed her light-brown
hair over her shoulder and tried to smooth the wrinkles out
of her jacket.

Marvel clapped her hands together. "How is The Castle? I
miss that place. Heck, I miss your grandmother. I loved that
woman's spirit fiercely. It's so wonderful that you're able to
come back for a visit. Are your parents coming for the holidays as well?"

Nola shook her head. "I wish, but they are on a tropical
vacation in a Costa Rican cloud forest for the month."

"Costa Rica?" Marvel lifted her graying brows. "I'm surprised you're not there with them!"

"They offered, but I wanted a bit of old-fashioned holiday spirit this year." Though, the truth was she was going
to be preparing the home to be sold. She wasn't quite ready
to tell that to Marvel, however. She wasn't sure why, but it
just felt like a decision that might cause some backlash...
Better to put it off. "Plus, they've never had much time just
to themselves. I think they deserve a romantic trip in their
retirement."

"You're absolutely right, darling. I always said I was going to travel the world one day, but here we are." Marvel shrugged her shoulders, then pointed to a back aisle. "Hey, do you know what they just started stocking? Plant burgers. Can you believe it? It looks like meat, except without the murder and torture of innocent animals."

Nola snorted, trying not to laugh out loud. Marvel was a staunch vegan and only recently had more and more options become available to her in such a small town. "I have heard of them before but never tried one," she admitted.

"Let's do tea at The Castle later this week. I'll bring some with me and we can sit out on the porch overlooking the water. That view of the lake...can't beat it!"

She nodded, though she wasn't interested in making big commitments with her time right now. "Sure, we can do tea."

"Great! I'll give you a call a bit later. I have to dash, darling, but we have so much to catch up on!" Marvel gave her an exuberant wave and then headed out into the cold air.

Nola turned back toward the store and grabbed a small cart as she began wandering the aisles. The selection was limited compared to what she was used to in Chicago, but she did manage to find a few favorites—a few bags of rice cakes, some holiday-themed Oreos, and a couple of frozen dinners. Plus all the wine. She'd stocked up on several bottles of red, as well as some dark roast coffee.

Priorities.

"Why, Magnolia Bennett! Aren't you a sight for sore eyes?" Perry Mott stood in the middle of the liquor aisle holding a bottle of rum. As Heart Lake High School's beloved woodshop teacher, Perry was a favorite among every alum.

"Hi, Mr. Mott," Nola greeted the older gentleman, wondering when he'd aged so much. She'd only seen him a year ago or so, but he seemed more frail and tired than before, despite the big smile on his face. "I see you're stocking up for your famous eggnog."

"Perry, please." He lifted the bottle of rum proudly. "My annual Heart Lake High School faculty party is coming up! You should come!"

"I'm not faculty," she reminded him.

He waved a hand like that was nonsense. "But you like eggnog, and that's all that really matters."

"Thanks, Mr. er...Perry. You'll have to save me some!" Nola gave him a quick hug before snatching up a fourth bottle of wine and heading back to the cashier. She had always loved Heart Lake, and there was no doubt that the people of this town were kind and loving. But she was here on a mission. She wanted to get in and out and call it a day. Honestly, every time she ran into someone she knew or thought of walking into The Castle, her heart squeezed a little with the painful thought that Gigi wouldn't be wandering these streets anymore.

Climbing into her car with her purchases, Nola set off for The Castle. Her route took her back down Main Street. The quaint shops lining the street had the perfect small-town charm that was classic Americana, and they were all beautifully decorated for the holidays with lights, wreaths, trees, and more. But Nola knew behind each shop window was a struggling small-business owner trying to stay afloat. In Chicago, her job was to help mom-and-pop businesses build and grow, so it was impossible not to see her hometown and think of how much they were missing out on. A few small changes to diversify sales and build a robust commerce platform with a little out-of-the-box thinking could revive these little businesses into national treasures.

Ideas for improving the small businesses in Heart Lake

began churning in her brain, but her thoughts were interrupted by the loud ringing of her cell phone. Her car was
equipped with Bluetooth, so she clicked the button on her
steering wheel to connect the call over her speakers.

"Hello?" Nola answered, mentally praying, *please don't
be work, please don't be work.*

"Nola, darling, I was just inquiring… have you managed
to send Spades the plan for their new social media han-
dles?" Her boss—Charles St. John, the British-born CEO
of St. John Consulting, one of Chicago's biggest marketing
firms—had a discordant, reedy voice that had the same
effect on her ears as an elementary schooler playing the
recorder. No doubt he was calling to mansplain something
she already knew perfectly well. Charles didn't even bother
to say hello or ask how she was doing. "It was due today, you
know."

"I sent it to them yesterday," she confirmed. Spades was
a new distillery company that they were helping to promote.

"And did you include the promotions with the other businesses from the local bar and restaurant association? It's
very important to have cross-promotion from related businesses in a launch like this one. We need them all to want to
stock this brand."

Nola rolled her eyes, her nostrils flaring at the useless
information. Still, she kept her tone steady and professional
as she responded, "Yes, Charles. Everything is ready to go."

This was exactly why she needed to sell The Castle and
leave her job. She wanted to start her own consulting practice where she'd be the boss, rather than doing all the work
while men like Charles took the credit. There wasn't a doubt
in her mind that she'd do all the legwork, and then he'd take
credit in front of the clients as though he'd done the entire
project himself. In a male-dominated industry, she was

beginning to see a pattern of that happening, and it was time to make some changes.

But first, she needed to find the resources to launch her own female-forward small-business consulting firm.

"Great," Charles responded, then launched into a long tirade about business-to-business sales that she'd heard a dozen times. Heck, she'd probably written the script. She gripped the steering wheel a little tighter, trying to practice slow belly breathing to keep herself from snapping at him. All that yoga and meditation came in handy sometimes.

Suddenly, a snowball flew out of nowhere and slammed into the driver's side window.

"Shit!" Nola yelled, completely caught off guard by the loud *thunk*.

"Excuse me?" Charles responded. "Did you just say my pitch was shit?"

Nola grimaced. "Oh, no! Sorry, Charles. I'm driving and something hit my car. I'll call you back!"

She definitely was not going to call him back but quickly hit the end button and pulled her car over to the curb to ensure everything was fine. Her heart was still pounding in her chest at the scare, but she tried to shake it off as she unbuckled and stepped out into the snow. Her toes immediately curled in her heels at the cold moisture seeping through.

"Aunt Magnolia!" Little voices cheered her name as another snowball whizzed right past her head.

Becca and Zander, her best friend's twins and her god-children, were waving to her from a few yards away. Piled high in jackets and outdoor gear, their little cherub faces were rosy from the cold as they bounced toward her with arms wide open. Her first instinct was to scold them for hitting her car and causing a potentially dangerous scenario, but the look of adoration in their eyes was enough to still her annoyance and make her open her arms to them for a hug as well.

"Becca, Zander! Oh, I've missed you!" She wrapped the twins in her arms and squeezed them.

They squealed and squirmed, soaking her dress with their snow-covered jackets.

"Who is supposed to be watching you two?" Nola asked. "You can't be out here all by yourself. You could have caused an accident!"

"Uncle Tanner is babysitting while Mama's at the store," Becca informed her, and Nola immediately gritted her teeth.

Of course Tanner would be somehow tied to this fiasco. He might be Heart Lake's favorite bachelor—and one of the hottest, most ruggedly handsome men she'd ever seen—but anytime he was around Nola, all they did was bicker. She was going to find him and give him a piece of her mind.

Chapter Two

"It's still leaning to the left!"

Tanner Dean rubbed a calloused hand across his forehead and brows, trying to swallow the irritation building in him, while his other hand held steady a twenty-foot-tall Christmas tree in his father's vaulted-ceiling living room. He pushed the tree more toward the right. "How's this?"

"Now it's too far to the right. The base isn't even. You'll have to take it down and cut it," Thomas Dean replied, barking orders from the stuffed recliner that had definitely seen better days. The rest of Thomas's living room and his entire house was professionally decorated—Tanner's sister, Rosie, had enlisted their cousin Amanda's help with that—and it was beautiful enough to be photographed in *Home Digest*, except for the plaid recliner with loose threads and faded patches placed in the center of the living room with perfect proximity to the fireplace to feel the warmth on cold winter nights. With the damn chair aimed squarely at the television, it was a safe bet that is where Tanner would find his father if he ever needed him.

Tanner still had memories of his mother arguing with his father over how ugly the chair was. In fact, he was pretty sure that his father had kept it all those years just to annoy her. After she'd passed away from breast cancer while Tanner was still in high school, his father had never really been the same. He was pretty sure he kept the chair now as a token of her memory. If there was one thing he'd known about his parents, it was how deeply they loved each other—and how passionately they argued with one another. He didn't remember a day when the two weren't on opposite sides of an issue, but their love and dedication to each other and their children was unwavering.

Tanner and his father weren't in complete agreement about everything either, but Tanner did appreciate how his dad had stepped up and taken care of Rosie and him after their mother had died. He cooked dinner for them every night, always welcomed their friends over with a hot pot of chili, and still made it to watch every game Tanner played while also running a successful local business. He was ornery in his old age, but there was no doubt that he was a good man and an even better father.

"Dad, it's even. I already made sure of it before I put it in the stand. Just tell me if it's straight, will you?" Tanner grabbed the saw and went to work at the base of the tree, attempting to flatten the trunk to allow for a straighter edge. Hopefully then it would stand up in a simple line and his father could return to his shows.

"No, I think the base is uneven," Thomas remarked before taking a sip of his dark beer.

Tanner sent up a silent prayer for patience before shifting the tree a bit to the left and then back to its original spot. "Now?"

He was trying his best to be understanding, but a *please* or *thank you* here or there certainly might have helped the situation. Tanner knew that his father's bad back was keeping him from being part of the holiday prep, as well as from his work at Dean & Son Custom Construction. That didn't make it any less frustrating to get unsolicited advice on how to saw a tree when Tanner himself was a professional woodworker. Dean & Son Custom Construction wasn't a one-man show, and Tanner had come on board against his better judgment at the behest of his father. It wasn't that he hated it—in fact, he was very talented at all things construction and woodworking. Genetics clearly carried skills down a generation. But Tanner also didn't love it. He saw the passion in his father's eyes when he used to work, and that same feeling was missing for Tanner. Still, however, it was his father's dream to leave the company to him. So, here they were.

"If you're going to do something, do it right," Thomas continued to rant from the recliner.

A loud pounding came from the front door.

"What in the heck?" Thomas jolted in his chair and turned to look at the door. "Who is that?"

Tanner stood up abruptly and unceremoniously dumped the tree on the living room carpet to go find out the answer.

"You can't just leave it like this," his dad protested. "You're getting pine needles all over the carpet!"

Tanner shrugged his shoulders. "I have to answer the door. It's probably some carolers from Grace Lake Church down the street."

Truthfully, some young kids singing Christmas songs badly would be an enjoyable break from the tension in the Dean household. Tanner swung open the large wooden front door, smiling wide when he suddenly froze.

Nola Bennett was standing on the front porch with his niece and nephew in either hand. Former queen bee of Heart Lake High School, Nola had been his teenage crush for as long as he could remember. She was older now as she stood in front of him with her jaw tight and her nostrils flared—the typical irritated expression she always had when they were around one another. But age had done nothing to dim her beauty. Her brown hair now had red highlights that perfectly matched the rosy tone of her flushed cheeks, and her deep-brown eyes were as piercing as they always were. Her nose was pointed, but in a way that fit her face perfectly and gave her an edge that matched her personality. Despite their history of bickering over literally everything and the fact that there had never been so much as a single romantic moment between them, Tanner had never found anyone who interested him half as much as she did.

"Tanner Dean, you are the worst babysitter I have ever seen," Nola announced without waiting a beat.

Tanner quickly pushed aside his thoughts, because clearly this was not a social visit. "Excuse me?"

Nola dropped the children's hands and pointed a finger at Tanner. "Rosie left the twins in your care and I find them out in the street throwing snowballs at cars? Alone in the dark? I almost swerved off the road and crashed!"

"I told them to stay in the front yard." Tanner shot a disapproving look at his niece and nephew, his head cocked to the side.

"I couldn't help it, Uncle Tanner! It's so snowy!" Zander ducked his gaze, ran off the porch, and threw his body into a snow pile. Pushing up out of the cold fluff, the young boy launched a snowball directly at Tanner. It landed square on his chest, startling him.

"Gotcha!" Zander squealed.

"Oh, now you're going to pay." Tanner used his deepest voice, the one the kids thought was hilarious when he was actually trying to sound scary. It rumbled in his chest and he didn't miss the surprised look on Nola's face as she considered him. He hadn't been able to hit those deep notes in high school, but it was a different story now, and he could tell that she recognized the change. "Let me grab my gloves."

"Wait, this is not—" Nola looked between him and the kids, but Becca had run to join her brother and they were stockpiling snowballs in a hurry. "Okay, I guess we're doing this. Tanner, time to dig deep and show 'em what you got! Are you ready?"

He tossed her a pair of gloves from the closet by the front door and pulled on his own worn leather pair. "Born ready."

Nola lifted one brow, but a smirk quirked the corner of her lips. She pulled on the gloves he'd given her and grabbed at some snow on the railing to begin rolling into a ball. With one swift move, she chucked it right at the side of his head. Icy cold dripped down his stubbled cheek and neck, sliding under the collar of the thermal shirt he was wearing. He shivered as the cool liquid trailed down his muscled chest.

"Hey!" Tanner shouted, amused but pretending not to be. "You're supposed to be on my team!"

She shook her head, but her eyes were sparkling with enthusiasm. "Never. Kids, let's get Uncle Tanner!"

"Yay!" Becca and Zander both began launching snowballs at their uncle as Nola hid behind the porch post and tossed a few his way as well.

Tanner grinned and tried to take cover behind a bush, but three-to-one was a losing battle. "White flag! White flag! I admit defeat," he finally said after his shirt was entirely soaked with icy slush. He waved his arms ceremoniously at the kids, dodging a few last throws. "Time to go inside and get some hot chocolate. It's too cold out here!"

"Hot chocolate with marshmallows!" Zander screamed, instantly forgetting about the snowball fight. He and his sister raced into the house, cheering and shedding wet clothes and outerwear with each step.

"I didn't say anything about marshmallows," Tanner shouted back, but the kids were out of earshot at that point. And there was no way he wasn't going to give them an entire scoop of marshmallows each anyway. While he may not have any kids of his own, Tanner adored his niece and nephew with his whole heart and it was impossible not to spoil them as much as he could.

Nola stepped back onto the porch, batting some snow off her jacket. She shook out her thick brown hair, small snowflakes clinging to her extra-long eyelashes, the cold reddening the tip of her pert nose. With a tired sigh, she arched one of her thick brows that seemed almost too perfect. This woman in front of him felt so much like a stranger. "So, okay, that was fun, but seriously, Tanner. You've gotta watch them more carefully. They could have caused an accident."

She handed him back the gloves he'd given her, then pushed her hands into her jacket pockets for warmth. Although *jacket* was a stretch, because it was more of a windbreaker. Of course she'd come back to town in December only to forget to bring proper gear for the snow. He didn't understand her sometimes. It's not like Chicago was a beach town—plus, she grew up here.

Annoyance tightened his gut as his gaze traveled down to her inappropriate footwear. "My apologies. I wasn't expecting the queen to arrive on her sleigh from the big city. Maybe you forget how we roll out here by the water, but in Heart Lake, kids can play in their neighborhood without adults helicoptering around."

Nola lifted her chin slightly, a look of both frustration and guilt crossing her face. "I'll have you know that Rosie and I keep in touch via text, and we try to do video calls with the kids at least every other month. I may not always be around, but I am still their godmother."

That, he did know. Despite her city lifestyle and complete lack of interest in all things Heart Lake, Nola had always treated his niece and nephew with the most love and affection he'd ever seen. Second to himself, of course. She was undoubtedly an amazing godmother, and anytime he saw her at a family gathering, she was usually fawning over the twins or laughing with his sister.

Admittedly, he found himself watching her a lot longer than he'd like to at those events. They were just so few and far between, considering she'd come to town for a day and then be off to the city again for months. The last time he'd seen her had probably been at her grandmother's funeral. It was a rare occasion where they hadn't fought at all and had been quite civil, actually. He had loved Gigi just as much as everyone in town had, and there was no doubt the loss was hard on Nola. He knew too much about losing a loved one to see it as anything other than completely heart-wrenching.

"Well, why don't you come in for some hot chocolate with us, then? I'll even throw in a few marshmallows," he offered, realizing too late that he wanted her company a lot more for himself than he did for the kids.

"Next time," she said, quickly rejecting his offer with a small wave. "I have to run, but I'll catch up with Rosie and the twins later."

"When I'm not around?" he asked, lifting one brow.

"It would certainly be preferred that way," Nola shot back over her shoulder as she walked to her car.

Tanner chuckled lightly as he watched her tread through the snow in heels, nearly falling a dozen times before she finally made it to her vehicle. God, that woman irritated him so much, and yet…he'd rather watch her drive off into the cold night than return to the Great Tree Debate with his ornery, old father.

Chapter Three

Nola pulled into the circular driveway and stared up at the great three-story Victorian home. When she was little, she imagined the house looked like a fairy-tale castle, and honestly, the description was still accurate. It was too dark to see the lake, but she could tell it was down the hill from the vast black expanse, framed in the distance by twinkling lights from houses on the other side of the water.

"Hey, Gigi, I'm home," she said to herself, a pang in her chest at the fact that all the large windows were dark. Normally, there would be at least three trees decorated for Christmas and a blow-up Santa that was equal parts hideous and hilarious waving from the porch.

The pang in her chest increased as she bumbled through the large, antique front door of The Castle with her arms full of grocery bags and suitcases. Almost dropping everything several times, she made it to the ornamental table in the center of the foyer and placed her items down on and around it. Nola closed the door behind her with a swing of her foot and then let out a deep exhale as she examined her surroundings.

She'd been in this foyer more times than she could count, but it felt different tonight. It *smelled* different—there was a musty scent, probably from the faint film of dust that coated every surface. The curtains were drawn and the darkness added eerily shaped shadows to the walls. It hadn't always been this way. In fact, when Gigi had occupied The Castle, the delicate floral scent from her favorite French perfume had infused the air. Gigi had worn the same signature scent every day of her life, and it was absolutely impossible for Nola to remember her grandmother without thinking of jasmine and ylang-ylang. She took in a deep breath but couldn't smell those flowers, and her heart ached a little at the expectation.

This seems like a good excuse for wine. Nola left her suitcases in the foyer but hauled her groceries to the kitchen. Depositing the bags on the long marble countertop, she fished out a bottle of red wine and went in search of a bottle opener. Gigi had always been more of a tea snob than a wine drinker, so there were dozens of strainers, kettles, and other tea accessories...but Nola couldn't find a bottle opener anywhere.

"Magnolia Bennett!" A high-pitched shriek sounded from the front of the house.

Nola lifted her head and smiled, immediately recognizing the voice of one of her best friends. "In the kitchen!"

The kitchen door flew open seconds later and Rosie Dean walked in, followed by her cousin, Amanda Riverswood. She'd already texted her two lifelong friends the moment she stepped foot in Heart Lake, but their impromptu visit tonight was a welcome surprise. Rosie was the mother of Becca and Zander, and she owned the local bookshop, Fact or Fiction. At thirty-three, Amanda was a year younger than them both and was single, married instead to her very successful interior designer business both locally and throughout the state.

"How are you skinnier every time I see you?" Rosie opened her arms to embrace Nola. "Those damn twins gave me a mommy pouch that is here to stay."

"Worth it, though?" Amanda chimed in, hugging Nola next.

Rosie sighed with a big smile on her face. "Yep. Every tiger stripe. It's all worth it for those little semen demons. Did I tell you that Zander put plastic wrap over the toilet seat last week? I went to sit down and do my business and suddenly there is pee all over the floor. It was a mistake letting him take home that book about pranks."

Nola laughed at Rosie's story but silently thanked the good Lord that she didn't have children yet. "I don't know how you do it. You're an absolute superstar raising those kids alone."

She was one of the only people in the world who knew the real father of Rosie's twins, but that was a topic that her bestie wouldn't entertain for even a moment.

Rosie perched on the stool at the island countertop, leaning forward on her elbows. "Yeah, well, someone's gotta do it. You two aren't adding to the population anytime soon."

"Definitely not." Amanda made the sign of the cross over her chest and forehead. "Don't put those fertility vibes on me."

"Speaking of the twins," Nola continued, opening more drawers in the kitchen in an attempt to find a corkscrew. "You need a new babysitter. The current one has attitude."

She wasn't about to admit that her blood was still pumping after her encounter with Tanner in the snow...in that perfect olive-green thermal shirt that hugged every muscle in his arms and chest. Not that she had noticed his muscles. Jesus, he had so many of them. Sure, he did physical labor every day, but the physique on that man seemed criminal. The adrenaline pumping through her right now was from the exhilaration of the snowball fight, and that was all.

"Hmm. A little birdie told me that you had a run-in with my brother tonight," Rosie teased, wiggling her eyebrows suggestively. "Tanner gave me quite the earful about your encounter and ensuing argument. What are you looking for, by the way?"

Nola held up the wine bottle. "A wine opener, but I swear Gigi might not have one."

"Oh, I do!" Amanda opened her purse and pulled out a corkscrew.

Rosie and Nola both looked at her for a moment, puzzled expressions on their faces.

Amanda shrugged her shoulders and handed over the device. "What?"

"Should I ask why you carry around a corkscrew with you?" Rosie questioned.

"I had more Girl Scout badges than the two of you put together," Amanda replied. "I'm always prepared. Now, crack open that wine because we need to catch up! What's the plan with The Castle? How long are you staying? How are the men in Chicago? How are you?"

Nola chuckled at Amanda's barrage of questions—some things never change—and opened the bottle. She hadn't found wineglasses, but regular glasses would do just fine.

"I'm selling. I'm not sure. Men are men. I'm exhausted." She poured the wine and handed each woman a glass, then took a sip of her own. Warmth slid down her throat and sat in her chest, bringing a dreamy smile to her lips.

"This was exactly what I needed after today," Nola remarked, holding up her glass.

"You and me both," Rosie agreed. "Things are really beginning to stress me out. Don't get me wrong—I love running a bookshop. But with all the big online mammoths in the bookselling space, it's hard to get a foothold as an indie."

"What can you give readers that big retailers can't?" Nola asked, her mind already flooding with ideas of how to improve Rosie's current business plan.

"Uh...late fees on all my bills?" Rosie joked, though Nola could hear the hint of stress behind her words.

"Or...personality. What about making Fact or Fiction

a destination spot? Bring in big authors to do signings or donate time for a meet and greet? People would travel from all over the country to come here!" Nola suggested.

"Hmm...I haven't done an author signing yet." Rose's full lips pursed. "It's such a small store. I don't think authors would be interested."

Nola waved a hand. "That's even better. Exclusivity. Only allow a certain number of people in the store at a time. The rest can wait in a line outside. Then blow up your social media with pictures of the long lines. Everyone will be wondering what they are missing."

"You should definitely do that, Rosie," Amanda agreed. "People love things that are unattainable. Makes it even more desirable."

Rosie nodded, clearly pondering the idea. "Nola, you're pretty good at business consulting. You're obviously in the right field."

"I freaking know it." Nola took another sip of her wine, bigger this time. "You'd think my boss would appreciate me a bit more, but Charles is so old-school. I swear he secretly thinks women should only be in the kitchen."

"Well, if you ever get tired of the big city, I'm sure Heart Lake could use that genius brain of yours," Rosie hinted, though not at all being subtle.

Nola smiled. "You know, if you came to visit more often, you'd see how wonderful Chicago is, too. I know I'm complaining, but also, it's realistically the best place for me to advance my career."

"You try traveling with twins and let me know how that goes," Rosie countered. "But I think I'll definitely be giving your suggestion a shot once the renovations are done."

"Renovations?" Nola asked. She'd assumed her frequent texts with her friends had kept her in the loop, but now she could see there was plenty she was missing out on. How long had it been since she'd caught up with these ladies face-to-face?

It had been a while. Too long.

"Rosie gave me carte blanche to redecorate Fact or Fiction." Amanda clapped her hands together. "I'm going for literary chic—small town meets Hemingway meets *Walden*."

"It's actually not as pretentious as it sounds," Rosie added. "She finally wore me down."

Nola lifted her brows. "How's business around here been going for you, Amanda?"

Her friend gave a weary shrug. "Same old story. It's not like Heart Lake is a thriving metropolis in need of design services regularly. I branch out to some surrounding towns and cities, though, so it's not too bad. Focusing on the state as a whole has been going well, but it's...not a lot. Driving all around isn't that fun."

"I recently saw some interior designers doing everything online, like selling look books and discounted pieces through an online portfolio. Those designers can work globally—location doesn't limit them." Nola picked up her cell phone and typed in a few search terms, then pulled up some recent websites she'd noticed. She pointed her phone toward Amanda. "I wonder if you could add something like this to your business model?"

Amanda took the phone and scrolled through the pictures. "Interesting...I could do my business mostly remote. Or I could offer online services as an additional option to current clients."

"This is why we've missed you," Rosie chimed in before finishing off the last of her wine. "Honestly, it's been way too long since we've all been together in person."

"Agreed on that. Let's not ever let this much time go between catching up." Nola poured her friend another glass.

"And I hope you miss me for more than my sparkling business acumen." She pushed aside the uncomfortable thought that she didn't have much else going on these days but work, work, and more work.

"Of course we do," Amanda assured her while topping off her own glass as well. "I miss having another single gal to gossip with."

"Uh, I'm single?" Rosie looked at her cousin. "You gossip to me all the time."

Amanda waved her hand. "Yeah, but you're a mom. You're not on the market."

"Apparently my lady bits were a one-and-done kind of show," Rosie said with a sarcastic laugh, but a noticeable flinch revealed the comment had hit bone.

"No, no, no. You know what I mean!" Amanda insisted.

"Are you dating anyone back in Chicago?" Rosie seemed determined to take the focus off of herself.

Given they were just catching up, Nola decided not to push. There would be time for that later. Instead, she shook her head. "Nothing serious since Dalton. I don't really have the time—plus, everyone in my circle is a corporate bigwig. They're not really my type. They are driven and successful, sure, but...I don't know. They are more interested in the bottom line than the people behind it."

It seemed like a nice, well-reasoned answer, and it was the truth—*mostly*.

The uncomfortable part she didn't share was that she could make time. In fact, she often *wanted* to coordinate schedules with someone else, come home at the end of the day to more than a quiet condo and a take-out menu.

She was...lonely.

"You know who is down-to-earth and cares about people?" Rosie quipped. "Tanner."

"Ooooh, yes." Amanda waggled her brows. "And as far as we know, he's still free as a bird."

"Honestly, that does surprise me," Nola mused, blaming the wine for the sudden dark flush on her cheeks. "I'm always waiting to hear that he's been snatched up by some cute ex-cheerleader turned preschool teacher with a way-too-perky personality."

"Tanner?" Amanda laughed. "I don't think that's his type. I can't even remember the last time I heard of him dating."

"Maybe he's still holding out for a supersmart woman with business savvy..." Rosie added with an insinuating shrug.

Nola eyed her friend with a small smile. Was Rosie implying that she and Tanner would make a good couple? That was definitely not possible. Nola had certainly had secret teenage girl fantasies about him many, many years ago. Hell, everyone in Heart Lake had. Her best friend's big brother was—and was apparently still—the town's favorite bachelor.

She didn't want to admit it to herself, but her heart beat faster even when she saw him today. Still, she didn't have time to sit here pining over a high school crush. She had to get this house sold and her life back in order. After all, her life wasn't in Heart Lake anymore. She needed to move her focus back to Chicago and put down roots in the Windy City.

"I'd assume he's too busy to date anyway," Amanda added. "Dean and Son has seen some big changes lately."

"It has?" Nola asked, wondering why she hadn't kept up-to-date on Tanner and his father's company recently.

Rosie nodded. "They brought in a new employee—Blake. He's actually been incredible. Dad's been slowing down, given his health lately. He just can't keep up with the growing demand, but bringing on Blake really helped with that.

He's fired up about the company, so it's nice to see that passion again. God knows Tanner doesn't have it."

"What do you mean?" Nola remembered nothing but talent when it came to Tanner's history with construction and building. "Tanner is great with wood."

"Oh, definitely," Rosie agreed. "But he doesn't like the business side of things. He loves the craft, but not the paperwork. Maybe I'm reading into things. I don't know. He just seems a bit restless or unhappy. Thankfully, Blake keeps that place running no matter what."

"Hmm. Well, I wonder what that's all about," Nola mused. "I should catch up with Thomas while I'm in town. I haven't seen your dad in a while."

Rosie pulled up a picture of her father with the twins on her phone and showed it to Nola. "He's doing okay, but definitely not as young as he used to be. His back is giving him a lot of problems."

"He always was a hard worker. I'm not surprised it caught up to him eventually. Well, ladies, as much as I've enjoyed our chat, I'm going to have to head to bed soon." Nola finished off the last of her glass of wine and then placed the empty wine bottle—or two—in the recycling bin. "I've got so much to do tomorrow to inventory everything in this place."

"I don't envy that task." Rosie looked around the expansive kitchen. "Gigi had a lot of stuff."

Nola snorted a laugh. "That's an understatement."

Amanda picked up their glasses and went to the sink to begin washing them. "I've got work early tomorrow, too. But let me know if you need help selling any of the antiques. I know some great vendors in the area."

"That would actually be amazing," Nola replied. "And, of course, if there is anything here that you two want, let me know. You all get first dibs."

Rosie nodded, but her face was pulled into a frown. "I still can't believe you're going to let go of this place."

"Yeah," Amanda agreed as she looked around The Castle. "We made a lot of good memories here. Probably half the town could say that."

"You're definitely serious about selling it?" Rosie asked Nola.

Her tone was kind and lacked judgment, but Nola still prickled at her friend's words. Irritation swam through her at knowing her friends weren't completely on board with her plan. It was the right choice from every logical standpoint. For some reason, she continued to feel a need to justify her actions...and was beginning to wonder who she was trying to justify them to.

"I'm absolutely sure." Nola lifted her chin as she walked her friends back toward the front door. "It's definitely the right move. I know Gigi would have supported it."

Amanda nodded before giving her a hug goodbye. "If there is one thing that's for sure, it's that Gigi always wanted the best for you."

"Exactly," Nola agreed.

And selling The Castle was the best for her and her future. She was sure of that. She just wished her friends were, too.

Chapter Four

"Anything else I can get ya?" Mattie, the Black Sheep Diner's bubbly redheaded waitress, leaned closer to Tanner. Her upper arms pushed in tightly to ensure her cleavage was on display, but Tanner kept his steel gaze trained on her face.

"I'd actually love some of that blueberry syrup you all have." Tanner looked down at the stack of pancakes in front of him and felt his stomach growling in response. His sister had always teased him for eating like a kindergartner, but there was nothing better than a stack of sugar-filled pancakes to start the morning. Thankfully, his metabolism was a hard worker and the manual labor aspect of his job meant he burned off every calorie he consumed and more.

"Coming right up." Mattie deflated a little when he didn't take the bait, before stalking off toward the kitchen.

Tanner lifted the ceramic mug to his lips and sipped the black coffee. It was typical diner quality and certainly never going to win any awards, but Tanner loved everything about it. The bitter taste felt like home, just like everything in Heart Lake. He gulped the hot liquid as he glanced around his favorite eatery. The Black Sheep Diner was always packed, no matter what time of day. Being open around the clock meant that it was perfect for every crowd, and right now it was full of hardworking men and women steeling themselves for the day ahead.

"Here you go, Tanner." Mattie returned with the blueberry syrup and deposited it on the counter next to him. "I made sure to get a fresh one just for you."

"Thanks, Mattie." Tanner grabbed the bottle and opened it, pouring a healthy helping onto the top of his short stack.

Mattie paused a little while longer, watching him pour his syrup, before another server called her attention away. Tanner appreciated the reprieve. Mattie was certainly nice, but he wasn't interested in anything romantic with her. She was way too young for him—hell, he'd watched her be crowned homecoming queen a few years ago. Honestly, he wasn't really sure why he was so hesitant to get back into dating. It had been over a year since his last relationship. His ex-girlfriend, Emma, had been kind and personable, but there just hadn't been much of a spark there.

Not like the spark he felt when a certain intense brunette stormed up to his door to yell at him yesterday, the light catching on the subtle red highlights in her hair.

Tanner tried to push the thought of Nola away, but seeing her for the first time in so long had opened floodgates he'd kept barricaded for years. She was back in town to sell her late grandmother's house—and then she'd be gone again. Logically, Tanner knew that there was no way anything beyond being her best friend's brother would ever happen between them. First of all, her entire life was in Chicago now. Tanner absolutely hated big cities. But more than just the location, they were too different. They wanted different things out of their futures.

He had other things to focus on now anyway—like Dean & Son Custom Construction. His father was pushing hard for Tanner to take the lead as his own health declined, and while Tanner certainly wanted to help his father . . . he couldn't say his heart was truly in the construction business.

"How's that syrup?" Mattie returned to the other side of the counter across from him, her eager smile not even slightly dimmed.

Tanner finished a bite and swallowed. "It's delicious. Always is."

"Good." Mattie beamed, as if she had made the syrup herself. "Hey, are you ready for the storm coming our way early next week? I heard the weatherman calling it a 'snow-pocalypse.' Seems like a lot of hoo-ha over a little normal Michigan winter weather."

"Actually, I've been looking at the models." Tanner put down his fork for a moment. "The name's a little silly, but he's right. The coming storm could be really dangerous. Have you checked your generator lately?"

Mattie shook her head, a coy look crossing her face. "I haven't. Maybe you could come over and make sure the motor's running well. I would hate to be stuck without heat. How would I stay warm?"

Tanner didn't miss any of her innuendos, but if there was one thing he was serious about, it was safety during the difficult weather Heart Lake frequently encountered in the winter. He might not be romantically interested in Mattie, but he was still always available to help a neighbor. "I can stop by later today."

"Oh, that would be amazing," Mattie began, but he didn't hear the rest of her sentence as the tinkling entry bell to the diner caught his attention.

Tanner glanced toward the entrance and saw Craig Blasco, former Heart Lake High School quarterback, walking in. In a smooth three-piece suit that seemed out of place for a diner, Craig adjusted his tie and then glanced toward the counter. Their eyes locked for a moment, and Tanner felt his chest tighten with irritation and his jaw clench. It was no secret that he and Craig hadn't been friends in high school or anytime since. Or that he didn't like that Craig had dated Nola once upon a time. He wasn't jealous. Tanner did not get jealous. But he still hated everything about what Craig represented.

The former football star was now an investment developer and he was dead set on turning the sleepy hideaway of Heart Lake into a destination location for well-heeled Chicago tourists. Sure, Tanner could understand wanting to bring more business to the town, but Craig wanted to demolish everything that made Heart Lake special. He planned to turn their favorite fishing spots into pontoon-rental docks with buzzing Jet Skis and chase away any bit of wildlife. The fact that someone from Heart Lake couldn't even appreciate how special this town was . . . It frayed Tanner's last nerve.

"Hey there, Tanny." Craig nodded his head in Tanner's direction.

Tanner hated being called that and knew Craig was well aware of the fact.

"How's the coffee?"

Tanner looked away, focusing his gaze on the dark color of his coffee swirling around in his mug. "Hot."

"Mattie Baby, be a doll and grab me a mug, will ya?" Craig slid into the seat next to him and there was no mistaking where his eyes were roaming as he took in Mattie's low-cut uniform shirt. "I've got a big day."

Tanner felt the muscles in his shoulders tighten as he tried to keep himself from saying something he shouldn't. He tapped his fingers against the side of his mug, trying to find something to say.

"Any new deals, Blasco?" Tanner didn't really want to know, but he was curious how much of his own town was going to be ruined by this frat boy.

"Did you hear about our plans to develop luxury condos on the lake? I'm acquiring a new piece of land that is absolutely perfect for the project." Craig took the mug of hot coffee from Mattie and began dumping pounds of sugar and cream into it. "I'm getting a hell of a deal on The Castle, too. Can't wait to get started on all the new construction. Cha-ching, cha-ching, cha-ching." He mimed an old-fashioned cash register.

He wanted to build luxury condos where Nola's grandmother's house was? That was the last thing he'd expected to hear when he'd asked the question. Tanner's fist tightened and he pushed up from his seat so abruptly that his chair almost fell over. If he stayed here for one more second, he was going to deck the asshole. It had nothing to do with the fact that Craig was going to be working with Nola—nope, not at all. They were all grown up now, and their relationship was over back in high school. No, Tanner was pissed off that Craig didn't respect Heart Lake or its history. He blew into town for the sole purpose of razing historical sites and padding his wallet.

Tanner had no respect for someone like that.

He wiped his mouth with a napkin before depositing it on his plate. He hadn't finished his pancakes, but suddenly his appetite was gone and in its place was swirling fury. Tanner reached into his back pocket and pulled out his wallet, tossing some money on the counter for Mattie before storming out the door of the diner.

"Was it something I said?" Tanner heard Craig ask Mattie in the background, but he didn't stop. He needed out of there—now. Otherwise, he was going to teach Craig what integrity meant to a man.

"Watch it!" Nola nearly ran directly into his chest. "You nearly ran me over."

She was standing on the front sidewalk, wrapped tightly in her faux fur–lined jacket and wearing yet another pair of high heels. It was as if she refused to adjust to the fact that she wasn't in Chicago anymore. Hell, these ones were taller than the last.

"Well, at least I'd be doing my part to help Heart Lake, then," Tanner quipped back, struggling to keep his frustration under control.

Nola cocked her head to the side. "Excuse me?"

"You know, for someone who spent their whole childhood in this town, you seem oblivious to everything that makes it special." Tanner couldn't stop the rant bubbling up inside of him. Suddenly every frustration he'd had with the changing climate of his small town was bursting at the seams. "Heart Lake may be small, but that's where its charm lies. You can't run into a soul in this place who doesn't know every damn bit of your history, and your history's history. Imagine if half of Chicago used Heart Lake as a weekend hot spot? We wouldn't know a soul, but even worse—they wouldn't give two shits about the soul of this town."

"Uh…" Nola's brows furrowed and she looked confused, but he wasn't remotely close to done.

"And now, you're what? Going to sell what stake you have left in Heart Lake and go back to Chicago? Becca and Zander will just never see you again?" Tanner asked, knowing he was being overly dramatic at this point, but he couldn't seem to stop himself. It wasn't just the fact that she was allowing their town to be run over by strangers, but it was that she was cutting ties with Heart Lake.

With him.

"Tanner, I'm going to stop you right there," Nola cut in, putting her hand up between them. "I'm late for a meeting, and I really don't understand what you're talking about. And honestly? I'm trying to forget that you just insulted my god-mother status, because I would never abandon those kids. You, however, I would happily never see again. Now, if you'll excuse me, I have a meeting I'm late for."

"With Craig? Yeah, I heard all about it," Tanner called after her even as she walked past him and into the restaurant. "This conversation isn't over. You're not selling him The Castle."

He wasn't even sure that she heard the last part of his sentence as the door slammed shut between them. Tanner gritted his teeth and tried to take a deep breath but found his frustration boiling over anyway. He stalked over to his truck and decided he would head in to work early. If there was anything construction was good for, it was pounding away annoyances. And with Nola back in town? He was pretty sure he was going to be working harder than ever.

Chapter Five

How like Tanner to ruin a perfectly good mood. Nola let the diner door swing shut behind her, trying to let out a few deep breaths as she walked toward the counter. She didn't know why he affected her like that, but damn it, he did. What right did he have to say those things to her? Selling Gigi's house was her decision, not his. She was all tense and worked up now, which was not at all helpful, given her schedule for the day.

Her morning had been really wonderful up until Tanner had verbally accosted her on the front steps of the Black Sheep Diner. She'd woken up overlooking the lake from the guest bedroom in The Castle and reminiscing about staying up all night with her cousins when they were children and teenagers. She had so many memories in these old rooms, and she would be lying if she said that it didn't make her a bit sad to think of this as her last visit to a place she'd considered home once.

So when Tanner had started scolding her about not appreciating Heart Lake and all the charm it offered, it had hit a sensitive spot. In fact, it had hit a lot of spots. Tanner was not known for speaking his mind. In high school, he was the quiet and brooding type, always in the woodshop working on his latest project or tutoring another student. With his bulging biceps, faded flannels, shaggy dark hair, well-worn denim, and serious deep-set hazel eyes, he'd been the biggest target of every high school girl's crush back then.

Not that he knew it or really even paid attention to the popularity he had. In fact, it was probably his indifference that made him even more of a draw. Nola had certainly not been immune to his charms, especially considering her best friend was his sister and she spent a lot of time at his house. But he was closed off and off-limits. She would never admit to Rosie that she'd spent so many Friday nights sleeping over at her house and joining in her family's weekly board game night just so she could spend more time around Tanner. She even once volunteered to be part of the stage crew for the high school performance of *Romeo and Juliet* when he was leading the stage crew team. Still, he'd paid her no attention and barely said two words to her. It had been pointless, and for more reasons than just his obliviousness. Nola had big-city goals. She never planned to stay in Heart Lake, and there was no doubt that a dalliance with Tanner would derail those life goals. He was all wrong for her, even if he did make her blood pulse faster and hotter than anyone ever had.

But that was high school. Nola was a grown woman now, and she had no interest in revisiting old crushes. Except for the fact that she was about to meet her old high school boyfriend to discuss selling The Castle. Craig had been the popular senior quarterback when she was a sophomore, so when he'd asked her out, she had said yes immediately. Not only was Craig insanely attractive—like, front-cover-of-*GQ* attractive—but he was headed for success. He came from a well-off family who prioritized big business and even bigger goals. He would be the perfect guy to be at her side while she aimed for professional success as well. Hell, most of their dates had been her listening to his plans about how he was going to make a million dollars before he turned twenty-five and how he planned to own prime real estate in Heart Lake on Lake Shore Drive, an enviable well-off suburb at the edge of Heart Lake, as well as in big cities like Chicago.

She'd looked him up a few months ago when she had begun to consider selling The Castle, and it turns out that he'd made all his dreams come true. He was a millionaire multiple times over and living in a huge home on Lake Shore Drive on the weekends and a penthouse in Chicago during the week. Thankfully, though, he was married, so she didn't have to worry about him misconstruing her reaching out. This was business, and that was it.

"Magnolia!" Craig's voice caught her attention the moment she reached the counter at the diner. He waved her over and she nodded her head, moving toward him to take the empty chair beside him.

"Hi, Craig." Nola greeted her ex with a quick hug and then sat down. She picked up the menu but already knew what she was going to order. This menu hadn't changed in thirty years, and she'd been coming to the Black Sheep Diner since she was a baby.

"Good to see you again, Cupcake. You haven't changed a bit." Craig's gaze roamed across her body, and she stiffened under the old nickname and invasive scrutiny. "Big-city life agrees with you."

"Thanks, but it's probably because I slept twelve hours." She'd fallen asleep in Gigi's comfy guest bed and had been out like a light.

"Beds do a body good, am I right?" Craig chuckled, and Nola mentally wagged a finger at Teenage Nola, who'd been so impressed with Craig going to the state championship on the debate team and having a detailed five-year plan by eighteen. He might have been goal oriented, but he was also a douche canoe with a capital *D*.

"Look, I don't want to waste your time." Nola cut to the

chase for both their sakes. "Your offer is lowballing me and you know it. I'm not taking anything remotely close to that."

He didn't seem surprised, but a sly grin spread across his face. "You always were a whiz in business matters," he remarked. "Do you have a counter?"

She pulled a pad of paper out of her side bag and pushed it across to him. He lifted the top page, glancing at the counteroffer on the next page. He nodded slowly, and she could see him making calculations in his mind.

"This is steep," Craig stated, letting go of the paper and reaching for his cup of coffee.

"The Castle is worth it."

"The land is," Craig replied. "We're not planning on keeping the property up for long."

Nola lifted her chin slightly, swallowing at the information she already knew but that still felt…unsettling. She believed she was making the right choice—Gigi would want her to use the funds from the sale of this house to start her business, right?

"I understand," she replied. "But you're going to have to sweeten the deal to make this happen. Otherwise, I'm going elsewhere. I only came to you first as a courtesy because of our past."

The smile reappeared on Craig's face. "Well, I'll certainly run the numbers by our investors and see what they say. I appreciate the early offer. I didn't know you'd still been thinking about me after all these years."

She paused for a moment, unsure how to respond to that. "You always talked about being in real estate investment."

He nodded his head. "Did you hear that I got married about eight years ago?"

"I might have heard," she replied, lifting the glass of water that the waitress had dropped off for her to her lips and taking a sip.

Craig took a bite of the eggs on his plate. "We're wrapping up divorce proceedings. I'm separated now."

"I'm sorry to hear that." She frowned, wondering what it would be like to be married for that long only to have it all come to an end.

"Don't be," he replied. "It wasn't right from the start. I'm single and ready to mingle. In fact, maybe we should grab dinner later?"

Nola considered his offer for a brief moment. Going back to Craig made a certain amount of sense. He was still incredibly good-looking but in a more mature way. His boyish looks had been replaced by a roughness that no doubt helped him in the boardroom. There were small traces of silver on the edges of his temples, and his face was clean-shaven but sharp at every angle. He'd never been the bulky athletic type but instead had that slim, strong runner's body that all her friends had drooled over. These days he looked a bit like a politician—styled but smarmy.

"I'm pretty busy right now cleaning out the house," Nola finally responded, not ready to say no but also not ready to commit to a yes either. "If there's time, maybe. My schedule is just really jam-packed on this trip."

Craig nodded, but his expression clearly showed he was disappointed. "Another time, then. Don't worry about cleaning the house since we plan to just level it anyway. But yeah, make sure you pack away anything you want to keep."

Nola swallowed, discomfort swirling in her belly as Tanner's look of judgment crossed her mind. He obviously hadn't wanted her to sell The Castle, and neither had her friends. Her own parents had said that they'd support her choice but were sad to see the house go. She inhaled slowly through her nose, wishing she could hang out with Gigi one last time and talk through all her feelings, her dreams of her future, but also her deep love for her past.

"Will do," Nola responded, then stood and grabbed her bag off the counter. "Let me know what the investors say and when you're ready to sweeten the deal."

Craig's tongue slid out across his bottom lip and he glanced down her body again. "I'm sure we can arrange something that'll please you. Keep your cell phone on."

She gave a quick nod and then headed back for the diner door. She was starving and the food here was to die for, but for some reason, she just didn't want to spend forty-five minutes sitting there listening to Craig's latest get-rich-quick plans or his excitement for his newfound singlehood.

"Magnolia, I am so glad to run into you." Marvel appeared next to her and made her jump slightly. There was something a little off about the woman, a mysticism that allowed her to come and go with such a softness that most people missed it.

"Oh, Marvel. Hi," Nola greeted her, putting her hand on her chest to calm her racing heart. "How are you?"

"Good, darling. Oh, you've got a little…" Marvel started waving her hands around Nola's head, as if grasping at something in the air and throwing it over her shoulder. "Jumping jalapeños, sweet girl. Your aura is flaming red with these little orange bits—like it's fizzling."

Nola frowned. "Uh…"

"Hold on—I've almost got it." Marvel brushed her fingers through the tips of Nola's hair, bouncing it off her shoulders. "Yep, that's the last bit. You're dimming a bit now—softer, a spot of blue."

"Thank you," Nola replied, unsure of what else to say.

"We should catch up, dear. Your aura—it's calling out to me. Erratic…searching." Her face seemed to pale for a moment and she went quiet as she stared off into the distance over Nola's shoulder. Suddenly, a smile split across her face and she seemed to bounce back to life. "Are you free for tea tomorrow afternoon?

I know we said we'd get something on the books, and I don't want to miss you while you're here!" Marvel pulled an iPhone out of the pocket of her brightly colored caftan and Nola immediately noticed the bedazzled cover and socket on the back.

Nola tried to hide her smile but was not successful. "Marvel, since when do you have a smartphone?"

Marvel glanced up at her, then back down at the phone. "Oh, you didn't hear? I offer psychic readings online now. You can talk to people on a video as if they were right there in front of you."

"Ah, FaceTime. Yes, I may have heard of it."

"It's incredible," Marvel confirmed. "A bit more challenging to read energies but with some practice, I've been able to connect through the phone waves." She wiggled her fingers mystically.

Nola nodded, as if that made complete sense. "Of course. And the store? How is the store doing?"

"Oh! I didn't open it this morning." Marvel slapped her forehead. "I always forget I'm supposed to be there. I have to dash! But I'll see you tomorrow afternoon?"

"See you then," Nola agreed. "I'll be at The Castle all day."

"Perfect! I'll bring my latest blend!" Marvel called over her shoulder as she rushed out of the diner.

Nola tried not to laugh as she followed Marvel out but at a slower pace. The woman had long been a mentor of hers growing up, given how close she and Gigi had been. However, there was no mistaking the quirkiness that made Marvel...Marvel. She was one of a kind, and Nola loved her just the way she was.

She lifted her chin. Tanner didn't think she appreciated Heart Lake's charm, but here she was having tea with one of the town's most beloved community members. She loved Heart Lake, whether he believed it or not.

So why did she still care what he thought of her?

Chapter Six

"That's actually helpful," Tanner told Blake as he took the box of nails from him. He'd been right earlier today, good honest work helped him pound away his annoyances. Blake was the newest hire at Dean & Son Custom Construction, and honestly, he had been a great find. Normally Tanner was the one tutoring Blake, but the student had been catching up to the teacher quickly. The kid was young, but he was enthusiastic and invested in the company and their mission. In fact, he'd just given Tanner some advice on the custom cabinets he was working on that Tanner hadn't even thought of. The place still looked a mess—most job sites did until the final cleanup day—but it was coming along.

Tanner smiled as he watched Blake flip a hammer around in his hand before sliding it into his tool belt.

"Thanks, dude."

"No problem. I'll go finish up the banister in the front room," Blake replied, adjusting the tools hanging off his work belt. He was only five or six years younger than Tanner, but the age difference still felt cavernous. Blake was full of dreams and big ideas, while Tanner had already passed that period of his life. Sure, he still had dreams. Who didn't? But his dreams were quieter now. He enjoyed helping teach new employees, like Blake, about the business and working on custom pieces for historic sites. The cabinets he was currently remodeling were for a nineteenth-century lakeside house just outside of Heart Lake's town limits that had more charm than any of the shiny new condominiums going up in the area. He knew the family that had owned this property for generations, and their entire purpose behind hiring Tanner was to preserve the history. This was the type of house he wanted to move into one day. Not that he minded living in the small fishing cabin from the twenties that he currently had. It was out in the woods at the edge of a small cove that jetted off the water. Serene, silent—it was everything he strived for in life.

"Anyone home?" a female voice called from the front room just as Blake was walking in that direction.

"In here," Blake called out, then glanced back at Tanner. "We expecting anyone?"

Tanner nodded. "Amanda Riverswood. She's the interior designer on this project."

"Amanda? That doesn't sound familiar. Have I met her?"

He shook his head. "I doubt it. She was just hired. But get to know her because she's the go-to designer for most homes in this area, particularly those with a historical background like this one. She's really talented at showcasing new and old together. We work with her pretty often."

Tanner had always liked his cousin Amanda because she valued integrity when it came to her work. She was always following up with clients and making sure that they got the best products to match their needs. He appreciated that dedication not only to her work but also to Heart Lake.

His thoughts drifted to Nola...but he quickly pushed her image away. Not going there today.

"Hey, guys," Amanda said, greeting him and Blake as she walked into the grand kitchen. She plopped her large purse down on the unfinished countertop and began rummaging through it. "I just need to take some measurements in the bedrooms, then I'll be out of your hair."

"Amanda, this is Blake. Blake, Amanda," Tanner said, introducing the two as he pointed between them.

Amanda reached one hand over to Blake and he shook it. Her other hand pulled a tape measure out of her bag triumphantly. "Nice to meet you, Blake."

"You as well," Blake replied, his smile growing wider than Tanner had ever seen it before.

"How have you been, Amanda? Haven't run into you lately."

"Better than you, I hear," she replied, propping a hand on her hip. "I heard about you and Craig at Black Sheep. The whole town is abuzz."

"Seriously?" Tanner shook his head, letting out one long exhale. "No one has more exciting things to talk about than that? It was nothing."

Amanda shrugged. "Eh, that's Heart Lake. Apparently, Craig had a few choice words to say about you to Mattie after you left. And she told probably six other people, who then told six other people, and now here we are."

"I couldn't care less what Blasco thinks about me," he replied, returning to the cabinets he'd been working on. He didn't have time for or interest in small-town rumors. "His company just tore down the Manor on Eighteenth Street. They're putting a frozen yogurt shop in its place. The Manor was there for over one hundred and fifty years before he came along. A true piece of history—gone."

"I was sad to see the Manor come down," Amanda agreed. "But it sat empty for fifteen years, except when dumb high school kids went in there to party. And we need more businesses, and I love frozen yogurt, don't you?"

Tanner cut his eyes at her, as if to say, *Of course not*. He was a die-hard rocky road ice cream fan and not about to participate in the abomination that was the latest fake ice cream trend.

"Sorry I asked!" Amanda chuckled. There was no doubt that she was used to his gruffness at this point. "But yeah, I get where you're coming from. Honestly, I can't believe that Nola is really selling The Castle. I always thought she'd move back there eventually."

He scoffed, shaking his head. "That will never happen."

"Yeah," Amanda agreed, but there was a sadness and hesitancy in her voice. She turned back to her purse on the counter and rummaged through it a minute more, pulling out a notebook and pen to go with the measuring tape she already had. "Chicago is pretty enticing, I guess. I can see the appeal from a business mindset."

"Plenty of business right here," Tanner replied, but mostly under his breath.

"I'm going to go grab a couple sandwiches at Dickie's Deli," Blake said as he walked back into the room and dropped his tool belt down on the counter. "I'm starving. You want anything, guys?"

Amanda shook her head. "No. I'm just in and out for a few measurements. I've got plans later."

"Oh, yeah?" Blake eyed her for a moment, a small smile at the corner of his mouth.

"Grab me a country club sandwich. And a cherry soda," Tanner said.

Blake nodded. "I'll be back in a few."

With that, Blake left and Amanda headed upstairs to take measurements. Tanner had a few moments alone with his thoughts, and he was glad for it. The changing dynamic of Heart Lake and the urbanization creeping in had bothered him for years, but to know it was one of Heart Lake's own that was selling out the town? He couldn't handle the betrayal. He knew that Nola didn't see it that way, and she was probably trying to do what she thought was best…but it wasn't. Heart Lake was more than just his home—it was the last place he'd seen his mother. The last place he'd held her hand.

This town wasn't going to just become another Chicago suburb. It was his last connection to who he had once been. It was where he wanted to raise his children one day and walk them around all the places that their grandmother had lived and loved.

If he ever had children, that is. It wasn't like he was getting started on a family anytime soon, despite his father's wishes. Thomas wasn't getting any younger and he wanted grandkids from Tanner, but Tanner told him that Rosie had enough kids for the both of them. Luckily, that had bought him some time. Still, though, Thomas often asked him if he was getting ready to settle down. It wasn't that he wasn't ready, and he knew that it was something he wanted eventually, but no one had made it seem like an interesting enough option yet.

His mind flickered to an image of Nola's face, but he pushed it away quickly as Amanda walked back into the old kitchen. She was scribbling something in her notebook and the tape measure was wrapped around her neck.

"Just getting a few ideas," she said. "The children's bedroom upstairs would have to get redone, but we'll keep the historical authenticity of the house."

Tanner lifted one brow. "How do you plan on doing that? Kids are rarely into antiques."

"Actually, it was Nola's idea." Amanda began putting her stuff back into her purse. "She's helping me set up a section on my website dedicated to children's room decor themes. It's really going to help expand my business. There are quite a few ways to incorporate some modern-day things that interest today's children without harming the bones of the original structure. Nola was really helpful with that."

"Was she? How nice." Tanner turned back to his work on the cabinets, not really interested in hearing about how amazing Nola was right now.

"Yup," Amanda confirmed. "Oh, hey, did you hear about Mr. Mott?"

Tanner lifted his head in alarm. "Is he okay?"

Perry Mott was his high school woodshop teacher and a big reason he fell in love with woodworking. The old man was certainly an oddball, but he had a passion for teaching children, and he'd been at Heart Lake High School for longer than Tanner had been alive. He was by far one of the students' favorite teachers and a large presence in this town.

Amanda waved a hand as if it were nothing. "Oh yeah. He's fine. But he is officially retiring at the end of this school year in June. The school board announced it this morning."

He had not been expecting to hear that. "Wow. Retiring? I didn't think the day would ever come."

"Right?" Amanda shrugged her shoulders. "We were all sure he'd work there until he died. Which would be, of course, never. The man is immortal."

Tanner nodded in agreement. "I definitely wasn't expecting it anytime soon. He loves that shop. Those kids are basically his whole life."

"Apparently he met someone online and is moving to Boca Raton."

He eyed Amanda, his brow furrowed. "Old Mr. Mott met someone online? He's been single for seventy-something years."

She nodded her head. "Stranger things have happened."

"Have they even met in person yet?" Tanner asked, feeling a little strange that his old high school woodshop teacher had a more active dating life than he did. He'd always assumed Mr. Mott would be a lifelong bachelor. The man rarely even took a vacation, let alone went out on the town. He did throw an annual Christmas party for the teachers that was well-known as one of the hottest parties in town.

"I don't think so since he never travels, but I'm not really sure." Amanda grabbed her bag and slung it over her shoulder. "The school board said they are looking for his replacement."

"Can't imagine anyone else in that woodshop," Tanner replied. A small smile touched his lips as he thought back to the years spent in Perry Mott's class.

Amanda tilted her head to the side slightly. "I can think of someone."

"Who?"

She looked at him like it was obvious, but he had no clue who she was talking about. "You, obviously. Tanner, you'd be an amazing teacher. You tutor kids all the time in carpentry and take on new interns here. I've seen you working with people—like Blake—and you always look so in your element."

"When have you seen me around kids that aren't related to me?" Tanner asked, the thought of becoming a high school shop teacher being absolutely ridiculous. Technically, yes, he did tutor teenagers and young adults interested in woodworking and carpentry, but it was something he only took on occasionally as a favor to someone usually. His plate was full with Dean & Sons. "I barely have time for them with my schedule here anyway. Dad's not working anymore because of his back, and I have way too much on my plate to consider taking leave to do anything else right now."

Amanda headed toward the exit but glanced back at him briefly. "Hey, I'm just saying. It's something to consider."

Tanner nodded but then turned back to the cabinet he was working on. "Have a good day, Amanda."

"You too," she replied, only to be replaced moments later by Blake, who walked in with their sandwiches.

"Ta-da!" Blake held up the bag of food triumphantly. "Lunch is served."

"Thanks, man. Hey, Amanda just left."

"Dang, well I'm sure we'll run into each other on-site soon." Blake took such a large bite out of his sandwich that Tanner thought he might choke on it. "Hey, have you thought about setting up an Instagram for Dean and Son? I could do some reels of the work to show people what we do. Drum up some interest, some business."

Tanner lifted one brow. "I think we have plenty of interest the way we are now. Don't need to fix something that isn't broken."

Blake shrugged his shoulders. "Suit yourself."

Staying in the Dark Ages suited him just fine. Tanner put his tools away and then washed his hands before grabbing his sandwich from Blake. Pulling his phone out of his pocket, he walked out of the kitchen to the expansive back deck this home boasted. It was one of his favorite spots, and he was pretty sure that this deck alone could sell the house in an instant.

Sitting on the ledge, Tanner let his feet hang over and unwrapped his food while checking his phone for messages. No new calls. Not that he was expecting one, but he wondered if Nola had more to say after their encounter. As frustrated as he still was with her decision, he was wondering if maybe he should apologize for the way he approached her. He'd been fired up from Craig, and somehow, she'd ended up the target.

Maybe she would be more open to a text message. Tanner pulled up her phone number and tapped to open a new conversation.

We should talk.

A few bubbles popped up on the screen before her response came back to him. I have absolutely nothing to say to you.

Tanner let out a frustrated sigh and placed his phone down on the deck beside him, then took a bite of his sandwich. He wasn't going to respond to her message, and she clearly wasn't interested in talking. Not that she'd ever listened to a thing he'd tried to tell her.

As soon as his mouth was full of the last bite of his sandwich, his phone began ringing. *Of course*, he thought. *Guess she does have something to say*. Swallowing quickly, he answered the call.

"Tanner, I need your help." He tried to ignore the pit of disappointment in his stomach upon hearing his sister's voice. "This renovation at Fact or Fiction is a nightmare, and I have to stay late to make sure that they finish the plumbing in the bathrooms correctly. We had a complete water explosion earlier today and I'm on my last nerve."

"Sorry to hear that," Tanner replied before sipping some cherry soda from a can. "I can try and help, but I'm not exactly a plumber."

"No, I have workmen here for that," Rosie replied. "I need you to go pick up the twins. I said I'd get them by one, but there's no way I'm getting out of here that early."

He glanced back at the house, contemplating leaving work early to help out his sister. Technically, he had come in early today and gotten a lot done. They wouldn't be that behind schedule if he left now and Blake kept going for a few more hours. "Yeah, I guess I can do that. Want me to just bring them to your house? Or Dad's?"

"My home is fine. If you could stay there with them until I get there, that would be perfect. There's a lasagna in the fridge that just needs to be heated up for about thirty minutes or so. Don't forget that Zander needs his medications, too."

Tanner nodded. His nephew struggled with asthma, but he was a strong and determined young boy. He never let his medical issues stop him, and Rosie never let him think that they could. It's something he admired about his sister. Not only did she kick ass as a single mother, but she took care of Zander's health like it was the easiest thing in the world. These days, it wasn't so bad, but when he'd been younger, it had been quite a lot of work. There were hospital and doctor visits, but Rosie's smile never faded once.

"Yeah, I know the drill," he replied. "I'll grab the twins. Are they at Ruth's?"

Ruth was a local babysitter who ran one of the most popular day cares in town, especially when schools were on winter break like now. Her house was nothing short of a kid's playland and her patience seemed to have no ending. She had a soft spot for Rosie, understanding she was a single mother and making sure her services were affordable for Rosie's budget. Tanner appreciated her kindness and how much love she poured into his niece and nephew.

"Not today." Rosie paused for a moment and Tanner's stomach sank as he guessed what she was about to say. "Uh, I actually let them stay with Nola. She wanted to spend some time with them, but she has plans this afternoon. Can you grab them from The Castle?"

Tanner groaned and rubbed a hand across his forehead. "Seriously?"

"What?" Rosie's voice went up an octave, like it always did when she was pretending not to know what he was talking about. "You love The Castle."

That was true. It was a beautiful piece of work—one that was about to be torn down. But Rosie was fully aware of

Tanner's hesitation with being around Nola. They bickered at every family gathering, annoying everyone else to no end.

"You *seriously* owe me." Tanner let out a long exhale. "You should have led with that information."

"You'll be fine," Rosie assured him. "Plus, it would be nice for you and Nola to catch up a bit."

This was beginning to feel like a setup, but he'd already said yes. "Mm-hmm. I bet it would. I'll go grab them now."

"You're the best! Thanks, Tanner." Rosie hung up the phone quickly, probably to give him less of a chance to back out. There was no doubt in his mind that his sister was orchestrating something, but he didn't have the heart to say no to his niece and nephew. Spending time with those kids was the best part of his week.

Seeing Nola, however? That might be even better. And worse.

Chapter Seven

It was settled. Rosie was a certified, full-blown saint. Nola was standing in the dark pantry in her grandmother's kitchen eating a white cheddar–flavored rice cake that she'd grabbed from Hobbes Grocery Store earlier today. With every bite she took, she moved slower than molasses to avoid making a loud crunching sound that might alert her godchildren to her location. She loved those kids with every fiber of her being, but there was definitely a difference between their once-in-a-while FaceTime calls while she was in Chicago and an entire day alone with them. The amount of energy these twins had? She had no idea how Rosie handled it day in and day out. It was barely past lunch and Nola felt like she could easily spend the rest of the day napping.

"Aunt Nola!" a little voice called out from somewhere in the house.

She froze midcrunch on her third rice cake, debating whether to give herself a few more blissful moments of solitude, or to charge out into the wild kingdom that had once been Gigi's calm and quiet home.

"Aunt Nola! Look what Zander found! I think he broke it." Becca was calling her this time.

And that's my cue, Nola thought as she shoved the rest of the rice cake down her throat before slipping out of the pantry to go find the latest mess made by the twins.

"I'm coming," Nola called out, winding around the hallway

toward where she heard the kids playing in a back bedroom upstairs. "What's broken?"

She walked into the guest room to find the kids standing in the middle of the space wearing vintage adult dresses that pooled around their feet and were baggy on their tiny frames. Zander had longer hair than the average young boy, thanks to Rosie's encouragement to allow him to make his own decisions about his body—something Nola admired about the young mom. But right now, Becca was putting his hair in pigtails that looked so tangled it was likely she'd have to cut the rubber bands out of the poor kid's hair eventually.

"Zander pulled the zipper too hard," Becca said, outing her brother. She pointed to the back of the dress he was wearing where a zipper was clearly off its tracks. "It's not zipping now."

Nola came over and messed with it, trying to get it back on. "I see you found Gigi's old clothes. What happened to hide-and-seek? I've only been in the pantry ten minutes."

"We wanted to play dress-up!" Zander announced, wiggling and making it difficult for Nola to get a grip on the broken zipper. "We're going to a tea party."

"You are?" Nola asked, feigning excitement at the concept. "Do I get an invitation?"

Becca put her hands on her small hips and rolled her eyes like the answer was obvious. "Yeah, if you dress up. And I get to do your makeup."

She lifted her brows. This kid had the makings of an expert negotiator. "Is that so? What should I wear?"

"There's a lot of dresses in here!" Becca ran over to the large closet, almost tripping several times on the long velvet gown she was wearing. Nola remembered seeing Gigi wear that dress to a Christmas party once, but she couldn't recall how long ago that had been. Gigi had always loved to dress to the nines, even though she rarely went anywhere that required such formal clothes. It didn't matter to her, though. She had worn lace gloves anytime she left the house and always had a perfectly coiffed hat at church on Sundays.

"How about this one?" Becca emerged from the closet dragging a long silver dress behind her. It was a slinky sheath and one that Nola had never actually seen Gigi wear. It looked like it came off the red carpet of Hollywood in the 1940s and was certainly more sensual than anything she'd ever seen her grandmother in.

She took the dress from Becca and held it up. "This one is gorgeous," she admitted, wanting to try it on just as much for herself as for the kids now.

"Put it on, and I'll get the makeup ready!" Becca had several old containers of makeup lying out on top of the long dresser. Nola was quite certain that they were all expired at this point, but Gigi had always had trouble throwing things away.

"Okay, I'll be right back." Nola headed for the bathroom down the hall and quickly slipped into the sheath gown. She surveyed herself in the mirror for a moment. The dress fit her perfectly and hung off her in a way that seemed almost effortless. She wondered what Gigi had been doing with a dress like this and what stories she'd never heard about Gigi's life. A pang hit her in the chest at the thought. She would never be able to ask her, never be able to know more than she already did. It felt so strange to be in this home with just the memory of her grandmother, and she wondered if she knew all there had been to know about her in the first place.

"Aunt Nola!" The kids were getting impatient.

"Coming!" She exited the bathroom and returned to find that Zander had used Gigi's dark-red blush to make his nose look like Rudolph's. She laughed. "Zander, what did you do?"

"I'm a reindeer!" Zander grinned and held up his nose for her to see.

"Way to get into the holiday spirit," Nola replied, shaking her head at his antics. She sat on a small bench beside the dresser and made herself accessible to her goddaughter's cosmetic artistry. "Okay, Becca. Do your worst."

"I'm going to be a famous makeup artist one day," Becca commented as she grabbed some eyeliner and began working on Nola's face. "I'm going to work in Hollywood and do all the famous people."

"Of that I have no doubt." And that was the truth because Nola was sure that both of these kids were destined for success and something bigger than this town. Their mother had made sure of that. She had certainly instilled in them a love for Heart Lake and their community, but Nola had always heard Rosie encouraging her kids to dream big and take chances. She loved that about her, but it only made it more frustrating that Rosie was giving Nola a hard time for doing the same in her own life.

She stayed quietly in her thoughts for a few moments as Becca continued to work and watched out of the corner of her eye as Zander added accessories from Gigi's costume jewelry to his outfit. So far he was up to a tiara, a bauble necklace, and a ring that he was wearing on his big toe. She tried not to laugh, but man, she loved his creativity.

"Are you ready to see?" Becca picked up a handheld mirror from the dresser but pointed it away from Nola so she couldn't look at her reflection just yet. "I did a really good job."

"I can't wait for the reveal!" Nola reached for the mirror. "I'm sure I look beautiful!"

"You do!" Becca confirmed as Nola lifted the mirror to her face.

Oh. My. God. A laugh caught in Nola's throat but she quickly pushed it down. Becca was clearly very proud of her work, and Nola was not about to tell her that she felt reminiscent of the Joker going to prom right now.

"It's...wow. It's very talented." Nola tried to find the words but was struggling to keep a straight face. "You worked so hard!"

Becca beamed and clapped her hands. "Do you love it?"

Nola nodded, not minding a little white lie to make her goddaughter feel confident. "Oh, I *love* love it."

"I do, too," a deeper voice said from the guest room doorway.

She turned her head to see Tanner standing there with a huge grin on his face, staring at her with wide eyes. He was clearly trying to muffle his own laughter but doing a piss-poor job as he attempted to cover his snickers with a cough.

"Tanner! What are you doing here?" She tried to forget the message she'd sent him earlier, saying she had no interest in talking to him. Honestly, she was a bit embarrassed at her overreaction, but he had had it coming. "I wasn't expecting you."

"Rosie asked me to swing by and grab the kids. She's working later than expected." Tanner stepped farther into the room and opened his arms as Becca and Zander both ran to hug him. "There was no answer to my knock at the door, so I just came on in."

"You just came on in?" Nola shook her head. Typical Heart Lake resident thinking doors were for opening rather than keeping people out. Not that she really minded, but she would definitely never see someone doing something like that in Chicago. At least not without the police being called.

"Uncle Tanner, do we have to leave right now?" Zander asked, pulling on Tanner's arm to bring him farther into the room. "We're still playing!"

"Come play with us!" Becca offered, then ducked back into the closet where Nola could hear her rustling around in the bins of clothes. "Oh, I found one!"

Becca bounced back out of the closet dragging a long garment bag with her. "Try this one!"

Tanner lifted the bag from her arms and unzipped the front. Inside was a gleaming tuxedo that had Nola more than a little curious. Who had worn this in Gigi's past? It looked like it hadn't been touched in fifty years. "You want me to put this on?"

Becca nodded. "Then we can play 'red carpet'!"

"What's that?" Tanner eyed his niece, but Nola was very familiar with their Hollywood-themed game of pretending to pose and take pictures on a fake red carpet. The kids always got such a kick out of it, and she'd played it with them quite a few times over the years.

"You'll see!" Zander pushed Tanner with the garment bag toward the bathroom and encouraged him to hurry up and change.

A few minutes later, Tanner waltzed out of the bathroom adorned in the vintage suit. She took one glance at him before instantly looking away. There was no doubt in her mind that if he saw the look on her face right now, he'd know exactly what she was thinking. And *Holy shit, he's the sexiest man I've ever seen* was not the thought she wanted to convey to a man she could barely stand most days.

He had wet his hair and slicked it back while he was getting ready. That, in combination with the well-fitting tuxedo, made him look like a sexy Italian mobster from half a century ago. That was certainly a fantasy she'd never known she had...until right now. Trying hard to keep her composure, she turned back to look at Tanner. He grinned at her, but that's when she noticed his feet. Nola laughed at the sight of someone so dressed up also being barefoot.

"Where are your shoes?" Nola asked, putting a hand over her mouth to hide her smile.

Tanner shrugged. "Whoever wore this suit last had tiny feet. There was no way those were fitting on me."

Nola lifted one brow, definitely sure that she should keep her mouth shut instead of saying what she was thinking. There were children around them, after all.

"Red carpet time!" Becca announced, leading the small group down to the living room where she had laid a red blanket in front of the fireplace. It was knitted and awkward to step on in heels, but Nola made the best of it and strutted across the blanket like it was a real Hollywood red carpet.

Zander was holding Nola's smartphone, aiming the camera at her and Becca as they posed together. Nola gave her goddaughter a few ideas for fun poses, like silly faces, vogueing, and more. Becca was laughing hysterically after a few minutes before she switched with Zander.

"Now you and Uncle Tanner," Zander exclaimed, motioning for Nola and Tanner to come together in front of the fireplace.

"Us?" Nola pointed between her and Tanner, as if the possibility were insane. "We should take more pictures of you guys!"

"No, you!" Becca agreed with her twin brother. "You can be the lead actor and actress! You just won an Oscar."

"Wow, Tanner. You're quite the talent, aren't you?" Nola teased as Tanner joined her on the blanket.

"I keep telling you, but you never listen," Tanner replied, clearly getting into the act and being more playful than his normal stern self. "I'm going to need to build a new shelf to hold all these awards of mine."

"What a hard life." Nola chuckled and struck a pose next to Tanner as Becca snapped a picture.

Tanner wrapped an arm around her waist and pulled her against his side, and Nola suddenly felt like her skin was on fire. He smiled wide as Becca took another picture, not seeming to notice how off balance Nola was. They'd never been this close...ever. She couldn't think of a time they'd even hugged politely in greeting. At the most, he'd maybe patted her on the back or shoulder. Or she had one time swatted a bee away from his cheek a few summers back. But other than that...nothing. Yet here he was, holding her against him like it was the most natural thing in the world.

"Aunt Nola, you have to smile!" Becca called her out and she snapped back to reality.

She forced a smile across her lips and leaned a bit more into Tanner, hoping they looked more natural on the camera than she felt. Tanner glanced down at her and she caught his gaze. He wasn't smiling, but there was something behind his stare that made a warmth spread through her that she hadn't felt in a long time. His gaze traveled from hers down to her lips, then returned to her eyes, and she felt herself shiver involuntarily. There was no way he hadn't felt her reaction, because his jaw tensed in response.

A knock on the front door pulled her out of the trance she was in.

"Hello?" a familiar voice called from the front hall. "Nola, are you home?"

She blinked, trying to recall who she had plans with today, but she was coming up blank. "In here!" she called out, quickly pushing away from Tanner and straightening her dress.

Craig Blasco, her high school ex-boyfriend, rounded the corner and walked into the living room as if he owned the place. Which he sort of almost did. Though she felt weird at the tightness in her chest at the thought.

"Craig?" Nola greeted him with a question, confused about why he was here. And even more confused about why he was holding a bouquet of flowers and a bottle of red wine.

"Oh." Craig paused midstride as he took in the rest of the room full of dressed-up children and Tanner in a tuxedo. His gaze settled finally on Nola. "Am I interrupting something? What happened to your face?"

She felt a warmth creeping into her cheeks as she remembered the makeup job her darling goddaughter had blessed her with. "Uh, I was just babysitting the kids for the day. Tanner was picking them up."

Tanner's face was stone-cold, and he ran a hand through his hair, mussing up the slicked-back look. "Come on, kids. Aunt Nola has plans. Get back into your normal clothes and let's go home like we planned."

"Let's get ice cream!" Zander exclaimed, quickly disrobing from the vintage duds he was wearing and running half naked up the stairs to get the rest of his clothes on.

Becca followed more slowly, looking a bit downtrodden at the idea of their play coming to an end.

Tanner looked between Nola and Craig. He cleared his throat. "Uh, tell the kids I'll be waiting on the front porch when they're dressed. I gotta change quick, too."

"Oh, you don't have to wait outside," Nola said, attempting to smooth the discomfort that was hanging in the air between them.

"Probably for the best," Craig volunteered. "See you later, old buddy."

Nola didn't miss the tension in Tanner's jaw or his small nod as he walked briskly past them and headed for the front door. She wanted to call after him, chase him down and ask him to stay...but she didn't. And she wasn't sure why.

"Poor guy is still holding on to that high school crush, huh?" Craig shook his head as he watched Tanner leave, then turned back to look at her. "It's like he never grew up and found a real woman."

She blinked, absorbing his words for a moment. *High school crush?* "A real woman?"

"Not that you're not real," Craig backtracked. "But, you know, high school was a long time ago."

"*We* dated in high school," Nola reminded him. Was he insulting her straight to her face? Honestly, she wasn't sure how much of his personality she could handle these days, but she just wanted to focus on the thing he was good at—real estate. She could ignore the unpleasantness if it meant he'd give her a great deal on this property. She needed that for her future business.

Craig chuckled and handed her the bouquet of flowers. They were lilies, and while beautiful, they were one of her least favorite flowers.

"Just wanted you to know I was thinking about you. Maybe we could go out sometime and talk again."

She'd rather eat three-day-old oatmeal. "I actually have a lot I need to get done, sorting through all of Gigi's things." Nola gestured at the room around her. "There's a lot to do before I head back to Chicago."

"I did want to talk to you about that," Craig said. He leaned forward and put his elbows on his knees. "While I was married, I split my time between the house here and the penthouse in the city during the workweek. But now that my divorce is almost final, I'll be in Chicago permanently."

"Okay...do I say congratulations? Or sorry?" Nola wasn't sure what point he was trying to make.

Craig shook his head. "It's a good thing—believe me. But I think when we both get back to Chicago in the new year, we should spend some time together. See if that old spark is there. We've gotten older, but we're not that different than when we were teenagers."

She certainly felt different. "We'll see. I want to focus on the deal for The Castle first."

"All right." Craig stood up and shoved his hands into his pockets. "I have a call with the investors this afternoon. I ran your proposal by them this morning. They are considering budging a little bit, but you won't get everything you want."

"Then I'll find someone who can get that for me," Nola quipped as the kids ran down the hall and burst into the room.

Zander looked around. "Where did Uncle Tanner go?"

"He's out there waiting for you two." Nola pointed toward the front of the house. "Thanks for playing with me today! See you tomorrow!"

"Bye, Aunt Nola!" Becca waved as she followed her brother out of the living room to the front door.

"Cute kids," Craig commented after they'd left. "But hey, listen—I'll get out of your hair since you're busy. I'll call you later to tell you what the investors said."

Nola nodded, appreciating that he was finally taking the hint. "Thank you."

"Sorry I didn't make it to your grandma's funeral. She was always nice to me in high school." He glanced around the room again, then looked back at her, his gaze softer. "It's weird being here and not having Gigi rounding the corner every few minutes to make sure we're leaving room for Jesus."

Something caught in Nola's throat—both laughter and sadness. Gigi had never been a fan of her dating Craig and constantly monitored them together to make sure they weren't too physically close. She insisted that there always be "room for Jesus" between the two of them. Nola had found it very irritating as a teenager, but now she would give anything to have Gigi scolding her again and pushing them apart on the couch.

With that, Craig nodded toward her and then exited out the front door. Nola followed him and then locked the door behind him. Turning, she caught a look at herself in the hall mirror—sheath gown and Joker makeup. She let out a small chuckle and then headed upstairs to wash it all off.

It had been fun playing red carpet with the kiddos. She couldn't believe Tanner dressed up, too. What a surprise—she didn't think the grump had it in him. But even more strange was why she kept wondering what Tanner thought of Craig's impromptu visit.

Chapter Eight

For pretty much his whole life, Tanner had been a great sleeper. It was actually a point of pride for him. The moment his head hit the pillow, he was out. He'd been told he had a tendency to snore when he was in a very deep sleep, but thankfully it hadn't seemed to bother his bed partners in the past. Tonight, however, sleep was elusive. Tanner was stretched out across the top of the plaid duvet on his bed, still fully dressed and staring up at the open-beamed ceiling. There was no doubt that he would normally be asleep by now, but his mind wouldn't quiet down.

After thirty minutes of not feeling remotely tired or motivated to undress and climb under the sheets, Tanner pushed up off the mattress and plodded into his living room. The cabin was small—only two bedrooms, one bathroom, and an open kitchen and living area. He'd built most of the furniture and cabinets, and the leather recliner he'd scored at an estate sale last year was one of his favorite things he owned. Outside, snow was falling on his big deck, and the moon shone over the shoreline, the ice going silver in the wintry light.

Tanner grabbed himself a glass and a bottle of whiskey from the cabinet above his stove and walked over to the recliner. Turning on the television, he changed it to the weather channel and sat down for a slow drink.

"Snowpocalypse is almost upon us!" the weatherman announced, pointing to an infographic on the green screen behind him. "This blizzard is going to be one for the record books."

Anyone from Michigan wasn't a stranger to the cold, but this blizzard had him more concerned than most storms. It had been a while since they'd had a projection like this, and he made a note to himself to check his father's and sister's generators and emergency supplies tomorrow to make sure they were ready in case the power went off. His mind flitted to Nola, wondering how prepared she was...or if she'd even still be here by the time the storm rolled through.

Leaving the television on, Tanner stood and walked over to the dark wooden bookshelves that covered the far wall of his living room. It took a minute, but he located what he was searching for on the bottom shelf—an old high school yearbook from his senior year. Returning to the recliner, he began leafing through the pages. His portrait was not that far away from Craig Blasco's. Tanner didn't look much different, but there was a boyish innocence to him at seventeen that was long gone now in his late thirties. He had a more mature look now, his facial hair fully grown in and his eyes darker and more experienced.

He glanced at Craig's photo, his jaw tightening in irritation. Craig looked like a soon-to-be frat boy back then, and he was certain that the football star had lived up to his reputation. Tanner had always hated running into the pompous jerk, and those feelings had only increased now.

He flipped farther back in the yearbook to the sophomore section. Nola was easy to find and his eyes immediately went to her sweet smile. She'd had braces at that time, but he'd thought she looked adorable in them. It had been a short phase for her, but it had never seemed to bother her like it would a lot of teen girls. They hadn't had any classes together or anything like that, but he'd seen her often in the halls or at sporting events, not to mention all the evenings she spent at his house with Rosie. He remembered how kind she'd been to him after his mother had died. Nola had supported Rosie through that period of their life and that's something he would never forget.

Despite all of their overlapping, Nola had still been a completely different person back then. Popular, outgoing, dating the football star and not at all shy about telling everyone of her dreams to move out of Heart Lake. Her eyes had always been set on a big city, whereas he'd never planned to go more than down the road. This was his home, and he had no desire to be in a large, crowded metropolis. Heart Lake was where he felt comfortable…at least, it had been for the last couple of decades. Lately, he'd been feeling restless, but he couldn't pinpoint a reason why. Work certainly was the biggest component, but he enjoyed what he did—it just hadn't felt like enough. The challenge was gone, and the excitement waned as he was taking on more administrative work to help out his father after his back injury.

His busyness at work had been an easy excuse to get out of relationships he hadn't felt were a good fit. He'd ended things with sweet Emma a year ago—or more accurately, she got tired of waiting for him to commit. He wasn't sure what was holding him back, but there was something in him that made him keep his distance from others. A hesitancy to trust, maybe, or perhaps a leftover wound from losing his mother. Or maybe it was something else entirely. Maybe he was waiting for something to feel like it fit in a way that nothing else had so far.

Tanner sighed and placed the yearbook on a side table. He stood and stretched his arms, then downed the rest of his whiskey. Placing the empty glass in his sink, he noticed through his kitchen window that a light was on in the ice fishing shanty he shared with a few local guys. It was a bit of a distance from his cabin, but there was no mistaking the flickering glow. Tanner glanced at the clock on the kitchen wall. It was pretty late, but he certainly wasn't going to sleep anytime soon. Grabbing a jacket off the hook by the back door, he bundled up and headed outside toward the shanty. The full moon lit up the lake and everything around him. He could see the edge of The Castle farther down on the water's edge, and he hated that the first thing he thought was, *Is Craig still there?* The lights were all off, but Tanner's stomach churned. He looked away and put the thought of Nola and her rendezvous out of his mind.

Reaching the shanty, he knocked lightly and then entered the small room. Perry Mott was sitting in the center of the room with his feet propped up and a beer in one hand.

"Hey, son," Mr. Mott said, greeting him with a small nod. "Want a beer?"

Tanner shook his head, knowing it would make him too cold. He was more of a liquor guy instead of a fan of ice-cold beer. "No. Thank you, though."

"Pull up a seat." Mr. Mott pointed toward a few chairs stacked in the corner.

Tanner grabbed one and dragged it closer to his old teacher. "I heard about your retirement news."

"Never thought you'd see the day, huh?" Mr. Mott laughed, a low rumbling chuckle that came directly from his chest. "Believe me, I didn't either. Thought I'd die right here in this ice fishing shanty one day."

Tanner grimaced. "I hope not. I'm not cleaning that up."

Mr. Mott laughed again. "Well, I'm Boca's problem now."

"And it sounds like a new mystery someone, too?" Tanner pried, but then instantly regretted it. He wasn't the gossiping type, and honestly, it was weird to ask his old teacher about his love life. It really wasn't any of his business. Damn Amanda for putting the question in his head. "I mean, you don't have to tell me about her."

"Her?" Mr. Mott lifted a brow as he took another sip of his beer. "I'll tell Ronald you called him that."

Tanner paused in surprise. "Oh. I didn't know."

Mr. Mott shrugged. "I'm not super open about my private life, but I'm not ashamed of it either."

"Well, good. No need to be." Tanner cleared his throat. "Has Ronald ever visited Heart Lake?"

"He hates the cold," Mr. Mott replied. "That's why I'm moving to Florida. It's about time I felt the sun on my face all year round."

Tanner could certainly understand that, but he had no desire to leave Heart Lake for longer than a vacation. "I can't remember the last time I got a tan."

Mr. Mott chuckled low and throaty once more. "I'm not sure my skin is going to know what hit it."

"We'll certainly miss you around here. Especially at the high school. You're important to those kids." Tanner wanted to say he was important to him, too, but the sentiment caught in his throat.

"These kids need someone invested in them, and patient enough to teach," Mr. Mott mused, taking another sip of his beer. "That's why I told the school board to hire you as my replacement. You'd be perfect for the job."

Tanner furrowed his brow. Hadn't Amanda suggested the same thing? "What? I can't take that job. I've got Dean and Son to worry about."

"You enjoy working there as many hours as you do?" Mr. Mott asked pointedly, as if he already knew the answer.

"It's not that I don't enjoy working there," Tanner said, fumbling to find an answer that would be truthful. "It's Dean and Son. With Dad's back being the way it is now, he needs all the help he can get there. It's the family business, and he's wanted me to take it over my whole life. Now we're finally there, and I can't back out. My father would be devastated. Plus, we have employees who depend on us for their livelihood. I recently hired a new kid—Blake—who's been really great and voluntarily taking on a leadership role in the company."

Mr. Mott didn't say anything. He seemed to be waiting for Tanner to explain further.

Tanner cleared his throat. There was an unsettledness in his stomach that he couldn't pinpoint. "It's just not an option. At least, not right now. My father needs me."

"Well, just think it over." Mr. Mott finished the last of his beer and tossed the bottle into a nearby recycling bin. "You'd be a good fit, and I think you'd enjoy it. But they can always find someone else, too."

Something about that response frustrated Tanner, though he wasn't sure why. Sure, they could *find anyone*, but Perry Mott had been a significant influence in the lives of a lot of Heart Lake high schoolers. He wasn't someone easily replaced. Tanner suddenly realized that he was feeling sadness—he was going to miss Mr. Mott when he moved.

"Thank you," Tanner added finally. "I don't think I'd have loved carpentry as much as I do now if it weren't for you and your classes. I don't know where I would have ended up, honestly. After my mom...I was headed in a bad direction."

Mr. Mott didn't say anything, but he opened a cooler next to him and pulled out another beer. He cracked it open and took a sip. "It's been an honor being part of this community for the last fifty years. It's been very fulfilling."

Tanner nodded slowly, wondering what that would feel like. He pictured his father's face if he told him that he would be walking away from the family business for a teaching job. He could see the hurt and disappointment etched into his father's wrinkles already. As tempting as the offer was, Tanner knew it wasn't an option. He couldn't do that to his father, and truthfully, he wasn't sure he had what it took to replace an icon like Mr. Mott. He knew what he needed to do and who he was.

Which made it stranger that he felt so lost right now.

Chapter Nine

"I think she kept the tea set somewhere in the butler's pantry," Nola said as she pulled open random cabinet drawers in The Castle in an attempt to find Gigi's famous set of teacups and matching kettle.

Marvel shook her head and waltzed past Nola directly to a cabinet on a side wall over a small counter. She pulled a stool up to the front of the counter, then climbed up it to reach the cabinet. Marvel was a small woman, barely over five feet, so a stool was a necessity for her in any kitchen. Nola suspected that Gigi had that stool for that reason exactly, given that Gigi had been quite tall and certainly never needed it. Without a doubt, Marvel knew her way around this kitchen better than Nola did, and she imagined how often Gigi and Marvel must have done an afternoon tea like this.

"Here it is!" Marvel crowed as she pulled out a teakettle and matching set of ceramic cups that were ivory white with delicate tiny pink flowers hand-etched onto the sides. "This was her favorite. Mine too."

Nola took the set from Marvel so that she could climb back down off the stool easier. She walked it over to the table in the breakfast room—an insulated sunroom in many ways that overlooked the lake. Nola set the cups up on the table with the required cutlery, sugar, and honey. There was an elegant wooden tea box that held six different assortments of tea, and Nola took a deep breath as she opened the lid and inhaled the aromas.

Marvel took the teakettle and brought it back to the kitchen to fill it with the water boiling on the stove. "Your grandmother was always a stickler for her tea. No tea bags allowed in this house. Loose-leaf, hand tied—only the best for her. That's why I brought you the same blend. I think it'll fix your aura problem, too. It's still up in flames, baby girl. We're going to need to work on that."

Nola laughed as she remembered her grandmother's affinity for special teas. Gigi had taught her as a young child how to use a tea strainer and bag her own tea leaves. She insisted that premade tea bags were basically chemicals and the worst pick of the tea leaves. Nola didn't know whether that was true, but she knew that Gigi did always make a delicious cup of tea. Of course, when she was younger, Nola had always loaded it with honey or sugar, but these days she tended to like it with maybe a small dash of milk and that was about it.

"You're going to love these," Marvel said as she walked back into the breakfast room with a pink box tied with a ribbon. "I got them down at Skippity Scones—you know, the new bakery off Fifth Street?"

Nola nodded, familiar with the place, but she would hardly call it new. It had been around at least ten years, but there was little explanation for how Marvel's mind worked.

After a few more trips back and forth from the kitchen to the breakfast room, the table was set with tea, scones, and every accoutrement an afternoon high tea might require. Nola smiled, wishing Gigi could see the setup. She certainly would have approved. Marvel and Nola sat on the soft cushions that decorated each of the thick wicker chairs that surrounded the wicker-and-glass table. They both paused for a moment, admiring the view of the lake through the long glass windows that spanned from the ceiling to the floor on three walls.

"I can still feel her here." Marvel let out a slow exhale, and there was a small smile on her face. "We used to look out on this view more than a time or two."

Nola understood what she meant. While Gigi might be gone, this house still felt like her. "I sifted through her closet yesterday with the twins. We played dress-up in some of her old gowns. The kids got such a kick out of it, but it was certainly strange to remember all the things she used to wear."

"Her closet was a thing for the mystery books," Marvel replied with a hearty laugh. "I swear I never saw that woman dressed in anything less than black tie. My closet is all caftans and ponchos, but she never went anywhere without a pair of lace gloves."

Nola giggled. "I remember. She had so many more gowns than I even remember her wearing. Seemed like she was always red-carpet ready. Not that she ever saw an actual red carpet in her entire life. I mean, Gigi was a schoolteacher before she married Grandpa, right?"

"She was, but she spent the first five years of her career at the Silver Slated School—one of those prestigious etiquette schools for girls back in the day." Marvel rolled her eyes and Nola tried to imagine the woman in the clothes Gigi used to wear. "Your grandmother...she certainly had a flare for the dramatic, you know. She'd come to one of my clay classes wearing all silk. I told her she was going to destroy the fabric, but she insisted she was fine." Marvel paused for a moment, a small sigh escaping her. "Damn it if she wasn't always right. Always left without a drop on her."

A lump formed in Nola's throat as she thought of her grandmother. A bittersweet nostalgia passed between them and Nola allowed the feelings of grief and love to mingle together inside of her without trying to push them away.

"Enough of the past," Marvel said, interrupting her thoughts. "Tell me what is new with you. What are you looking forward to?"

"Well, I'm assuming you know I've been talking to Craig about selling The Castle..." She paused for a moment, glancing over at Marvel to see her reaction.

Marvel didn't look at her, but rather lifted her cup of tea to her lips and sipped slowly.

"I think he might want more than just a business deal," Nola concluded. "He came over unannounced yesterday to check out my interest. I quickly sent him on his way, though. My focus is on the business deal and then getting back to Chicago and starting my company."

"More women should be in charge these days." Marvel placed her cup down on the table and then tucked her hand into the box of scones, lifting one out. "You've got ambition. You're going to go places, and I admire that about you. I know Gigi certainly did."

Nola smiled. "Thank you. I do want to make her proud."

"You did. You will," Marvel continued. "Though, I must admit that a part of me wishes you could stay around town. It's been nice seeing you in passing this week."

"It's been nice being back," Nola agreed. "But I'm so close to my dreams. My own consulting business in Chicago? It's all I ever wanted."

Marvel nodded slowly, as if thinking carefully. "With your talent, maybe you can give me some tips for Dirty Birds. Hell, I bet a lot of Heart Lake could use some business consulting."

Dirty Birds Clay Studio was Marvel's pottery place, and there were certainly ideas she could come up with. Nola had considered bringing her business to Heart Lake, but not for long. Her life was in Chicago now. Her client list and contacts were there. And the large influx of cash she'd get from the sale of The Castle would surely set her up for success in the city.

"Ooh, you know what I forgot?" Nola lifted a finger in the air and then stood up. "I'll be right back. I wanted to go through some of Gigi's jewelry with you. I know she would want you to take your favorites."

"Your grandmother and I had very different tastes in accessories," Marvel replied with a laugh. She shook her arm that was lined with wooden bangles and pointed to the necklace on her chest that looked like a homemade dream catcher. There was no doubt that Marvel had a more eclectic style compared to Gigi's highbrow elegance. "But you're right. I would love a piece to remember her by."

Nola chuckled, then dashed off to grab the jewelry box in Gigi's room. A minute later, she was walking back into the breakfast room and placed the box on the table. She opened it carefully, sighing at the mess inside. "You know, for someone as put together as Gigi, her jewelry box is a disaster."

Marvel peeked over. "I think every one of those necklaces is tangled with six others."

"Want to help me try and gently pull them apart?" Nola gave Marvel her best pleading pout.

"Putting a lady to work, huh?" Marvel leaned over and grabbed a mass of chains and spread it out on the table. She slowly began untangling the different lines. "I ought to make you come down and volunteer to clean stations at Dirty Birds."

Nola had nothing but fond memories of every visit to Marvel's studio, though she certainly didn't have an artistic bone in her body when it came to creating things. Every project she did ended up looking like a child had completed it, but she didn't mind. "I do need a ceramic pencil holder for my new office."

"We're having a smash-the-art night in January." Marvel lifted a necklace and squinted at the tight knot as she worked it out slowly. "Figured it would be a good way to get rid of all the unclaimed pieces and start fresh for the new year. Plus, people always have a ton of frustration built up after the holidays with family."

"Still one of your best business ideas," Nola commented, pulling a ring from a tangle of bracelets. Marvel had started holding quarterly events at her studio where she allowed people to come in for one hour and break…everything. She called it a cathartic release, but Nola had always ended up laughing every time she went. Gigi had loved it, which was an odd fit with her poised personality. Watching her grandmother chuck ceramic plates against a wall was still one of her favorite memories.

"Will you look at this?" Marvel held up an audaciously large pink diamond ring. "Where do you think she even got something like this?"

Nola looked closer, examining the shiny piece. "Wow. Do you think someone gave this to her? That would have made quite an engagement ring."

"Still could," Marvel teased, handing her the ring. "You'd look quite dashing with this on your finger."

Nola tucked her chin down, hoping to hide the crimson that was no doubt spreading on her cheeks at that comment. "I always wondered if Gigi had ever been in love."

"Well, your grandfather didn't wear his heart on his sleeve. Maybe he did in his own way, but he was married to his career in the merchant marine. I think he wasn't ever home more than a few weeks at a time over all the years I knew them. He loved being a captain. Being out on the Great Lakes was his happy place." Marvel handed her an untangled necklace. "After he died, I never saw her with anyone else, nor did she ever mention an interest in finding another man."

Nola held the ring up higher, watching the light reflect off the surface. This ring screamed romance. It wasn't the type of ring someone bought for themselves or just gave as a random gift. This meant something, and Nola couldn't help but wonder who had meant this for Gigi.

"Did she ever talk about anyone before my grandfather?" Nola asked.

Marvel sat back for a moment, looking off into the distance. "You know, she did. I remember a story she told me once—must have been decades ago. I haven't thought about this in so long. It was a high school sweethearts romance. She said he was her first love—a boy who appeared young and living in her heart instead of her head. He asked her to marry him at their high school graduation. It was a big deal back then, because they were so young and he was considered one of the most eligible young men in town. He was going big places."

She'd never heard this story before. "Did she say yes?"

"Absolutely," Marvel replied. "They were set to move to Philadelphia because he'd gotten into a university there. She pushed off further education to become a teacher just to follow love."

"I had no idea Gigi lived in Philadelphia when she was younger." Nola wondered how much she hadn't known about her grandmother. The more she looked back on things, the more she realized how much she depended on Gigi...but had Gigi depended on her? It made her glad to know that she'd had friends like Marvel to be that for her.

"Oh, no. She never went." Marvel shook her head as she handed her another untangled necklace. "He died in a bar fight—shot by another drunk patron in some stupid Russian roulette–type game on a dare. He died quickly—immediately, actually. He wasn't even twenty years old. I remember her face when she told me—I'd never seen anything so haunted. Blue aura that day—very dark, dark blue."

Nola felt a lump in her throat. This was certainly not a story she'd ever heard from her grandmother. "That's heartbreaking."

"She didn't talk about it much. Really only the one time, I think. I'm not sure she ever opened up to loving a man again after that." Marvel let out a sigh. "Your grandfather was a nice enough fellow. Helped keep away the loneliness, I'm sure. Gave her your father, which was her whole world until you came along. She told me once she was born to be a mother and a grandmother."

"She was certainly the best at that," Nola agreed. She couldn't help but feel an ache in her chest as she imagined the pain Gigi must have felt at such a young age. Gigi had never gotten the chance to leave Heart Lake and follow her dreams or build a life with the man she loved.

Nola wondered what this young man had been like, and what Gigi had been like when she was in love. She lifted the beautiful pink diamond ring back up to the light. It was fun to imagine this was a ring that he'd given her. Her mind drifted unwillingly to Tanner's face and she found herself wondering if he would have ever been the type to fall in love in high school and run off on a romantic elopement. She pictured him giving a ring like this to the woman he might love...to her. A shiver went through her as she realized what she was thinking.

Ridiculous. Childhood crushes stayed where they were—in the past. Gigi might have fallen in love at a young age, but Nola was long past that now. She scolded herself for even entertaining the idea for a moment.

Still...it was a beautiful ring.

Chapter Ten

The next day, Tanner's old truck pulled to a stop in front of the first available pump at the one and only local gas station, eloquently named the Gas and Pass. He pushed the truck into park and then unbuckled himself, sliding out of his seat and pulling his wallet out of his back pocket. He made quick work of propping the fuel nozzle up into the side of his truck and getting the pump going. As he leaned against the driver's side door, he heard a clanging sound coming from the other side of the pump.

"What the heck!" A very familiar voice rang out, causing him to look up.

Tanner stepped across the median and saw Nola perched on the back bumper of her car, trying to pull the gas hose across the roof. "What in God's name are you doing?"

She jumped as she let out a loud shriek.

He was behind her in less than a second, holding her up as she tried to regain her balance. He tried his best not to think about how soft her hips felt beneath his hands, or the warmth spreading through him at the proximity.

"Nola, seriously. What the hell are you doing on top of your car?" he asked her again as he helped her back down. "You could hurt yourself."

She waved a hand dismissively. "I would have been fine if you hadn't tried sneaking up on me. And since when do cars have gas tanks on the left side now?"

He glanced at the rental car she was driving and realized

that her gas tank was on the side facing away from the pump. "Uh, depends on the car. But it's certainly not unusual. That's why you check your dashboard to see what side of the car the tank is on before you pull up to the pump."

Nola's hands went to her hips. "I know how to pump gas, Tanner."

"You sure about that?" He lifted a brow as he pointed to the spectacle in front of him, which was now a very short gas hose dangling over a too-large car. "Seems you might have missed a step here or there."

"I'm sure you're loving this," she replied as she pulled the hose back to the pump and put it away. "I'll just turn the car around. It's not that complicated."

"Okay, but next time look at which way the arrow is pointing on the dashboard next to the gas pump sign. That says which side of the car the tank is on." Tanner heard the clink of his gas pump as it finished and shut off. "Did you grab some extra fuel for the generator? The storm coming in is going to be rough. Might need to sit it out for a few days."

She scrunched up her face. "I have a generator?"

"I would hope so . . ." Tanner ran a hand over the back of his neck in an attempt to soothe his irritation. This woman was clearly too used to the luxuries of living in a big city. Had it really been so long since she'd lived here and remembered battling the storms by candlelight? "Please tell me you are ready for the storm with all the supplies you might need."

Nola shrugged. "The thermostat works just fine. I press a button and I'm warm. Plus, we have plenty of candles. I could build a fire if I needed to, you know."

"*You* could build a fire?" Tanner lifted his brows and tried not to smile, but the idea seemed far-fetched. "Since when?"

She narrowed her eyes at him. "I was a Girl Scout for six years, Tanner. Of course I know how to build a fire."

He shook his head and started to walk back to his truck. "Well, good for you. I'm sure your candles will be very helpful. Don't freeze to death out there."

"Thanks for your concern," she snapped back, climbing into her car.

He could practically feel her shooting daggers at him as she slammed the door closed and glared at him. As she pumped her gas, he offered her a wave and way-too-wide smile that he knew would just piss her off more. She practically spun her tires trying to get out of the lot as quickly as possible. Tanner finished putting his gas hose away and closed his tank. His jaw was clenched and he took a deep breath as he climbed back into the driver's seat of his old truck. Christ, everything about that woman got on his last nerve. He was just trying to look out for her, but of course she had no interest in his help.

She had no interest in Heart Lake in general.

Thankfully, he was quickly distracted from his thoughts when he arrived at his father's house and opened the front door to hear the bustling commotion of his family preparing for their usual Sunday-night dinner. The twins were fighting over something in the living room, so he bypassed them and went straight to the kitchen where his sister, Rosie, was standing in front of the stove.

"Smells good in here," he commented as he swiped a finger through the big bowl of mashed potatoes sitting on the counter.

Rosie flailed a hand at him, trying to push him away. "Don't stick your grimy hands in my hard work!"

"Okay!" He put his hands up in defense and then snuck another swipe the moment she looked away. Honestly, his sister was one of the best cooks he knew, and if Sunday dinners weren't already a tradition for them, he'd still be stopping by just to get a home-cooked meal from her.

"Tanner, is that you?" Thomas called out to him from the open doorway to the back porch. A cold draft was coming in, so he pulled his jacket tighter around him.

"Yeah, Dad." Tanner left Rosie's side and stepped out of the kitchen onto the porch. It was his father's favorite part of his house and spanned the entire back length. There was a set of steps on the left to walk down to the grass that jutted out to the end of the ledge overlooking the water, but Thomas hadn't been able to take them on the boat in years, not since his back injury. Last summer, however, Tanner had helped put in a ramp at the other end of the porch and then put a paved path down to the fire pit that sat near the water. His father used it often now, spending his evenings sitting out by the flames with a cold beer. At least, when he wasn't sitting in front of the television and snoring, ignoring the physical therapy and chiropractor pamphlets Tanner would leave on the coffee table.

"Hey, son." Thomas nodded at him from where he was sitting in a large wooden chair, his feet up on a wooden stool and a wool blanket across his lap. He had a hot cup of coffee, or maybe tea, in his hand and a thick sweater on, but Tanner was still confused as to how he wasn't freezing out here. "How's the house on Valley coming along?"

Tanner plopped down in the chair next to his father. "We're almost done with the renovations. We will be about a week ahead of schedule, actually. Hoping to wrap up in the beginning of the new year, though our deadline is February first."

Thomas looked pleased. "Great. They're good people."

He agreed but didn't respond. They sat silently next to each other for a bit, just taking in the view. The ice coated the surface of the lake, looking like glass. The sky was gray and Tanner thought back to his conversation with Nola only a few minutes ago. He hoped she was getting ready for the storm.

Not that he was admitting to caring about Nola. No, that wasn't it at all. He just cared about his sister, and his sister cared about Nola...so, for his sister's sake, he needed Nola to stay safe. At least, that was the story he was going to go with.

"Dinner is ready!" Rosie called out the back door. She paused and placed her hands on her hips. "Christ, it's chilly out here. Dad, you need to come inside before you freeze to death."

"What about me?" Tanner asked as he got to his feet and then helped his father to do the same. He handed him his cane and walked beside him as they reentered the house.

"You can stay out there," Rosie teased, pretending to close the door behind her and lock him out.

Tanner knocked his shoulder into hers slightly, laughing. "You wish."

"I need a head count for the Yule Log Dinner, by the way." Rosie pulled out their father's chair at the dining room table and helped him settle into it. "Are you inviting Blake this year? I know he's new, but he doesn't really have anyone else in town. I think it would be a nice gesture, don't you?"

"That's a good idea," Tanner confirmed. The annual Yule Log Dinner was a simple tradition their family had done every year on Christmas Eve for as long as he could remember. Once upon a time it had been their mother's tradition, and she loved bringing over as many neighbors, friends, and family as possible to celebrate. Since their mother's passing, Rosie had mostly taken the reins, but Tanner tried to help where he could. He knew how much it meant to their father to keep their mother's traditions alive. "I don't know if he is staying in town for the holiday or not, but I'll ask."

Rosie called the twins into the dining room and instructed them to take their seats as she began bringing food in from the kitchen and filling the table. "What about a date, Tanner?"

"Is Blake dating anyone?" He hadn't asked his employee about his love life, nor did he really care to know. "I don't think he's married. I haven't asked him about his relationship status."

"Not for Blake." Rosie rolled her eyes as she took a seat across from him and began piling food onto their father's plate. She gave a stern look to Zander when he shoved an entire roll in his mouth before even getting to his vegetables. "You. Nola's single, you know."

Tanner ignored the comment, though he knew his sister was more perceptive than he gave her credit for.

"Nola is back in town?" Thomas looked up, a forkful of mashed potatoes in his hand. "I haven't talked with that girl in a few years. She was too busy when her grandmother passed. I'm still sad about that loss. Gigi was a force to be reckoned with."

"She's selling The Castle," Tanner volunteered, then took a swig of his drink. "Making a pretty penny off it, too. So, I'd say she's doing just fine."

Rosie frowned. "That's not really fair. She needs to sell it."

"Does she?" Tanner countered, not backing down.

His sister shot him an annoyed look but didn't respond.

"Well, bring her to the dinner," Thomas continued. "I would love to see her again. She always was a good kid." He pointed at Rosie. "Helped keep this one here in line."

"Me?" Rosie balked, her hand on her chest. "I was practically a saint."

Tanner let out a loud laugh that startled one of the twins. Thomas grinned and shook his head.

"You? A saint?" Tanner winked at Zander and passed

him another roll. "I never thought I'd see the day. Sheriff Etson knew our address by heart thanks to the number of times he dragged you back home."

"That never happened. Kids, your uncle is making up stories. Your mother always followed the rules." Rosie bristled, but she was smiling, too. "This is exactly why we need more women in this family. You all gang up on us. Right, Becca?"

"Right!" Becca reached up and high-fived her mother. "Can Aunt Nola be in our family? She is fun!"

"Sure," Rosie replied. "Just ask Uncle Tanner to marry her."

Tanner coughed, the piece of steak in his throat suddenly lodging in place. He pounded on his chest for a moment, trying to clear his airway. It finally came loose and air poured back into his lungs. Christ, the very thought had nearly killed him.

"Uncle Tanner, can you marry Aunt Nola?" Becca had her hands clasped together like she was praying. "I want to be a flower girl! Or a bridesmaid. Wait, can I be both?"

"Ignore your mother," Tanner replied once he was finally able to breathe again. "No one is getting married in here."

"Speak for yourself, son." Thomas let out a low chuckle and then dug back into his food. A glob of mashed potatoes fell off his fork and back onto his plate. "I'll be bringing a guest to dinner as well, Rosie."

Rosie and Tanner both turned to look at their father, eyes wide.

"What? Who?" Rosie scrunched up her brow as she examined Thomas. "Oh my God, Dad. Are you dating someone?"

Thomas was avoiding both of their gazes, however. "Just make sure to add a space next to me at the table."

While their mother had always invited half the town to this dinner every year, his father had always been the opposite. It wasn't that Thomas wasn't social, except that he...

wasn't social. Hell, the only people who knew him had met him through his late wife or through Tanner and Rosie. He could be a bit of a grump, but more than that, he just kept to himself. He was a quiet man who didn't need a lot, and people respected that about him. If Tanner was being truthful, he knew that he had a bit of his father's reputation as well. He tended to keep to himself, even back in school. He was much more at home in nature or in the shop than he'd ever been at a party. He certainly couldn't say the same for his sister, since she'd definitely inherited their mother's social butterfly personality.

"Dad, you can't just drop a bomb like that and expect me not to ask questions," Rosie said, continuing to pester their father. She was pointing the end of her spoon at him with her eyes narrowed. "Are you talking about a date? Are you dating? Since when do you date?"

"Rosie, leave the poor old man alone," Tanner interjected. He popped another roll into his mouth, grinning at Zander, who was trying to sneak his third when his mother wasn't looking. "He's entitled to a private life."

"Well, now you have to bring a date, Tanner," Rosie shot back at him, pointing her spoon in his direction now. "You're going to let your father show you up as the most eligible bachelor in Heart Lake?"

Both Thomas and Tanner laughed at that one, but Zander quickly interjected that he was eligible, too. Soon the whole table was laughing and moving on to talk about tomorrow's annual eggnog contest in the town square. Their family had entered his mother's recipe for years, but they always came in second place to Perry Mott. This year, however, Rosie was determined to best him. Tanner smiled at the lively conversation, but he couldn't help picturing Nola at the table with them like part of the family.

They'd had so much fun dressing up with the twins—the banter and camaraderie had been easy. Things felt seamless between them, at least when they weren't bickering. It hadn't been like before... It was more than just the memories from childhood or the way she'd cared for him when he'd been hurting the most. The way she'd helped him after he'd lost his mother—he wasn't sure she even remembered making those parking signs with him. But he did.

He'd never forget, especially when he saw those same moments of kindness and support in her now around the twins and his sister. Tanner tried to shake the thought from his head, but... he wasn't sure he could anymore.

Chapter Eleven

"I will never understand this town's obsession with eggnog." Nola wrinkled her nose and huddled under a portable space heater while sipping a sample cup of one of two dozen varieties entered into Heart Lake's annual eggnog contest. The town square's historic gazebo had been completely decked out in Christmas decorations, and every entrant had their own table with samples of their eggnog for people to try and vote on. Along with their eggnog drink, every table had one dessert that was eggnog flavored to try and bribe voters even more—everything from cakes to coffees to ice creams. The Rotary Club donated the grand prize: a winter of free snow plowing for the winner's driveway—a coveted award in a place like Heart Lake.

"Eggnog is everything good about Christmas," Amanda countered, grabbing a second sample and chugging it in seconds. "Creamy, nutmegy richness—it's the very definition of holiday cheer."

"Well, of course you would love eggnog," Nola teased, nudging her friend with her elbow before adjusting her shades—the sun was bright against the snow. "You're basically Santa's elf."

Amanda grinned and shook her head just enough to make her jingle bell earrings clink. "Ho ho ho. Oh, by the way, the Christmas decoration idea was genius."

"I told you that service would be popular," Nola replied,

then gestured around the town square. "Just look at what you did with this area in just a matter of hours. It's beautiful."

Nola had suggested a while back that her friend offer interior and exterior holiday decorating as an add-on service in her business. Amanda had been a bit unsure of it at the time, considering that it was such a seasonal offer, but she'd given it a try anyway. It had been a hit, and this year, she'd even done the exterior Christmas decorations for the contest.

"It really exploded," Amanda agreed. "I didn't realize there was such a demand for it, but I've decorated damn near half the houses in this town at this point. In fact, business has been booming so much I had to hire two high school kids to help keep up."

"We'll need to go on a drive later to see all the lights." Nola glanced up at the sky and the clouds creeping in on the horizon. "If the storm doesn't come early, that is."

Amanda nodded. "Yeah. The storm is only a few hours away, from what the weatherman said. Also, I have a new baby to take care of."

"I'm sorry—can you repeat that?" Nola gaped.

Amanda gave a sheepish shrug. "A fur baby. I adopted a rescue puppy yesterday. It's a French bulldog—mostly."

"Are you kidding me? Those dogs are the cutest! What's its name?"

"Waffle."

Nola burst out laughing. "You're kidding."

"Hey!" Amanda pretended to be miffed. "That's my child you're laughing at."

"I'm sorry. I am not laughing to be mean. It's just…Waffle."

Amanda pulled up a photo of the pup on her phone and held it out to Nola. "That was the name the shelter gave him. Poor thing was abandoned outside of a Waffle House. So, Waffle it is."

Nola fawned over the adorable picture. "Well, congrats. I'm excited to meet the new addition."

Amanda tucked her phone back into her pocket. "Yes, for sure. After the storm you can meet his royal cuteness."

Nola was charmed. She wasn't used to seeing her independent friend so doting and nurturing. "Okay, you can go soon. But Rosie's eggnog and cookies are next." Nola pointed at the closest table in the line. "Remember, she really wants to win this year."

"Hey, I am an honest judger," Amanda replied, chuckling lightly. "I won't allow friendship to sway my vote."

Nola shushed her as they approached Rosie's table. "Hey, Rosie. What do you have for us this year?"

"New and improved!" Rosie handed both of them a small paper cup of dark-colored eggnog. "It's my mom's recipe but with a little something extra."

"What's the secret ingredient?" Nola asked, sipping on the creamy treat. "Mmm, this is good."

"Secret means *secret*." Rosie grinned and put her hands on her hips. "But I expect you both to give me tens across the board on the voting card."

Amanda held up her card. "I cannot be bought. My judging is always ethical."

"As ethical as that time you puked peppermint schnapps into the principal's desk drawer after prom?" Rosie tilted her head to the side and grinned. "They couldn't figure out where the smell was coming from for a week."

Amanda laughed. "I cannot be blackmailed either. Principal Mullins is retired anyway. What's she going to do— put me in detention?"

Rosie shrugged, then handed them both a cookie wrapped in a napkin. "Well, try the eggnog cookies because there's no way you'd vote that anything other than a ten. It's got a nutmeg-sugar sprinkle on top and is truly perfection."

Nola hesitantly took a bite of the cookie. It was pretty good, honestly, but eggnog was still her least favorite flavor.

"Nola Bennett." A familiar voice rose from behind, and Nola turned to see Craig standing there with a silver flask in his hand. "Funny running into you here."

"Is it?" Amanda cocked her head to the side, then waved her hand around the square. "Literally everyone in town is here."

Nola shot her a stern look. She knew neither of her best friends were Craig's biggest fans, but she still wanted the sale to go through. "Hi, Craig. Nice to see you again. Did you try some eggnog?"

He lifted his flask. "I did. And I brought a little additive for it as well. Care to join me?"

"Actually..." Nola glanced furtively toward Rosie's table, pleased to see her helping someone else and not paying attention to them. "I'll take a little."

She held out her cup of eggnog to Craig and he poured in a dash of liquor.

"This is really bringing me back." He capped the flask and tucked it into his pocket. "Remember when we stole my pop's liquor and replaced it with water?"

Nola grinned, scoffing lightly. "He figured it out right away. I had no idea the container would burst in the freezer like that."

"I really shouldn't have skipped science class so often," Craig joked as he watched her down the drink. "That should warm you up a bit, anyway. There's a storm coming, you know."

"I've heard," she said, her mind immediately going to Tanner and his repeated warnings about being prepared. "Rosie's going to lend me some flashlights and batteries."

Craig nodded, and there was a softness to his gaze that she remembered from years ago. It was hard to believe, but there was a sensitive side to him under there somewhere.

She'd seen it before, mostly when his father had screamed at him. She remembered the way he'd shown up on her doorstep, disheveled and tearstained with a black eye. He hadn't wanted to talk about it, but Nola knew his father had a temper. "That's one option," he replied. "I'm headed back to Chicago after this. Going to beat the storm home and ride it out in my penthouse. You should come join me."

"Shouldn't you ask your wife before inviting guests over?" Amanda cut in, smirking.

Nola felt her cheeks heat. "Amanda!"

He leveled a look at her friend and cleared his throat. Any gentleness was long gone and a stony gaze was plastered in its place. "I would ask her, but she's in the Mediterranean with her tennis instructor."

"Oh." Amanda looked slightly uncomfortable now. "Well, that sounds like an expensive lesson."

"It was," Craig agreed, now laughing lightly. "It only cost me half my assets. Too bad I can't return the boob job I paid for."

Nola cringed, remembering the time that Craig's father had told him that he shouldn't date a girl with no tits—while she'd been standing right next to him. At the time, she'd just been embarrassed and felt gross. She'd begun stuffing her bra whenever she went over to his house and tried to avoid his father as much as she could. It had taken her a while to move past that time in her life, to love herself the way she was, and living in Chicago had certainly helped her achieve that. But being back in Heart Lake around all the same people tended to make her feel like the younger version of herself and reminded her that she absolutely couldn't wait to get back to Chicago.

"Wow." Amanda shook her head with disdain, then grabbed Nola's arm and steered her toward the next table.

"See you later, Craig. I can't believe you ever dated that douchebag."

"He wasn't always so...crass," she replied, following Amanda to the next table where Mr. Mott handed her a cup of eggnog ice cream. "His dad was sort of the worst, so maybe it rubbed off on him."

"I never really liked the guy, but you were too busy paying attention to his six-pack," Amanda joked.

"Amanda," Nola chastised, though she couldn't help but laugh a little. "I mean it—his dad was pretty toxic. Not exactly role model material."

"Well, he's a grown man now who stands on his own two feet." Amanda took a scoop of the ice cream. "And I swear to crackers on Christmas that I will never speak to you if you date Craig again."

"Never going to happen in a million years." Nola shuddered, then tried her ice cream. "Oh wow. Mr. Mott, this is very good!"

The older man raised his brows and grinned. "Is it, now?"

"I mean..." Nola stammered. "Of course it's good. I just am not an eggnog person, so I'm surprised I like this so much."

"I've been known to convert a few lost souls in my time." Mr. Mott winked and handed her a cup of eggnog. "Here, try my eggnog. It's even better than the ice cream."

Nola didn't hesitate and took a swig. Its flavor was similar to the ice cream but even richer and denser. She smiled and nodded her head at him even though she preferred the ice cream by far. "You're a top contender again this year."

He grinned and handed Amanda a cup. "It would be nice to go out undefeated on my last Christmas in Heart Lake."

"I heard Boca is calling for you," Nola replied. "You must be thrilled to get out of here."

Mr. Mott frowned slightly. "Well, I wouldn't say I'm thrilled. I've loved every minute of being in this town. This place is special—mark my words. But sometimes in relationships you make compromises. Ronald doesn't like the cold, and I don't mind the heat, so Boca it is."

Nola nodded and a strange feeling of guilt swelled in her chest. For some reason, she'd assumed anyone moving out of Heart Lake was as eager as she was to start fresh and new in a better place, but the expression on Mr. Mott's face said the opposite. Her thoughts drifted to The Castle and the pending offer from Craig's company that had just come in, now that they'd worked out details. Somehow her excitement over it seemed to have dampened slightly, and she wondered if she was going to miss Heart Lake in the same way Mr. Mott would. She glanced around the square, trying to see the town the way he must see it. It wasn't hard to do. Heart Lake was beautiful—that was impossible to deny—but it wasn't just the way the town looked or how the historic structures mixed with the modern in a way that was quaint and assertive. It was the people milling around the town, laughing and chatting with one another—it was the atmosphere around them.

It felt so much like Gigi, and her heart squeezed at the reminder.

"Come on." Amanda nudged Nola toward the next table as she thanked Perry. "Marvel's next."

"Girls!" Marvel waved them over with a crooked grin and handed them both a small cup. "Tell me what you think!"

Nola sniffed the concoction, confused as to why it looked more like apple juice instead of eggnog. "This is eggnog?"

Marvel shook her head. "No, it's my apple cider. I put a scoop of my eggnog ice cream in it like a root beer float. Here, try some."

She dropped a dollop of the ice cream in both of their cups.

Amanda made a *cheers* motion with her cup and then drank hers. "Ooh, Marvel, this is tasty."

The woman beamed and lifted her chin. "Didn't I tell you? Perry thinks he can win the pity vote because it's his last year in the contest. Think again, Mott!"

She yelled the last part loud enough for him to hear her from his table. He just laughed and waved her away.

"You should see what I do with a hot cup of joe and eggnog," Marvel continued, returning her attention to the girls. "You will see stars."

Nola chuckled. "I'll have to try that someday."

Or not.

"Make sure to give me a ten on the scorecard there." Marvel pointed to the cards in Nola's hand. "I'm counting on your vote."

Nola chuckled and nodded her head as she followed Amanda to the next station. "Voting is cutthroat this year!"

"Yeah, right?" Amanda tasted an eggnog muffin at the next station thanks to Ruth, the owner of Itty Bitties Day Care. "I can't vote ten on all of them."

"At least the voting is anonymous," Nola replied, smiling at Ruth and thanking her for the eggnog and muffin, which she would absolutely not be finishing because it sank down her throat like a brick.

"Aren't you going to miss this?" They walked around the corner and Amanda grinned at her as she discreetly tossed her muffin into a nearby trash can. "This town has character."

"You're not wrong there," Nola agreed. "But Chicago certainly isn't lacking in personality. And imagine—if I make it big there, I can make it anywhere."

"I guess." Amanda wrote a few notes on her scorecard. "But what do you define success as? Is it about that recognition and title? The money? Or is it about making a difference in people's lives and having an impact? I could move to New York or Los Angeles and charge insane prices to decorate rich people's houses. I could make a name for myself that way if I wanted to—I know I have the talent to do it. But there's something about being here in my hometown and around people who truly appreciate me and my work—it adds another level. Bringing beauty and stress relief to people in Middle America has become my definition of success."

Nola thought about what her friend was saying, and she certainly didn't disagree. She'd never thought of Amanda as less successful because she'd stayed local. And still . . . something in her gut told her she needed to be more, see more, do more. Her mind flickered back to her earlier thought of how Craig's bigger dreams influenced her when they dated. But Craig's dreams had been an escape for him . . . Nola wasn't sure she had the same motivations with The Castle.

"That's lovely," Nola finally replied.

She glanced up after their next two table visits and noticed Tanner standing on the sidewalk talking to Mattie, the waitress from the Black Sheep Diner. He was leaning in close to her and showing her something on his phone. It was innocent enough, but she felt a prickle go down her spine at the thought of Tanner potentially being involved with the young woman. Not that he couldn't be. He was free to date whoever he wanted, and Mattie was certainly pretty and sweet. Nola didn't care one bit.

So why was the scene bothering her so much right now?

"Ready to go?" she said to Amanda, dropping her scorecards in the ballot box. "I don't think I can eat any more eggnog anything. I'm going to dream of nutmeg tonight."

"You go. I have to stay behind to clean up after," Amanda reminded her. "I'll catch you after the storm. You've got enough supplies to ride it out, right?"

Nola nodded, not wanting her friend to worry about her. "More than enough," she promised. "Candles, flashlights. The whole nine yards."

Amanda looked a bit skeptical but shrugged. "Okay, well, call me if you come across any binge-worthy shows. This weather is perfect for hibernating in front of the television with a bowl of popcorn."

"Will do." She gave her friend a quick hug and then waved goodbye to Rosie as she headed for her car parked on a nearby side street.

"Nola!" Tanner jogged down the sidewalk to catch up to her, but she didn't slow down or wait for him. "Whoa, whoa, whoa—wait up. Why are you running?"

"I'm not," she replied haughtily, though she was visibly picking up her pace even more. "I've just got places to be."

He finally caught up and let out a breath. "Great, but I wanted to stop by and drop off a generator before the storm. Do you have extra gas or should I bring that, too?"

"Didn't we already have this conversation?" She stopped and turned to face him, her hands on her hips now. "I told you I was just fine. I've lived in Heart Lake for most of my life. I know how to handle a little snow."

"Yeah, but it's been a good ten years since you've lived here," he began. "I'm not sure Gigi had her generator serviced in the last few years, and it would be good to have a backup."

"Honestly, Tanner, I'm not your problem and it's none of your business," she shot back. "You clearly don't approve of me and my choices anyway, so why bother me now?"

He stepped back slightly, looking surprised. Irritation

flooded his expression seconds later. "Fine. Have it your way. You always know best, right?"

Tanner shook his head and walked away with firm stomps against the sidewalk. Nola watched him for a moment, trying to figure out why she felt guilty...again.

She turned and walked back to her car at a slower pace. When *was* the last time Gigi had had the generator serviced? Nola sighed and hoped she hadn't bitten off more than she could chew.

Chapter Twelve

Tanner pulled into the only empty parking spot at Hobbes Grocery. It seemed half the town was here prepping for the incoming storm—not that he was surprised. Heart Lake wasn't a town that panicked. They were always prepared for weather emergencies. No one was a stranger to this type of storm, and people were always willing to lend a hand in times like these. There was no hoarding of supplies or price gouging—only sharing, distribution to those who couldn't afford it, and friends checking in on each other to make sure everyone was holding up well.

He loved a lot of things about this town, but their neighborly concern was his favorite.

Tanner thought of Nola again as he stepped out of his truck and headed into the store to grab a few additional snacks and some extra batteries. An older woman handed him a basket and smiled. "Hey, Sherry," he said, greeting her. "You ready for the storm?"

"Oh, we're more than ready. It's supposed to be a doozy, so we've stocked up on enough gas for the generator to last to Armageddon." Sherry looked toward the cash register and smiled at her husband running the till, Old Man Hobbes.

Tanner realized he didn't actually know her husband's name. He had always just gone by "Old Man Hobbes" and no one ever questioned it. "Good. Well, I'm glad you're going to be safe."

She nodded and then greeted the next customer coming in behind him. Tanner headed down the closest aisle and snagged a few boxes of his favorite cereal—Cheerios, multigrain, of course—and then grabbed a gallon of milk. He could live off of cereal for a few days just fine, but he figured it was probably best to grab some fruits and veggies as well. Of course, he snuck a pack of Double Stuf Oreos into his basket before he went to the register—his one guilty pleasure that he had to hide in a high cabinet in his kitchen or lose it to the twins every time they came over.

"Cereal and cookies? Certainly sounds like a bachelor." Craig Blasco sauntered up behind him in line at the register, holding nothing but a six-pack of beer.

Tanner eyed him skeptically. "Just beer? Certainly sounds like a bachelor not ready for a storm."

"Oh, I'm getting the hell out of Dodge before this storm rolls in," Craig replied, leaning against the conveyor belt. "This storm is coming from the east. I'll be holed up in Chicago with DoorDash delivering my meals."

"What the hell is DoorDash?" Tanner furrowed his brows, confused.

"Don't worry about it." Craig laughed and shook his head. "It's really more for us city folk. Heart Lake's too much in the middle of nowhere to have it, I bet."

Tanner bristled at Craig's condescending tone but just turned back to the cashier and smiled at her as he handed over his purchases.

"Once all this house business is finished, Nola and I can get snowed in together in Chicago. I guarantee she's a frequent DoorDash user. I wonder if I should get some wine for her when she comes over." Craig seemed to be musing out loud rather than talking to Tanner specifically, but it still pissed him off. "We'll practically be neighbors soon."

"Good for you." Tanner gritted his teeth and let out a low exhale in an attempt to keep from telling Craig what he was really thinking right now. Honestly, the image of him and Nola curled up together on a couch in some high-rise was enough to make his blood boil. He couldn't understand why she'd dated him in high school, but to continue to give him the time of day now? He felt beyond frustrated. "Have fun with that."

"What about you?" Craig continued, despite everything in Tanner's demeanor saying he didn't want to talk. "Who are you holing up with during this storm?"

"Just me," Tanner replied. "Maybe my sister if she needs me."

"Right, right." Craig nodded. "Rosie, huh? Good girl, that one. Shame about what happened with her baby daddy back in the day."

Tanner could feel his fists tighten almost automatically, but he made every attempt to force them to release. He just made a *hmm* noise in response. By this point, the cashier had finished ringing him up and was handing him his bags.

"Nice to see you as always, Craig." Tanner gave him the fakest smile he could muster and then walked out of the store. Once he was safely in his truck, he let out a low groan, almost a growl. He inhaled slowly, allowing his lungs to fill and release the tension in his muscles as he cracked his neck from side to side and then stuck the key in the ignition.

It wasn't that Craig was a monster. He wasn't. But he valued things that Tanner—and Heart Lake—just didn't stand for. Online food delivery. Fancy, showy things that showed off his wealth. And then the big one...the desire to run away the moment things got hard. Plus, Tanner had never liked the way Craig had treated Nola when they had dated. He never saw him being unkind to her, but she seemed to always act differently around him. Hell, everyone did. Craig demanded attention and anyone around him just had to deal with the leftovers.

Tanner's phone rang, pulling him out of his thoughts. He fished it out of his pocket and answered the call. "Hello?"

"Hey, Tanner," Blake boomed on the other end. "The guys finished weatherproofing the place on Sycamore. It should be fine during the storm."

"Good. What about you?"

"I think I might have overprepared," Blake admitted, chuckling lightly. "Where I'm from, people panic at the sight of rain. I've got enough toilet paper in my bathroom for six months. You know, just in case."

Tanner laughed, shaking his head. "In case of what?"

"Hey, you laugh, but toilet paper could be a hot commodity in the end times."

"Well, I'm glad you're stocked up on the essentials, but what about heat, food, and flashlights?" Tanner glanced in his rearview mirror, noting that the generator he'd been planning to bring to Nola's was still in the back of his pickup. He clenched his jaw, wondering if he should just ignore her and bring it over anyway. Or maybe Blake needed it.

"I've got two generators, a weighted blanket, about eight bags of chips, and, most importantly, a Wi-Fi hot spot to make sure I can keep watching ESPN during this whole mess." Blake began rattling off a bunch of sports stats, which Tanner only half listened to.

"Cool, glad you are all set. Call you when it's over." Tanner tossed his cell into the cup holder in the center console and then pulled out of the parking lot. Snow was already beginning to fall, though it wasn't quite sticking to the roads yet. He should have just enough time to do a final check on his father and Rosie. He'd already set them up with fully functional generators and every supply they could possibly need, but he still wanted to double-check. When it came to family, he wasn't going to mess around.

He pulled into his father's driveway and parked, dashing into the house before he froze.

"Hey? Dad?" Tanner called out as he shook the snow-flakes from his hair. "You here?"

"The living room," his father hollered.

Tanner walked in, expecting to see his father watching television from his recliner as usual. Instead, his dad was standing on a mat in the middle of the living room and had pushed the furniture out of the way. He had his hands over his head and was squatting low. "What the heck are you doing?"

"Yoga," his father responded, moving into another position with his arms stretched out to the side. "Don't start. It's good for the back. Gotta rebuild that core strength."

He frowned. "I'm not going to laugh. I'm just…surprised." That was the understatement of the year.

"It's a young man's game out there, Tanner," his father responded, now balancing on one foot. "Shape up or ship out."

Tanner watched him for a moment, concerned he might be having some sort of stroke. "Okay, well, I just wanted to make sure you were ready for the storm. Are you sure you don't want to come stay with Rosie or me for a few days? You don't have to be alone if you don't want to."

Thomas smiled and shook his head. "Don't worry about me, kid. I've been through more blizzards in my lifetime than you could count."

Tanner shrugged and tossed up his hands. "Okay, well, I tried. You have fun…downward dogging."

Tanner walked into the kitchen and checked that the fridge was fully stocked and that his dad had everything he needed. Once he was satisfied, he passed the living room to head toward the front door, pausing again to watch his father chanting some sort of mantra under his breath as he moved on the mat. Tanner shook his head. Honestly, he had no idea what the hell was going on anymore.

"Bye, Dad," he called out. "See you in a few days."

"Namaste, you son of a gun!" his father called back.

Chapter Thirteen

A loud thump jarred Nola awake as she sat up quickly in the large, quilted guest bed. There was no obvious cause for the noise as she looked around the room, but the thumping continued and seemed to be coming from the outside wall. She slid out of bed, shivering the moment her bare feet touched the freezing-cold wood floor, and walked over to the window. With a quick slide of the curtains, she pulled them open to look outside.

Except...that was pretty much impossible.

One of the tall trees by the house was banging against the siding every few moments, shaking off heavy clumps of snow that were trapped on its branches. In fact, snow was... everywhere. She could barely see a few feet past the window, as the storm was coming down in thick blankets and piling higher and higher on the ground with every passing moment.

Nola shivered and pulled the curtains closed again in an attempt to keep in the heat. She pulled on some fluffy socks that in no way matched the flannel pajama bottoms she was wearing. Wanting to bundle up further, she grabbed an old wool cardigan from the back of the closet and wrapped it around her shoulders. Covered completely now, she headed downstairs and started playing with the coffee machine. Gigi had been a tea drinker, so while she did own a coffeepot for guests, it had hardly ever been used and was an ancient relic at this point. Back in Chicago, Nola had a Keurig and made her coffee in a matter of seconds—something she definitely missed. Convenience was basically her love language when it came to anything in the kitchen.

After a few minutes of tinkering, however, Nola was able to get the machine to start brewing, and she grabbed a mug from the cabinet while she waited. The snow was still coming down outside the kitchen window, but she had turned up the thermostat on her way downstairs. Thank God Gigi had modernized the HVAC five years ago. There was a beautiful magic in watching the cold snow surround her as she was safe and sound inside.

She chuckled as she thought of Tanner's doomsday attitude while she poured herself a steaming hot cup of coffee. She didn't bother adding cream or sugar. That would only cool it down, and she wanted to feel the burn against her throat and warmth filling her belly. He was probably at home prepping his storm kit, or whatever emergency supplies he needed, while she was just fine in the warmth of The Castle. Honestly, she'd been through quite a few storms in her youth in this house, so she wasn't sure why he suddenly thought this one would be any different.

Her phone vibrated against the marble countertop and Nola glanced down at the screen. A silly picture of herself and her mother appeared alongside her mother's name, and Nola smiled at the memory of taking that photo a few years ago on her birthday. Baby Bennett was a wild soul—she'd have to be for someone who'd gone her entire life with that name. Legally, her name was Barbara, but if anyone dared call her that, there would be hell to pay.

"Hello?" Nola said, answering the video call and pointing it toward her face as she continued sipping her coffee.

Both her mother and father came on the screen, waving to her. "Hi, sweetheart! How are you doing?"

"Good!" She sat down at the kitchen table and tucked her legs beneath her. "We're getting a doozy of a storm. Quite a bit has fallen already. Perfect weather to cozy up and sort stuff. I've gotten through about half of Gigi's things at this point, though. It's coming together."

"Good work, honey," her father, Riggs Bennett, said, lifting what looked like a margarita to the camera. "Look what they give us for free at this resort."

"Dad, isn't it seven o'clock in the morning in Costa Rica?" Nola tried not to be jealous of the beach she saw behind her parents.

Her mother laughed. "Darling, it's five o'clock somewhere. You know we're early risers. We already had a sunrise swim. We might go back for round two in a bit."

"Well, Dad's going to drown," Nola teased. Her father wasn't much of a drinker, but he never turned down anything that was free. She had no doubt he'd have one margarita and be flat on his back asleep before their swim time.

Baby looked at her husband, grinning. "Maybe we'll get a handsome lifeguard who can save him? Or teach me while he's passed out."

Riggs scoffed. "I won't need saving. I'll be the *Baywatch* king out there, running through the sand in slow motion. You'll be having to push the ladies off of me."

Nola rolled her eyes, laughing at her parents' antics. "Okay, you guys be safe. I'm going to try and get through some more boxes this morning. At this rate, I'll be done before the new year with some time to spare."

"If you find a large box of bottle caps, make sure to save those," Riggs added. "Very important."

She scrunched up her nose. "Bottle caps? Really? Why?"

Her father shrugged. "I collected them as a kid."

"Riggs, you can't be serious." Baby looked at her husband. "Do you want to just collect more things for Nola to have to get rid of again when we die?"

"Morbid much?" Nola cringed at the thought, but she was certainly used to her parents' brash honesty at this point.

"I'll display them somehow. We can hang them up in the living room," he insisted to his wife. "They could be a collector's item. You never know."

"Nola, honey, listen to Mama. If you find them, throw them away." Her mom elbowed her dad, but they were both laughing. "We have to go, darling. But check in with us later. I want to know you're safe!"

"I will," she assured her parents before hanging up and tucking her phone into the pocket of her cardigan.

Grabbing her coffee, she headed down to the basement and opened a few boxes. Some of the things she found she could clearly give away—in fact, she wasn't even sure why her grandmother had six sewing machines. She'd only ever seen her do minor patchwork here and there on clothes by hand but certainly never with an entire machine. Rosie, however, sewed often and made most, if not all, of her children's clothes. Nola picked out the sewing machine in the newest condition to set aside for her. She pulled out her phone and snapped a quick picture of it, then texted it to Rosie to ask her if she wanted it.

Within seconds, her phone rang.

"Hello?" Nola answered, turning on the speakerphone and putting the phone down as she continued to go through more boxes.

"I'm adding Amanda in," Rosie said, not even bothering to say hello. "Oh, and yes, save me that machine. I can pick it up later. I totally need it."

"Okay," Nola agreed. The next box she opened was small but filled to the brim with unused plastic cutlery. "What the heck?"

"What happened?" Amanda's voice came on the phone alongside Rosie's.

"I'm going through Gigi's things, and she collected the oddest items. I swear, it's ridiculous the things she saved." Nola put that box aside in a donation pile. "At this point, I could basically start a random hobby shop out of the basement alone."

"If you come across any pet supplies, let me know," Amanda replied. "Waffle is turning out to be a handful!"

Rosie laughed. "I still can't believe you own a dog."

"He's a Frenchie," Amanda clarified. "And he ate two pairs of my heels. But he is adorable."

"The cutest alien I've ever seen." Nola giggled, remembering the adorable photo Amanda had shown her at the eggnog contest. "But it kinda looks like his eyes are about to pop out of his head."

"He hasn't grown into his face yet," Amanda huffed. "Anyway, how do you take a small dog out in the snow? I've tried to take him out to pee twice already and he won't take a single step out the front door."

"I mean...neither would I," Rosie chimed in. "There's already, like, two feet of snow out there. The kids are bouncing off the walls, but I'm a few minutes away from tossing them in parkas and throwing them into the snowbank."

"I think you have to use those indoor puppy pads for times like these," Nola advised, though she wasn't the person to ask about pets. Her family had had a cat at one time, but it passed away when she was a teenager, and they'd never gotten another. Her parents said they wanted to travel, and pets make that harder. Now she was on her own, but she kept putting off getting a dog for fear that she wouldn't be able to handle the responsibility. After all, starting her own business was going to require a lot of time and manpower. That didn't mean that she didn't occasionally find herself drinking a glass of wine and browsing pet adoption sites just to coo over the sweet little furry faces.

"I've got newspaper... Would that work?" Amanda asked.

"I think so," Nola replied. "But I'm not an expert. Puppies are difficult. It's like having a baby."

"The hell it is," Rosie practically squawked into the phone receiver. "You try pushing two watermelons out your lady bits and then chasing them around for seven years while being covered in unidentifiable bodily fluids and having a tear straight to your butthole. Then tell me that's anything like having a goddamn puppy."

Nola winced. "Okay, so maybe it's not the exact same thing."

"Sorry, just one sec. Zander, we do not shoot Nerf bullets at the television!" Rosie hollered. "I don't care if you're playing war! Anything over twenty dollars is in the safe zone."

Nola chuckled as she listened to her friend, wondering what it would be like to have children of her own one day. She certainly wanted them, but the older she got, it seemed less and less likely. She wasn't even dating anyone, let alone having sex. It had been... too long. She sighed. "Do you remember when we had snow days as kids?"

"Oh man," Amanda said. "I would sit in front of the television watching the news and waiting, waiting, waiting for our school to come up in the banner at the bottom as 'closed' or 'delayed.' Whenever it wasn't there, I was devastated."

Nola laughed, because she certainly remembered the days of limited technology and not having the Internet to answer all her questions in seconds.

"These days, we all get a text alert in the morning if school is closed," Rosie confirmed. "Plus an email and a notice on the school website. Kids have it so easy now. They'll never understand holding rabbit ear antennas and praying for a miracle."

"Have they made a snowman yet?" Nola asked. That had

always been one of her favorite activities as a child, and she'd made entire snow families on the front lawn of The Castle once upon a time. Tanner often helped back then, which she always found to be super sweet. Until he'd ruin the moment with a surprise snowball to the back of her head. No matter, she always got him back ten times worse when she, Amanda, and Rosie teamed up against him in an all-out snowball war.

"Not yet," Rosie replied. "But, I'm—"

Nola waited for Rosie to finish her sentence, but she just heard a lot of unintelligible shouting in the background for a moment before Rosie finally returned to the phone.

"Rosie, you okay?" Amanda asked.

"I have to go. Our power just went out," Rosie explained. "Thanks to Tanner, our generator should kick on fast. But my backup plan is to head over to his place with the kids before the storm gets any worse."

Nola said her goodbyes and hung up the phone. Getting back to work, she dug through a few more boxes and sorted things between the keep and donation piles. Finally, she decided it was time for a lunch break and headed up the stairs.

Or at least she was halfway up the stairs before everything went dark.

Crap! Nola grabbed the wall and slowly made her way up the rest of the steps in the pitch black. Thankfully, it was easier to see on the main floor since the daylight was coming through the windows. But it was clear that the power was completely off in the entire house.

A shiver ran up her spine and goose bumps rose on her arms. She sighed as she realized she was going to have to make a fire in the fireplace to stay warm. And that the wood to build the fire was out in the shed behind the house. She had meant to bring it in just in case but had forgotten entirely. Clomping upstairs to the bedrooms, Nola made quick work of bundling herself into multiple pants, shirts, sweaters, and jackets. She was so layered it was almost hard to move.

Her first step out the back door toward the shed was when she realized she'd made a huge mistake. Not only was the snow up around her knees, but it was coming down so heavy that it was hard to see more than a few feet in front of her. She was pretty sure she knew the direction of the wood-shed, but...

Pulling her hat tighter on her head, Nola lifted her legs high and trudged through the snow for what seemed like an hour. By the time she stumbled across the shed, she could hardly feel her legs, and her nose felt like it might fall off. It was damn near impossible to get the door open with how much snow was piled in front of it, but she managed to pry it just far enough to reach inside and grab as many logs as she could reach. Tucking them under her arms, she headed back to the house. Thankfully the trip back was a bit easier now that she'd already carved a small walking path on her way to the shed.

The moment she got inside, she shed all her wet layers directly on the mudroom floor and ran upstairs to jump into a steaming-hot shower. After she was warmer, she bundled up into just as many clothes as before and went to grab the logs she'd left by the door. She placed them carefully in the fireplace, then went to look for a lighter.

Fifteen minutes later, she had found a few matches. She dragged one across the striker and held it up to the log.

And nothing.

Frustrated, she tried again. And again. Until she was down to her last match and began considering the possibility that a wet log might be pretty difficult to light... and that she actually couldn't remember how to properly light a fire from her Girl Scout days.

Never mind that—Google was still her best friend. The Internet had an answer for everything. She pulled out her phone and typed *how to build a fire* in the search bar. An error signal appeared on the screen. Nola frowned as she looked at the top bar on her phone and realized that the Wi-Fi was not connected and she had no service outside of that.

She glanced back down at the wet logs in her fireplace and the useless phone in her hand. A chill crawled across her skin and she went to sit on the couch, pulling a throw blanket tight around her. She wasn't going to panic. The power would come back on soon. She was sure of it.

She grabbed a paperback off the end table next to the couch and angled herself to get enough light from the window to read a few chapters. She added another blanket around her shoulders and cozied up to the story. Surely she'd find the candles before the sun set. At least, that's what she hoped—a few candles and a warm fire weren't a lot to ask for.

Chapter Fourteen

"Uncle Tanner?" Zander stepped into the garage from the side door that attached it to the house. He was bundled up in a sweater and thick pants, but he really didn't need to be. The power might be off for most of Heart Lake, but Tanner had seen to it that his generator was working properly. Not only did he have power, but he had heat... and lots of it. Including in the garage, which technically was more of a workshop for him than anything else.

"What's up, buddy?" Tanner turned to look at his nephew. "You guys finished lunch?"

Zander nodded but then looked bashful for a moment, wringing his hands together. "I had a question."

"Shoot."

Zander walked over to the workbench and ran his hand along the chair leg that Tanner had been carving. "I didn't get Mom anything for Christmas."

Tanner frowned. "Is that your question?"

"No," Zander continued. "I need your help to make her something. I spent my whole allowance on new ice skates, and I don't have anything left over. Can you help me?"

Tanner chuckled lightly. "Kid, you have perfectly good ice skates from last year."

"But Robby got new ones and said mine looked old." Zander picked up a hammer and twirled it around in his hands.

Not ready to see Zander hit himself, Tanner reached

forward and took the hammer. "We'll have to teach you to budget another time, but we can do a project for your mom in here. Did you ask your sister if she needs one, too?"

"Oh, let me check!" Zander ran back inside the house.

Looking around the workshop, Tanner assessed what scraps he had leftover that the kids could fashion into a simple gift for Rosie. His eyes passed over the fuel in the corner he used for his generator, and Nola's face crossed his mind from their conversation in town yesterday. He clenched his jaw as irritation rumbled through him. He shouldn't even be thinking about her, let alone worrying about how she was managing in the storm. She'd insisted she would be fine. She *had* been a Girl Scout, after all.

Tanner snorted at the thought, remembering her spending a lot more time eating cookies with Rosie that they were supposed to be selling, instead of learning wilderness skills. And Michigan in December? Everyone in Heart Lake had to know how to tough out a difficult storm... or three.

The garage windows were already piled high with snow, and the roads were impassable. Still, he wondered if he should check in on her and see if she was okay. He grabbed his phone off the nearby bench and sent a quick text message asking if she had power. It said *sending* but not *delivered*. He felt a slight worry in his gut but tried to push it away. Maybe it just took longer than normal to deliver because of the storm.

"Becca said she wants in!" Zander said as he burst back into the garage with his twin sister in tow.

"But I get to paint it," Becca added. She already was grabbing one of the grubby work aprons hanging off a hook on the wall by the door. "Zander can do the hammer stuff."

Tanner smiled at that, but there was no doubt that his niece was certainly skilled when it came to anything artistic.

"Well, I was thinking we could make a spice rack. Your mom has all her spices on the kitchen counter—and this could help."

"Yes! She would like that," Zander replied, his expression all-knowing as he climbed onto the bench and sat at the worktable.

Tanner grabbed the pieces of wood that they would need, as well as a few tools. It didn't take long for him to show them how to start putting it together. Zander struggled staying focused, but Becca kept showing him what to do when he snapped back to attention. Their dynamic was heartwarming, and Tanner felt that familiar realization that he loved this. There was something about teaching children, but particularly teaching woodwork, that hit his soul in a way nothing else did. These moments reminded him of learning from his own father, and how confident he'd felt as a young boy in shop. He didn't necessarily have that confidence in other aspects of his life, but with a piece of wood in his hand, he felt secure in who he was and how good it felt to create something.

"Uncle Tanner, Becca isn't letting me help!" Zander tried yanking a paintbrush away from his sister.

"I said I wanted to paint!" Becca pushed him away, focusing on the task at hand. They'd put together a quaint spice rack in record time, and now Becca was painting it deep red.

"How about Zander does the accent colors when you finish the base?" Tanner found a middle ground he thought they could agree on. Zander wasn't thrilled but settled for the compromise.

"Uncle Tanner, what are you going to give Nola for Christmas?" Becca asked a few minutes later as she handed her brother the brush.

Tanner blinked. "What?"

"You haven't gone shopping yet?" Becca put her hands on her hips like a tiny diva, and Tanner wanted to laugh, but he was still reeling over why he'd be getting Nola a Christmas gift. "Girls like presents, you know."

"I hadn't planned on getting her something," Tanner admitted. "Why do you ask?"

"Well, remember back when you got Emma the bird feeder?" Becca tilted her head to the side. "She didn't like that. It wasn't romantic. I like you with Nola a lot better than Emma anyway. She was boring."

"Uh…" Tanner stammered for a minute, trying to place how or why his niece knew so much about his love life—or lack thereof. "Nola and I are not dating."

"Okay, yeah," Becca replied. "But you should be. Don't you love her?"

If he hadn't already been thrown off by this conversation, that statement certainly would have done it.

"I like Nola as your mom's friend," Tanner tried to explain, though the words didn't feel genuine even as he said them. "It's not a love like that. Where would you even get a crazy idea like that?"

Becca rolled her eyes and then grabbed the paintbrush back from her brother. "I just know these things, Uncle Tanner. It's obvious."

"Hey, Tanner?" Rosie's voice called out from the house and seemed to be moving closer.

Tanner put a finger to his lips to silence the kids and quickly placed a box over the spice rack so that she wouldn't see her Christmas gift early.

"Are you in here?" Rosie popped her head into the garage. "Oh, hey, kids. I've got some snacks ready if you want to go eat."

"Yes!" Zander rushed past her, shedding his apron on the way. Becca followed him, but a bit slower.

Tanner chuckled, picking up the apron from the floor and hanging it back on the hook. "What's up, Rosie?"

"I'm worried about Nola. This storm is getting worse by the minute. It's been a long time since she's lived in Heart Lake. She's used to the city and landlords and all that jazz." Rosie crossed her arms over her chest, her lips turned down into a frown as she glanced out the window. "What if she lost power? What if she doesn't know what to do? She's not responding to my calls."

Tanner glanced down at his phone, also silent with no incoming messages. "She isn't answering the phone?"

"The call isn't even going through for her to be able to answer it!" Rosie paced back and forth. "Can you go over there? I know it's a lot to ask, and the weather is terrible. But maybe if you took the cross-country skis?"

Tanner followed her gaze out the window, where the snow was piling high. There was certainly no way he'd be able to drive to The Castle in the current conditions, but he was no stranger to using other ways to get around in a snowstorm. Cross-country skiing wasn't his favorite, but he was good at it when he needed to be. The fact that Rosie was sharing the same worries he had been having earlier only cemented it for him. Someone needed to go check on Nola despite the fact that she'd *insisted* she'd be just fine. Honestly, he was irritated that she hadn't just listened to him in the first place.

Then again, she never had.

"Yeah," Tanner agreed. "I can go check on her. I'll go get dressed, but can you pack a small bag of some basics? Matches, blankets, batteries, some food?"

Rosie nodded, a look of relief washing over her face. "Can you message me when you get there and let me know if she's safe?"

"I'll try." Tanner couldn't promise his phone would work

any better than hers out there, but he was more used to this area than she was. "But you owe me."

Rosie smiled and threw her arms around him in a big hug. "You can be grumpy all you want, but you are the best big brother ever."

He huffed and rolled his eyes but let her hug him anyway. "Okay. Let's go. We're wasting time."

Secretly, he was excited to see Nola as much as he wanted to also ease his sister's mind. Heck, he'd really be easing his own mind. He had a bad feeling that she wasn't doing as well as she'd pretended earlier.

He needed to make sure she was safe.

Chapter Fifteen

The blanket she had wrapped herself in might as well have been tissue paper. Nola pulled it tighter around her shoulders as she sat on the floor in front of the fireplace. She'd found more matches buried in the kitchen and she'd put them to use. Small embers were pulsing and little bits of smoke puffed out every once in a while, but there were no warm flames. Despite her best efforts, she hadn't been able to figure out how to build the fire, only light it.

That was at least a start.

Her stomach growled and she glanced toward the kitchen, wondering if it was worth it to leave this spot to find something to eat. She had already gone through most of the food she'd bought on her first day here, and what was left were a few rice cakes and a couple bottles of wine. Not really substantive in her last moments alive. Not that she was worried about dying, but the thought had crossed her mind. If she were to freeze to death right now, how long would it take for someone to find her? She shivered at the thought and checked her phone again. It was on its very last bit of battery, working overtime in an attempt to connect to any network.

Bang! A noise from the front porch caused Nola to jump. It sounded different than the noises she'd become accustomed to of the trees rubbing up against the siding or the snow falling off the roof. She pushed up to her feet and walked slowly to the front hall, peeking around the corner.

A large, dark figure moved across the porch. She couldn't make out who it was, given that the windows were all stained glass, but there was no mistaking the fact that it was clearly an axe murderer. A true-crime podcast junkie, Nola had heard stories like these one time too often. Woman stranded in a snowstorm, murdered by a serial killer on the loose? It was classic fodder for the shows she listened to.

Not today, asshole. Nola ran quickly toward the mud-room and grabbed the first thing she could find to use as a weapon—a badminton racket that Gigi had used in the summers to play her favorite game. Okay, so it wasn't perfect, but she wasn't going down without a fight.

The killer pounded on the front door again, and Nola lifted her racket high, ready to strike. Why the hell was a serial killer knocking on the door anyway? Or was he trying to bang it down? She could feel the goose bumps breaking out across her skin.

Suddenly, the door flew open and the figure stepped inside with a gust of snow.

Nola went feral. Screaming like a banshee, she waved the racket around, smashing it against the intruder as hard as she could.

"What the hell!" The intruder pushed his hood off and she recognized Tanner's voice and familiar handsome face. "Did you just hit me... with a racket? A very tiny racket?"

She paused, glancing down at the weapon of mass destruction in her hands. Grinning sheepishly, she lowered it. "To be fair, you were supposed to be an axe murderer."

"Sorry to disappoint," he replied, pushing the door closed behind him. "The night is still young, though."

Nola dropped the racket and resumed pulling the blanket around her shoulders as the cold air from the doorway had caused her to shiver harder than before. "Ha ha. You're hilarious. Why are you even here? How did you get here?"

"Skis," he said nonchalantly as he worked himself out of his wet boots and gear. "Rosie said her calls weren't going through. She insisted I check you were alive."

"Well, a few more minutes and you might have found my frozen corpse." Nola gestured to the house around her. "As you can see, no power, no heat, and no idea what I'm doing."

Tanner smiled, but it was that cocky smirk that always pissed her off. "Ah, so your days as a Girl Scout didn't prepare you for this?"

Nola rolled her eyes and walked back to the living room as he followed closely. "Again—hilarious. But since you are here, help me build a fire before I literally freeze."

He looked at the few embers sparking in the fireplace. "What's that?"

"My fire."

"Is it, though?" He scrunched up his face and then laughed. "Christ, you seriously would have frozen to death."

"Again, ha ha." She plopped down on the couch.

Tanner shook his head. "No, come here. I'm going to teach you how to build a fire correctly."

She wasn't in the mood for anything but a warm drink. Still, she sighed and joined him by the hearth. He wasn't wrong—she did need to learn if she wanted to survive the next few days in this storm.

Despite their usual annoyance with one another, Tanner was actually quite helpful and slowly walked her through the steps to not only lighting a fire, but building it. The living room fireplace was basically roaring in minutes and it felt delicious against her skin. They repeated the process in the bedroom fireplace, this time with Tanner supervising as she did it herself.

It wasn't as hard as she'd remembered, but without his help—or a YouTube tutorial—there was no way she'd have figured this out on her own.

"I feel like I'm coming back to life," Nola said, rubbing her hands in front of the fire in the living room where they'd returned. "It's so warm in here."

Tanner glanced out the window, the snow still piling high. The sky had darkened now. "Glad I could help. I'd better hurry home before it gets worse."

She followed his gaze, but a ball of nerves rolled around in her stomach. It was almost completely dark at this point, and she couldn't imagine how much snow was out there. Trekking back to his house in that seemed very dangerous. She wasn't sure she'd ever forgive herself if something happened to him because he'd come to help her.

"Or you could stay here? You know, at least until the storm clears?"

Tanner lifted one brow as he turned back to look at her. "What?"

"It's just very dark outside already." Nola pointed to the window but now felt like she didn't know what to do with her hands. Fidgeting seemed the best choice. "It's really too dangerous to go back out there. Heck, it was too dangerous to travel here in the first place. I don't want to think about what could happen."

His face softened slightly, and his shoulders dropped. "You'd worry about me?"

She lifted her chin, avoiding eye contact. "I mean, yeah."

They were both quiet for a moment, and there was a strange shift in the air between them. It was as if her admitting a small bit of vulnerability, of care, had melted the tension that was normally pushing them apart. It wasn't the first time she'd felt that way around him, but the moments had been few and far between. An occasional favor back in high school when she'd needed a ride somewhere and he'd been old enough to drive, or the time she and Rosie had snuck out after dark and he'd helped them sneak back inside without ratting them out to their parents. And more recently... they'd spent time softening to each other in a way they had never managed before.

"It is getting pretty late," he finally agreed. "I can sleep on the couch by this fire. You've got the one upstairs. In the morning, I'll try and get your generator started. We should be able to get the power back on."

She nodded. "How about something to eat? I have rice cakes."

Tanner laughed, then went to retrieve the bag he'd brought with him. "Rosie sent me with some supplies."

"Bless her!" Nola clasped her hands together as if praying, but the relief was palpable. Not only was Rosie an incredible cook, but there was no doubt she'd overloaded Tanner with more food than any one person could eat. It was her way. "I'll grab some dishes and silverware and we can eat in here by the fire. It's too cold in the kitchen."

He nodded and pulled a few blankets from a basket behind the couch. Tossing them on the floor, he spread them out. Nola watched for a moment, then quickly ran to the kitchen to grab the necessary items. She didn't forget the bottle of red wine and two glasses either. That would certainly warm her up.

"All right, here we go." Nola deposited the supplies on the blanket in front of the fireplace.

Tanner lifted up something small to show her. "Did you lose this? I found it under the coffee table."

He was holding the large pink diamond ring that Gigi had left her. She hadn't even realized it had gone missing. She paused as she took in the scene in front of her—Tanner down on his knees on the blanket, holding a ring up to her. Admittedly, her stomach was doing something weird she wasn't sure she liked... but she also wasn't sure she *didn't* like it.

"Uh, yeah." She stumbled over her words as she took it from him. "That was Gigi's. It's one of my favorite pieces of hers."

He nodded slowly. "It's lovely—perfect for you."

She flushed, feeling heat push into her cheeks. She wasn't sure whether she felt embarrassed at his comment or understood. This ring *was* perfect for her and her personality. It seemed Gigi had always known that.

"I guess it is," she admitted. "Maybe someday."

Though what someday might hold for her romantic future was a complete mystery to her.

"What about a game of Scrabble while we eat?" She changed the topic quickly, not sure she had any more answers to give in that moment. "Gigi has a ton of board games in the hall closet."

Tanner pulled some containers of food out of his bag and began setting up their fireplace picnic. "Sounds good."

"I'll grab it," she offered, hopping to her feet and heading to the hallway. She managed to pull down the game, even though it was on a high shelf, and found a few candles as well. "These are essential oil candles I got Gigi two Christmases ago. Looks like she never used them!"

Tanner looked dubious. "What's an essential oil?"

"Seriously?" Nola shook her head and got to lighting a few of the short, stout candles and placing them around the room. "These are supposed to be very relaxing and calming. Given the stress of the storm, it's perfect for tonight. These are lavender, I think. Or eucalyptus."

She sniffed one of the candles to be sure.

"Is this some weird Chicago thing? Sounds very 'city' to me." Tanner was smiling now, so she knew he was just teasing her. "Come and eat some of this lasagna before Rosie kills me. She made it this morning."

"I will. It smells amazing. Does your phone work? Mine is dead." Nola sat down next to him on the blanket and took a plate of the warm pasta from him. "I know she's probably worried."

Tanner nodded. "Yeah, I texted her as soon as I got here. It took a while, but it went through. She said she was glad you're safe."

Nola put her hand on her chest, appreciating how good of a brother he was to her friend. "I don't know why I always fight with you. You're actually a pretty decent guy and a really great brother and uncle."

He paused, midbite of pasta, then swallowed slowly. "Wow...yeah, uh, thanks. I guess I try to not be a dick as much as I used to be."

The more she thought back on it, the more she wasn't sure he'd ever been a jerk at all. Grumpy, sure. Standoffish as a teenager? Definitely. But softhearted and caring...always.

She cleared her throat after a silence fell between them. "So, they are staying at your house? Do you have power?"

He chuckled and looked up at her like it was the dumbest question in the world. "Of course I have power. I tried to remind you about your generator, too. Remember?"

Warmth pooled in her cheeks. "Hey, I wasn't doing too bad before you got here."

"You were nearly an icicle, but okay."

"I'm pretty sure I would have been just fine." She rolled her eyes and placed the game of Scrabble down on the blanket between them. "Also, I have to warn you—I've never lost a game of Scrabble."

He shrugged. "Then get ready to lose, Magnolia. You've never played me."

Chapter Sixteen

"*Quixotic* is not a word," Nola insisted, pushing his Scrabble tiles off the board.

Tanner nodded his head. "Yes, it is. And it's seventy-six points. Mark it down."

"Okay, then tell me what it means. What's the definition?" She crossed her arms over her chest, looking smug.

Tanner had played Scrabble so many times with Rosie and his mother that his vocabulary was extensive. "It means idealistic, or not sensible. Something I think you'd be very familiar with."

She narrowed her eyes at him. "Normally I would look it up on my phone to see if you're right or not, but my Wi-Fi signal keeps going in and out."

"Gasp!" Tanner said melodramatically. "What will you do without the Internet? How will you survive? Will your Instagram followers worry?"

"You know what Instagram is?" She lobbed back a hardball and he grinned as he took it.

To be fair, he had no social media and was not interested in getting it. However, he'd certainly been around his niece and nephew long enough to know that they were very invested in a video-sharing app called TikTok and had already forced him to star in several of their mini clips.

"Play your word," he replied, tossing a few tiles at her.

She stuck out her tongue but then pulled some tiles off her rack and placed them on the board. "Jukebox."

"That's a proper noun. You can't play those."

"No, it's not." Nola pointed to the board. "That's seventy-seven points and you can bite me."

Tanner swallowed hard, not expecting the wave of heat that rushed over him at her words. He knew she hadn't meant it literally, but...biting her was...Well, he hadn't really thought about it until just this moment. And now, he couldn't *not* think about it. He cleared his throat as he tried to push the image out of his head—her porcelain flesh beneath his hand, soft and inviting.

Christ, he didn't have time for thoughts like those.

"I'll, uh...I'll mark it down." Tanner picked up the scrap piece of paper that they had been using to keep score. "I'm still in the lead anyway."

She glared at him, her brows furrowing. "What? Let me see that!"

With a quick yank, she took the paper from his hands and examined it carefully. After a moment, she tossed it down. "You cannot give yourself points for *sthenia*. That is not a word."

"Look it up." He crossed his arms over his chest. "Oh right. Spotty Wi-Fi. Guess you'll just have to trust me."

Nola huffed. "You're cheating."

"You're an even worse loser now than you were at family board game night when we were kids," Tanner said, referring to the infamous Friday evenings that always ended in someone having hurt feelings.

"When have I ever lost?" She picked up the empty bottle of wine in front of both of their almost-empty glasses. "Should I grab another?"

Tanner shrugged and stretched his long legs out. "I could drink another."

"Don't get too tipsy. I wouldn't want anyone to say I took

advantage of you," she teased as she pushed up to her feet and headed for the kitchen.

He followed her movements with his eyes, knowing she wasn't serious, but also struggling with where his mind went. She returned a moment later with a second bottle of red wine and popped it open, refilling both of their glasses.

"How's it been going down at the new renovation site?" Nola asked as she plonked herself in front of the roaring fire, putting her hands up to pull in a bit more heat.

Tanner took a sip of his wine before answering, rubbing a hand against the stubble on his chin. "Blake has been a pretty great hire. He's very eager. Learns quick on his feet."

"That's good," Nola replied. "Is your dad able to do much anymore?"

He shook his head. "I mean, he's an expert at complaining about what I'm doing. Other than that, his back has him mostly out of commission. Although, he's been doing yoga lately."

Nola frowned. "Like, *yoga* yoga?"

"Yeah," Tanner replied with a wry grin. "*Yoga* yoga."

"How flexible of him." Nola giggled.

Tanner let out a little laugh. He forgot how funny this woman could be and how light things could be around her. They had always fought and were tense with one another in the past, but the few times he saw her uninfluenced by him...she was quite endearing. "But yeah. Blake has been helpful. I wish I could give him more responsibility, but he's still so new. I don't want to put too much pressure on him until he's ready."

"Why do you want to give him more?" There was no judgment in her voice, but rather just curiosity. "Are you thinking of leaving?"

"No..." Though even as he said it, he wasn't sure he

believed it. "But maybe branching out a bit. Not leaving entirely."

She didn't say anything, her face expectant.

"Perry Mott is retiring from the high school." Tanner took a larger gulp of his glass of wine this time. "He's put my name in for his job."

Nola clasped her hands in front of her chest, smiling wide. "Oh my gosh, that would be *perfect* for you! You'd be incredible as a teacher."

"Really?" He furrowed his brow. "What makes you say that?"

"I've seen you with the twins—plus, you tutored all the time in high school. You seemed to really like it back then. I know everyone said you were the person to go to if they needed help in woodshop." She shrugged her shoulders like it seemed obvious. "I mean, don't you think so?"

He wasn't really sure how to answer that. She wasn't wrong—he had tutored a lot of peers back in the day. He'd also taught many employees and interns who had come and gone through Dean & Son Custom Construction. "I do enjoy teaching, in a sense. But full-time? I'm not sure my dad would be thrilled with that. He expects me to take over the business entirely one day."

Nola shrugged. "You can still run a business and not have to work at it every day. You just hire other people. You said Blake is eager. I bet he'd love to be a manager and take on more of the daily operations one day."

Tanner paused. He leaned back slightly, pushing his feet closer to the fire. "It's something to think about, for sure. I'd never really considered it."

She was quiet for a moment, watching the flames flicker as she sipped her wine. He hadn't thought of Nola as a good listener before, but she really was. Her advice was kind and helpful, and she didn't push or judge. She just accepted what he was saying, and was supportive. Tanner wondered if he'd underestimated her all of this time. Maybe they weren't so different. Maybe she wasn't some stuck-up city girl who'd forgotten her roots.

"You know, you were pretty different in high school," Tanner mused.

Nola's head tipped back and she let out a small laugh. "God, I hope so. I've done a lot of work to become the person that I am now."

Tanner leaned in, propping his elbows on his knees. "How's that?"

"I've always been in the shadows, you know? Growing up as Baby's daughter—my parents are wonderful, but they are like giant planets and I was just in their orbit." She looked off in the distance, and her voice became softer. "In high school, I dated Craig and he was always center stage. I guess I was used to that position, but with Gigi? I was always the star in her eyes."

"She had a unique way of making people feel special," he agreed.

Nola nodded. "She's the one who inspired me to move to Chicago. She paid for graduate school. She told me my dreams were important." Her voice caught for a moment and she cleared her throat. "I owe it to her to pursue all of the things she dreamed for me."

"I guess I agree with Gigi on that front," Tanner admitted before letting a low sigh escape his lips. "There's no doubt you'll meet any goal you set for yourself. I guess I'm just sad to see Heart Lake change. This place is a part of me. I have memories here that I can't get a redo on."

She was quiet for a moment, and he wondered if she was thinking of his mother or her funeral. It felt like they were both holding on to the dreams of a woman they'd admired, and his heart swelled at the mutual understanding between them.

"Change can be upsetting—I've certainly been there," Nola finally admitted. "But there's a beauty to experiencing something brand-new, pushing yourself out of your comfort zone. It doesn't always have to be a bad thing."

Easier said than done. The biggest change in his life had been losing his mother, and he'd give anything to never have to have left the comfort of her arms.

"Rosie says the same thing," Tanner remarked. "She's always sending me links to self-help books and growth podcasts, or whatever the heck those things are called."

Nola chuckled. "She sends me some of those, too. Do you ever listen to them?"

He shrugged. "I've had them on in the background on a long drive a time or two . . . nothing major. I know she wants me to embrace change, settle down . . . I think she's never forgotten how rough things got back in the day. She's always trying to keep me on the straight and narrow."

"You?" Nola scoffed. "Since when were you *not* on the straight and narrow? You basically spent all of high school in Mott's woodshop. Craig and I were at the parties on the lake, drinking and dancing—you were never there."

"I wasn't that kind of extroverted teenage delinquent," Tanner admitted with a laugh. "But I still pushed the limits in my own ways. I used to run bets on the football games. Students would give me their wagers and I'd pay out the winners after the game. Eventually parents and teachers started using me, and the pot grew almost out of my control."

Nola blinked hard. "You . . . you what? Oh my gosh, Tanner Dean . . . Were you a bookie?"

A sly grin spread across his face. "I wasn't *not* a bookie,

I guess. More like the mathematician behind it all. Made a good bit of dough betting against your boy toy there before it all blew up in my face."

"I had *no* idea you were such a bad guy." Nola gave him a slight shove, her hand pushing against his shoulder. "What happened?"

"After my mom, I stopped responding to clients... Things sort of fell apart and I ended up owing a lot more than I could pay." Tanner didn't like to reflect on that time of his life, and he still carried a small amount of shame over his actions. "Thankfully, my father and Mr. Mott got me out of that situation. Mr. Mott gave me a new activity to take my mind off everything, and, well, here I am today."

"I had no idea that's how you got started in woodworking," Nola replied. "Sounds like that change really worked out well for you."

A warmth settled over the two of them that had nothing to do with the fire they were seated in front of. It felt like the long years of frosty tension had melted between them and things were... comfortable. Tanner felt at ease. He felt happy. And honestly, that wasn't a feeling he was familiar with too often. It's not that he wasn't happy in his life, but he was just... content. He was okay.

But right now? Right now, he was feeling joyful. He felt full, in the warmest way. And he couldn't help but wonder if Nola was responsible for this moment. And if maybe he wanted more moments like right now.

"You know, it's funny... I think we could actually be friends if I lived here." Nola lifted the glass to her lips as she gazed into the fire. "Maybe we're not as different as I thought."

The reminder of her coming departure felt like a brick on his chest. "You could move home, you know. It is still an option."

She shook her head emphatically. "The sale is almost complete. We're still negotiating terms, but I think it won't be long now. It's time to move forward. I have a vision for what I want my life to be, and a housewife isn't part of that."

He furrowed his brow. "There's more in Heart Lake than being a housewife—though there's certainly nothing wrong with that either."

"There's not. You're right," she agreed. "But the job opportunities in Chicago are incredible. I could make a real difference there—a female-led consulting company. They wouldn't know what hit them! You've got to have vision for the future, Tanner. Not everyone has a father's company to inherit."

Tanner swallowed hard, pulling back the retort that was so close to leaving his lips. Those familiar icy feelings of tension spread back across his chest and he wondered if it had been a good idea to stay the night. Clearly, they had both changed a lot since high school.

A buzzing sound filled the air for a brief moment, and the lights flickered back on. The heater could be heard churning back to full power, and the ice maker in the kitchen clattered.

Nola jumped slightly at the sudden change. "The power is back!"

He stood and walked to the window, surveying the snowfall. "Maybe I should head back home."

"I doubt the roads are any more passable just because the power is back on," Nola pointed out, joining him at the window. "Look—it's waist-high out there."

Tanner rolled his eyes because while it was certainly deep, *waist-high* was a bit of an overreach. Still, it wasn't passable at the moment. "The plows will be out overnight. I'm sure it will be clear by morning."

"Okay, well…might as well make the best of it." Nola plopped down on the couch and picked up the remote control to the small television in the corner. Gigi had never been big on technology, but she did like watching her soaps during the day. "Let's watch a movie!"

He nodded slowly, pacing for a minute or so before joining her on the couch. "Yeah, I guess that's fine. What movie?"

"I'm not sure what's on, but we can browse through a few." Nola pointed the remote at the television and flipped between a few channels before settling on a romantic comedy that he had seen before. His last girlfriend had made him watch it, so it certainly wasn't his first choice.

"Is this okay?" Nola asked.

Honestly, he wasn't interested in arguing right now. Nor was he that interested in watching a movie. He leaned back into the couch cushions and kicked his socked feet up on the coffee table. "Yeah, it's fine. I think I've seen it before."

"We can pick something else," she offered, holding the remote out to him.

He shook his head. He could feel himself getting really tired, but he just didn't know how to stop it. "Nah, this is fine."

"Okay." She placed the remote down on the table as the movie played. Settling back into the couch, she tucked her feet up underneath her and pulled a blanket across her legs. They sat there in silence, partially watching the movie and partially fighting off sleep.

Eventually, sleep won.

Chapter Seventeen

Nola stretched out her legs, desperate to shake off a cramp that was setting in, but they were immediately met with resistance. She opened her eyes and took in her surroundings, only to find herself tucked up against Tanner on the couch with the television playing an infomercial in the background. The television host was currently putting a line of spray-cheese product on apple slices, and the audience was losing their minds.

The sun was still low in the sky, so it was clearly morning. She yawned and stretched her arms above her head for a moment, careful not to disturb Tanner.

He was leaning back into the couch, fast asleep, a blanket over his chest and lap. He wasn't exactly snoring, but his gentle breathing made her heart pound a little harder. He seemed peaceful, calm...and that wasn't an emotion she'd seen very often on his face. The last few years, he always looked stressed and occupied with his thoughts. She really hadn't focused on it too much, but she had noticed it. She figured it was just his way—always stern and stoic. But now? Seeing him asleep in a moment of vulnerability...This was how she wanted to see him more often. He deserved this moment. He deserved the peace.

She wasn't sure when that shift had happened inside her, feeling compassion and understanding for a man who had previously annoyed her every time he breathed in her direction.

"Are you watching me sleep?" Tanner spoke, but his eyes remained closed.

Nola jumped, pulling away from him as she startled. "No! Are you trying to give me a heart attack?"

He grinned as he sleepily opened his eyes and yawned. "At least I'm not the one with a Scrabble tile stuck to my face."

She ran a hand across both of her cheeks, and sure enough, there was the letter *Q* stuck to her left one with a paste of what appeared to be dried drool. Warmth rushed to her skin as she plucked it off and debated whether she should just jump off a cliff right now or wait and double down on her humiliation. Holding up the tile, she wiped at the drool on her cheek. "At least it's ten points."

Tanner laughed as he stretched his neck from side to side. "Looks like we fell asleep out here."

Nola nodded and pushed up to her feet. "Do you want breakfast or something? I think I have some eggs."

"I should probably be heading back," Tanner replied, joining her on his feet.

He walked toward the window and she followed him, eyeing the early morning sun. It sparkled over the thick layers of untouched snow, the road completely invisible.

"I want to look over your generator before I go," he added.

"Please, have something to eat first." Nola headed for the kitchen, feeling a growl in her stomach that some rice cakes were just not going to fix. "It's the least I can do."

He didn't argue but instead went to find the generator out behind the house. She could hear him clattering around against the siding as he made sure it was working properly. Scouring the cupboards, she didn't find much, but there were ingredients for pancakes with chocolate chips. She piled everything on the counter and found a mixing bowl and a pan.

Cooking had never been her strong suit, but pancakes were pretty basic. Surely she could make a few of those work. Grabbing the bag of flour, she strained to get it open. Finally, the top gave way suddenly and Nola coughed as a cloud of flour masked her entire upper half.

"Great." She wiped off as much as she could from her face and neck before quickly trying to mix the ingredients from a recipe she found on Pinterest. She had plugged her phone in to charge and propped it up so she could see the recipe while she worked. Honestly, it didn't seem to be going too badly until she reached the actual cooking stage.

First of all, how do people make perfectly round, golden pancakes like it's nothing? Nola was on her third black, crispy cake before her frustration nearly sent her over the edge.

"Smells interesting in here," Tanner remarked as he walked into the kitchen after he was finished working on the generator. He headed straight for the sink and washed his hands. "What did you make?"

She stammered, trying to flip the other pancakes she had in the pan. "Um…well, I was attempting pancakes. I got a few that I think are edible."

Tanner followed her gesture as she pointed to a plate of misshapen pancakes that were more charcoal than cake at this point. He glanced back at her, his eyes raking across her body. "Uh, did you…did you get a little flour on you?"

She grabbed a hand towel, dampening it in the sink and wiping her face again as well as trying to fluff the remainder off of her shirt. "It puffs out of the bag without warning. They should tell you that ahead of time."

"Okay," Tanner replied, smirking slightly. He walked over to the stove where she was working on her current batch and shook his head. "You've got the heat up way too high. Can I?"

She moved aside and handed him the spatula. "Go for it. I can't flip them without them falling apart."

"My dad used to always leave the pancakes to me on Sunday mornings," he mused as he got to work taking the burned pancakes off and wiping the pan down. He poured more batter at a lower heat, and sure enough, they began to bubble golden brown. "It was one of my favorite things to make for my mother when she was sick. She'd always ask me for them."

Nola felt a squeeze in her heart as she thought of Tanner and Rosie's mother, who had passed while they were in high school. She'd always been a really kind woman and a fantastic mother, and Nola missed her, too. Hearing stories of how Tanner took care of her made a lump form in her throat, and she couldn't help but wonder if that loss wasn't part of the reason why he was so stoic and guarded around most people now. "That's really sweet. I'm glad you were able to have that time with her."

He flipped a few perfect pancakes onto a fresh plate and poured more batter. "It will never be enough," he admitted. "But it was something."

"I feel that way about Gigi," Nola agreed. "Honestly, I miss her more than I let on."

Tanner looked up at her for a moment, his gaze studying her face. He set his jaw, and there was a flicker of something in his eyes that she couldn't identify. "I'm glad you came here for Christmas."

Nola paused, taking in his words. It was probably the nicest thing he'd ever said to her . . . and also the most intimate. "I'm . . . I'm glad I did, too. Last night was fun. We haven't really hung out one-on-one before."

He flipped the last few pancakes onto the plate and then turned off the burner. He pushed the pan back on the stove top, making sure it wasn't next to the edge. Wiping his hands off on a towel, he deposited it back on the counter and stepped closer to her. His voice was low, almost husky, as he finally spoke. "I wonder if we didn't miss a lot of opportunities."

She swallowed hard, unable to find the words to respond. All she could think about was the way his eyes pierced through her and made her feel shaky, like her knees were going to wobble and give way at any moment. He reached forward and ran a hand down her arm, starting at her shoulder and ending at her fingers. Then his fingers were intertwined with hers and he was pulling her to him.

And she went.

She didn't hesitate but rather melted against his chest. His free hand found her chin and tilted her face up to look at him. She wasn't sure she could, but when she finally lifted her gaze to his, she could see flames flickering in his irises. He leaned forward slowly, tempting, waiting...wanting. It was as if he was asking her permission for what he was about to do, and there wasn't a single bit of her that wasn't begging him to keep going.

Pushing up slightly on her toes, Nola leaned toward him, closing the gap. He met her halfway and their lips collided. Everything seemed to freeze around her in that moment, like someone had pressed pause and all she could do was feel her mouth against his. The stubble from his chin scratched her skin in the best sort of way. The soft woody smell of his cologne, or maybe just his natural musk, seemed to envelop her as his arms wrapped around her. He was a brick wall, firm to the touch, but there was something inviting about him in that moment. An openness that wasn't normally there, and Nola wanted to dive into his vulnerability headfirst. Hell, she wanted to be open and give just as much as he was.

What had started slowly and passionately, deep with

emotion and desire, pummeled forward into a frantic grabbing at one another's clothes in urgent, furious motions.

She'd worked his shirt up over his head, tossing it onto the floor as they stumbled out of the kitchen and up the stairs toward the bedroom. By the time they'd reached the second-floor landing, she was only in her bra and panties and he was only wearing his jeans. He lifted her to him, letting her wrap her legs around his waist as he carried her the rest of the way.

The moment her back hit the comforter on the king-sized bed, she pulled him down on top of her, needing to feel him against her. Tanner kicked off his pants as he leaned over her, his mouth finding more to taste. He started at her jaw and worked his way down her neck slowly, tantalizingly. She writhed beneath him as her skin felt like it was deliciously burning at every swipe of his tongue.

His strong, calloused fingers hooked onto the sides of her panties and slid them down her legs, discarding them who knew where as she pressed upward to feel him against her. Tanner was panting now, like he was putting forth every effort to control his movements and slow his pace. She didn't want him to. He reached behind her, pinching the clasp of her bra and pulling it off. Nola wriggled free and then gripped the fabric of his boxer briefs and yanked them off.

His brows lifted at the suddenness of her movement, and she grinned in response. "Christ, Nola…" His voice was a low growl that rumbled through her body and skittered across her skin, leaving small goose bumps behind.

"Too fast?" She bit the corner of her lip, trying to calm her breathing.

He pushed his pelvis down against her, rubbing circles against her core. She could feel how badly he wanted her. "Not fast enough," he said in a low grumble, his lips mere centimeters from her ear.

Skin to skin, they were sealed together by sweat and desire as their tongues tangled around one another. She pushed against him, rolling them over so that she was straddling his waist as he lay back on the bed. Being above him was enticing...like he was hers to control for just a moment. His defenses seemed lowered in the way he was gazing at her—soft, open, willing.

Nola placed a hand on either side of his face, cupping his jaw. Her thumbs brushed gently against the stubble on his chin as their eyes locked.

"Tanner..." she whispered, but then went silent. There was nothing she could say that could accurately describe how she felt.

His large, calloused hands were rough against the sides of her ribs as he slid them slowly up her skin. He was gentle and the way he caressed her was tender and made her heart swell. His hands slid up to her breasts and he cupped them— every graze and squeeze sent rivers of tension through her body, landing directly in her core.

A moan left her lips as she dropped her head backward.

"Perfect..." Tanner murmured, and his eyes were dark as they pierced through her. "You're so incredibly beautiful, Nola."

Shivers ran across her skin and she ran her tongue across her bottom lip. She couldn't believe she was here...with Tanner...on Tanner. It felt surreal, and yet, everything about this moment felt right. Despite the fact that they'd rarely spoken nice words to each other before this week, the way his body melded against hers felt natural. It felt needed, like she'd gone her whole life missing something she was always supposed to feel.

Tanner reached over the edge of the bed to grab his jeans and pulled his wallet from his back pocket. He slipped out a condom from the folds and ripped it open. Her insides clenched with anticipation as she watched him put it on. Then he grabbed her hips and placed her down on top of him. Slowly, carefully, then all at once.

Her back arched instinctively at his intrusion as every part of her body felt like it was coming alive for the first time. He groaned deeply, gutturally, and she could feel the rumble of it as her hands pressed against his chest. With slow movements, she pushed up on her knees just enough before sinking back down and relishing the fullness.

"Nola..." Tanner's voice was low—almost a growl— and his eyes were closed. His fingers dug into her hips as he moved with her. "You feel so amazing."

"Mmm," she agreed with a soft moan, unable to find the words to express how she was feeling. It was intangible, unexplainable, and she felt a tension forming in her chest at the weight of it all. She let her head drop back as she closed her eyes and concentrated on the pulsing feeling in her body as waves of pleasure grew through her. She didn't want to stop and assess why her heart felt like it might explode out of her chest, or why tears felt too close for comfort.

They moved as if they had done this a thousand times, as if his body was meant for hers, and she couldn't stop her heart from screaming that it was...he was. She edged toward the cliff, spiraling as he pressed in deeper and sent her tumbling over the edge.

Her gasp blended with his groan as they unraveled together, her body both tense and liquid all at once. She slid down onto his chest as the sensations overtook her, trying to breathe as her face was buried in his neck. They stayed that way for a while—she wasn't even sure how long. When they finally separated, they curled against each other and just let silence fall over them.

Nola's eyes closed peacefully. Tanner's arms wrapped around her waist. Her body was sated, but her heart was throbbing as if it had been overfilled and she couldn't take one more second of emotion. She slowed her breathing and allowed herself to drift off to sleep, not thinking about what any of this meant but rather just enjoying how perfect he felt beside her.

He felt right.

Chapter Eighteen

Tanner watched Nola sleeping soundly next to him. Her head was lying on his bicep and he was pretty sure he'd lost all the feeling in that arm, but it didn't matter one bit. His other arm was wrapped around her waist, pulling her close to him as they spooned together. Her brown hair was tousled across the pillow haphazardly, and her chest rose and fell slowly with each breath. Waking up with her beside him was the first time in his entire life that things felt right. He felt rested, calm... at peace. There was nothing empty about this moment.

In fact, it felt almost overwhelmingly full. His heart was pounding in his chest and screaming at him—*how did this happen?* He wasn't sure what had possessed him this morning to kiss her, but it felt like something that had been bubbling under the surface for years until it finally broke through. The way she'd responded to him, melted into him—he wasn't sure he would ever experience something of that magnitude again.

And as odd as it sounded, he didn't want her to wake up. He didn't want to let go. He wanted this day to last forever, and yet, everything about that terrified him. Nola *wasn't* forever. She was going to sell the house and head back to Chicago. Heck, without The Castle to return to in the future, she might not ever visit Heart Lake again.

Nerves stirred in his gut as he realized that this might have been a mistake. She was leaving. This was nothing more than a fling to her, but everything he was feeling right now didn't feel fleeting. It felt forever. She felt rooted in his heart and there was no way forward.

"Now who is watching the other one sleep?" Nola's voice was a soft murmur as she roused from her sleep with a small smile. She turned around to face him. "How long have you been up?"

"Not long," he replied. When he looked out the window, it was clear that the sun was in an entirely different place than before he'd fallen asleep. He leaned over to the nightstand and grabbed his phone to check the time. "Oh wow. We slept the day away. It's almost dinnertime. It'll be dark soon."

"I was supposed to get some packing done today." Nola's brows lifted. "Oh well—this was better."

She pushed up off his arm and rummaged for a T-shirt in the dresser. She pulled it on quickly and then stood up. "I . . . uh . . . I should probably get to that."

There was a shift in the air, and Tanner felt it the moment the door slammed shut between them. Their eyes met, gazes pensive. He nodded slowly, grabbing his own clothes. "I should be heading home. Rosie's probably lost her mind alone with the kids."

"Yeah, okay." Nola chewed on the end of her fingernail.

They dressed in silence.

"Thanks for . . . uh, breakfast?" Tanner stumbled over his words, unsure what to say as he finished dressing and headed for the door. "Although, I guess we didn't end up eating those pancakes."

She let out a forced chuckle, avoiding his eyes. "Yeah, I guess not."

"I'll see you around," he said.

"Tanner?" she called as he reached the door. "Would you mind . . . would you mind just keeping this between us? You know . . . last night and everything. Don't tell Rosie. Please?"

It hadn't even crossed his mind what to say to other people, if anything, but damn if her request didn't feel like a punch in the gut. Tanner steeled himself as he pushed away the feelings of discomfort that were entirely too confusing to sort through right now. She was just being practical. They didn't have a future, and there was no point getting everyone in Heart Lake involved in their temporary business.

Despite the validity of her request, it didn't make it sting any less.

"Yeah, that's fine," he said with a clenched jaw. He avoided looking at her. "I have to go before it gets too late."

"Oh, okay." Nola didn't move to stop him, not that he wanted her to. But there was something so uncomfortable in the way this moment was ending.

He gave her a small nod of his chin before grabbing his things and heading back home. Thankfully, the snow was easy to navigate with his cross-country skis, and there was still enough light in the sky to guide his way back home.

As he stomped up the steps to his front door, he was wholly unprepared for the welcome wagon that greeted him.

"Uncle Tanner!" Zander was standing on a chair propped up against his kitchen counter, leaning over a large mixing bowl filled with a brown, gooey substance. It was clearly supposed to stay in the bowl, and yet it had traveled to almost every surface of his kitchen and the twins' faces and hands. "We're making brownies!"

Becca grinned at him as she licked the batter off of a spoon. "Mom said we could."

He walked over and swiped his finger through the edge of the mixture, bringing it to his mouth. "Mmm. It tastes good. Where is your mom, anyway?"

"She's in the living room watching Bravo. She said she

needed thirty minutes of alone time if she was going to stay sane," Becca explained nonchalantly as she helped Zander pour everything from the bowl into a baking tin.

Tanner smiled, enjoying his sister's candor and capacity for self-care. He headed for the living room to find her with her feet propped up on his homemade coffee table, a blanket wrapped around her, and a glass of red wine in her hand.

"Well, you look cozy," Tanner remarked as he dropped down onto the couch next to her.

Rosie glanced at him, and there was a weariness on her face and dark circles under her eyes. "Remind me to buy more wine next time I'm trapped in a snowstorm with the twins. Also, did you realize that your television didn't get Bravo? How was I supposed to watch my housewives reality show? Don't worry—I added it to your cable subscription."

"Gee, thanks." Tanner wasn't surprised, but he honestly didn't mind too much. Rosie worked so hard and so much, if a television channel made her happy, he was more than willing to supply it.

Rosie looked over at him, eyes wide. "So…how was Nola?"

"Hmm?" He reached over and stole a handful of popcorn from the bowl beside her.

"Did you stay the night with Nola?" Rosie sat up straighter, the blanket falling around her waist, and gave her brother an appraising stare. "Oh my gosh—did something happen between you two finally?"

"Finally?" Tanner's brows furrowed as he frowned at his sister. "What are you talking about?"

Rosie rolled her eyes as if it were obvious. "Literally *everyone* has been waiting for you two to get together."

"Nola and me?" Tanner shook his head, confused as to how this was even possible. He had made damn sure that he wasn't the source of gossip around Heart Lake, so for Rosie to insinuate that people had been talking about his love life...hell, no. "Seriously, what are you talking about?"

"Okay, so you're telling me that you've been gone for more than twenty-four hours...at Nola's house...and *nothing* happened?" Rosie laughed and shook her head. "You are such a liar."

Tanner huffed. "I didn't say anything one way or the other."

"I don't even understand why this is still a question. Everyone knows that you and Nola are perfect for each other. At what point are you two going to realize it?" Rosie leaned back into the couch again and grabbed a handful of popcorn. "I don't know anyone else who could handle your stubbornness aside from her."

"I'm the stubborn one?" Tanner scoffed at the audacious statement from the sister who had refused to eat her vegetables for the first twelve years of her life. He couldn't remember a time she'd ever listened to *no*.

Rosie rolled her eyes. "This isn't about me. It's about you and my best friend. When I was a teenager, it pissed me off so much that Nola looked at you with googly eyes."

"She what?" Tanner frowned. That was news to him.

His sister nodded. "And don't think I didn't see you doing the exact same thing. I'm not upset about it anymore. Honest. I actually think it makes a lot of sense. The two of you?"

"Rosie, I hardly think—"

"Ugh, there you go again." Rosie let out a loud, exaggerated sigh. "You're not in high school anymore. You're both adults. And you have a lot more in common than you think. She would challenge you, and you know damn well you need that."

He didn't respond this time, turning back to watch the television instead. His sister's words stuck with him, and he wondered if he was the last person to know that there could really be something there. There was no doubt that Nola had always pushed him his entire life. He'd resented that some-times, but in the latter years he'd really begun to appreciate it. Most people saw him as stoic and quiet and didn't take the time to reach out to him or get to know him. Some had even called him intimidating on occasion, which he tried not to find offensive...but it was, a bit. He was nice to everyone he met, so to know that some people were nervous around him didn't make him feel great.

But that was definitely not the case with Nola. At least, it hadn't been until today.

"She's going back to Chicago," Tanner said after several minutes of silence.

Rosie tossed her hands up. "Well, it's not like Chicago is that far away. And I know there's something more between you two."

Tanner couldn't argue with that. Nola had always dished back everything he'd given her, not standing down once. And last night? It had been one of the best nights he'd had in his life. It had felt like he'd come home, even though he wasn't home at all. Then this morning...God, he couldn't get over how she'd felt beneath him. The way her body had responded to him made everything in him begin heating again. Cer-tainly nothing had been held back in those moments, and she'd willingly given him every part of herself.

"There might be something there..." he admitted, though he wasn't even sure what he was saying. "It's just not that simple, Rosie."

"Nothing with you ever is." Rosie chuckled. "You guys will figure it out."

Tanner inhaled slowly, filling his lungs with the possibility of tomorrow. The decision his sister laid out crossed his mind slowly, but then it was settled with a comfort he'd never felt before. He was going to do this—what *this* was, he didn't know.

But he knew that he wanted to try. He knew he wanted to be with Nola, and if she wanted that, too, then he was going to figure out how to make it work between the two of them.

There was no easy answer for how. After all, Nola was still moving back to Chicago right after the new year. It was a few hours' drive, though. Not impossible. He'd never been in a long-distance relationship before, but he'd also never been in a relationship he felt so strongly about. He'd never been around someone he felt so strongly for.

"Tanner?" Rosie waved a hand in front of his face. "Are you listening? The kids are calling you. Brownies are ready."

He snapped out of his thoughts, turning his head to look toward the kitchen. Sure enough, Becca was walking over with a plate full of brownies that honestly could probably use another ten minutes in the oven. They had a bit of a soupy consistency and were oozing across the plate.

"I saved you some, Uncle Tanner!" Becca held the plate out to him triumphantly.

He smiled and took it, even though he had no intention of eating the chocolate lava. "Thanks, Becs. It smells amazing."

"Maybe you can bring some to Aunt Nola and share!" Becca volunteered.

Rosie turned to look at him. "Yes, Tanner. Maybe Aunt Nola would like to sample your goodies."

He cut his eyes at her. "What incredible advice. I'll have to keep that in mind."

She grinned and shook her head before taking a big bite of the liquid brownies to appease her daughter. Tanner pretended to do the same, but all he could really think about was what his next steps should be.

He knew what he wanted, but how did he tell someone he wanted her when he'd spent his whole life actively convincing her of the opposite?

Chapter Nineteen

"Anyone in here?" Marvel walked through the back door of The Castle as if she owned the place, startling Nola, who was standing at the stove waiting for the teakettle to finish heating. "Nola, you here?"

"In the kitchen," Nola called back.

"Hey, Sugar!" Marvel waltzed into the kitchen in full snow gear carrying a large wooden picnic basket that looked like it had been well loved in its day. "How'd you manage through the storm? It was wicked out."

"We lost power for a while," Nola confirmed. She glanced out the window, wondering how Marvel traversed the snow-covered roads to get there. "How'd you even get here with so much snow?"

Marvel slid the basket onto the countertop. "You should come home more often, darling. And you know I use my Viper to get around everywhere in the winter."

An image of Marvel's old snowmobile came to Nola's mind. She smiled as she remembered the woman flying across piles of snow at breakneck speeds with her rainbow-colored ponchos flapping in the wind behind her.

"I brought you some sugar cookies," Marvel continued, pulling open the basket and lifting out several containers of colorful, elegantly decorated cookies that each looked like different patterns of lace on a red or green backdrop. "I whipped these up during the storm and figured you could use a few. I know Gigi used to always send some cookies your way down there in the big city."

Nola felt that familiar ache when she thought about her grandmother. "Yeah, she did. I miss that."

Marvel gave her arm a sympathetic pat. "What do you say we get together on Christmas Eve? Have some tea and cookies, toast Gigi, and start off the holiday on a sweet note?"

"I'd like that," Nola replied honestly. "I'm not sure how much longer I'll be in town, but I'm hoping to have everything wrapped up with the house by the new year."

Marvel nodded but then moved on to discussing Perry Mott's upcoming Christmas party for the staff at Heart Lake High School. After a bit more gabbing and snacking on a few of the delicately decorated sugar cookies, Marvel took her leave.

Nola watched her jet off on her snowmobile, and decided it was time to get to work. Coincidentally, her boss seemed to be on the same wavelength.

Her phone pinged with a new text message, and Nola walked into the kitchen and slid it out of her pocket to read it. The client dinner moved up. I need you back here in two days.

Part of her wanted to go, to do whatever her boss said she needed to do. It was her job . . . her whole future. But another part of her told her that she wasn't ready to leave Heart Lake.

Not yet. Not now.

I won't be back in Chicago until the New Year.

Three dots appeared after her response, and they seemed angry. Not that she could really tell what her boss was thinking. Somehow, she didn't care, though. The dots disappeared and she was glad for a moment that she didn't have to explain herself. Hell, she wasn't sure she could. All she knew was she wasn't ready to return to Chicago yet.

With Christmas right around the corner, Nola needed to finish wrapping the presents she bought for the kids and her best friends. Another cup of tea and two rolls of wrapping paper later, she had managed to fill a bag with perfectly coiffed gifts for everyone.

Everyone except for the man with whom she'd undoubtedly had the best sex of her entire life.

Her cheeks flushed warm as her mind replayed clips from their brief tryst. Tanner had always had the ability to get under her skin, but now his hands had touched every inch of her. And he was still her best friend's big brother. She sighed as she thought of the complicated situation she'd put herself in.

Steeling herself, Nola stood resolute as she placed the bag with the gifts by the front door. She knew she had to go back to Chicago eventually if she wanted to pursue her dreams. There was no future for her here—and stringing Tanner along certainly wouldn't help. Instead, she was going to see this as a nice moment of closure. Their quick fling would be the bow on the chapter that was her life in Heart Lake. The thoughts rang hollow in her heart, though. Something about this felt more like leaving something she wanted rather than returning to something she wanted. Everything inside of her felt twisted up in knots, and she couldn't stop thinking of the way his hands had held her as if he never wanted to let go…as if she never wanted him to let go.

Nola glanced out the window on the snow jutting up against the icy lake. A heaviness settled in her chest as she thought of the fact that this might be one of the last times she'd see this view. She shook the thought out of her head and headed upstairs. There was one gift left to wrap, and she knew exactly what it would be. She'd come across an object in Gigi's collection of miscellaneous pieces she treasured that would be perfect—an engraved whittling knife. It was small and sturdy with a tiny quote: HOME IS IN THE HEART. She wasn't sure where Gigi had gotten this, or why she had it, but she knew Tanner would love it. Carefully, she wrapped it with the remainder of the red-and-green paper she had left over.

After packing and inventorying more of Gigi's things, Nola took a break for a snack. She put together a quick sandwich—which was about the extent of her culinary talent—and stared out the kitchen window as she ate. The snow was still piled high, but the roads were well plowed and salted by now. Michigan was never one to be kept down for long.

Nola eyed the multiple containers of sugar cookies that Marvel had dropped off earlier and decided to bring a box with her as she took the gifts for the kids to Rosie's store. Twenty minutes later, she was stumbling into Fact or Fiction with an armful of gifts and cookies. A shrill bell rang above her head as the door flew open and she almost tripped on the giant welcome mat that said READ OR LEAVE.

"I don't remember ordering a Santa," Rosie teased as she came over to the entrance to take some of the items Nola was balancing in her hands. Nola was dressed in all red and had jingle bells for earrings that clinked with every move of her head. She even smelled like cinnamon and sugar and everything holiday spirit. "Where's your big white beard?"

"Freshly plucked," Nola replied, only partially teasing because tweezing her chin was becoming more and more of a necessity with each passing year. "Marvel brought me a few hundred cookies, I swear. Figured I'd share some with you and the kids."

Rosie pulled open the container and snaked out a cookie, popping the corner into her mouth. She sighed as she leaned her elbows on the live edge wooden countertop that lined the front half of the store. "Mmm. She makes the best cookies. It's crazy how fast she decorates them. I would never have a skilled hand like this."

Nola certainly agreed that the lacework in the icing on the cookies was incredible. "That woman is beyond a mystery."

"Do you have Christmas Eve plans yet? The kids would love to see you," Rosie said, polishing off the last of her cookie. She picked up a pile of books and began returning them to the hand-carved wooden shelves, which, when combined with the scent of paperbacks, made the entire place smell like a forest. "They can open their gifts in front of you. Plus, we invited Marvel. And, of course, my brother will be there."

Rosie wiggled her eyebrows suggestively as she returned to the counter.

Nola scoffed. "Why would I care about Tanner being there or not?"

"I'm not blind, Nola." Rosie leaned forward against the counter. "He was over at The Castle for, like, twenty-four hours."

"It was a snowstorm," Nola protested, walking over to the plush bright-orange couch on the opposite wall. "There wasn't much of a choice."

"Suuuure. Blame the snow." Rosie winked and then grabbed another cookie, pointing it at Nola as she sat down. "You have gossip, and you owe it to me. I know what happened."

Nola could feel her cheeks heating as she looked away and tried to think of a good excuse to give, but her brain seemed to go blank. "It's not gossip... It was just... I don't know. It was just a one-time thing. A mistake, really. I can't believe Tanner told you."

"I dragged it out of him." Rosie frowned and crossed her arms over her chest. "You think it was a mistake?"

Nola cleared her throat, trying to figure out how to back-track. "I mean, not a *mistake* mistake...but it never should have happened. Everything is all complicated now."

"How?" Rosie was not one to let things go. "You and Tan-ner have had chemistry for years, and you know it."

Nola felt a bit defensive being put on the spot, but she couldn't exactly argue with that fact. She plucked at a loose thread on the couch. "Sure, but that's all it was. It's not like I date a lot in Chicago. Work is so busy. It's been..." She paused for a moment, trying to count how long it had been since the last time she had sex. "I don't know, but it's been a while. I got swept up in the snowstorm, the fireplace lighting—all of that. I cannot be blamed for my actions."

Rosie laughed loudly at that one. "Oh, okay. Sex-starved is your excuse." Rosie then wrinkled her nose and recoiled slightly. "Ew—gross. We're talking about my brother. I don't want to picture that."

It was Nola's turn to laugh now. "You're the one who asked me!"

"I regret my life choices," Rosie joked, shaking her head. "But either way, I don't think this was a mistake. And I don't think it's a one-time thing."

Nola stood up and grabbed a cookie. "Let's change topics."

"Okay. When are you going to move back to Heart Lake?" Rosie grinned like she knew the answer already but wanted to push Nola's buttons. "You know, we could use your business smarts here. Local mom-and-pop shops can't stay open."

"Well, there was just a snowstorm," Nola reminded her. "It's understandable."

Rosie shook her head. "Not in Heart Lake. A storm never stopped anyone here."

That was certainly true if she considered a woman in her fifties on a snowmobile delivering cookies.

"What would you do to get more business in here?" Rosie asked. "You can send me an invoice for your advice."

Nola grinned. "I'm sure I can extend a friends-and-family discount."

"Well, obviously I wasn't going to pay the invoice," Rosie teased. "But seriously, what would you do?"

Nola paused for a moment and looked around the bookstore. Stepping into one of the aisles, she put a hand to her chin and considered the options for a moment. "Honestly, I think I'd give people reason to hang around more."

"What do you mean?" Rosie stepped around the counter and came to stand next to her.

"Have you thought about adding a small sitting section for people to eat or drink? Maybe serving some coffee, wine, a few cookies?" Nola pointed to Marvel's cookies. "I bet Marvel would supply them at cost. Everyone would come by to have some of her cookies. This would be the new hot spot. Even if they didn't end up buying a book, you'd still make a profit off of the food and beverages. Though, honestly, I think it would be hard to sit here and *not* buy one of these books."

Rosie surveyed the bookstore, clearly taking Nola's suggestion into consideration. "You know what? If I moved that bookshelf to the back, then there would be enough room for a few tables and chairs."

"When the weather is nicer, you could add tables outside, too." Nola pointed toward the front of the bookstore, which had a very wide sidewalk and long awning. "Maybe invest in a few standing heaters and then people could sit outside in the cold, too."

Her friend walked toward the window that looked out on

the sidewalk. "You know what? Heart Lake people *would* sit outside in the snow . . . *if* they had a hot beverage."

Nola shrugged. "So, offer a hot toddy along with some hot chocolate and espresso. Maybe some mulled wine?"

"Do I need a liquor license for that?" Rosie asked.

Nola nodded. "Yes, but that shouldn't be hard to get. We've known the mayor since we were babies."

Rosie clapped her hands together. "See? This is exactly why Heart Lake needs your expertise. Since I'm already in the middle of renovation here, it would be perfect timing to add a café component. I'm having a big reopening launch to show off the new interior in the new year, so I can have it ready to go by then!"

"The liquor license might take a bit longer than that, considering the holidays," Nola warned. "But you could certainly try!"

"Don't poop on a dream you just created," Rosie teased. "Okay, so help me move that bookshelf, because we have work to do."

"Wait—what?" Nola's eyes widened. "I provide consultations, not manual labor."

"Time to expand your business model, too." Rosie grabbed her arm and pulled her toward a heavily packed bookshelf. "I hope you've been going to the gym. These things are heavy. And we have to take all the books off first, then put them back on after."

"Wonderful," Nola said, jokingly gritting her teeth. "I can't wait to be your free labor."

"Just like old times, huh?" Rosie laughed and then began instructing her on what order to remove the books in. Putting on a smile, Nola decided to make the best of it and help her friend—after all, it was her idea.

Chapter Twenty

"Mattie?" Tanner waved a hand toward the waitress at the Black Sheep Diner after almost twenty minutes had gone by without service. "Can I grab a coffee?"

Mattie turned to him, a frazzled look in her eyes. "Uh, yeah. I will. One second."

She disappeared into the kitchen and was quickly replaced by Felecia, one of the co-owners. She and her twin brother, Felix, owned the diner together, and it was well known that the two hardly ever got along. Despite their constant arguments, they ran a mean business and there was nothing better than bacon and eggs at the counter.

"Dean!" Felecia greeted him by his last name, and he noticed that she had the same frenzied look in her eyes. "If you want to complain, I'm going to put in a suggestion box at the front."

"What?" Tanner knit his brows. "No, I just want coffee."

She looked relieved. "Thank Christ. I can't handle one more goddamn complaint about this avocado toast."

"Avocado toast?" Tanner gratefully accepted the mug of black coffee she poured him. "Is that new?"

"Brand spanking," Felecia confirmed. "That Bennett girl is a business consultant now. She told me it was a must-have item on the menu, along with a few other hippie-dippie selections that are just taking up inventory space. No one in Heart Lake wants a fancy toast. They want bacon and eggs. Extra greasy."

Tanner chuckled, because that was certainly the truth and exactly what he was about to order. "So, Nola's giving you business advice?"

"It was a one-time free consultation," Felecia replied. "Don't worry. I'll be giving her my feedback."

He grimaced as he thought about that conversation. "Well, I can try it if you've got inventory to burn."

Felecia's brows rose. "You want avocado toast? You know that's what young city folk eat, right?"

"I mean, I like guacamole and chips. How different can it be?" Tanner shrugged, but Felecia just laughed and told him his order would be right up.

"Eat your words, Dean," Felecia teased as she walked out of the kitchen a few minutes later with a plate of green mush. "Enjoy the latest trending menu item in the Midwest."

Tanner examined the plate as she put it down in front of him. On it were long oval pieces of bread topped with mashed avocado and sesame seeds. There was a sauce drizzled on them as well, but he wasn't sure what it was.

"I can add a fried egg on top if you want, though Bennett suggested they be 'poached,' " Felecia explained, using air quotes. "Who wants runny boiled eggs? I swear, I don't understand the city."

He didn't respond but took a bite of the toast. His mother had often made her own version of eggs Benedict when they were kids, so he was partial to poached eggs in that dish at least, but he certainly wasn't going to tell Felecia that. He swallowed his first bite, and admittedly, the toast wasn't awful, but it was pretty tasteless. It just seemed bland, and he wondered what the attraction was to unflavored guacamole on a piece of limp bread.

"Hey, Brother!" Rosie slid into the seat at the counter next to him. She flagged down the waitress. "Mattie—the usual bacon and eggs, please!"

Tanner eyed his sister as he swallowed his last bite. "What are you doing here?"

"Just dropped the kids off at Dad's house." Rosie started pouring way too much sugar into the coffee Mattie had just placed in front of her. "I need a few hours off mommy duty to buy their Christmas gifts."

He laughed. "Christmas is tomorrow."

"Which is why I need some nourishment before I hit the stores," Rosie replied. "It's going to be an insane crowd out there. Hey, why is it so gloomy in here today? Everyone seems in a sour mood. What are you eating?"

"Felecia is in a mood today," Tanner explained, but didn't go further into details on the avocado toast debacle. "How's the bookstore? You ready for the relaunch yet?"

"I'm actually going to push back the grand reopening until the new year—maybe mid-January?" Rosie took a sip of her coffee, then added even more sugar. "Nola gave me the *best* idea for the store—add a little café area for customers!"

Tanner furrowed his brows. "What?"

"Like coffee, wine, little cookies made by Marvel," Rosie explained. "Give people a reason to come and hang around a bit."

"But does that mean that they buy books?" He felt himself bristling at the suggestion and he wasn't entirely sure where the animosity was coming from.

Rosie shrugged. "Well, hopefully. I mean, if they are there longer, then they might want something to read. I've got magazines and newspapers for sale, too."

"Everyone is on their phones these days." Tanner finished the last of his coffee. "Books are basically obsolete."

His sister's face scrunched tightly and she turned to him with fire in her eyes. "Books aren't going *anywhere*, you dick. Everyone loves a bookstore. It's home. It's heart. It's happiness. I don't know why I even talk to you."

Tanner grinned, knowing he pushed his sister's buttons anytime he spoke about paperbacks. He personally stuck to digital e-books when he had a free moment to read, but he understood that his sister was nostalgic about printed words. One of her favorite places growing up had been the library. His thoughts returned to Nola's suggestion about adding a café at Fact or Fiction. Irritation nestled further under his skin. He couldn't understand why Nola didn't see the good in this town just the way it was. She'd been here a few days and was already trying to change everything—first, the avocado toast, and now the bookstore? Not to mention The Castle. What was next? What was so wrong with their small town...with him?

He wanted to show her that there was value in Heart Lake, and there was value in him. He deserved a chance as much as this town did, and he was going to prove it to her. In that moment, he knew exactly what to do—and it involved the perfect Christmas present. He said goodbye to his sister and headed home to his garage workshop to make the gift. It was small, and maybe a little cheesy, but he couldn't wait to give it to her. After several hours of working on it, he wrapped it in some gift wrap and stuck it in his truck so he could give it to her next time he saw her.

Later, Tanner found himself on his way to his family's annual Christmas Eve Yule Log Dinner. A yearly tradition for the Deans, everyone came together on Christmas Eve to have an incredibly filling, overindulgent homemade dinner. By the time he showed up, the twins were on their second hot chocolate and Rosie was pulling the roast beef dinner out of the oven.

"You realize I've been over here cooking all day since

you saw me," Rosie quipped, eyeing her brother with a look of annoyance.

Tanner grinned. "I thought you were gift shopping?"

Rosie glanced toward the living room, as if making sure no one had heard him. "Uh, of course not. All my gifts were purchased weeks ago. You think I'd wait till the last minute for my precious children?"

He laughed, knowing the ruse. "Ah, what was I thinking? Of course you were prepared ahead of time as usual."

"Exactly," Rosie confirmed, a tiny smile on the corner of her lips. "Put your gifts for the kids under the tree. We'll open them after dinner."

Tanner was holding a brown paper bag full of wrapped gifts for the kids and his sister and father. Since he wasn't great at wrapping, he'd convinced Amanda to help him so that the packages would look aesthetically pleasing. She'd done an amazing job, and he placed the beautifully bowed gifts around the tree with pride.

Of course, there was one still in the bag for Nola... but he figured he would give her that when he saw her.

Which turned out to be right now.

"Nola, you made it!" Rosie greeted her friend as the beautiful brunette waltzed in through the front door carrying a glass dish full of what appeared to be some type of casserole. Marvel was directly behind her with a large tin of what was undoubtedly her traditional holiday cookies. "Ooh, what did you bring?"

"Green bean casserole," Nola replied with a proud smile on her face as she handed the dish over to his sister.

Rosie frowned, peeking under the tinfoil top. "Why is it red?"

Nola frowned back. "The spaghetti sauce. Right?"

"You put spaghetti sauce on green bean casserole?" Rosie

asked, then let out a little laugh and shook her head. "Well, I'm sure it tastes delicious. I can't wait to try some."

Tanner stayed off to the side, nursing the beer his sister had handed him after he'd distributed his gifts. Nola hadn't caught sight of him yet, and he didn't mind the chance to see her unencumbered by his presence. She looked the perfect image of a snow angel, dressed in a white flouncy sweater and white jeans that hugged her legs. In a striking juxtaposition, her lips were painted bright red, making it absolutely impossible to ignore her mouth. His mind immediately went to what it had felt like pressed against his, and all the things she'd done with those sinful lips.

He cleared his throat and pushed those thoughts away. Now was *not* the time. "Hey, Nola."

She turned to find him standing a few feet behind her. "Oh. Tanner. Hi. Funny seeing you here."

"At my family's house on Christmas Eve?" He furrowed his brows and allowed a small smile to slip across his lips. "Yeah, what a crazy coincidence."

Her cheeks blushed crimson. "Oh, right. Well, I mean... it's good to see you. Merry Christmas."

He tipped his chin toward her. "Merry Christmas to you, too."

"Christ, this is awkward," Rosie teased as she walked between them and handed Tanner a basket of rolls. "Can you put these on the table and then come help me bring everything else?"

"Sure," he agreed, swiping one of the rolls and popping it into his mouth. "Mmm, kudos to the chef."

"You can't wait five minutes until we're seated?" Rosie huffed, and rolled her eyes but then started passing dishes to everyone to bring to the table. A quick caravan of helpers started until the dining room table was piled high with food and every chair was filled. A shorter table was pushed up against the large dining room table, and the twins were seated there after much argument about being sat at the "kids' table."

Marvel took the seat next to Thomas at the top of the adult's table. "Can't wait to dig into these mashed potatoes. They look perfectly scrumptious!"

Tanner's father smiled at Marvel, and there was a glint in the way he looked at the eccentric woman that gave Tanner a moment's pause. He felt there was more to that story, but he didn't have time to dig into his father's personal life right now. Not that his father would discuss personal matters with him anyway. He was a private man and Tanner had adopted some of those same characteristics.

Nola was seated diagonally across from him, and it seemed she was doing everything she could to avoid looking in his direction. He didn't mind, though, since it gave him more opportunity to watch her out of the corner of his eye. This was far from being Nola's first family dinner with the Deans, and yet, she fit in as if she'd been at every one. The way his father interacted with her, or how Rosie would lean over and clink her wineglass against Nola's—all of it was so homey, so comfortable. She fit in in a way few people ever had.

None of his previous girlfriends had had this level of ease with his family. He wasn't sure he'd ever given them the opportunity to, and that told him something right there. He *wanted* Nola to be part of his family, and he liked her sitting at the table where she belonged. This was her home as much as it was his. His heart had already come to this conclusion, but as Tanner watched Nola pass a basket of rolls to the twins even after Rosie had told them they had already had enough, his mind knew it, too.

This felt right. This felt like he could do this forever.

After lots of laughter and gorging themselves on Rosie's delicious meal, the Dean family worked together to help clean up the kitchen and table. After doing most of the heavy lifting—like putting the leaves back in the table—Tanner stole away to his father's office to grab the gift he'd made for Nola. He had tucked it away in a cabinet at the bottom of the built-in bookshelves against the far wall. He pulled it out and paused for a moment, looking around the room that had sat unused for a while now. He wasn't sure what was going to happen with his father's business, but he knew that a decision would need to be made soon. He let out a long exhale and tried to clear his mind. He wasn't going to worry about any of that right now.

The office door opened and Nola's head poked inside. "Oh, I didn't know you're in here. I saw a light on."

"Yep. Just me," Tanner replied, turning the gift over in his hands absentmindedly. "Actually, uh, I have something for you."

"For me?" Her brows shot up and she stepped into the office, allowing the door to close behind her.

The air in the room hung stiffly between them for a moment, and Tanner cleared his throat and stepped closer to her, extending his hand out to her with the gift. "It's not much. But...here."

A smile pulled at the corners of her lips as she took the wrapped package and looked it over. "You really didn't have to get me anything."

"I didn't," he replied, rubbing a hand across the back of his neck. "I, uh...I made it."

"Oh." Her smile widened and she pulled at the wrapping paper until it came apart to reveal a long wooden name placard he had carved and stained for her future office desk.

Underneath her name was the acronym CEO. When her eyes lifted back to his, there was a shimmer against her lower lashes as tears welled. "Tanner...this is really sweet. This means so much."

He looked away, uncomfortable with the display of emotion he wasn't sure how to handle. He wanted to wrap his arms around her and kiss the hell out of her, but he just felt...stiff. "Yeah, well, I just thought you needed a bit of us down there in Chicago. I wanted you to know that I support your decision, your career. All of that. You're going to be amazing as your own boss. I have no doubt."

She rushed forward unexpectedly and threw her arms around him. "Thank you, Tanner."

He leaned into her hug, accepting the warmth of her closeness. The way her body fit against his was natural, expected, as if this was how it was always meant to be. He closed his eyes, savoring the moment. His hands found their way around her back and brought her in even closer.

When they finally pulled apart, he watched as her smile disappeared and was replaced with something heavier. Her eyes hooded as her gaze traveled down to his lips, and he felt a stirring in his chest that he didn't want to end. She bit the corner of her lip, pulling it between her teeth as she let out a small exhale.

"Tanner..." She said his name barely above a whisper, but it was like she was shouting at him.

There was no chance he could hold back now. Giving in to their exchange, Tanner lowered his mouth to hers for a small, gentle kiss. Her eyes fluttered closed and a happy sigh came from her as she melted into him. It was a single perfect kiss—almost a goodbye—and Tanner wanted nothing more than to wrap his arms around her and make her his.

Her hand lay flat against his chest, and he wondered if

she could feel his heart pounding. He leaned in toward her, removing any gap between them as he touched either side of her face with his fingertips. Gently, he tilted her face toward him as their kiss deepened. His entire body felt electric, and there was no way to soothe the longing he was feeling except with her.

But then it was over as quickly as it had begun.

Nola pulled away and clutched his gift tightly in her hands as she cleared her throat. "I actually, uh, got you something as well."

"Really?" He hadn't expected to be on her Christmas list.

She reached into her pocket and pulled out a small rectangular item wrapped in red and green foil. "It's not much..."

Tanner took it from her gently and pulled at the tape adhering one side together. The wrapping paper fell apart and a small whittling knife rolled into his hand. He lifted it to take a closer look. A small engraving on the side—HOME IS IN THE HEART—made his own heart thump loudly in his chest. It wasn't just that this was a beautiful gift but rather that it was the perfect gift for him. It was sentimental and practical and showed that Nola knew him in a way he rarely allowed people to.

"Nola... I don't know what to say," he admitted, clearing his throat. "This is an incredibly thoughtful gift."

She fidgeted with the edge of her sweater, but her smile was clear. "It made me think of you, and of Heart Lake."

"You think you'll miss us?" He meant it as a joke, but the words tumbled heavily out of his mouth and sat between them.

"I will," she replied without hesitating. "I know I will. But I, um... I should probably be heading home. It's been a long day. I've been doing so much organizing at The Castle, you know? I should probably get to bed early."

He noticed that she was rambling and not making eye contact, but he didn't force the issue. He was just trying to focus on not embarrassing himself as he readjusted his junk stealthily. "Thanks for coming to dinner, Nola. I know it meant a lot to my sister to have you here."

Her eyes flicked to his, a nervous smile returning. She heard what he wasn't saying, and he felt exposed in a way he never had before. "I enjoyed tonight," she finally replied.

With that, she left the office, and he watched her go, restraining himself from begging her to stay. There was no doubt in his mind that there was only one place he wanted to spend Christmas tomorrow.

He would deal with the inevitable heartbreak later.

Chapter Twenty-One

Mariah Carey's swoon-worthy voice crooned from the small radio sitting in Gigi's kitchen as Nola swayed side to side, humming along to "All I Want for Christmas Is You." She sipped at the hot tea she'd made to ease the tension in her chest and shoulders after her kiss with Tanner in his father's office earlier tonight. The fire in front of her was crackling and warm, and she felt comforted by the heat—and the knowledge that she finally knew how to make a fire all on her own. She didn't need anyone, but, God—she wanted one person...one person specifically. Despite the fact that being with him was an impossible dream, he still had wiggled his way into her heart, and she was pretty sure he was there to stay now.

She inhaled the soft floral aroma of her drink, proud of herself for finally perfecting Gigi's art of tea making. If her grandmother had been there, Nola had no doubt she'd be proud, too. Nola's heart ached as she thought of the woman who had meant so much to her. With only a few days left in Heart Lake, Nola knew she needed to move more swiftly with packing up the house. The attic was next on the list of areas to tackle, but she just couldn't summon the energy to do it tonight.

A knock on the front door caused her to jump, but when she walked into the foyer and saw Tanner on the other side of the glass, she couldn't deny the surge of happiness she felt.

She opened the door to find Tanner leaning against the frame. Her heart skipped a beat. "What are you doing here?"

"There were a lot of leftovers from dinner at the house." He lifted a plastic container that looked overly full. "Rosie said you forgot to take some home with you."

"You're here to bring me food?" She lifted one brow, a smirk on her lips.

He grinned sheepishly and shifted his weight from one foot to the other. "It seemed like a good excuse to come over."

She stepped back, pushing the door open wider to allow him room to enter. "I never turn down food," she teased.

He handed the container to her and they walked together into the kitchen. She stored the food in the fridge and glanced around for something to offer him.

"Are you thirsty?" she asked. "I could make tea?"

Tanner shook his head and then pulled a thermos out of his jacket pocket. "I snuck some of Marvel's spiked eggnog out with me. Thought we could have a small nightcap."

"That sounds perfect." Nola grabbed two glasses from the cabinet and placed them on the counter as he portioned out the drink for them both. She could smell the nutmeg almost instantly and a warmth filled her at the memories of Christmas with her family. It might not be her favorite beverage, but it did taste of nostalgia.

He lifted his glass to hers. "Cheers."

"Cheers." Nola clinked the edge of her glass against his, then took a long sip of the creamy drink. She wasn't sure if it was the alcohol filling her stomach or the way Tanner was looking at her over his glass, but her body felt lit on fire in the best way. She swallowed hard, pushing any nerves away. "So, Tanner, tell me something I don't know."

He laughed lightly, familiar with her request. Ever since she'd been a child, she'd ask people to tell her something she didn't know when a conversation lulled. She'd always found it to be a way to get people to open up unexpectedly, and she loved digging into people's stories.

"I'm thinking about getting a cat."

"Since when are you a cat person? Or an animal person at all?" Nola laughed lightly. "I can't picture you just sitting in your armchair petting your cat in a cabin in the woods."

"Stranger things have happened," he joked. "I think I'd get a tomcat—a big fellow. Name him Lizard."

Nola snorted. "I can't wait to see Becca's and Zander's faces when they hear that. You've got to create your cat's own Instagram page—thelizardcat! I bet you could gain a ton of followers and then you'd be set."

"I have no interest in Instagram... or a new career, if you can even call it that."

"Ah, you're so stuck in the past." Nola was joking, but she could see that something about her comment irked him.

"Why do you do that?" he asked, swirling the remainder of the drink in his glass around the edges.

Nola frowned. "Do what?"

"Want everything to change, to move forward to something new." Tanner cleared his throat, and when he looked up at her, there was a sadness in his gaze that made her stomach sink. "Me, this house, this town... Why isn't it enough the way it is? The avocado toast at the diner nearly ruined Felecia. And The Castle? Blasco is slime, and he's going to turn this land into a money pit. Why can't things just stay the way they are? What's so wrong with how things are?"

She wasn't prepared with an answer to his question,

but she took a moment to think it over. He certainly had a point—she was always trying to improve things and one-up herself. "Admittedly, Heart Lake was not ready for avocado toast," she agreed, trying for a joke to ease the tension she felt. "Sometimes I can get a little swept up in things."

He exhaled sharply. "You think? Old Man Hobbes about had a heart attack when Felecia told him they were considering adding turkey bacon to the menu in place of his usual pork bacon."

Nola chuckled. "Okay, but some healthier options certainly could benefit people, too."

He didn't argue but finished the rest of his drink and placed the empty glass on the counter.

"Maybe the answer is somewhere in the middle," Nola continued. "You're right...I do push for things to evolve and change. I'm not entirely sure why, but I think I struggle with being content. And I'm not entirely sure that's always a bad thing. Just sitting in these good feelings and being happy with what I have—you know?"

Tanner shook his head. "Not really. I love what I have."

"Do you?" She probed a little, knowing he wasn't telling the full truth. There were more layers to Tanner than he wanted to admit, but she'd peeked behind the curtain earlier this week and she knew where to look now. "Are you happy with things as they are right now? Running your father's business? Living alone in that cabin on the water? Or is it easier to play it safe? To not reach for what you really want in fear of losing it...like how you lost your mother."

He looked away but didn't argue with her. She could see conflicting emotions cross his face as he let out a low sigh.

"I saw how badly Rosie was affected by your mother's death in high school. You held it together, and I never saw you break. None of us did. I can't imagine what you went through." Nola stepped closer to him and placed her hand on his forearm. "If loving someone means losing them eventually, isn't it still worth it for the time you do have?"

His voice was a husky growl when he finally responded, as if there were a lump stuck in his throat. "Nola . . ."

"Tanner, tell me the truth." She moved her hand down to his palm and interlaced her fingers with his. "Is this the life you want? Are you living your dreams?"

He wrapped an arm around her waist and pulled her flush against him. His eyes pierced through her and she felt a fire building in her core.

"Sometimes I think maybe things could be different," he admitted quietly. "I guess I've gotten so used to being by myself, being lonely, that I don't really question it anymore."

"Well, you don't have to be lonely tonight," Nola told him, barely above a whisper. "Stay with me."

She pushed up on her tiptoes and brushed her lips against his. His body stilled against her, and she splayed her hands against his chest. It was like pressing against a brick wall, impenetrable and stoic, and yet she knew there was a heart beating beneath her fingertips that had a softness she'd only just met.

In a quick sweep, Tanner's hand caught the back of her knees and lifted her up against his chest. He headed for the stairs but paused at the bottom step. "Are you sure about this, Nola? You're leaving soon . . ."

Her hand cupped his jaw. "Heart Lake will always be a second home to me. You can't get rid of me that easily."

Something flickered in his gaze, and she wanted to ask him what had happened. What thought had just run through his mind? But as they ascended the staircase together, she pressed her lips to his instead. She didn't want to dig into the deep emotions tonight. She just wanted to feel him around her, to feel held.

The way he laid her against the comforter on the bed was delicate and gentle. He took care with every move he made as he climbed on top of her. His hand slid down the length of her side until he found the bottom hem of her shirt. His fingers moved beneath the fabric and spread across her skin like he was reclaiming her. She shivered as her body responded to his touch and her back arched off the mattress.

"Christ, Nola." Tanner's voice was a low, guttural moan as he said her name, his lips against her ear as their bodies pulled against each other. "I need you."

"Take me," she responded in a breathy whisper.

As eagerness overtook them, they both made quick work of shedding their clothes. Nola pushed against his chest, pressing his back to the mattress as she straddled him. She ran her fingers lightly across the skin on his chest, starting at his collarbone and moving to his abdominal muscles. He was rock solid beneath her and she pressed her hips harder against him for the tiniest bit of relief.

When she raised her eyes to his, she found his gaze dark and brooding and his jaw tight as if he was exercising every bit of control he had not to flip her over and press inside of her right then and there. Instead, he waited and watched as she took her time exploring every inch of his body. Her fingertips caressed the skin on his arms as his biceps flexed against her palms.

"I want to remember everything about this," she whispered, though she wasn't sure if she was telling him or trying to soothe herself.

Tanner's hands gripped her hips and dug into her skin as he watched her. "We have all night."

Even that didn't seem like enough. Nola swallowed hard

as she felt her chest tighten, her heart pounding hard against her rib cage. "All night…"

Her vision clouded for a moment and she realized that tears were beginning to well on her bottom eyelids. Tanner seemed to notice and the tension in his body shifted. He went from restraining himself to suddenly caressing her and pulling her against him with a softness that made her feel delicate in his arms. He rotated their bodies, turning her back onto the mattress as he slid his body across her and knelt between her legs. She gently pressed her knees against the sides of his thighs, and he placed slow, gentle kisses down the length of her neck.

She held her breath for a few seconds, trying to keep the tears at bay. Honestly, she wasn't even sure where they were coming from. The thought that maybe this was the last time, that this wasn't a permanent part of her life, seemed painful in a way she'd never felt before. She writhed beneath him as his tongue slicked against her breast, twirling around her nipple and sending shooting pleasure through her body in sharp waves. He took his time, paying attention to every inch of her until she was panting and begging him to give her the release she so desperately needed.

After quick work securing protection, Tanner pressed against her entrance and then consumed her. She moaned as he filled her, and she wrapped her arms around his body, clutching him to her as if he wasn't close enough. But he was completely intertwined with her, and with every thrust, she only came closer and closer to losing herself in him entirely.

His mouth found hers, and there was a hunger inside him that matched how she felt. Tension pulsed through her body as she skittered to the edge of the cliff and threatened to fall over. And then it was too late.

She was free-falling and nothing could stop her as she

trembled against him and waves of ecstasy slammed through her in quick succession. Similarly, his body tensed and stilled as he drove as deep as he could inside her and his teeth sank gently into the skin between her shoulder and neck. After what seemed like an eternity and only seconds all at the same time, he moved to her side, collapsing on the mattress with half his body still draped over her like a heavy, weighted blanket.

She smiled, her eyes closed as her fingers ran up and down his arm softly. Her body slowly regained control, the tremors of pleasure slowing to a warm throb that satiated deeply in her core. She concentrated on the feeling of his skin as she ran her hand across him. He was solid—hard muscles pressing back against her—and his skin was soft and rough all at the same time. The hair on his arm was thick, but she could see the dots forming across his skin as he responded to her touch even as he dozed off. His eyes stayed closed, peaceful, as his breathing deepened with every inhale.

Nola closed her eyes and allowed herself to be in the moment, to just enjoy the feeling of being here with the man she...The word stuck in her throat as it crossed her mind. She wasn't going to allow herself to go there. She wasn't going to allow herself to even think it. Right here, right now...this was enough.

It had to be.

Chapter Twenty-Two

The sound of bells pulled Tanner from his sleep as he stretched out his arms with a long yawn. Every Christmas morning, the bells on top of Grace Lake Church rang to celebrate the holiday, and it usually drew a crowd of families with young kids who loved to watch the massive bells move. He hadn't gone in a few years, but as he rolled over and watched Nola sleeping next to him, her hair spread across the pillow behind her, he remembered the times she'd tagged along with him and Rosie as children. Sometimes he forgot how big a part of his life she'd been because she just seemed...right. She fit. She belonged there, and that seemed even more true now that she was lying beside him.

Careful not to wake her, Tanner slipped out from beneath the sheets and found his pants. He slid them on and tiptoed downstairs in search of his phone and a good cup of coffee. He made quick work of setting up Gigi's old coffee machine and brewing a pot as he checked his messages.

"Hey, Rosie," Tanner said, voice texting his sister as he tucked the phone between his ear and shoulder. He found a small container of plain eggnog in the fridge and poured it into his cup of black coffee. A quick stir with a spoon and he had a Christmas-flavored treat. "Merry Christmas!"

Almost immediately after he sent the text, he got a call from her. "Merry Christmas, ya grinch!" Rosie teased, and then her voice pulled away as she scolded someone in the background for putting their hands in the pancake batter. "What time will you be home? Should we wait for you to get here to open presents?"

"Nah," Tanner replied. "Go ahead and open them after breakfast as usual. I probably won't be back until later."

Rosie giggled, and he immediately rolled his eyes, knowing what was coming. "Ah, okay. Someone has you occupied, huh?"

"I just thought she might want some company." Tanner tried to keep the defensive tone out of his voice, but he could feel his cheeks beginning to heat anyway. He wasn't one to kiss and tell, and it felt strange that people were keeping tabs on his love life since he'd always kept it so private. Of course, he'd never dated his sister's best friend before either. "It's her last Christmas here, after all."

"Sure it is." Rosie sounded less than convinced. "But good for you two. I hope you all have fun! Let me know if you want me to drop by some more food. Nola never has anything in her fridge."

"She's got my cookies!" Marvel's voice could be heard in the background.

"Yes, you guys can just eat Marvel's cookies all day," Rosie repeated with a small laugh. "There are no calories on Christmas."

Tanner was surprised to hear that Marvel was still over there since last night. She must have decided to join the family for Christmas breakfast as well. He made a mental note to ask Rosie about it later.

"Thanks. I'll keep that in mind. Tell the kids Merry Christmas for me," he said before saying goodbye and hanging up the phone.

He walked over to the fridge and took a peek inside, not surprised to see only a scarce collection of random groceries and a few plastic containers of leftovers from his sister.

He opened one container and found some sort of bell pepper stir-fry. Deciding to be a bit creative, he pulled it out and grabbed the carton of eggs sitting on the door of the fridge. It took a few minutes to orient himself to the kitchen, but he was soon able to find a pan and some supplies to put together some stir-fry omelets. It was a trick his mother had taught him many, many years ago when Rosie had gone through a phase of refusing to eat any leftovers. She'd always been a picky eater, but there were a good two years in middle school when she would rather eat nothing than eat day-old food. His mother had had the patience of a saint when it came to his sister, and so she'd use any leftovers in brand-new recipes instead. Once repurposed, Rosie often didn't even recognize the ingredients as leftovers, but if she did, she seemed not to mind. Honestly, it had turned into some pretty delicious creations, and if there was one thing he knew, it was that you could put pretty much anything in an omelet and have a hit.

While the eggs were cooking, Tanner mixed some coffee with hot chocolate and eggnog for a Christmas-themed mocha drink. He poured it in a mug for Nola and placed it on a small tray, along with some silverware and napkins. When the two omelets were done cooking, he plated them and added that to the tray with some blackberries he'd found in the fridge as well. Taking care not to stumble, Tanner balanced the tray in his hands as he walked up the stairs to the bedroom.

When he entered, Nola was still asleep, but she was sprawled out on the bed like a starfish. He chuckled low, wondering how she hadn't kicked him out of bed in the middle of the night with all her stretching. Tanner placed the tray on the nightstand and then crawled back into bed next to her, lifting her arm to give himself space to scoot in.

"Mm," Nola moaned lightly, rousing as she stretched her

arms and legs even further. "Why are we awake? Isn't it too early?"

He laughed at her disgruntled mumbles. "Nola, it's ten o'clock. I can't remember the last time I slept in this late."

"Ten o'clock on a holiday is basically dawn," she argued with a yawn, pulling herself up to a seated position next to him as he leaned back against the headboard. "This is anti-Christmas."

Tanner shrugged and then lifted the breakfast tray onto the bed and placed it between them. "Hey, Santa's been up for hours. He pulled an all-nighter."

"You made breakfast?" Her eyes went wide and her tongue slid across her lower lip. It was like he could see her ravenous thoughts on her face as she eagerly examined the contents of the tray. "Oh, man. This looks amazing. I'm freaking starving."

"Help yourself." Tanner handed her a plate and fork, then took his. He took a few bites while watching her devour half her omelet so quickly he wondered if she'd had time to breathe. "Like it?"

She looked up sheepishly and then swallowed her cheekful of eggs. "Love it. Thank you."

"No problem." He continued eating and they sat in silence for a few minutes as they both just enjoyed their food and each other's company.

"What is the family up to today? Do you all have plans?" Nola didn't look at him as she asked.

Tanner finished the last of his eggs and returned his plate to the tray. "They're opening presents by now, I'd guess. Normally they spend Christmas Day watching a Christmas movie marathon and playing in the snow. Rosie will probably spend the day reading and asking everyone to leave her alone as her gift. I imagine they'll do a small dinner tonight and then head to bed early, since the kids probably got up early today."

Nola nodded and took another bite. "So, I guess you should be heading back soon?"

"I could," Tanner acknowledged. "But I was thinking it might be nice to spend the day here instead."

Her head lifted quickly, a smile spreading across her face despite her attempts to hide it. "Oh yeah?"

"If that's okay with you," he added, teasing slightly now. "I mean, if you have plans with someone else..."

She laughed and shook her head. "No plans. Just snow and Marvel's cookies."

"That sounds like a pretty good day to me." Tanner took her empty plate from her as she finished and returned the tray and its contents to the nightstand. He pulled her back down under the blankets and wrapped an arm around her as she laid her head on his chest. "Merry Christmas, Nola."

She traced circles on his bare chest with her index finger. "Merry Christmas, Tanner."

They stayed that way for a while, quietly holding one another and falling in and out of sleep as they allowed peace and comfort to eclipse everything they'd been worried about in the past, or were worried about in the future. Nola roused an hour later and kissed Tanner awake for a very special Christmas Day celebration—the best he'd ever had.

By the time they had both gotten out of bed, showered, and dressed for the day, it was already well into the afternoon. Nola rummaged through the pantry and snacked on some rice cakes as the two sat together on the couch and watched an old Christmas movie.

"What do you want to do for dinner tonight?" she asked as she polished off the last rice cake.

He could practically hear her stomach growling, and

based on the contents of the fridge—or lack thereof—he was going to have to get creative with food choices. "Hobbes Grocery is closed for the holiday today, but we can go scrounge something up from my dad's house or Rosie's. Or we could go ice fishing and catch dinner."

She lifted one brow as she turned to look at him. "Catch our dinner?"

"I could show you how," he offered with a slight shrug of his shoulders. "I share a small ice fishing hut out on the lake with a few other guys from town. It's usually a good spot to catch. Have you ever been?"

"Not in a long time," she admitted. "But I'd be open to that. As long as you know how to cook the fish."

They bundled up in warmer clothes and set off toward the ice hut in his truck, which was equipped with chains on the tires for driving through snow. He'd lived in Michigan long enough to always be prepared, and so his fishing equipment was already in the back, waiting for any excuse to get out there. When they arrived, he circled the truck and opened the door for her, helping her get down from the high height.

"Thanks," Nola said, taking his hand. She leaned into him and placed a small kiss on his cheek.

He felt warmer immediately. "I'll get the fishing rods. Why don't you head out to the hut and I'll be right behind you."

He pointed out the small ice fishing hut on the lake not too far away. She nodded and began the trek while he rounded the back of the truck and began pulling his gear out. A few minutes later, he followed her only to find that she'd stopped at the shoreline and was rolling a large ball of snow across the ground.

"What are you doing?" he asked, dropping his equipment to the ground.

She looked at him as if it were obvious. "Building a snowman. Duh. Go find a few sticks for the arms."

Tanner smiled and shook his head but followed her lead. He walked a bit closer to the water's edge where the trees ended and kicked the snow around in an attempt to find some sticks under it. He didn't have much luck, however, so instead, he reached up and snapped two medium-sized branches off one of the trees. He also scooped up a few pine cones and some small rocks from the shore. By the time he'd returned to Nola, she'd already placed the torso on top of the bottom sphere, and she was now rolling a smaller ball of snow for the head.

"Can you hold the bottom two snowballs still while I put this one on top?" Nola asked, lifting the head in her hands. "I'm worried it's going to all collapse."

He inspected her work so far and packed a few areas that looked weak. "I think it's good. Go for it."

She carefully placed the head on top and he helped secure it with some more snow in between. "Did you find some arms?"

"And some eyes," Tanner replied, grabbing the rocks he'd collected and handing them to her. "Or buttons, maybe. I figured we could rip up some of the pine cones and use the pieces for buttons if we need to."

Nola got to work placing the rocks carefully on the snowman while Tanner stuck the sticks in the sides for the arms. Soon, the project was complete and they both stepped back to admire the end result.

"It's missing something," Nola mused, tapping a finger to her chin. "Ah, I know."

She walked over to where he'd dropped the fishing equipment and rummaged around in the long, thin bag. She pulled out one of his oldest fishing rods and held it up. "This will work perfectly!"

"For what?" he asked.

Nola leaned the fishing rod against one of the snowman's

stick arms to make it look like he was holding it. "He's going fishing!"

Tanner smiled and shook his head. "You're ridiculous."

"Wait—we're not done." She pulled a red plastic package out of her jacket pocket and held it up. They were red Twizzlers, one of his least favorite candies. She slid a piece out and placed it across the snowman's face in a slight curve to resemble a mouth smiling.

He cocked one eyebrow. "You just carry Twizzlers around with you all the time?"

"Never know when you'll have a licorice emergency. Always best to be prepared," she replied in a tone so serious he couldn't tell if she was joking or not. "Come on! Let's go fishing."

They headed across the ice to the small hut and he opened the door to usher her in. "It's warmer inside."

"Hey, folks," Perry Mott said, greeting them as they walked in. He was seated on a wooden box and drinking a beer—not a fishing pole in sight. "Fish are biting well today."

"Certainly looks like you're catching a lot," Tanner said, teasing his friend.

Perry lifted his beer in salute, a crooked smile on his face that seemed slightly more magnified lately. "Taking a mental health break. You should try it sometime. You never get a day off over there at your dad's place."

"Tell me about it," Tanner replied, then gestured toward Nola standing beside him. "You remember Nola Bennett, right?"

He tipped his baseball cap. "Nice to see you again, Nola. How are the folks?"

"On vacation at the beach right now, so I'd say doing pretty good compared to us," Nola said with a small chuckle.

"Don't I know it," Perry replied. "I'm headed south myself at the end of the school year."

"I heard!" Nola confirmed. "That's so exciting."

"It would be more exciting if this kid would agree to take my job next year." Perry pointed at Tanner. "Don't you think he'd be perfect for the role?"

Nola glanced sideways at Tanner. "We have, uh, discussed that a bit."

He could tell she was restraining herself from what she really wanted to say. In fact, she looked about ready to burst at the seams. "It might have come up."

"The board is just waiting for your application. It'll get fast-tracked right to the top of the pile," Perry promised. "Well, technically, there is no pile yet. But still...it would be a great fit if you want it."

"I promise I'm thinking about it," Tanner repeated, hoping to change the subject. "But tonight, I'm going to teach Nola how to fish."

"*You're* going to teach *me*?" Nola shook her head. "Step aside, buddy."

He grinned as she grabbed the equipment from him with all the confidence of a pro fisherman. This was the Nola he'd known all his life. She was a constant challenge, and he wanted every moment of it. He wanted every moment of her.

Chapter Twenty-Three

"I'm not sure I'm a fan," Tanner said, placing his mug down on the coffee table.

Nola settled back farther into the couch and kept her eyes on the flickering fire as she continued sipping on the mulled wine they'd picked up from a neighbor on the way back to The Castle from ice fishing. "It's not for everyone," she admitted. "But it always reminds me of Christmas. My mother makes a big batch on Christmas Eve most years. When I was a kid, she always made a nonalcoholic batch for me, too."

"Have you spent a Christmas apart from your family before?" he asked her. "I was surprised you didn't go with them on their trip. Sounds like something you would enjoy."

He wasn't wrong. She did love to travel, and warm weather was certainly a plus. "It is. I'm not entirely sure why, but it just seemed...final. You know? Like this was my last chance to spend Christmas here in Gigi's home like I always used to."

Tanner was quiet for a moment before a soft exhale escaped his lips. "It doesn't have to be the last."

She didn't respond to that. There wasn't much she could say. She knew his feelings on the matter, but she felt...differently. At least, she was pretty sure she did.

He stood and walked over to the bar cart, pouring himself a stiff whiskey before returning to the couch. She didn't turn to look at him but felt the couch depress next to her as he moved closer and placed his arm behind her shoulders.

"Rosie says Blake is really excelling in the business," Nola said, changing the subject, though an awkward tension had settled between them. It felt like after everything they'd experienced in the last twenty-four hours, that certainly shouldn't be the case ... and yet, everything hung awkwardly between them now. "So, how's that working out?"

Tanner crossed one ankle over his opposite knee. "Blake is a good man. He's doing well. Eager to learn."

"Amanda's been asking about him," she added. "She says he's ambitious."

"He is," he confirmed, still staring straight ahead toward the fire.

What was he thinking? Every time things seemed to ease between them, the snap back seemed harder and harsher.

"About what Mr. Mott said..." Nola awkwardly inter-jected the comment after a few moments. "Have you thought more about his offer? The job at the school?"

"It's not really his to offer," Tanner replied, taking another sip of his drink. "The school board makes the final call. I'm sure they have candidates in mind."

"Yeah, like you," Nola pushed back. "I bet you're top of their list. You'd be amazing as a high school teacher. You're so good with kids, and you have the patience of a saint."

He eyed her, one brow raised and a slight smirk on his lips. "I do?"

"Well, with kids." She gave him a wink, but he had a point. When it came to adults—or her, specifically—patience didn't seem to be his strong suit. "Have you told your father about the job? I bet he'd be supportive if that's what you wanted."

"Nola, stop pushing me. Can't you just leave well enough

alone? It's my life." Tanner pushed up off the couch and walked back over to the bar cart, where he poured himself a refill. His tone was sharp and cutting, and Nola felt herself freeze. "Besides, you're not even planning to stay here. You shouldn't be telling other people what to do with their life when you're so focused on your own."

She swallowed hard, a seething response bubbling up inside her, when her phone pinged next to her and diverted her attention. She gritted her teeth and exhaled slowly as she read through the text message she'd received from Craig.

"Holy shit." Her eyes widened and she gasped as she read the new offer on The Castle. This time he was not messing around—apparently business didn't stop on Christmas in real estate. Not only had Craig's company met every qualifier she had insisted on, but his offering price point had skyrocketed. The offer was huge and more than enough to fund her business in Chicago. She felt a twinge of excitement that her dreams were all falling into place…This was everything she'd been waiting for. And yet, sadness eclipsed any happiness she might be feeling. Where was this coming from? All she knew was that it felt like there was a rock sitting on her chest, and she wasn't sure she could keep breathing. "I can't believe it."

"What?" Tanner turned around to look at her. He seemed to understand from her expression that it was something serious, so he put his glass down. "What is it?"

"Craig upped his offer—by a lot. It's everything I asked for and more." The news blurted out of her before she could even digest what it all meant.

The concern etched on his face hardened to stone. "Well, sounds like you got everything you wanted. Guess your mind is all made up about this place…about everything."

His words clearly pointed to more than a real estate sale, or moving out of town. He was talking about them. That's not what she had meant at all, and the familiar feeling of frustration began bubbling inside her once again. The judgment on his face—as if he'd already decided who she was—irritated the hell out of her. She was suddenly reminded of everything she'd always disliked about him when they were younger—his self-righteousness, stubbornness, and the way he made snap judgments as if he knew everything.

"That would be easier for you, wouldn't it?" she snapped back. "If you could just write me off as if I never existed—as if *this* never happened."

"I think it's time I head home." He didn't bother to answer the question and began to walk away.

Nola wasn't about to let him off the hook that easily, and she followed him. "God, Tanner, you're so stubborn. I don't understand why you see something good and you throw dynamite at it. The job at the high school? Me? It's like you refuse to let yourself have anything you actually want, like some martyr who has to sacrifice everything...for what?"

He pushed his clothes into a duffel bag and shook his head. "Just because you and I have different values doesn't mean I'm sabotaging my own happiness. Maybe I just value things that are more important than my name on an office door. Maybe I value people and traditions more than a cash offer to sell away my history."

His accusation knocked the wind out of her. He stormed past her and back down the stairs, and she continued to chase after him. She was so angry she couldn't think straight, and her words were clustering together before she could get them all out.

Tanner swung open the front door and came to a dead stop. "Rosie?"

"Tanner!" Rosie was standing on the porch with Becca and Zander in tow. There was a panicked look on her face.

"We need to go to the hospital. Dad was having chest pains. He got so dizzy he fell over! Marvel took him to Heart Lake Hospital."

"What?" Nola gasped behind him, her hand flying to her chest. "Oh my gosh, Rosie. Is there anything I can do?"

"Yes, actually," she began, pushing her children forward into the house. "Can you watch the twins until we know more about what's happening? That's why I came here. I don't want them at the hospital unless...unless..."

The words caught in her throat, and a sob escaped her lips.

Nola waved her hand and ushered the kids inside. "I've got them. Go. Take your time. Focus on your dad."

Tanner glanced at her, and his stony expression from moments before was gone. In its place were fear and a vulnerability she'd only seen once before at his mother's funeral. "Uh, thanks, Nola. We'll keep you updated."

With that, he hurried off after his sister and they climbed into her car. Zander and Becca turned their faces up to look at her. Fear was etched there as well, and Nola swallowed hard.

"Well, uh, kiddos...how about some dinner? Did you guys eat?"

Zander shook his head. "We were about to, but then—"

"Grandpa's going to be fine," Becca interjected, cutting off her brother. "We said a prayer for him. Everything is going to be fine."

The young girl seemed to be convincing herself more than she was convincing Nola, but Nola certainly wasn't going to disagree. "That's right. Be positive. But I say we fill our tummies with something yummy while we wait!"

"Cookies?" Zander asked. "Mom lets us have cookies for dinner."

Nola laughed, knowing that was far from the truth. "I bet she lets you order pizza, too?"

"Definitely. She definitely lets us have pizza," Zander confirmed as he kicked off his shoes and ran into the living room. "And soda!"

She pulled out her cell phone and called a couple of pizza places in town. Everything was closed, but she finally found one just outside of town that was willing to deliver. She placed the order and then headed to the kitchen in search of cookies to tide them over.

"Aunt Nola?" Becca walked into the kitchen behind her and was looking down at her fidgeting hands. "Can I ask you a question?"

"Sure, baby," she replied, placing the container of cookies on the counter. "Want some hot cocoa and cookies, too?"

Becca nodded and sat herself on one of the stools at the island, pulling the container of cookies closer to her and lifting one out. "My mom told me about when her mom died. She said you were there for her when that happened."

Nola frowned, the memories of that time coming back in a sad wave. "I remember."

"I was wondering," Becca continued, but she paused to take a bite of the cookie in her hand. "If Mom's mom died, does that mean my mom could die, too?"

The little girl turned big eyes toward her, tears welling in the corners as she waited for an answer to a question Nola had certainly not prepared for.

"Um, well…" Nola cleared her throat and then inhaled slowly. "Life is…uh, well, it's hard to imagine knowing that the people we love might die one day. But the good thing is that we have them now. Your mom isn't going anywhere. We have to spend as much time with her as possible while we can—spend as much time with everyone you love. That's the most important thing."

Nola's mind flicked back to her earlier conversation

with Tanner, and how he'd been saying almost exactly that.
Something clicked in her that she hadn't considered before,
and she felt a pull for home she'd not felt in years.

"I'm with Mom all the time," Becca replied. "So, that's
good, right?"

"That's very good," Nola confirmed, handing her another
cookie. "Come on. Help me make some hot cocoa."

Becca hopped off the stool and came over to the stove
to help Nola begin boiling the milk. She handed Becca a
box of cocoa and gave her a tight squeeze. She wasn't sure
she'd said all the right things, and now that she was looking
at things in a different light, she was wondering if she'd been
off base all along.

Chapter Twenty-Four

"Thomas Dean." Tanner repeated his father's name to the hospital admitting clerk at the desk. "He just checked in not that long before we got here. They were only a few minutes ahead of us."

"Check under Tom or Tommy, too," Rosie added, leaning across the counter in an attempt to see the clerk's computer screen. "He sometimes goes by those names."

"When has Dad ever gone by Tommy?" Tanner furrowed his brow and shook his head. "Thomas Dean. That's what it will be under."

"Folks, I understand your rush in this moment, but if you could please just give me a minute to look through our records," the clerk said. "I promise I'm looking as fast as I can."

Tanner nodded and pulled Rosie gently away from the counter. "Sorry about that."

Rosie glared at him and crossed her arms over her chest but didn't say anything.

"Okay, so it looks like he's in ER room two," the clerk confirmed, handing them a small map to show where they were going to go. Tanner didn't need it since this hospital was pretty small to begin with and he'd spent his fair share of time at his mother's bedside while she was here.

"He's still in the ER?" Rosie asked. "Why hasn't he been moved to a room yet?"

"I'm not a doctor, ma'am," the lady replied, pointing them in the direction she'd highlighted on the map. "They can help you in the emergency room."

Rosie took off and Tanner had to jog to keep up with her. It only took a few minutes to finally find the right room, and his sister tossed open the curtain drawn over the door.

"Dad? Are you—?" Rosie began to ask, and then came to a dead stop in the middle of the doorway. "Oh my God. That is disgusting."

Tanner frowned and walked past her. "Christ, Rosie. What's wrong with you?"

Then he saw what she'd been looking at—Marvel was seated on Thomas's lap and they were sharing a very, very open kiss. Tongue, saliva—all of it permanently seared into his brain for the rest of time. He quickly turned around and faced the door.

"Uh, Dad...you okay?" he asked.

"Hey, kids!" Thomas seemed to be in a cheery mood, and there was no indication that he was on his deathbed. In fact, he seemed downright happy as Tanner turned back around to look at them now that the tongue-sucking had ceased. "Nice of you to come check on me, but there's no reason to worry. I'm healthy as a horse."

"Wait a second. I suspected something was up, but, oh my God, is this for real?" Rosie asked, pointing between their father and Marvel. "Are you two really dating?"

Marvel's face lit up with a wide grin and she nodded. "You kids can call it dating," she confirmed. "We call it unifying our hearts and bodies."

Tanner's stomach churned at the mental image. "Um, okay. What did the doctors say, Dad? Was it a heart attack?"

Thomas shook his head. "Nah, just a medication mix-up."

"What medication?" Rosie was lifting up the chart from the slot next to the door and began flipping through it. "Oh my God. Dad, you took expired Viagra?"

Marvel giggled. "Technically, it still worked."

Tanner ran his hand over his forehead, wishing he could just disappear into thin air and never have to bear witness to this conversation again. He couldn't even identify what he was feeling right now. Nausea, certainly. But also discomfort with the idea of his father being with another woman. He'd never seen his father date after their mother had died, and he'd never imagined that it would happen. "Christ, Dad. What the hell?"

"If I'd known, I never would have let him take it," Marvel added. "I'm going to take good care of him going forward. You have my word that I will pay deep attention to every inch of your father's body."

Rosie made a gagging sound. "Oh God. I need a coffee if I have to keep thinking of my father's body."

"I'll show you where the machine is that the doctors use," Marvel said, ushering Rosie out of the room. "Much better than the swill they serve down in the cafeteria."

The room fell silent as the two women left. Tanner glanced at his father to find him staring at him.

"Son, you're clearly upset," his father began.

"Am I upset?" Tanner snapped back quicker than he'd intended. "Yeah, I'm freaking upset that my father took expired Viagra on Christmas and made me think he was dying."

"An unfortunate turn of events, to be sure," his father joked, a lightness in his voice that Tanner hadn't heard in a long time. The usually stoic and grumpy man he knew seemed to be gone. "I'm sorry I frightened you and your sister like that."

"Yeah, well..." Tanner crossed his arms over his chest. Everything he'd been pushing down seemed to well up inside, and he knew in that moment that it was time to say something. Things hadn't been well between him and his father in years, and it went way beyond a health scare or a new love interest. "I guess I'm upset about more than that, too."

"I had a feeling," his father said with a sigh. "What happened between us, kid? We used to be close a while back. Things seem like they've shifted in the last few years, though."

Tanner wasn't sure where to begin, so he just spit out the news and let it hang heavily between them. "Perry Mott is retiring, and the school board is talking about potentially offering me his job."

"You're leaving Dean and Son?" His father's eyes widened for a moment as he absorbed the news.

Tanner shook his head. "I haven't taken the job. I told you I would keep your legacy going, and I am not going to walk away from my responsibilities."

His dad was quiet for a moment, rubbing his hand across the stubble on his chin. "I think you should take the job."

"What?" Tanner balked. "I'm not taking the job, Dad. I promised to help you run the company."

Thomas waved a hand at him and shook his head. "I should never have asked you to promise me that, Tanner. After your mother passed away, I think I clung a little too tightly to the idea of family...of not letting anyone else in, and not letting anything else change. Lately I've been wondering if maybe that was the wrong idea all along, and if maybe teaching that to you kids hurt you more than it helped you."

Tanner took a seat in the chair beside the gurney his father was sitting on. "What do you mean?"

"Spending time with Marvel more and more lately, it's shown me that new can be pretty great. Change can lead to some wonderful moments and wonderful people." Thomas smiled and looked toward the doorway, as if hoping Marvel would walk back in at that moment. "It's funny. I've known Marvel around town for years and never gave her the time of day. Never even tried to look past what I thought my life path would be and should be. I almost missed something really great because I was clinging so hard to tradition and history."

The sentiment felt familiar and Tanner's mind wandered to Nola. He swallowed hard as he wondered if he'd been doing the same thing as his father all this time.

"Blake's been taking a leadership role lately," Thomas continued. "I bet he'd take on more responsibility if you asked. He's an incredible young man. And so are you. You've always been amazing with kids. Teaching the next generation is really the perfect fit for you. Hell, you could even give the most promising students internships at Dean and Son. We should maybe rethink the name, too. Blake deserves to be added to the marquee at some point."

Tanner couldn't believe what he was hearing. He'd pictured running his father's business his whole life. Not because he wanted to but just because it was expected. He hadn't even allowed himself to dream of anything else. "I don't know what to say, Dad."

"Say you'll call the school board and submit your application," Thomas replied. "We can meet with Blake after the holidays to see if he's interested in more. If not, we'll figure it out. You can always stay as part owner and leave the day-to-day operations to someone else, or I could buy you out. Maybe talk to Nola about it. See what she thinks."

"Nola?" Tanner looked up at his father in confusion.

His dad nodded. "Aren't you two together? Or was Rosie pulling my leg?"

"We're not together," Tanner replied, though the sorrow in his voice was more evident than he'd intended. "She's selling The Castle and moving back to Chicago to start her own business there. She doesn't want to stay in Heart Lake."

"Okay, so she's moving a short distance away," Thomas replied. "What's that got to do with the two of you being together or not? Do you like her?"

"Of course I do, Dad. It's not that simple." He swallowed the lump forming in his throat. "She has plans that don't involve me."

"Did she say that? All I hear you talking about is business. You can't date long-distance or move down there with her?" Thomas shook his head and let out a long sigh. "Honestly, I have not taught you well if you're going to just give up on the girl you've been pining for your entire goddamn life like that. What the hell is wrong with you?"

Tanner's mouth fell open, but he didn't know how to respond. His father had a point—several good points, actually.

"Go talk to her, son. Fight for her. You love Nola. You always have." Thomas smiled as Marvel walked back into the room and took his hand. Rosie was behind her and still looked a bit sullen. "You never know what you've been missing out on until you open yourself up to love, Tanner."

"Ooh, what a romantic," Marvel teased, seating herself on Thomas's lap again.

Tanner sighed. "I wish it were that easy. We had a fight before all of this. I said things..."

"So?" Rosie jumped into the conversation now. "Go unsay them. We're talking about you and Nola, right?"

"I've been wondering when those two would get together

already," Marvel mused. "I've been making love potions for years."

Tanner leaned forward, his elbows on his knees as he hung his head in his hands. "I really messed up, guys. I'm not sure she'd take me back at this point. I don't even know if she ever wanted to be together in the first place. She has plans and goals that don't include me, and I don't want to be the one who stands in the way of everything she's dreamed of."

Rosie snorted. "Believe me, big brother—nothing you do is going to stop Nola from chasing her dreams. She's a strong, independent woman."

He chuckled lightly, because that was certainly the truth. Once she set her mind to something, she went after it with all the fierceness of a bull in a bullring. He loved that about her. Hell, he loved her.

Holy shit, I love her.

Chapter Twenty-Five

"Simon says, 'Dance like a monkey!' " Zander giggled as he shouted out the instructions to Nola and his sister, who were standing by the fireplace in the living room. Zander was on top of the ottoman over by the L-shaped sectional couch, which almost made him as tall as Nola when he stood on it.

Nola dutifully swung her arms around and made monkey sounds as she and Becca both played along. She nearly knocked over an ornamental vase on a side table and scooted over to the center of the room to avoid knocking anything off the bookshelves that lined the far walls.

Zander was nearly falling over in a fit of laughter. "Simon says, 'Roar like a lion!' "

Nola made a loud roaring sound as she pushed out her chest.

Rosie walked into the living room just as Nola reached the lowest pitch she could manage. "Is this Nola's house or the zoo? I think I'm in the wrong place."

Nola laughed and then collapsed onto the couch with relief, nearly knocking Zander off with the weight of her body plopping onto the soft surface. She'd loved spending the evening with her godchildren, but, man, in a house full of breakable items, expensive paintings, and huge windows, it was enough to increase anyone's anxiety tenfold.

"You're back," Nola said, trying to catch her breath. "How is your dad?"

"He's fine. False alarm." Rosie rolled her eyes. "I'll fill you in later."

She smiled, happy to hear that it had been nothing serious. "I'm glad he's doing well. Did you tell Marvel?"

"Did you know that they are *dating*?" Rosie said with exaggerated effect. "I knew something was up, but not to that extent, damn."

"Mom said a bad word!" Zander called out. "We get cookies!"

Rosie sighed and leaned against the door frame. "Shit."

"That's another cookie!" Zander started adding his cookie total on his hands. "Becca, we get two cookies each."

"I never should have come up with that rule," Rosie said with a chuckle. "They've been eating more cookies than ever before."

"Well, you've already had quite a few today," Nola reminded the kids, giving them a stern look. They'd spent plenty of time raiding the kitchen cabinets already. "I'm sure we can let your mom's indiscretion go this one time."

Zander frowned. "Fine, but I call shotgun."

"What?" Becca shrieked. "That's not fair. I'll get there first!"

The kids took off at a sprint for the car, racing each other to get to the front seat. Nola lost sight of them, but she could hear them bickering in the front yard.

"Never have kids," Rosie joked. "I swear I'm going gray faster than I can count, thanks to them."

"What happened with your dad?" Nola asked now that they had a moment alone. "Marvel told me they've been seeing each other for a while now."

"You knew and didn't tell me?" Rosie huffed.

Nola shrugged, running a hand across the side table she often placed her purse on when she came inside. "I thought you knew. It didn't exactly seem like a secret. She's always over there."

Rosie tapped a finger to her chin. "I guess that was kind of a giveaway if I look back at it. But yeah, he's fine. He was just trying to get some and took an expired Viagra. Doctors gave him a new prescription and sent him on his way. Never seen him giddier as he and Marvel practically skipped to the car hand in hand. It was gross."

Nola laughed at her friend's discomfort. While she had never experienced her parents being with anyone but each other, they were certainly very affectionate, and Nola always avoided eye contact when they displayed it publicly like that. "Well, I'm glad he's doing well. It sounds like he's happy."

More shouting came from the front yard and Rosie sighed. "I have to run. I'll see you later."

Nola said goodbye and closed the door after she watched them get safely in the car and drive away. It was getting pretty late at that point, and Nola found herself just crawling straight into bed with all of her clothes still on. She pulled the blankets up around her and tried to close her eyes, but her mind was on overdrive. She needed to make a decision about what she wanted to do going forward—accept Craig's offer or not. She wasn't even sure why she was questioning it, because it was literally everything she'd asked for and more.

But lying in the bed she'd spent last night in with Tanner, all she could feel was a heavy throbbing in her chest as she wished he were there with her again. Despite the words they'd exchanged earlier, she missed him. She wanted to apologize for the things she'd said and assure him that she truly did care about him. In fact, she loved him. The realization hung in the silence for a moment as she digested the thought. Slowly, she fell asleep as thoughts of her future began molding into something she hadn't dared let herself picture before.

When she opened her eyes the next morning, she found the sky gray and overcast out her bedroom window. She pushed the covers off and realized she was still in her jeans and T-shirt from yesterday. Nola hopped into the shower and refreshed, then headed down to the kitchen to find something to eat. She frowned as she looked in the fridge. Seemed like she'd need to hit up the grocery store again soon. Turning instead to the coffee machine, she loaded up some coffee grounds and grabbed a mug from the cabinet while she waited for it to brew.

Her phone buzzed, pulling her attention. More messages from Craig. She'd told him yesterday she needed time to think about his offer, and he'd only doubled down on his pushiness since then. His latest message warned her that it was a time-sensitive offer and she shouldn't pass it up.

She sighed because he was right. It was what she wanted. Though she wasn't sure why she no longer felt as confident in that plan as she had before. She began to type a message in response to Craig, letting him know that she would accept the offer, but her phone rang and interrupted her.

Nola saw her boss's name on the phone and answered quickly. "Hello?"

"Bennett, I need you back in Chicago by close of business today," Charles St. John demanded from the other end of the line without so much as a hello. "We've got a dinner scheduled with the clients from Taiwan. We're *this* close to closing the entire thing, and it's been hell trying to get all the moving parts working right since you've been off gallivanting around small-town America."

"Charles, I'm still scheduled to be off until the new year. I have a lot of paid time off saved up for this. I haven't taken

even a sick day in years," Nola began protesting as her anxiety spiked. There was no way she'd be able to finish packing everything up today or get all the paperwork complete.
Not to mention she wasn't ready to say goodbye. She wasn't
ready to leave.

"Christ, Bennett. I'll send packers and movers up there
to do it for you. Why do you want to stick around that dump
anyway? I bet there is only one stoplight in that town, and
you certainly can't get good sushi up there. Fucking hillbil-
lies. You belong back in Chicago."

Anger seethed in Nola as her boss ripped apart her hometown. "I grew up here, Charles. Heart Lake is an incredible
place full of incredible people. I'd be damn well lucky to still
be living here."

As impulsive as her statement had been, she'd never meant
anything more. This town had been everything to her for
years, and she'd walked away from it without so much as a
thank-you. Being home, being here…it had awakened a nostalgia in her that she hadn't known she'd been ignoring. Heart
Lake wasn't just her home—the people of this town were.

One in particular, especially.

Charles laughed. "Great. So what time should I tell the
restaurant we'll do dinner with the investors?"

"I don't know, and frankly, I don't care. I won't be there."
Nola swallowed hard, trying to digest everything she was
about to say, but she couldn't hold it in a second longer. "I'm
a senior manager at this company, Charles. I've pulled in
more business than most of my coworkers combined, and yet
I'm still spoken to like a secretary or an intern. I deserve
to work for, or with, someone who respects me, and I don't
think that's ever going to be you. So, you know what? I quit."

"Excuse me?" he balked on the other end. "You can't
quit. I respect you just fine."

"This isn't up for negotiation. I quit." Nola held the phone tighter in an effort to keep from dropping it. "I'll be following up this phone call with an official letter of resignation via email later today. Thank you for all the opportunities, but I have somewhere else I need to be."

With that, she hung up the phone despite the fact that she could still hear him arguing on the other end of the line. She placed her cell phone on the kitchen counter and let out a long exhale.

"Holy shit."

She had just quit her job. The job she'd been working at for years, trying to move up the ladder. The job she'd dreamed of being a partner in one day. All of that work—gone.

And she couldn't be happier. She had another plan—one that didn't involve being disrespected forty hours a week.

For a woman who lived and died by to-do lists, the impulsivity of her decision was not lost on her. Anxiety and terror were trying to steer the ship, but she wasn't going to allow that. She had the perfect idea for a new business. Sure, it was terrifying, but there was an exhilaration in starting something new, too.

Now she just had to figure out a plan and put it in motion. It wasn't going to be quick or easy, and her mind was already going a million miles an hour with everything she'd need to accomplish to achieve her goals.

Nola poured herself a cup of freshly brewed coffee and grabbed a notepad.

It was time to get to work on a brand-new future.

Chapter Twenty-Six

Tanner noted the list of repairs that he needed to do on his deck as he sat outside his cabin and looked out on the lake. The wooden dock that jutted into the water was sagging, and a storm had knocked off one of the railings. He hadn't had time to get to it yet, but he certainly had the time now. Now that he was looking at life alone permanently.

He wasn't sure when it had happened, or how he knew so confidently, but Nola had been the end goal for him. Tanner wasn't sure how he'd move on without her, but he knew it wouldn't be with another woman. He'd rather live out his days alone in this cabin than try to replace the hole she left in his heart with anyone else.

Still, he knew he needed to keep busy for his own mental health.

"Mott here," Perry Mott said, answering the phone in the same kindly tone that Tanner had always received from him.

"Hey, Mr. Mott," Tanner replied, holding the phone between his ear and shoulder as he seasoned the steak he was about to sear on the stove. "It's Tanner Dean."

"Tanner, buddy—please call me Perry!" His former teacher greeted him with a friendly chuckle. "Nice to hear from you. You coming to the pine cone drop tonight to celebrate the New Year?"

"Rosie's in charge of the confetti, so I'd lose my head if I wasn't there," Tanner joked, although it wasn't exactly untrue. The annual pine cone drop in the center of town celebrated the New Year in Heart Lake fashion. Everyone gathered around before midnight to count down to the New Year as the pine cone lowered down a pole. It was as simple as it was quaint. "Listen, I wanted to talk to you about the position."

"I'm all ears," Perry responded.

Tanner took a deep breath as he pulled a pan out of the cabinet and placed it on the burner. "I am going to submit my application when businesses reopen after the holidays. I've decided to stay on as part owner at Dean and Son but turn over the day-to-day operations to someone else. I'll have to go to night school to get my teaching certificate, but I think it's doable."

Perry whooped on the other end of the line. "Heck yeah! I've had my eye on you for this role since you first entered my classroom twenty years ago."

"Really?" Tanner found that suspect, but he had done a lot of tutoring back in the day. "Well, I was thinking I could also offer internships at Dean and Son for promising students looking to go into construction. Kind of utilize both roles to benefit the other."

"That's a fantastic idea," Perry agreed. "I've already sent my recommendation letter for you to the board, so submit your application and I bet all this gets wrapped up real quick."

"Thanks, Perry. I really appreciate the opportunity."

"You're the one doing me the favor, kid." Tanner could hear the smile in Perry's voice. "I'd hate to move away and think this place would fall apart or the program would end. I'll feel so much better knowing these kids will be in the hands of someone who will care about their futures as much as I did."

Tanner felt assurance in that moment that he was making

the right choice. He wanted to be everything Perry had seen in him, and he wanted to give the confidence to another generation that Perry had given to him all those years ago.

The two men said their goodbyes and Tanner hung up the phone. Just as he was heating the pan and preparing to place the steak on it, he heard his front door open.

"Tanner, you home?" Blake's voice called out from the front hallway.

"In the kitchen!" Tanner shouted back, then went to the fridge to pull out a second steak.

Blake rounded the corner and placed a six-pack of dark beer on the counter. "I figured I'd stop by and we could pre-game a bit before this pine cone thing."

Tanner took a beer that Blake held out to him and cracked it open, taking a long swig. "I could certainly use it today."

"You and me both," Blake agreed. "I'm a little nervous about this event tonight. I've never been to one before, and everyone in this town seems to know each other so well. It's odd being the new man."

Tanner placed the two seasoned steaks on the hot pan and smiled at the sizzling sound they made. "You'll be fine. Heart Lake is very welcoming."

"I guess." Blake opened his own beer and took a few gulps. "What's got you tense today? Lady troubles? You're dating Nola, right?"

Tanner frowned and looked at him. "Who told you that?"

"I heard Felix talking about it at the diner the other day," Blake replied.

"How the hell does Felix know about my personal life?" Tanner shook his head, though he certainly wasn't surprised that the news in this town spread so easily. "But no. We're not dating. She's leaving tomorrow to go back to Chicago, from what I understand."

"Really?" Blake cocked his head to the side. "I thought she lived here."

"Used to," Tanner corrected him. "She's been a city girl for a while now. She grew up here, but her life is in Chicago."

Blake was quiet for a moment, watching as Tanner flipped the steaks over. "I don't get it, man."

"Get what?" Tanner took another swig of his beer as he watched the steaks cook.

"The bachelor life, you know?" Blake sat in a chair at the small table in his kitchen. "You don't go out and date. I never see you with anyone. This is the first person I've heard you've been with since I moved here. I figured she must have been pretty special to pull you out of your hibernation like that."

"She is special," Tanner quickly replied, because there wasn't a doubt in his mind that Nola was absolutely everything he wanted. "But it's not always that simple. She wants to move away. My life is here."

"It doesn't have to be, though," Blake replied. "I've noticed you've been wanting to take a step back from the business. I'd be happy to handle more day-to-day operations if you wanted a break."

Tanner pulled the steaks off the pan and plated them. He grabbed some silverware and brought the plates over to the table and sat down across from Blake. "Actually, I was going to talk to you about that. I think I am going to pursue other things right now, so if you are open to more of a management role, we can talk."

"I'm in," Blake responded immediately. "So, you're going to do it? Move to Chicago with her?"

"What?" Tanner furrowed his brow and then paused as he thought about Blake's comment further. "Move to Chicago...I *could* move to Chicago."

"Well, duh," Blake said with a laugh as he took a big bite of steak. "Isn't that what we're talking about?"

Tanner just nodded but focused on eating his steak as his mind tried to work out the details. He certainly couldn't take Perry's job if he moved to Chicago, but he could always find a teaching job down there. He could come back up here on some weekends if work at his dad's company was needed. He'd want to keep visiting his niece and nephew anyway.

The thought of moving away from Heart Lake had honestly never crossed his mind, but the more he thought about it, the more it made sense. Nola had dreams in Chicago that he wanted her to pursue, but his dream was to be with her. He didn't really care where that took them. Sure, he wasn't a city person, but if it meant sleeping beside her every night…he could certainly do it. Hell, after everything she'd done throughout her life to support him and Rosie, he owed this to her.

No, he *wanted* to give this to her.

"Shit, I'm dumb as hell," Tanner said, only realizing once the words had left his mouth that he'd said them out loud.

"You're just realizing that now?" Blake laughed and opened another beer. "We've all been telling you that, man."

Tanner grinned and shook his head. "I can't believe I'm that stubborn. I always said my dad was a stubborn bastard, and look at me now."

"Your dad is a man in love," Blake replied. "I've never seen a grosser public display of affection than the two of them sharing the same side of a booth at the diner last week. They were practically procreating in the middle of the table."

He grimaced. "Yeah, I've witnessed them a few times now. I mean, good for him. He's certainly happy. I guess if he can do it, I sure as hell can."

Blake nodded. "Nola seems like a great girl, too. Do you think she's open to you moving down there with her?"

He exhaled slowly, because that was the part he'd been avoiding thinking about. He'd left her two voicemails and sent her a text message asking her to call him over the past week. All had gone unanswered. He'd even gone by The Castle and she hadn't been home. He had seen that the FOR SALE sign in the front yard was gone, though. She must have accepted the offer from Craig that she'd told him about.

His last exchange with her had certainly not at all gone the way he'd hoped, and his guilt was at an all-time high for the things he'd said to her. Rosie had assured him that Nola would be at the pine cone drop tonight, however, so he'd been hoping to pull her aside there. He wanted to apologize. He wanted to tell her that he'd realized how much he wanted her in his life—how much he wanted *her*.

He wanted to tell her that he was in love with her, and he couldn't keep it to himself anymore.

"I have to talk to her," Tanner admitted. "Our last conversation wasn't great. She's been keeping her distance."

"You fucked up, didn't you?" Blake tapped his beer against Tanner's. "Man, if there's one thing I know about women, it's how to apologize. I've made more mistakes than a weatherman when it comes to relationships."

Tanner lifted one brow. "I can see that."

Blake scoffed. "Ignoring that. Anyway, my advice is to write her a song. Sing it to her and seduce her back with your dulcet tones."

"Are you joking?" Tanner's eyes widened. "Have you heard me sing?"

Blake touched a hand to his chin as if in thought. "I don't think I have."

"Yeah, and there's a reason for that," Tanner replied. "Believe me—no one wants me singing to them."

"The worse it is, the better," Blake reasoned. "She's going to appreciate the effort. And the chance to laugh at you."

"Finish your goddamn steak so we can go to this festival." Tanner took the last bite of his own steak and followed it with the rest of his beer. "I'm not turning into a musical greeting card for you."

Blake's eyes lit up. "Ooh, what if you wore a costume during the song, too? Something historical, like Romeo-and-Juliet kind of style. Women love that kind of thing. Dead teenagers and all—super romantic."

"Our company has great health benefits. Maybe you should use them and see a doctor." Tanner took his plate to the sink. "Or maybe a whole team of doctors."

Blake joined him at the sink, dropping his plate in. "No medication can fix what I have," he joked. "But if you're not going to serenade her, what are you going to do?"

He had no idea. All he knew was that he needed to see her as soon as possible. He needed her to know how he felt, and he needed her to know he was more than ready to support her in following her dreams.

Chapter Twenty-Seven

"You quit your job?" Amanda smoothed the edges down of the red gingham blanket that she had spread across the grass in the main courtyard in town. It was nighttime, but there were string lights across the entire area that lit the place up as if it were day.

Nola placed the picnic basket—which was full of mostly wine and cheese—down on the blanket and took a seat where she would have a good view of the pine cone drop. Piles of snow from the last storm's dump were stacked high, but the weather was still much too cold for her liking, so she was bundled in a thick jacket, leg warmers, and fuzzy boots. "Yep. Didn't even give two weeks' notice. Just said that I was done."

"Holy shit." Amanda opened the picnic basket and pulled out a bottle of red wine and held it up. "Well, that's reason to celebrate!"

Rosie sat down on the blanket across from her, her eyes on where her kids were playing not too far away. "I always thought that St. John bastard was overlooking how valuable you were," she agreed. "What are you going to do next?"

Nola pulled out the glasses as Amanda opened the bottle and began to pour some for the three of them. "I've actually already started a new plan. I literally haven't come up for air since the day after Christmas because I've been working on it."

Rosie lifted one brow as she glanced at her. "Spill!"

Nola took a sip of the wine, letting it warm her before she took a deep breath. "I'm not selling The Castle. I'm going to convert it into a bed-and-breakfast-style retreat center for small businesses. I'm still going to live there, of course, but my goal is for it to become a place that big-city people—and small-town businesses, of course—can come and build team morale as well as business strategies. I'm going to offer business consults as part of the retreat package as well. Not only that, but I'm also going to add an online component and do virtual retreats and seminars offering business advice so that anyone all over the world can attend."

Amanda smiled, and both she and Nola looked at Rosie. Her approval was what they were always looking for as the resident mom of the group.

"Gigi would have loved that," Rosie said softly. She wiped a tear from her eye. "So...you're staying in Heart Lake?"

Nola nodded. "If you'll have me."

Rosie jumped forward and threw her arms around Nola. Amanda was close behind, and they all bear-hugged. "I can't believe the whole crew is back together again!"

Nola went on to explain further details about her plan, including how she was going to be able to utilize a lot of Gigi's old treasures in decorating the retreat center, as well as in the programs. Nola fiddled with the large pink diamond ring that she'd slipped on her finger earlier this week when she'd begun planning this entirely new strategy. It had felt strangely right at the time—a piece of her home with her forever. In fact, everything felt strangely right in this moment—everything except one thing...

Nola looked up when she heard a commotion off to the side and saw Heart Lake's mayor, Larry McStill, arguing with a teenage guitarist about his song choices. She grinned, all too familiar with the quirky personalities that made up this small town, and wondered how she ever could have thought to leave. Tanner had tried to tell her how special this place was, and somewhere deep down, she'd known that to be true all along. But for the first time in a long time, she really felt it in her soul. This place was her...

She turned back to look at her friends, only to realize that they were both looking up at Tanner, who was standing beside the picnic blanket.

Home.

His eyes smoldered as their gazes met, and something inside of her simply knew that this was everything she had ever wanted. *He* was everything she'd ever wanted. None of this had been in her plans, but nothing had felt more right than it did in this moment when he smiled at her.

"Nola." He said her name with a gruff rasp that made her shiver in the best way. "Can we talk?"

She handed her glass to Rosie for safekeeping and stood up. "Sure."

Amanda gave her a silent thumbs-up and Rosie winked at her as she followed Tanner away from the courtyard to a more secluded area of Main Street. He stopped at the base of the large clock that adorned the square and turned to face her.

"I've been trying to reach you this week," he began, his hands shoved into his pockets. "I was hoping I could talk to you before you left."

"Tanner, I'm—"

"Would it be okay if I went first?" he asked, cutting her off. "I just...I've been practicing what I want to say all week."

She nodded, her heart already swelling at the nervous way he was looking at her. There was a vulnerability in his expression that she rarely saw, and she wanted to go with it as long as he'd stay open to her.

"The things I said last week," he continued. "They couldn't have been further from the truth. I was an asshole, and I was also being incredibly selfish. I love that you have big dreams, and I love that you're so ambitious that nothing could stop you. Part of me saw that ambition as a threat to what we had...or maybe have? That it was going to take you away from me. That you were going to leave and I'd have lost the only person who has ever made me feel whole."

Nola's heart pounded in her chest, and she wasn't sure if her knees were going to buckle or if she was going to cry.

"But I realized that if I did convince you to stay and give up your dreams, you wouldn't be the person I've fallen in love with." Tanner stepped closer to her and reached for her hand. "Nola, I love you. I'm in love with you. If you'll have me, I'd like to come to Chicago with you. I'd like to give us a real chance. I'll go wherever your dreams take you, and I'll be cheering you on every step of the way."

He lifted her hand to his lips and kissed her knuckles. "I love you, Nola Bennett."

"Tanner, I..." The words got stuck in her throat as emotion overwhelmed her. She shook her head and took a deep breath, trying to keep the tears at bay. She couldn't believe what she was hearing—that he was willing to give up his entire life here in Heart Lake to be with her. No part of her could picture Tanner in Chicago, and the absurdity of the image made her smile. "I don't want you to come to Chicago with me."

He paused for a moment, as if hoping she would say more.

"I don't want to go to Chicago," she continued. "I want to stay here in Heart Lake. You were right—I didn't see how special this place was, and I didn't see that sometimes things are perfect just the way they are."

"You're staying here?" His eyes widened as he squeezed her hand tighter. "But your dream..."

She shook her head. "Dreams change, evolve. I'm still going to be starting my new business—but here, at The Castle."

"You didn't sell?" He looked dumbfounded, but a smile began to creep over his face. "You didn't sell. You're staying in Heart Lake. You..."

"I love you, too, Tanner," she finished for him. "I love you just the way you are."

Nola saw a mistiness cross his gaze, and tears welled on his bottom lashes.

"You were right when you told me I needed to change—that I was stubborn." He shook his head and pulled her against his chest. "I'd been so stuck in my routine and how I thought things should be that I wasn't open to anything—or anyone—new. I've been realizing lately that new additions to our family are not only a good thing, but an absolute blessing. I'm applying for the teacher position—you gave me the courage to do that. I'll have to go to night school and things might be hectic for a while, but I know I can do it."

"I have no doubt," Nola replied, tucking her arms inside his jacket to wrap around him. "I'll be by your side every step of the way if you'll have me."

"I want nothing more," he replied, his voice low and husky as he leaned down to kiss her.

Just before his lips met hers, someone tapped her on the shoulder. She turned to see Craig standing there, his hands crossed over his chest and his foot tapping the ground.

"I've been trying to reach you all week, Nola," he began. "What the hell? My investors want an answer, and I'm not going back there without that property."

She shrugged, then looked at Tanner with a grin. "That's going to be hard for you because...offer not accepted. I'm not selling The Castle."

Craig looked between her and Tanner, his eyes narrowing. "Are you serious right now? That offer was everything you asked for."

"It was," she agreed, then looked back at Tanner. "But it wasn't what I truly needed. It took me a while to figure that out."

She'd come a long way since high school, when she'd dated Craig and had her eyes set on big cities and to-do lists. A sense of community surrounded her in a way she'd never stopped to appreciate before, despite living here for most of her life. But there was something new, too. There was an anchor, something to ground her in feeling at home and like she belonged.

She would never look the other way again when something as powerful as love came knocking on her door. In fact, she was going to learn to listen to the small voice in her head that not only helped shape her own life, but could also help shape others' lives in business consulting. Things were certainly going to change—The Castle being one of the first. But it wouldn't be gone and replaced by high-rise condominiums. It was going to be used to enhance the community, bring tourism and more business to Heart Lake, and expand her dreams in an entirely new direction.

Craig huffed, then nodded toward Tanner. "You're making a huge mistake—with the property, and with him."

Nola smiled and turned back to Tanner, wrapping her arms around him once more. "Goodbye, Craig."

"Where were we?" Tanner murmured as he pressed his forehead against hers.

She pushed up slightly on her toes and met his lips. A loud cheer suddenly came from the center of the courtyard, and Nola was startled to see that the pine cone had dropped. Her neighbors were laughing and setting off fireworks, and someone was singing in an off-key tune.

"I guess it's officially a new year," Tanner said, his hand touching beneath her chin and lifting her mouth back to his. He kissed her again, and this time nothing could stop them.

It was a new year, a new life, and a new love. She couldn't think of anything better.

Epilogue

Six Months Later

"What about cherry? Have we considered that stain yet?" Nola leaned back against Tanner's chest as they sat together on a reclining Adirondack chair on the dock in front of his cabin. They'd moved in together not too long ago since renovations had begun on The Castle to prepare it for becoming the retreat center she was dreaming of.

Tanner chuckled lightly and squeezed her tighter. "Nola, we've discussed every inch of the plans for the center. The colors, the stains, the everything."

She grinned. "I know. I'm just so excited. I can't wait until it's all finished and ready to go."

"We're going as fast as we can," he assured her, placing a small kiss against the side of her head.

She had hired Dean & Son to complete the job, and so far, Blake had been doing incredibly well taking point. Tanner had spent many nights and weekends over the last six months working toward his teaching certificate, and he was going to be starting at Heart Lake High as soon as summer ended. He still checked in on the business regularly—especially Nola's project—but he'd been more hands-off than ever before. She was proud of him for pursuing something he loved, and even prouder of the fact that he was more open than ever to new things.

Hell, she'd gotten him to eat avocado toast at least once a week for breakfast these days. It was a whole new Tanner, but she loved everything about him.

"We should probably get ready for tonight," she said after a few more quiet moments staring out at the water and watching the sun begin to set. "Your father said he purchased a new game for us to try."

"Yeah, he got Cards Against Humanity," Tanner clarified. "But he hadn't checked to see if he got the original. Still isn't used to online shopping."

"Which one did he get?" Nola asked, pushing up from the chair so that she could head back inside to get ready.

Tanner stood up as well, his gaze focused out on the water. "The Disney expansion pack."

She pumped her hands in the air. "Yes! I'm going to crush that one."

"Nola!" A familiar voice yelled out her name behind her.

Nola turned to see Rosie in a canoe with Becca and Zander, paddling toward them. She waved, though she wasn't sure what they were doing here when game night was at their house and Rosie usually prepared all the snacks and food for everyone.

Another canoe appeared not too far behind Rosie's, and Nola saw Amanda and Blake paddling that one. Then a small rowboat joined the canoes, and in it were four passengers—her parents, Thomas, and Marvel. Her eyes widened as she realized everyone she loved was making their way toward her.

What the heck was going on?

"Tanner?" She turned around to look at him for answers, but when she did, he was down on one knee on the dock. "Oh my God..."

"Nola, I asked everyone to come be a part of this moment because I have a very important question to ask you," Tanner

Sarah Robinson

began. He reached into his pocket and Nola was sure her heart was going to actually explode out of her rib cage. He pulled out a small booklet and held it up to her. "Which color do you think would look best on the walls of the bedrooms?"

She blinked, confused for a moment until she realized he was holding a stack of paint sample strips. She laughed, tossing her head back at the absurdity of the moment.

"I'm kidding, of course," he continued, reaching into his other pocket and throwing the paint sample strips onto the dock. He pulled out a ring box and held it up to her. "Nola, I've been in love with you my entire life. I want nothing more than to make you happy for the rest of yours. Will you marry me?"

Tears filled her eyes and she could barely see as she nodded her head and tried to get out her response. "Yes! Yes, of course!"

She could hear everyone cheering in the background as they figured out her response. Tanner moved to open the ring box, but she put her hand on his and stopped him.

"I have one condition, though. I'm sure you got me a beautiful ring, but I already have the perfect one in mind." She wanted to be with him forever, but she also wanted her history to move forward with them. She wanted to wear Gigi's pink diamond ring as a symbol of her dedication to this town, and this man.

He laughed and pushed her hand away. "Woman, look."

When he opened the ring box, she saw Gigi's ring staring back at her. Her hand flew to her mouth and she had to steady herself as he slipped it on her finger.

"How did you know?" she asked through tears as he stood and wrapped his arms around her.

Tanner kissed her, and she didn't want him to ever stop. "I know you, Nola. I love you just the way you are. And look over there."

He pointed off toward the shore and she saw a small, freshly planted tree that hadn't been there before.

"I planted a magnolia tree in honor of today. We can watch it grow along with us and our life," Tanner explained. "I can't wait to spend the rest of my life with you."

She couldn't believe he'd planned all of this so perfectly, but then...she *could* believe it. She believed in him, she'd learned to believe in herself, and most importantly, she'd learned to believe in home.

Don't miss the next feel-good romance in the Heart Lake series!

AVAILABLE SUMMER 2023

About the Author

Bestselling author **Sarah Robinson** is a native of the Washington, DC, area and has both her bachelor's and master's degrees in criminal and clinical psychology. She works as a counselor by day and a romance novelist by night. She owns a small zoo of furry pets and is actively involved in volunteering in her community.

You can learn more at:

Website: BooksbySarahRobinson.com
Twitter: @Booksby_Sarah
Facebook.com/BooksbySarahRobinson
Instagram: @BooksbySarahRobinson
Pinterest.com/BooksbySarahRobinson

**For a bonus story from another author that
you'll love, please turn the page to read
"The Christmas Wish" by Melinda Curtis.**

Rosalie Reyes has big plans to open her new pet
shop during the Christmas parade. But it seems
like Everett Bollinger is determined to sabotage
the parade and her business too. With the help
of the local matchmakers and a rambunctious
Saint Bernard named Remy, Rosalie is about
to unleash the town's holiday cheer and make
it a paws-itively amazing Christmas for all.
Including a certain town manager who's about
to discover the reason for the season... is love.

FOREVER

Prologue

How did it get to be Christmas again so soon?" Bitsy Whitlock organized her cards while her friend's granddaughter serenaded the card players. Bitsy had a pair of threes, an ace of spades, plus a jack and eight of hearts. In other words, *nothing*.

"*Ho-ho-ho. Cherry nose.*"

"Time flies when you're a widowed grandma." Mims Turner set down her cards, casting a grin toward her granddaughter, otherwise known as their songstress—Vivvy, a blond cherub cuddling a plush Santa.

"*Ho-ho-ho,*" Vivvy crooned from her seat on Mims's hearth. "*Cherry nose.*"

Cute as Vivvy was, cute as Bitsy's own grandchildren were, cuteness didn't make up for the empty space in Bitsy's king-size bed. At the holidays, the loneliness of widowhood tended to creep up on her.

"Are we finishing the game now? Or taking a break?" The red-and-green tie-dyed shirt Clarice Rogers wore hung loose on her shoulders compared to the last holiday season. "I think the eggnog needs more nog."

"*Ho-ho-ho. Cherry nose.*" Four-year-old Vivvy sang louder. She'd inherited her loopy blond curls from Mims. "*Gammy, sing!*" As well as her grandmother's take-charge attitude.

"*Hat on head,*" Mims warbled dutifully, with head-shaking, gray-curl-quaking intensity.

"Eyes so red!" Clarice sang at the top of her seventy-something-year-old lungs.

"Those aren't the words," Bitsy murmured, staring at her cards.

"Go along with it," Mims urged before singing, *"Special night."*

"Beard bright white!" Clarice may have gotten the Christmas carol wrong, but she got an A for enthusiasm, just like Vivvy.

Won over by cuteness, Bitsy hummed along.

It was Black Friday, and instead of shopping, the three grandmothers in Sunshine, Colorado, were playing poker. There was business to be taken care of in addition to holiday planning. Business that rode on the outcome of their poker game.

Matchmaking business.

Bitsy, Mims, and Clarice made up the board of the Sunshine Valley Widows Club, which was open to anyone who'd suffered the loss of a spouse or partner. But they were playing poker as the sole members of what they privately called the Sunshine Valley *Matchmakers* Club. The winner of the pot of pennies earned the right to decide who they were going to help find love this holiday season.

Bitsy had someone in mind—a young widow who probably laid a hand on an empty bed pillow every night like Bitsy did and wished...

"Must be Santa." Little Vivvy rocked back and forth. *"Must be Santa."* She got to her feet and danced with her plush Santa. "Gammy, sing again."

Mims obliged her granddaughter, embellishing the song with arm movements and googly eyes that made both Bitsy and Vivvy giggle.

"My eggnog needs more nog." Tossing her gray braids

over her shoulders, Clarice hobbled to Mims's kitchen, where they'd left the bourbon.

At this rate, the trio of matchmakers would be passed out on the floor with Vivvy at naptime, game still unfinished. Bitsy was fond of Vivvy but the sweet girl stood in the way of serious matchmaking decisions. If only she could be distracted long enough for them to finish the poker game.

But how?

Bitsy rummaged around in the black leather bag at her feet. She may be thrice widowed, but she was always prepared—Band-Aids, hair spray, clear nail polish, antacids, and… "Vivvy, I have a candy cane in my purse. Would you like it?"

Vivvy gasped, dropped Santa, and ran across the wood floor, blond curls bobbing. She put her little hands on Bitsy's leg and bounced up and down, no longer interested in singing.

Clarice returned with a bottle of bourbon just as Bitsy unwrapped the cane and handed it to Vivvy.

The little angel took a lick and then spun away like a ballerina, chanting, "*I love Bitsy. I love Santa. I love Christmas.*" And then she was silent.

"Back to the game, ladies." Clarice topped off their eggnogs and settled into her chair. "Per the rules, once we start the game, we must finish the game." Clarice was their secretary and the keeper of club rules. She nodded toward little Vivvy. "Nice save, Bitsy."

Bitsy inclined her head. "I think we need to add an event to the Widows Club schedule. Our account balance is low." As treasurer, Bitsy managed club funds. She sipped her eggnog and glanced at the cards she'd been dealt. She had a feeling about that ace. She kept it and the pair of threes, weak though they might be.

"Let's postpone new events until next year." After reviewing her hand, Mims discarded two cards. Didn't mean the club president had three of a kind. She had a tendency to keep face cards, even if they didn't match or were different suits. "I'm warning you gals. I have a good hand and a person in mind who needs Cupid's help."

Cupid, aka the Matchmakers Club.

"You should get better at the bluff." Clarice ran her fingers down one of her long braids and then discarded one card. Just one! She had a competitive hand, all right. "Last game of the year and it's going to be mine."

It wasn't an idle threat. Bitsy's pair of threes were worth nothing. She wasn't going to beat Clarice without some bluffing.

Clarice dealt their replacement cards. Bitsy glanced at hers.

For the love of Mike.

She'd received another three and a jack.

Why didn't I keep that handsome jack?

Bitsy bit her cheek to keep from frowning. No sense emboldening her opponents. "Are we doing a gift exchange this year?"

Mims rubbed the worry lines from her forehead. She had bubkes, for sure. "I liked what we did last year. Lunch at Los Consuelos."

"Boring." Clarice inserted her cards into her hand. She had something, all right. Either two pair or a full house. Nobody sorted a garbage hand.

Despite sagging spirits, Bitsy kept biting her cheek.

Clarice tapped her cards on the table. "Ladies, are you in or out?"

"I'm in." Bitsy went big, tossing in ten pennies, working the pretense of a good hand.

Mims folded.

Clarice slanted Bitsy a sideways glance. "You're looking to end the game on this hand."

"I've got some shopping to do." Another bluff. Bitsy had done all her shopping online this year.

Instead of folding, Clarice counted out ten pennies. "Let's see what you've got."

The moment of reckoning had come. There would be no more bluffing.

"Three of a kind." Shoulders drooping, Bitsy fanned her cards in front of her. "All threes. Pathetic, I know."

"My hand is more pathetic than yours." Clarice huffed and tossed her cards down. "Three of a kind. Mine are twos."

"I won?" Bitsy couldn't believe it. "With threes?"

"Merry Christmas," Mims mumbled. She'd been on a losing streak lately. In fact, Bitsy couldn't remember the last time the club president had won.

"I got sticky hands." Vivvy flexed her little fingers as she walked toward Mims, candy cane eaten.

With Mims about to go on grandma cleanup duty, Bitsy didn't waste time gloating. "I choose Rosalie Reyes." The widow who reminded Bitsy of herself.

"The gal with the dog?" Clarice sat back in her chair.

"I love puppies." Vivvy held her hands in front of Mims. "Sticky, Gammy."

"Rosalie is the *widow* with the dog," Bitsy confirmed. "She's only just come back to town. I was thinking Doc Janney would be perfect for her." He was so patient and intuitive. He'd know when a memory of a lost love lingered, and he'd be bighearted enough not to be jealous.

"It's flu season." Mims stood and gathered Vivvy into her arms, careful of her candy-cane-coated fingers. "Doc Janney is too busy for love this time of year. What about Noah Shaw? He's handsome and—"

"Not ready to settle down." Clarice scrunched her thin features. "What about that new man at town hall? What's his name?"

"Everett Bollinger?" Bitsy couldn't think of a reason why the man wouldn't work except "He seems like a bit of a stick in the mud."

"Scrooge-like," Mims agreed, clapping Vivvy's sticky hands together.

"Scrooge?" Clarice chuckled. "What better Christmas present for Ebenezer than the gift of love?"

Chapter One

Everyone in town knew Rosalie Easley Reyes.

And today, two days after Thanksgiving, Rosalie was making sure everyone in town *saw* her.

It was snowing, but only just, as if the sky above Sunshine, Colorado, couldn't decide if it should or shouldn't.

Shouldn't, please.

Rosalie walked the length of the town square, trying not to shiver.

Pearl, the oldest waitress at the Saddle Horn diner, came out of the pharmacy bundled up for the cold. "Well now." She handed out one of her rare smiles. "Don't you two have the Christmas spirit?"

"Yep." Rosalie glanced down at Remington, her dog, and kept walking. And walking.

Past the bakery. By Los Consuelos. Down Sunny Avenue. Up Center Avenue and past the dilapidated, empty warehouse. Back to Main Street and around the town square.

She approached the town hall, where the Widows Club board stood huddled as if planning their next event. They waved.

Shoppers got out of her way. Kids stared. The younger ones stopped playing in the snow in the town square and gawked.

"Are you Santa's helpers?" one of the kids asked, running over.

Two other boys joined the first, cheeks red from the cold.

"We are." Rosalie slowed, risking freezing. Her green flannel elf onesie wasn't as warm as Remington's thick fur coat. "This is Remy." She straightened the Saint Bernard's antlers and smoothed his plush sweater so the words *Merry Christmas from Sunshine Pets* were more easily visible.

"There's no reindeer named Remy," the young ringleader scoffed.

Before Rosalie could answer, Remy did. As dogs went, he was a talker, working his vocal cords up and down the spectrum like a baritone in the opera.

Ra-roo-roo-roo-arumph.

"Yes, Remy. I know." Rosalie leaned down as if imparting an important secret to the children. "Remy says he's no reindeer. He's Santa's dog, here to remind you not to forget your pets this Christmas. They need a gift under the tree too, which can be found right around the corner at Sunshine Pets."

"Subtle." The deep, familiar voice from behind Rosalie was loaded with sarcasm.

And just when she'd been about to hand out pet store flyers for the little tykes to give their parents.

Rosalie turned, bringing Remy around with her so she could face her nemesis—Everett Bollinger, the new town manager and all-around killjoy.

"Hey, kids," Everett said without taking his eyes off Rosalie, "there are free candy canes at the town hall."

The children scampered off.

"Free?" Rosalie gasped dramatically, which in the cold nearly gave her a shiver-spasm.

Everett had been hired to balance the town's budget. Nothing in Sunshine was free anymore.

"To promote the town hall toy drive." Everett was tall, broad-shouldered, and disapproving where he should have been tall, broad-shouldered, and kind. He had the appearance of a nice guy—balanced features, gray eyes behind wire-rim glasses, brown hair threaded with occasional strands of gray. It was just when he spoke that the façade of kindness cracked, and you knew ice flowed in his veins. People in town had taken to calling him Scrooge. "I admit, free candy canes were inspired by your Black Friday promotion."

"But you hated that idea." She'd given out a hundred candy canes on Friday, threading their red-and-white stems through white felt kitten faces. When he found one discarded kitten face in the snow, he'd claimed Rosalie was contributing to litter and had made her stop.

Since she'd opened her pet shop a few weeks ago, Everett had constantly trounced her efforts to market the business. The signs she put up on the way into town were against code. The sandwich board placards she placed on the corner of her street were trip hazards to shoppers. The flyers she'd left on car windshields were against the town nuisance ordinance.

Someone was a nuisance, all right.

Scrooge gave her a tight smile. "I made the candy cane idea fall within Sunshine's guidelines."

"Without branding," Rosalie pointed out, patting Remy's front flank, drawing him closer as the wind from Saddle Horn Mountain whipped though Main Street.

Remy stared up at Everett and spoke: *Aroo-arumph*.

Everett glanced from Remy to Rosalie.

Rosalie gave her adversary a half grin. "Remy says using my idea is stealing."

Everett's mouth formed a grim line.

Too late, Rosalie remembered Everett's history. "I'm sorry. I . . . I shouldn't have said that."

It began to snow in earnest—slow, silent flakes that swirled around them as if trying to block out the kids playing in the snow, the shoppers hurrying from store to store, and the painful memories of the past.

"You should get inside," Everett said in a husky voice.

"Walking my dog isn't against any ordinance in Sunshine." She gripped Remy's leash in her red-mittened hands. "Why are you trying to sabotage my business?"

"Rosalie." Everett moved closer and gave Remy a pat on the head, being careful of his antlers. "You're out here without a jacket, and it's below freezing."

He hadn't answered her question.

"Santa's elves don't wear jackets." Despite her best efforts, Rosalie shivered.

Everett sighed. "Santa's elves have Christmas magic to keep them warm."

Her chest constricted.

He'd mentioned Christmas magic, a clue that there might be a heart buried beneath all that frozen tundra.

Impossible.

Rosalie lifted her chin. "If you want to see Christmas magic, you should come to Sunshine Pets."

He sighed again, but it wasn't an angry sigh. In fact, a smile seemed to be lingering at the corner of his mouth.

She waited for that smile, despite snow and wind and cold. She waited and wondered if his smile would have the same impact as his use of the words *Christmas magic*.

The smile didn't come. "Don't you ever give up, Rosalie?"

"Nope." Rosalie smiled brightly at her adversary because no one ever beat city hall by shouting. "I'm looking forward to our next Holiday Event Committee meeting." The group he'd formed to plan celebrations of holidays year-round. "What time is it again?"

"Monday after you close up shop for the day." Everett left her on the sidewalk and headed toward the bakery.

"See you around." Rosalie breathed easier now that his back was to her. "Come on, Remy. Let's spread more holiday cheer"—and awareness of her pet store—"before I lose feeling in my legs."

Besides, there was bound to be an ordinance against frozen business owners on the sidewalk.

She traipsed around the town square at a good clip.

"Merry Christmas." One of the Bodine twins emerged from the bakery in a T-shirt and brown apron. The Bodine twins were identical, and it was impossible to tell whether this one was Steve or Phil since they both worked at the bakery. "Mr. Bollinger said to give you this." The tall teen handed her a cup with a lid.

Rosalie stopped. "Mr. Bollinger?" *Scrooge?*

Everett was nowhere to be seen in the bakery but the Widows Club board sat at a table near the window and waved to her. A toddler with blond curls and a wide smile sat in Mims's lap, waving too. The group caught Remy's attention. He pressed his face against the glass and gave them a doggy grin.

Rosalie accepted the cup, cradling its warmth in both hands. "Is it coffee?" A latte would be heaven about now.

"Hot chocolate with extra whip." The teen grinned. "Mr. B. wanted you to have something hot and sweet."

"Probably because I'm out here burning off too many calories," she mumbled. "I need the sugar to avoid freezing." Everett seemed the practical sort.

"No, no. Mr. B. said you needed a drink to warm you up and that you deserved something as sweet as you were on the inside." The Bodine boy darted back in the bakery, stopping to talk to Bitsy before returning to his place behind the counter.

Rosalie met Remy's gaze.

Her dog shook his head, a loud flapping of ears that knocked his antlers askew.

The candy canes. The mention of Christmas magic. And now this gift.

Rosalie straightened her dog's antlers. "I think you're right, Remy. It's hard to believe, but I think Everett Bollinger has a heart after all."

"I've gone soft," Everett muttered as he entered the town hall.

He no longer tolerated rule benders and rule breakers. And Rosalie...She challenged him on every ordinance, every regulation.

Which was why it made no sense that he'd spoken to Rosalie about Christmas magic.

At least I had the presence of mind to refuse the Widows Club suggestion that I buy her a hot chocolate. Still...

"I've gone soft," he muttered again as he removed his coat. Soft wasn't in his plans.

"Ev, you are anything but soft." Yolanda, his assistant and the front desk clerk, was decorating a Christmas tree in the lobby. She brushed back her shoulder-length gray hair, revealing dangly Christmas tree earrings. "I have people tell me that every day. Scrooge is the nicest name they call you."

"I'm not taking that personally." Everett hung his coat on a hook by the door, reminded of Rosalie, coatless, with gloves so thin they were unraveling, walking around outside in green long johns and freezing her heinie off. "I was hired to be the bad cop to Kevin's good mayor."

He'd been contracted to increase Sunshine's coffers, something Mayor Kevin Hadley had struggled with because he was a nice guy.

I used to be like him.

But nice guys always finished last. Everett wasn't going to be anyone's nice guy again.

He paused, surveying Yolanda's work. Twinkling lights on twisted cords, shiny balls that had seen better days, small paper snowflakes. Up close, he was pleased with the cost-cutting décor. "Where did you get the tree?"

"Never fear, oh mighty Ebenezer." Yolanda delivered her words with humor, not sting. "It's fake and came out of storage. I didn't spend a penny of the town's money on it. You know, you're taking all the fun out of Christmas."

"I like to think I'm cutting the fat from the budget." And none too soon. But Everett wasn't a total wet blanket when it came to Christmas. He went into his office and returned with a plain brown cardboard box and a simple sign that read, TOY DRIVE.

Yolanda glanced up. "Oh. That's nice. And just when I was convinced that I didn't like you."

"Contrary to popular belief, I don't reject Christmas." Everett placed a tin on the counter with child-size candy canes he'd bought with his own money. "Remember, I signed off on the expenditures for tree decorating in the town square."

"Uh-huh." Yolanda smirked. "Only after the mayor requested it."

Before Everett could reply, a man in his early thirties came in the front door. Beaming, he greeted Yolanda and then introduced himself to Everett with a firm handshake. "I'm Haywood Lawson, local real estate agent. I hear you're the one to talk to about special events."

"This ought to be good," Yolanda muttered, sprinkling the tree with tinsel.

"You want to hold a special event?" Everett leaned on the counter, unable to resist guessing what that event might be—beer fest, outdoor concert, community yard sale? Haywood had a strong grip. Maybe he was the athletic type. "We're in the initial planning stages for a mudder," Everett said. The outdoor obstacle courses challenged competitors physically and emotionally.

"It's not that kind of event." Some of the shine came off Haywood's smile, but then he brought it right back to beam-strength. "I want to propose to my girlfriend in the town square after the tree-lighting ceremony on Friday. The choir is going to be there and has agreed to sing when she says yes."

"You don't need my permission for that." *Or a permit of any kind.* Everett straightened, preparing to retreat to his office and the stack of paperwork that awaited him.

"Whew." Haywood grinned. "I'd heard—"

Yolanda coughed.

"And…um…" Haywood seemed to think better of what he'd been about to say and grinned some more. "Back in the day, my dad proposed to my mom in the town square, and then the town bells rang." At Everett's blank look, Haywood added, "There are bells in the town hall's belfry. They haven't been rung in years."

Everett glanced at Yolanda. "And that would be because…"

"It's a long story," his assistant hedged.

"And yet I have time." Not really, but enough time to hear why the town bells weren't used.

Yolanda gave Haywood an apologetic glance. "The last time they were rung…Well, it was over a decade ago. There was this group of athletic boosters from the high school. They'd been celebrating Kevin's recruitment to play quarterback at Western Colorado University. But they jammed too many people in the belfry, and things got a little…*squishy*… for the occupants as the bell swung back and forth."

Everett sucked in air and held himself still, preparing to hear the worst.

"No one was killed," Haywood was quick to point out, allaying Everett's fears.

"Understandably, we stopped allowing citizens to ring the bell after that." Yolanda made a weak attempt at a smile. "But this is different. We can have someone on staff ring the bell when Haywood pops the question."

That would be very Kevin-like, soft on regulations and protocol.

Everett frowned, not like Kevin at all. "I'd have to calculate the cost."

The pair blinked at him.

"What cost?" Haywood was no longer smiling, not even a little bit.

Everett didn't care. He didn't feel a twinge of remorse for being fiscally responsible. "I imagine this would take a fifteen-minute commitment from a town employee, so an increment of their hourly rate."

"I'll volunteer my time to do the bell ringing." Yolanda gripped the tinsel as if it were Everett's neck. "After all, it's for love."

And what fools did for love…

"I can't authorize that, Yolanda." There was nothing soft inside Everett. Nothing at all. "If you aren't on the clock, if things get…*squishy*…the town of Sunshine will be liable for your injuries—or death, should it go that far."

"It won't go that far." Yolanda shook her tinsel. "It'll just be me and the bell, which will give me about two more feet of clearance in the belfry."

Kevin came downstairs from his office. "What's up?"

"We're discussing the fee for bell ringing," Yolanda said darkly. "Things in this town didn't used to be so complicated."

Everett leaned on the counter and brought the mayor up to

speed. "There are two issues here: liability for *squishiness*"—
he raised his eyebrows Yolanda's way—"and *precedent*. If we
ring the bells for Haywood without charge, we have to ring
them for every happy couple who walks through our door."
Our. As if he were staying.

He wasn't.

"Precedent? You mean when our constituents enter
expecting a small service for free?" Kevin smiled. He was
a politician, and it was a good smile. But it was a smile that
had nearly pushed the town into bankruptcy. "That's a good
precedent to set."

"I'll pay," Haywood blurted, clearly uncomfortable.
"Will fifty dollars do it?"

"I think that's fair." Everett took a candy cane from the
tin and handed it to the would-be groom. "And now we know
the going rate for bell ringing. Yolanda, can you take Haywood's money and write him a receipt?" He told her which
fund to deposit it to. "Kevin, when you have a minute, I'd
like a word."

The door opened again. A uniformed deliveryman
entered with a clipboard. "Is there an Everett Bollinger here?
I've got a delivery in the truck."

"That's me." Everett reached for the clipboard, trying to
remember what he might have ordered and drawing a blank.

"I can't tell you how happy I am to find you," the deliveryman said. Once in possession of his clipboard, he hurried
back outside.

"We can talk in my office when you're ready." Kevin disappeared upstairs.

There was a commotion outside, like the sound of finger-
nails on chalkboard or...

It can't be.

Everett's view was obstructed by a tree. He rushed to

open the door, facing his worst fear. "I can't accept that." He had to shout to be heard above the scruffy little dog inside a plastic crate, who was yapping her displeasure with hoarse vocal cords.

Tinkerbell hated her crate.

"Too late." The delivery guy thrust the small cage into Everett's arms. "I drove over a hundred miles with her. You signed. She's all yours." He practically ran out the door, calling, "Merry Christmas!"

Yolanda said something Everett couldn't hear over Tinkerbell's protest.

He turned, hoping to be able to read her lips.

"No dogs in the workplace," she shouted, grinning. "Even on Saturdays."

"She's not my dog." But Tinkerbell was his problem.

Everett hurried into his office and closed the door. "Tink, calm down." His ex-wife's dog pressed her button nose through the bars and sniffed. Her little tail wagged over the remains of what looked like a pink sweater. "Come on out." Everett set down the crate and opened the door.

The brown terrier mix leaped out and piddled in the corner.

"Tink," he scolded, grabbing wads of tissue and mopping up the puddle.

Tinkerbell raced around him, yapping. There was no telling how long she'd been in her carrier. A quick search of the crate revealed nothing—no water bowl, no leash, no food. Only the remains of that sweater.

Kevin opened Everett's office door. "Everything okay in here?"

Tink barked and panted and ran in circles around Kevin's feet until Everett snatched her up.

"It's my ex-wife's dog." Sitting on the edge of his desk,

Everett poured water into his empty coffee mug and then gave her a drink. "Lydia's mother was supposed to keep Tink while she was... away." Something must have happened.

Tink stretched to lick Everett's chin as if to say, *It wasn't my fault.*

"I'm sure this is just temporary." Everett adjusted his glasses with his free hand.

"I don't know if it should be." Kevin stepped inside and closed the door. "This is just what you need."

Everett was quick to disagree. "Tink is..." High maintenance, like his ex-wife. "I work long hours. It's not fair for me to have a dog." Which was why his ex-mother-in-law had agreed to take Tinkerbell in the first place.

A few scratches behind the ears and Tink stopped giving doggy-shouts of displeasure.

Kevin settled down too, sitting in a chair on the visitor's side of Everett's desk. "Do you remember when we first met?"

"Yes." Everett fought a frown, confused by the change in subject. "At a conference in Denver."

His boss nodded. "You were speaking about the balance between fiscal responsibility *and* community building."

"Yes." That was back before Lydia had been arrested for embezzling from the city Everett had been managing. Before her conviction and the confiscation of 99 percent of their worldly possessions to repay what she'd stolen.

"Hiring you was a risk given what your wife..." Kevin trailed off. He'd been good about avoiding the topic, as had Everett. And then the mayor gave Everett his winning smile. "Hiring you has paid big dividends. You've done a great job finding places where money was leaking or where we can ask our businesses and constituents to pay for Sunshine's services. Your outreach for business development out by the highway has been stellar. For the first time in a long time, there's potential for growth in Sunshine's future."

Everett's chest swelled with pride. When he'd been hired, Sunshine was a town on the verge of bankruptcy. In nearly six months, he'd worked miracles. If he could unload one piece of property from the town books, there'd be a surplus in the budget and a shine to his tarnished reputation. And then he could make a move to bigger things and a bigger town.

"But, Everett, I didn't just hire you to adjust our financial course. What we're lacking here is the balance between the two—financial stability and community services." Kevin's smile sharpened to a point where Everett's pride was punctured. "I need community building, or come the next election cycle, I'm toast."

Everett would be long gone before the next election. "It hasn't all been about the finances. I started the Holiday Event Committee." The goal of which was to add events to Sunshine's municipal calendar that generated revenue year-round. But he'd also put events on the calendar that cost nothing, like Rosalie's upcoming evening dog walk through Christmas Tree Lane.

"You and I both know that's not enough." Kevin had a way of looking at Everett that cut through all the bull. "Yolanda needs to be empowered to grant small, personal requests like Haywood's."

"Like ringing the bells when someone proposes?" Soft. It was soft and lacked the structure to protect the town's economic interests.

Kevin nodded. "Or giving Yolanda more than one hour to decorate the office for Christmas. On a Saturday, no less."

"Strict performance guidelines means no one will shout about nepotism." The way they'd shouted at him after Lydia's crime had come to light.

"I'm willing to foot a few hours' bill to show some holiday cheer." Kevin's tone was cajoling. "The goodwill gained is worth it. Christmas spirit goes a long way around here."

Tinkerbell perked up her ears and tilted her head as if confused.

Everett could relate. "I don't follow."

Kevin stood. "Decorate your apartment's exterior for the season, for one. In a small town like Sunshine, people notice these things."

"But . . . I'm never there." Except to sleep.

"The bare minimum will do. Put a wreath on the door. Frame your window with holiday lights on a timer." Kevin patted Tinkerbell on her tiny head. "I'm not saying you have to get a tree. Unless of course you're planning to hold one of your committee meetings at your place."

"No." Everett's apartment was plain. Cast-off furniture and bare walls. As part of the agreement to turn state's evidence against Lydia, he'd had to turn over all their possessions. He'd come here with only a used car he made payments on and a suitcase of clothes. "No meetings at my place."

Kevin stared at Everett's shirt and tie. "And maybe you should loosen up and wear a tacky holiday sweater. I know you have a sense of humor. You should show it."

Everett stroked his designer tie, resisting the urge to try to loosen it. He was holding on to the few things the government had let him keep, his squeaky-clean image not being one of them. "Next thing you know, you'll be telling me to date."

"Great idea. It would prove you have a heart." Kevin moved toward the door. "But Tinkerbell is evidence of that too. It's clear that dog loves you. Why don't you bring her to the office these next few weeks? Show this town what you're really made of."

What Everett was made of was slugs and snails and puppy-dog tails, as his grandmother used to say, reciting a child's poem when he misbehaved. "You don't really want me to bring Tink to work." The noise and prancing would be a distraction.

"I do. I can't enforce a tight budget without some semblance of compassion." Kevin's no-nonsense tone reinforced that the point was non-negotiable. His boss hesitated, hand on the doorknob. "What was it you wanted to talk to me about?"

"Nothing." There was no way Everett was going to broach the subject of end-of-the-year layoffs after receiving a lecture like that.

Chapter Two

The bell over the front door to Sunshine Pets echoed through the store.

Remington turned his big, furry head to see who'd entered but remained seated next to Rosalie, who was lying on her side trying to connect the water supply to a pet fountain. He thumped his tail though, indicating he knew her visitor.

"Rosalie?" Her younger sister, Kimmy, came to lean over the counter.

Rosalie realized she'd been hoping it was Everett who'd entered the store. Sometimes it was the simplest of gestures that touched her. That cup of hot chocolate...Since she'd stopped walking Remy over an hour ago, she hadn't been able to stop thinking about Everett. Had she misjudged him?

"This place looks the same as when I left." Kimmy had watched the store while Rosalie was out playing elf with Remy. She ran the deli and lunch counter at Emory's Grocery store during the week and had been helping Rosalie on the weekends. Kimmy tugged off her green mittens and unwound her matching muffler. "Where is everyone?"

"Everyone as in customers?" Rosalie gave the pipe connector one last, good twist. After adding more ornaments to the store's Christmas tree, she'd tried filling the pet fountain, and water had gone everywhere. No way was she making that mistake again.

"Yes. The sidewalk over by the town square is busy with shoppers." Kimmy shrugged out of her jacket and laid it next to her scarf and mittens on the sales counter. "Stores on Center Street have good traffic. Is it too late to move your business onto Main Street? There's a space open by the thrift store."

It wasn't too late to move. It just wasn't an option. She was emotionally attached to this location. It was on this street that she'd decided she was going to marry Marty. Granted, they'd both been in high school at the time. And granted, she'd never imagined that years later she'd be widowed, her life forever changed by a bullet aimed at Marty and his badge.

"Earth to Rosalie." Kimmy rapped the counter with her knuckles, bringing Rosalie back to the present.

"I made a few sales." Most people seemed to be shopping for their two-legged family and friends instead. "And I've got a great idea to bring in more customers before the tree-lighting ceremony."

Rosalie turned on the spigot, her hand hovering over the handle. Thankfully, the pet fountain filled with a gentle gurgle of water this time, not a leak in sight.

With a soft grumble, Remy stood and lapped water spilling into the bowl.

"Do you know what's missing in this pet store?" Kimmy glanced around with a twinkle in her eye, fiddling with her long brown hair.

"There's nothing missing." Rosalie caught sight of her reflection in the decorative mirror on a nearby wall. She and Kimmy used to stare in the bathroom mirror and marvel about how much they looked alike. They both had the same brown eyes, the same friendly smiles, and the same long brown hair. But since Marty's death, Rosalie's reflection had changed. Her eyes were flat, and she'd cut her hair. When she looked in the mirror—heck, when she looked out on life—there was something missing, inside and out. And she couldn't quite put her finger on what it was.

"Nothing is missing," Rosalie reiterated, glancing out to the historic fountain on a brick island in the middle of the road before stowing her husband's tools in his beat-up red metal toolbox. The store was perfect. It was something inside of her that was incomplete. "I've got a great variety of merchandise." Collars and leashes. Pet beds and pet food. Key chains, T-shirts, and sweatshirts for humans. Fuzzy pet sweaters and snow booties, like the ones Remy had worn on his walk.

"I agree. You've stocked everything here a pet owner would want." Kimmy straightened Remy's sweater. "Except pets. What about people who don't have a fur baby? Or want another one? Isn't that why you built those enclosures in the front windows?"

It was. But that was Rosalie's expansion plan. She wanted to establish the pet-supply business first. "I don't want to bring in puppies, kitties, or baby bunnies and not have customers here ready to take them home." Because if they didn't find homes by Christmas, Rosalie would adopt them all. Not wise when she, Remington, and Kimmy were sharing the small apartment above their parents' garage.

"I think you should help rescue animals find homes." Kimmy waved toward the door. "And look. It's Eileen Taylor." Kimmy glanced back at Rosalie. "And before you say anything, yes, I asked her to meet me here. She works at that animal rescue on the outskirts of town. You want a business with heart? You can form a partnership of some kind and bring in animals ready for adoption."

On cue, Eileen entered the store lugging two pet carriers. "Merry Christmas, Rosalie."

Arr-aroo. Remington trundled toward their latest visitors, his big, bushy tail wagging.

"Merry Christmas, Eileen." Rosalie grabbed Kimmy's arm and whispered, "I hope you have it in your heart to take on whatever she's bringing in here." In case they failed to find a home for them due to a lack of customers.

"Trust me." Kimmy pried herself free.

"I brought some sweethearts in the hopes you can find them forever homes." Quiet and unassuming, Eileen was a sweetheart herself. She was several years younger than Rosalie and had been rescuing animals since she was a kid. "A pair of lop-eared bunnies the color of cinnamon toast. And a trio of kittens, including a three-legged darling."

"Bunnies and kittens." Kimmy grinned at Rosalie. "No one can resist bunnies and kittens. Just wait until we post pictures on social media."

"Okay." Rosalie relented because the animals were adorable. "If you're willing to trust them to my care, Eileen, we can put them in the window boxes and see if we can't find them forever homes."

While Eileen and Kimmy prepped the window space under the watchful eyes of Remy, Rosalie unpacked her latest delivery—holiday pet sweaters.

The front door opened, and Everett walked in.

All three women stopped what they were doing to stare. He stared back, adjusting his glasses and studying them as if they were an exhibit in the zoo. Remington meandered up to greet him, sniffing the air like a bloodhound.

Rosalie found her voice. "Can I help you?" Because he hadn't come bearing a gift of hot chocolate.

"Yes." Everett didn't sound happy. He unzipped his thick red jacket, revealing a small Yorkie mix with a happy dog smile and long, thin hair. "I need to equip my dog."

"You have a dog?" Kimmy blurted, cradling the three-legged gray tabby to her chest.

Rosalie couldn't fault her sister's outburst. She hadn't taken Everett as an animal person at all. Up until this afternoon's hot chocolate treat, he'd been Scrooge.

"Clearly, I have a dog." Everett drew the little thing from inside his jacket and held it to his chest with one arm. "This is Tinkerbell."

The dog shivered against what was certainly the cold outer lining of Everett's jacket. Remy stretched and touched his nose to Tinkerbell's delicate toes.

"We'll start with sweaters." Rosalie fought to contain her excitement. She could sense the opportunity for a big sale because Tinkerbell had hair, not fur. She'd need a wardrobe to keep warm. Waving Kimmy and Eileen back to pet duty, Rosalie leaped into action. She held up a small red sweater with a Christmas tree knit on the back. "I just received some thick holiday pullovers. But I also have plain pink fleece."

Everett winced at the word *pink*. He joined Rosalie at the box of sweaters and touched the red one. "I'll take this and a black fleece, if you have it."

While Rosalie hurried to check her display for a fleece jacket in Tinkerbell's size, Everett moved to the rack of hanging leashes, followed by Remy.

Rosalie could contain her grin no longer. Sunshine was a small town, and Everett was a prominent figure who made the local rounds. If she outfitted Tinkerbell well, it'd be great promotion for the store.

"I don't have black fleece but I found a red one." Rosalie placed her find on the sales counter, sweeping Kimmy's jacket, scarf, and gloves underneath.

"That'll do." Leash in hand, Everett moved to the aisle with bowls. He selected a set of copper ones, which weren't cheap. This was going to be her best sales day yet.

"Dog food and pet beds are mostly on the back wall."

Instead of joining him, Rosalie went to the display of leather-soled dog booties and selected a pair, adding it to the pile on the counter.

Facing the choices in bagged dog food, Everett set Tinkerbell down.

Yap-yap-yap.

Tinkerbell raced toward the pet fountain. She stood on her hind legs and stretched over the edge but she was too short for a drink because the water level was still low. Continuing to bark, she hopped in. She cringed and barked louder as the water splashed her.

Eileen rushed to the little dog's rescue. The last thing she needed was Everett annoyed because his dog was being made fun of.

Garumph-aroo. Remington moseyed over and put one foot in the water, as if in solidarity with Tinkerbell.

"Oh, no you don't." Rosalie grabbed the Saint Bernard's collar and urged him back while Tinkerbell continued to let them know she wasn't happy.

Yappy-yap-yap-yap.

"Tinkerbell," Everett chastised, carrying a bag of premium dog food toward the counter, "get out of there."

The small dog faced her master, yaps targeted at him.

"She's stubborn," Everett said loud enough to be heard over Tinkerbell's complaints. He paused at a display of pet beds.

"I think she's just anxious in a new place." If he wasn't going to make a big deal out of his wet dog, neither was Rosalie. She plucked a small towel with Christmas wreaths from a nearby rack and then picked up Tinkerbell and dried her off.

As soon as the dog was in Rosalie's arms, she quieted.

When Everett joined them at the register with the dog

food and a fuzzy brown pet bed, Rosalie set Tinkerbell on the floor and then held up a bag of dog treats. "These too?"

Everett nodded. While he paid, Tinkerbell barked and pranced adoringly around his feet.

"Thank you for the hot chocolate earlier." Rosalie rang up his purchases. "That was very thoughtful."

Everett opened his mouth but hesitated a moment before answering. "You say that as if you didn't think I had it in me." He stared down at his canine chatterbox with a long-suffering sigh.

"I've always thought you had kind eyes." Rosalie wanted the words back as soon as she'd uttered them.

"Kind eyes? My self-image is shattered," Everett said. But there was a look in his eyes or perhaps the beginning of a smile on his face that belied that statement. He picked up his dog and scratched behind her brown, silky ears.

Over at the window, Kimmy and Eileen were grinning.

Remy sat near Everett, glancing from Tinkerbell to the man with an occasional contented rumble deep in his chest. It was an approving sound.

If Rosalie had been able to growl in her throat, she'd have been doing it too. "You know, with a little work, Tinkerbell would get over some of her anxiety."

"Tink is untrainable." There was mutiny in Everett's tone, as if he was daring her to contradict him.

"No dog is untrainable...if their owners can be taught." *Right back at you, Scrooge.*

Kimmy made a strangled noise and tried to hide behind a kitten snuggle.

"Owner training?" Everett raised a brow. "Your dig is duly noted." He zipped Tinkerbell into his jacket as he headed for the door. "Can you deliver my stuff to my apartment after five thirty?"

"Yes." Everett didn't tell her his address, and she didn't ask. This was Sunshine. She knew where he lived. His apartment was in a small complex. His door visible from the street. But...he'd left all his purchases on the counter. "Don't you want to bundle Tinkerbell up and put on her leash?"

"You'd be surprised what I want," Everett grumbled as deeply as Remy but he stared at Rosalie when he said it, pausing with the door open.

A gust of wind rushed in.

But Rosalie's goose bumps had nothing to do with the cold.

"You need to grow up, Tink." Everett strung lights in his apartment window while Tinkerbell ripped apart the cardboard wrapper they'd come in. "You might get a day or two at the office but then it's home alone for you."

Tinkerbell tore a long cardboard strip free and then abandoned it to pounce on the empty light-timer box. Everett knew as soon as she lost interest in the cardboard, the barking would begin again.

The barking...

Tink had yapped up a storm the day Lydia had been arrested. The terrier had barked her upset at the world until her voice was a raspy squeak. And Everett had sat in a kitchen chair holding her as they'd led Lydia away, as the rug of his life had been yanked from beneath him.

"You can be on your own," Everett told Tink. He plugged the colorful Christmas lights into the timer. They came on, racing around his window frame like a video game in an arcade. "You can be quiet and a good dog." Just as Rosalie thought Tink could.

Rosalie. The petite beauty was a dreamer. She probably

still believed in pots of gold at the ends of rainbows. He should have confessed that he hadn't been the one to buy her a hot chocolate. What had the Widows Club been thinking to treat her in his name? He'd heard rumors of their matchmaking but one look inside her store with its pampered-pooch merchandise and Everett knew he and Rosalie were like orange juice and toothpaste.

Tink stood, ears forward, cardboard dangling out of half her mouth.

Footsteps sounded on the stairs.

Yap-yap-yap!

Tinkerbell bounded toward the door, destroyed boxes forgotten on the carpet.

Yap-yap-yap!

The little dog stood on her hind legs and pressed her front paws on the door, only to drop back down to all fours, circle, and continue to bark.

The doorbell rang.

Everett scooped Tink into his arms. Immediately, the barking stopped. He opened the door.

"Nice wreath." Rosalie swung the bag of dog food inside and followed it in, closing the door behind her and depositing a bag of goods next to it. "You left the price tag on it though." She glanced around, eyes widening.

The apartment was clean but dated—from the kitchen cabinetry and countertops to the used furniture he'd bought locally when he'd moved here.

"You were expecting a black leather sofa and glass coffee table?" He raised his brows in challenge.

"You aren't a stereotypical bachelor so why would I expect you to furnish your place like one?" She plucked Tinkerbell from his arms and knelt with her next to his dog supplies. "Honestly? I expected antiques covered in white sheets." She tugged the Christmas sweater over Tinkerbell's head.

"You expected Scrooge's mansion." Not a question. This Scrooge thing was going to haunt him until he left Sunshine.

Rosalie guiltily raised big brown eyes to his face.

"I know what people call me." He didn't much care what the populace of Sunshine thought of him. But Rosalie? For some reason, he cared about her opinion. "So you think of me as Scrooge too." Also not a question.

Rosalie tugged Tinkerbell's sweater into place and didn't answer.

He stared down at Rosalie's short, dark hair. It curled around her ears. And her long, dark lashes curled across her cheeks. And her optimistic determination tried to curl around his heart.

Don't go there. She thinks I'm Scrooge.

"I think my feelings are hurt." He hadn't meant to say that. He hadn't meant to say anything. He adjusted his glasses but he couldn't adjust his response toward her.

Rosalie stood, cradling a merry-looking Tink and flashing a half grin. "You have feelings?"

"If we're doing inventory of what I possess, you can start with a dog." Everett tried to smile, as if this was one big joke. But there'd been so little to smile about in the past eighteen months that he was sure his expression was on the fritz.

"A dog is a fine place to start after what happened to . . ." Her half grin flatlined. "Sorry. I didn't mean to bring up your past. I don't like it when people remind me of mine."

More than his smile was broken. There was his pride too. But the remnants of his pride also made him tell her, "You can say it." A part of him didn't want her to. A part of him wanted to believe that Rosalie hadn't searched out his history online. "I'm not running from what happened."

That wasn't exactly true. He wasn't running but he was regrouping.

And it was working. His shock over Lydia's crimes no longer haunted his dreams. He didn't wake up feeling hollow every morning. He had a reason to put one foot in front of the other.

Cuddling Tink close, Rosalie searched Everett's face as if looking for something she'd lost.

Being a man who'd lost everything, he knew her search would come up empty.

Sighing, she set Tinkerbell on the floor.

Tink began to bark, sounding like a broken record.

Almost without thinking, Everett bent to return her to his arms.

"You should really do something about that," Rosalie said unnecessarily.

"My ex-wife got Tink a month or so before she was caught." Everett stroked Tinkerbell's small head. "I think Lydia was worried things were about to go south. She had a doctor prescribe the need for a therapy dog." Which was literally a whole different animal than this one. "She carried Tink everywhere."

"And now you can't put her down." Rosalie nodded. "We can fix that."

We.

Everett stilled, aware of the warm woman who smelled of Christmas trees a few feet away, the small warm dog next to his chest, and the warmth blossoming where his heart used to be.

He should point out that there was no partnership between them, no *we*.

He should point out that he wasn't looking for anything long term, no *we*.

Instead, he said, "My wife's hobby was dressage."

"That's an expensive hobby." Rosalie opened the dog treats. She held a nugget in one hand where Tinkerbell could see it. With the other hand, she pointed her index and middle finger at her eyes. "*Watch*." The word came out like a growl.

Tink's ears pitched toward Rosalie, and she stared at her with bird-dog-like intensity.

"Good girl." Rosalie gave Tink the snack and then brushed a hand over her head, touching Everett's arm in the process.

Her touch immobilized him. It made his heart race. It was irrational. Rosalie was a permanent resident of Sunshine, a business owner. She had roots, whereas he had no intention of staying.

"Dogs want to have a purpose." Rosalie dug out another treat and said in that same growly voice, "*Watch*." Repeating the hand gesture toward her own eyes.

Again, Tink's attention focused on Rosalie. Again, she received Rosalie's praise and the snack. Again, Rosalie's hand brushed over Everett's arm.

His lungs burned from a lack of air. He couldn't move, not even his eyes. He couldn't remove his gaze from the delicate lines of her face.

"We just need to give them a role in our lives—companion, protector." Rosalie took Tinkerbell from him and put her on the floor, where the dog immediately began to yap and romp at their feet. "*Watch*," Rosalie growled.

Tink stilled, staring up at Rosalie.

Everett stilled, staring down at Rosalie.

"Good girl." Rosalie knelt to give Tink a treat and praise. All that affection...

It wrapped around Everett and made him long for a comfortable couch in front of a blazing fire with Rosalie by his side. He cleared his throat and straightened his glasses, trying to bring order to his wayward thoughts. *I'm too old for infatuations.*

Maybe Kevin was right. Maybe Everett should date. He could spare a night or two out, and there was probably a single woman in town his age who was looking for casual company.

As soon as Rosalie stood, Tink started barking again, albeit half-heartedly with one eye on her.

"You try, Everett," Rosalie said above Tink's complaints, pressing a small dog treat into Everett's palm. Her fingers were as soft and warm as the look she gave him. "Use a rumbly voice to tell Tink you're the top dog here and she needs to keep an eye on you instead of barking so much."

Everett didn't have much faith in the exercise, but he dutifully said, "Tink, *watch.*"

The little stinker sat down and panted at him.

"Wow, look at that." Everett laughed.

When he didn't immediately give Tink the biscuit, she stood and barked at him. Once. Sharply.

Everett started to give her the reward but Rosalie stayed his arm.

"Tell her to do it again." Rosalie gave his biceps a squeeze, and even through his dress shirt he could feel the unexpected strength in those small fingers. "Repeat the command, and then be fair and feed her if she earns it."

Tinkerbell waited for Everett to speak, watching him the entire time. It hardly seemed fair, like she knew the drill. But since the dog was staring at him when he said, "Tink, *watch,*" he gave her the treat.

"It's a miracle," he said. Now he could take Tink to work with fewer concerns that she'd disrupt the workplace and derail his carefully reconstructed image. "You're a lifesaver, Rosalie."

Before she could say any more, before he said something he'd regret to her, and before Tink could have another meltdown, he ushered Rosalie out the door.

And when she was gone, his apartment seemed as sterile and unaffected as before.

Except for the vaguest impression—like the scent of a Christmas tree—that warmth and happiness had been within reach.

"What took you so long?" Kimmy asked when Rosalie climbed into the passenger seat of her older-model car.

The gray, three-legged kitten was asleep in Kimmy's lap. Rosalie's sister had fallen for one of Eileen's furry orphans and was taking her home.

"I was about to text you to see if you needed rescuing." Kimmy smirked. "Or more time with that handsome man. Spill. Which was it?"

Remy's curiosity was in sync with her sister's. From the back seat, the dog nuzzled Rosalie's shoulder, emitting a grumble as soft as the snowflakes falling on the windshield.

"I gave Everett some dog-training tips, that's all." Rosalie wasn't going to admit he'd shared some insight into his past. If she told her sister that, Kimmy would get ideas about romance and second chances. Rosalie was at peace with widowhood, her plate full with the launch of Sunshine Pets.

Kimmy's gaze searched Rosalie's face, as if she already had romantic ideas and was looking for proof. "I'd hoped Scrooge was asking you out."

"Please. Let's not go there." Rosalie could admit to herself that she felt attracted to Everett but the last thing she wanted was for her sister to latch onto the idea. She'd never hear the end of it. "Does Everett look like the kind of guy who'd ask the delivery girl out?"

"No." Kimmy backed out of the parking space. "He looks like the kind of guy who'd overthink a first kiss." She pulled out of the parking lot and turned toward the south side of town and home. "He has that intense stare. I saw him stare at you back at the store. I can imagine how it'd be. Your gazes would linger while the wheels of his brain would turn."

Holy how-to-read-a-situation. There had been prolonged gazes.

But Kimmy wasn't finished. "And you'd be staring into his eyes waiting to see what would happen, because you're polite and a little clueless."

And because I'd be slow on the uptake, focused on the dog.

"And then Everett would swoop in for a kiss you'd have had no inkling was coming."

Rosalie resisted the impulse to touch her lips and give her sister's fantasy credence. Nevertheless, the notion of kissing Everett had been planted in Rosalie's mind.

The clouds above them parted. A star twinkled in the velvet sky. A single star as bright and shiny as Marty's love for her had been.

Her eyes burned with tears.

My future wasn't supposed to be like this. In my thirties. Alone. Starting over.

But it was. And even the memory of her dead husband's love couldn't wipe away the attraction she felt for a quiet man with a loud dog.

"Or I could be misreading the town Scrooge completely." Kimmy laughed, unaware of the tenor of Rosalie's thoughts. "After all, I'm the woman in the car who's never been married."

Chapter Three

It's my first meeting, so I brought fudge." Bitsy Whitlock set a plate of fudge in the middle of the town hall's conference room table and sat next to Rosalie.

Everett liked Bitsy. Fudge. No more needed to be said. He hadn't had dinner yet.

"And I brought dog treats." From her seat next to his, Rosalie passed a small plastic bag to Everett. Despite the upbeat impression made by her green Christmas sweater with Rudolph's blinking nose, Rosalie seemed tired. Her big brown eyes had circles under them that were nearly as dark as her short hair. She opened her mouth to say something and then paused and cocked her head. "What's that sound?"

Everyone on the Holiday Event Committee went silent. Muted yapping could be heard down the hall.

"It's...uhh..." Everett wondered how he could phrase the truth without looking like a jerk. "I put Tink in time-out in the bathroom with a dog chew." Because she panicked in her crate, and regardless of what Kevin said, Everett needed to project a businesslike impression with his committee. "The *watch* command you taught me only worked during the first hour this morning. And before you judge, she's only been in there about ten minutes." He'd waited until the last possible moment to put Tinkerbell away, hoping she'd take a nap.

"Oh, poor thing." Rosalie stood and swiped the treat bag. "Moving is super stressful for pets. I'll get her."

"Make sure you bring my guilt back with you too," Everett called after Rosalie, who quickly returned with Tink barking excitedly at her feet.

Everyone admired Tinkerbell and her holiday sweater, not seeming to mind her prancing about and yapping. Finally, Rosalie sat between Bitsy and Everett with Tink in her lap. The little dog wagged her tail and stared adoringly at Everett until he gave her a friendly pat, and then she was all about the dog treats Rosalie slipped her.

"We'll start with the events this month before moving on to events for the first half of next year," Everett said, dragging his attention back to his agenda. "This Friday is the tree-lighting ceremony and—"

"The Widows Club usually sells hot chocolate." Bitsy extended the full plate of fudge in front of Rosalie and toward Everett.

Finally.

Everett extended his hand. And then the meaning of Bitsy's words sank in, and he paused midreach. "Did your club pay the city for a permit?" He didn't recall one being issued.

"No." The warmth left Bitsy's tone. She withdrew the plate. "We donate all proceeds to charity."

"That doesn't mean you don't need a permit." Everett spoke slowly and deliberately, the way he did when he suspected someone wouldn't be happy with his enforcement of a law.

Rosalie leaned toward Bitsy, slanting Everett an it's-coming-back-to-bite-you smirk. "Town hall has declared the tree-lighting ceremony a commerce-free event. Everett wouldn't let me hand out free dog biscuits that night or flyers about my organized dog walk through Christmas Tree Lane."

Tension balled in his chest. Rosalie was making him out to be a heartless ogre. "I explained—"

"Everett nixed me too." Paul Gregory nodded. He ran

an extermination business in town. "I was going to pass out magnetic chip clips with my logo."

Everett had no problem explaining town ordinances to Paul but he wasn't going to be the one to tell the man that a cockroach logo on a chip clip was in poor taste.

"What the Widows Club does isn't commerce." Bitsy's smile stiffened, and she drew the fudge into the circle of her arms. "It's charity. I can't remember a year the Widows Club didn't sell hot chocolate at the tree-lighting ceremony. Permitless, I might add."

Everett glanced toward the mayor's wife, who was his boss's eyes and ears on the committee.

Barb raised her finely arched brows as if to say, *If you're picking an argument with the Widows Club, you're digging your own grave.*

If that wasn't an indication of the power and popularity of the Widows Club in Sunshine, Everett didn't know what was.

"Perhaps we can make an exception for charity," Everett allowed carefully, eyeing the fudge. "I'll have to check with the mayor."

Bitsy passed the treats away from Everett to Paul.

"Moving on. There will be a marriage proposal at the end of the tree-lighting ceremony," Everett continued, giving Tink more pats despite her sitting in Rosalie's lap. He was finding he couldn't resist the tiny dog's big, pleading eyes. "And the bells will ring when the proposal is accepted."

"How romantic," Bitsy said.

"Super sweet," Rosalie agreed.

"That seems to be the consensus." Stomach growling, Everett eyed the plate of fudge, which was being passed around the table and had only a few pieces left. "Moving on to the Christmas parade. Did we garner enough volunteers for the event, Paul?"

"Yes." Paul waved a sheet of paper. "Volunteers will be stationed at the high school, where the parade begins, and at the town square. The latter is the toughest job since volunteers have to make sure when the parade ends, everyone disperses quickly and efficiently. We don't want a backup like we had last year. It took over an hour to unclog the streets and sidewalks in the center of town."

"I have a suggestion." Rosalie raised her hand. "Why not have the parade wind around the town square and end on Sunny Avenue?" Where her shop was located. She smiled her unflappable smile, tired though it was. "It eliminates the logjam."

And showed favoritism to businesses on Sunny Avenue. Everett's spine stiffened.

"What a lovely idea." Bitsy patted Rosalie's arm. "Isn't that a lovely idea, Everett?"

Everyone was agreeing it was a lovely idea, just like everyone agreed ringing the town hall bells after a marriage proposal was romantic.

Everett fought back a frown. "I'll have to conduct an analysis and run it by the mayor for final approval." Heaven forbid Everett found some cost associated with a new parade route.

"I'm sure everyone will appreciate the change." Barb was as open to pleasing constituents as her husband was. "It makes things easier on the *community*."

Everett didn't miss her hidden message or the gentle reminder that Kevin wanted to strengthen their community.

"Oh, and don't forget the Widows Club has a hot chocolate stand in the town square during the parade too." Bitsy's voice was as gentle as her smile. "Benefiting charity, of course. And speaking of which, we work a wrapping booth for charity at the local mall. Please don't tell me we need a permit for that."

The local mall being a three-story brick building on Main Street housing multiple small, independent retailers.

"No permit for that," Everett reassured her.

The fudge plate bypassed Everett and returned to Bitsy with one piece remaining. "We'd appreciate you volunteering for a wrapping shift, Everett."

How could he refuse? Unfortunately, it didn't earn him that last piece of fudge.

Next on the agenda was the committee's homework—compiling ideas for Valentine's Day. They did a good job creatively—from wine tasting in the local library to a Cupid-themed scavenger hunt with the town's businesses. The group was a bit deflated when Everett pointed out that none of their ideas required town hall's formal participation.

"Remember that we want events to build both a sense of community and Sunshine's coffers." Everett's comment was about as well received as Scrooge telling Bob Cratchit he could put only one lump of coal on the fire.

They finished the meeting by talking about Sunshine's Easter Egg Hunt. The committee felt it should continue to be free. Everett disagreed. Had none of them checked the price of eggs recently? Rather than argue, Everett tabled the decision pending financial review and made a mental note to seek sponsorships to offset the cost of eggs.

"Rosalie, can I have a word?" Everett asked after he adjourned the meeting. "About the parade…"

Perhaps having heard his words, Bitsy turned at the meeting room door and stared, holding the plate with that one last piece of fudge wrapped in cellophane.

"About the parade…" Everett lowered his voice and moved closer to Rosalie.

"You're going to veto my suggestion." Rosalie put Tinkerbell on the floor.

Yap-yap-yap.

Tink raced around the meeting room, from Bitsy to Everett to Rosalie and back again.

Yap-yap-yap.

Everett caught Tink as she circled his feet, bringing a welcome silence.

"You shouldn't pick her up." Rosalie crossed her arms over her chest. She plucked the small dog from his arms and set her down once more. "Let me tell you why ending the parade on Sunny Avenue is a win for you." She barely paused to take a breath before making her argument over the sound of Tinkerbell's barking. "There are charming and historic features on Sunny Avenue, places that are great for selfies and to start conversations. The lamppost clock, the barbershop pole—"

"The bench dedicated to the town's founding fathers," Bitsy cut in, also at a near shout.

Rosalie nodded. "The historic fountain in the middle of the street."

"And what should I tell other businesses on other streets?" His head began to pound from the shouting required to be heard. It had been an all-day occurrence, after all—people shouting over Tinkerbell's barks. "What should I tell the businesses that aren't going to have a parade finish nearby?"

Tink showed no sign of quieting, although neither did Rosalie.

"Tell them you'll end the parade elsewhere next year," she said.

"That's a brilliant idea." Bitsy moved to Rosalie's side.

"And fair." Rosalie nodded. "Plus the parade will look like a well-orchestrated event. This is a win for you and town hall."

The pressure to agree closed in on him. Simultaneously, the pressure to hold his ground kept his shoulders square.

Yap-yap-yap.

The soundtrack of his life lately. His temples pounded harder.

"I tell you what." Rosalie started to smile, as if preparing to sweeten the pot. "You're obviously too busy and stressed to make a decision now." She gestured toward Tink, who'd stopped running the racetrack and was prancing in front of Everett. "Let's take her for a walk to Sunny Avenue. You can see it through my eyes, and I'll give you some more training tips."

"Do not offer me free training," he said quickly. No way would he allow himself to be put in a situation where it might look like he was playing favorites. "I'm open to tips." From one business associate to another. Unable to stand her barking anymore, he picked Tink up. "I'll walk with you, Rosalie, because this dog needs an outlet. This has nothing to do with the parade or comped services."

"Of course not." Rosalie was quick to agree. "Why don't you suit up Tinkerbell in her booties? I'll go get Remington. He's still at the store."

Rosalie hurried out the door before Everett's stomach growled again.

"I'm so glad you two found common ground." Bitsy handed him the last piece of fudge and wished him a Merry Christmas.

Chapter Four

The temperature was falling. Rosalie's breath created visible clouds.

But the cold couldn't reach the warm feeling of excitement inside her. Everett was considering changing the parade route, which would help build store awareness and sales. That explained her eagerness, not the fact that she'd be walking with Everett.

She rounded the corner and saw him standing outside the town hall holding Tinkerbell.

Remington gave a soft grumble and picked up his pace.

"Put her down and let's walk," Rosalie instructed when she was a few feet away.

"Are you sure?" Everett glanced around. "I tried to walk her this morning, and she wouldn't stop barking."

There were several shoppers entering and exiting stores. They greeted Rosalie warmly, frowning at or ignoring Everett. He didn't seem to mind being snubbed but it bothered her.

"Put her down." Rosalie shoved thoughts of Everett aside, focusing on Tinkerbell. "Once we get in a rhythm, she'll quiet down."

Tinkerbell didn't prove Rosalie's theory. She yapped her way down the block next to Remington, who pitched his ears forward as if he was inwardly wincing. Likewise, Everett hunched his shoulders higher up toward his ears with each step.

"You know," Rosalie shouted above the barking as they

neared a corner, "dogs can sense when your stress is off the charts."

Everett blew out a breath. "If that's true, old Remington should be woofing nonstop like Tink."

"What do you mean?" She patted Remy's shoulder, not breaking stride. "I'm perfectly fine."

"Liar. You look like you haven't had a good night's sleep in weeks." They turned down a street toward Sunny Avenue. Everett glanced at her. "I've always heard starting a business is stressful. Go on. Admit it. It's not like anyone can hear us above Tink."

Before she could deny she was stressed, Tinkerbell stopped barking.

"Do you hear that?" Rosalie asked, grinning.

"No," Everett grumped. And then he looked down. "Oh."

"That is the sound of a happy dog." One that didn't bark. "Maybe you're the one who needed a walk. Are you feeling less stressed?"

"That's a chicken-and-egg question." His lips rose in an almost smile. "Did our walk relieve my stress? Or am I more relaxed because of Tinkerbell's silence?" He stared at her the way Kimmy had described. Lingering. Thoughtful.

Is he thinking about kisses?

Rosalie had trouble breathing.

"And what about you?" he asked. "I've seen you walk all over town with your dog. Why?"

"Besides the fact that he needs exercise, I..." She shouldn't say anything. "I..." For sure, Everett didn't want to hear about her feelings. "I wake up angry," she said anyway.

Everett's eyebrows arched.

"I'm angry at the kid who shot my husband, although I ache at the thought of him spending his life in prison." Rosalie should stop there but she couldn't. The anger that interrupted her sleep had invaded her mouth. "I'm angry at my husband for letting his guard down while on patrol, although he died doing a job he believed in and that makes me proud. And—"

Aruff-aroo.

Remington didn't like it when she released all these messy emotions. He crossed into her path, slowing her down.

Rosalie guided him back to her side. "And I'm angry with myself for wanting Marty to pick up an extra shift." She patted Remington's shoulder again. "I wanted to buy a new dining room table. I shouldn't have cared what we ate on. I should have been patient or found something used online. I should have been happy with what I had, because now what I have is anger and regret in the middle of the night."

They approached the corner at Sunny Avenue. All the landmarks came into view—the clock, the barbershop pole, the wrought-iron bench and historic street fountain.

Everett's silence said more than words. She'd made him uncomfortable.

Rosalie slowed and measured out an impromptu sales pitch. "This street is as wide as those around the town square, providing plenty of parking. And it's charming, don't you think?"

His gaze roamed the street. "I hear the fountain doesn't work."

Rosalie glanced up at Everett. "My husband hit the fountain years and years ago." The day she'd decided she was going to marry him.

Everett's eyebrows resumed the surprised position. "Joyriding?"

"He was learning how to drive, and I was walking our family dog."

"You stopped traffic." There was a teasing note in Everett's voice.

She elbowed him gently, as if they were longtime friends. "I had fewer miles on me then."

"You don't have many miles on you now."

Her cheeks heated. "But they're hard miles. I feel older than thirty-four."

Kimmy would be crowing at Rosalie fishing for Everett's age.

"Wife of a cop. Widowed." He shrugged. "Fair mileage."

He wasn't going to tell her how old he was? She tried to tell herself it didn't matter. She wanted him to change the parade route, not make a pass.

"Age is relative," Everett added slowly, coming to a stop in front of her store. "The day after Lydia was arrested, I could barely bring myself to get out of bed. Coming here... Let's just say I feel much younger now." He may have been looking at her shop but he didn't seem to see anything.

The chalkboard sign invited folks in. The bunnies and kittens were cuddling as they slept. The Christmas tree lights twinkled next to pet-themed ornaments. It was a beautiful façade.

She caught sight of his reflection in the window. He wasn't smiling.

His reflected gaze met hers. "I understand the anger. I understand sleepless nights and second-guessing. But what happened... You can't change that. You have to move forward with a more careful tread."

Watch your step.

The reason for all his rules became clear. She'd read about his past. His wife had been a city's longtime controller. He'd been hired to straighten the finances, same as in Sunshine. And according to the press releases, his wife hadn't stopped stealing after he'd come on board. She hadn't watched her step but Everett now made sure everyone around him watched theirs.

Tinkerbell barked impatiently, prancing. By unspoken agreement, they resumed their walk. They rounded another corner, heading back up Center Avenue toward the town square.

Everett slowed, staring across the street at the vacant warehouse.

"Does the city still own that warehouse?" At his nod, she said, "I've always thought it would be cool to turn that place into loft apartments with shops or restaurants below."

Before he could answer, a group of high school kids drove by in a car with the windows down, singing the *five golden rings* line at the top of their lungs. The rest of "The Twelve Days of Christmas" faded as they turned at the next intersection.

"Kids." Rosalie chuckled, although it sounded bittersweet.

"Lydia didn't want to have children," Everett admitted quietly, squelching Rosalie's desire to laugh. "Her horses were her babies. And then Tink, of course. Afterward, I was grateful we hadn't been parents. What do you tell a child about their mother when she goes to jail? What do you say when…"

"Their father is killed in the line of duty?" The words came out on a tight thread because Rosalie was angry about being childless too. "We always felt like we weren't at a place to afford children yet."

Aroo-ruff. Remington had something to say about that. Or perhaps he thought she'd said too much already.

They reached Main Street. The town square was dark. The trees wouldn't be lit until Friday. But the stores along the town square were open late, shop lights warming the sidewalk. Townspeople were bundled up and scurrying about with shopping bags. For them, it was just another normal holiday season.

But for Rosalie and Everett…

"There's something about you…" Rosalie couldn't look

at him. "I tell you things I should keep to myself." Things she hadn't even told Kimmy.

"Who says I don't want to listen?" Everett took her hand, the one that didn't hold Remington's leash. He slid his thumb over the hole in her mitten, touching her skin with his bare hand because he didn't wear gloves. "Or that I didn't want to be heard?" He stared into her eyes. There was no Scrooge, no ice, no frozen tundra.

Rosalie held her breath. Was he thinking about kissing her?

Why was *she* thinking about kissing *him*?

Somewhere nearby, a child belted out an energetic rendition of "Must Be Santa."

Somewhere, deep in her chest, Rosalie's heart belted out a strong cadence of attraction—*him, him, him*.

It's okay to move on. Marty's voice, as if he were reading a line from the love letter she'd found after he died.

Rosalie sighed.

"I'll see you around." Everett released Rosalie and walked toward the town hall. "Here's hoping you don't wake up in the middle of the night angry."

Rosalie stood staring at his retreating back, unable to move.

What was happening here? This morning he'd been Scrooge, more concerned with pennies than people.

It didn't matter what she'd thought of him this morning. The attraction...It wouldn't go away. It validated her hunch that there was more to Everett Bollinger than what he showed others.

Snow began falling. Several inches were predicted to come down before morning, enough to cover their footprints in the sidewalk and conceal all evidence that indicated Everett Bollinger had a heart.

Yap-yap-yap.

No matter how much Everett walked Tink, she was still yappy every time he put her down when they were inside.

"*Watch.*" He gave her a treat and then walked out of his office to the printer to collect the pages of a proposal for the town council to sponsor a mudder. The costs associated with setup were minimal, while the entry fees would generate much-needed income. Building and housing values in Sunshine were stagnant and had been for years, which meant tax dollars didn't increase when the town hall's spending increased. And then there was the vacant warehouse.

When Kevin's father had been mayor, he'd purchased that warehouse from a friend and proposed developing it into a second mall. The rents were supposed to pay the mortgage, and then tenant sales were going to be taxed. He'd claimed it'd be legal double-dipping. But while they were remodeling the building, there'd been a fire and a worker had died. Several years and one lawsuit later, the abandoned warehouse was a rock around the town's neck.

Kevin couldn't find a company who'd be willing to invest in the building and Sunshine. Without a buyer, the path to a balanced budget was nearly impossible. And without a balanced budget, the town wouldn't qualify for federal funding, which they needed to provide residents with other services.

Yap-yap-yap.

Tink pranced around his feet in her holiday sweater. She followed Everett back to his desk, where he put her in her pet bed, currently residing on the corner of his desk.

Feeling masculine much, Bollinger?

He'd seen Rosalie every morning and every night as they walked their dogs. They'd call out hello and by mutual agreement head in opposite directions, as if they regretted the confidences they'd shared on their walk around the block.

I regret it.

And yet his thoughts drifted toward Rosalie when he clipped on Tink's leash. Would she be out walking? Was the hole in her mitten unraveling further?

Unproductive, these thoughts. Not to mention soft. He was the hatchet man, not the mayor.

"Of course we still have places in the parade," Yolanda was telling someone in the outer office.

Everett pressed his lips together. The deadline for inclusion in the parade had been the Wednesday before Thanksgiving. Deadlines were rules and meant to be honored. He stood up and put Tink on the ground.

Yap-yap-yap.

"*Watch.*" Everett gave her a treat. Crunching the kibble, she followed him happily to the service counter. "Late entry?"

Twin teenage boys stood at the counter with paperwork and cash. They were the same boys who worked at the bakery after school.

Yap-yap-yap.

At Yolanda's frown, Everett scooped Tink into his arms.

"We forgot to turn in the paperwork." One teen tried to look contrite but he was doing a bad job of hiding a smile.

"It's for our FFA club at the high school," his twin said, doing a better job of looking meek and apologetic. He elbowed his brother.

"You're letting them in?" Everett fixed Yolanda with a stare. "Were you going to charge them a late fee?"

Yolanda had a hard stare of her own, one he'd been on the receiving end of from her all day. "You want to charge a late fee to students?" She crossed her arms over her chest and *tsk*ed. "During the holiday season?"

"We just want to make it right," said the first teen.

"Yeah," echoed his twin. "Just because we screwed up doesn't mean the rest of the kids should suffer."

Kevin would have given them an understanding grin and relented. Everett wanted to refuse them entry, teach them a lesson about responsibility, and send them on their way.

"We brought a toy." The first teen dug in his backpack and put a new Frisbee in the toy drive box.

It was the only thing in the toy drive box.

"You're gonna make them pay a late fee when they brought a toy?" Yolanda made another disapproving noise, strong enough to send her Christmas tree earrings swaying. "I need to consult with a higher power. And I don't mean God." She meant Kevin. She picked up the phone and punched in Kevin's extension.

"Hang on." Everett pushed down the phone button, blaming his sudden soft spot on Rosalie, who was kind to everyone. "I think there's a lesson to be learned here."

Yolanda's eyes narrowed.

"Boys." Everett fixed them with a no-nonsense smile. "We're trying to build a stronger sense of community in Sunshine. You missed the deadline to sign up for the parade, late or otherwise."

"Here we go," Yolanda muttered, picking up the phone once more.

"But..." Everett waggled a finger at Yolanda. "I'm willing to make an exception if you help us with the town hall toy drive." He rattled the near-empty box.

"You'll waive the parade fee completely?" Yolanda asked suspiciously.

"We'll take their fee, and if they fill this box with toys by the tree-lighting ceremony, we'll let them be in the parade."

"Toys in lieu of a late fee?" Yolanda still looked dubious.

"Exactly." Everett nodded. "No one gets special treatment around here."

Except maybe Tinkerbell.

Chapter Five

You know, this is ridiculous." Rosalie stopped on the corner of Sunny and Center Avenues and called across the street to Everett. It was Thursday and the third night in a row she'd seen him walking Tinkerbell after she closed for the night. "We're the only ones out here walking dogs. We should walk together."

The sheriff's car drove slowly toward them. It had snowed earlier, and the roads and sidewalks were slick. Sheriff Drew Taylor waved to them both as he passed. He had one of his deputies in the passenger seat.

"I don't think walking together is a good idea," Everett said, but he crossed the street toward her anyway.

"Why? Because you haven't decided about the parade route? You know it's a good idea."

Oo-oo-aroo.

"And Remy agrees with me." Rosalie patted Remy's shoulder.

Everett stopped a few feet away, staring at her. "And this is why I don't walk with you. I don't like to talk shop after hours."

"Please." Rosalie turned toward the south end of town and home. "You don't walk with me because you have your secrets, which you don't want to tell."

"And you have yours." He fell into step beside her. "Which you don't want to tell."

Rosalie could feel his gaze upon her face, as tangible as a caress. Her pulse quickened.

"The circles under your eyes are gone." Everett looked ahead. "You've been sleeping well."

She had been. Their conversation had loosened anger's hold on her dreams. "And you've been up to your old tricks in town."

He glanced at her. "Tricks?"

"Blackmailing kids into supporting the toy drive. Charging another couple to ring the bell after they become engaged in the town square." Rosalie whistled, long and low.

Both dogs perked up their ears.

"What is it with you and money?" Rosalie gently bumped Everett's arm with her elbow. "If I didn't know better, I'd still believe all the talk about you being Scrooge incarnate."

"Do you know what it takes to keep a town financially healthy?" Everett stared down at her through his glasses. It was the icy stare he'd often used on her prior to buying her that hot chocolate. "Much less to make it grow?"

"Nope." She was as immune to icy stares now as she'd been then. "I barely know what it takes to make a business grow."

"I was hired to get the town's finances in order." Each word he uttered was as sharp as a fresh icicle.

She nodded, still immune. "And you're doing a good job."

Everett's gaze thawed. "Did you have retail experience before opening your store?"

They stopped at a corner, waiting for a car to pass before crossing.

"Nope. I worked as a nine-one-one dispatcher before I moved back home." Rosalie slowed for an icy patch of sidewalk. "I worked at the Feed Store at first but Victor Yates treats pets like livestock." It had bothered her. "To me, pets are part of the family."

Ga-rumph.

Remington slid a few inches. Rosalie led him onto the fresh snow on her uncle Mateo's front yard. It was slower going but less slippery.

"Pets are family. Your attitude explains everything wrong with your business." Everett picked up Tinkerbell and fell into step behind Rosalie. "You've got too much heart invested in your store."

Too much heart? Those were too similar to Marty's words.

"Rosalie?" Everett was waiting for her defense.

She shook off the lapse. "You're supposed to be passionate about your business. The things I stock are meant to bring love to pet families and in turn that love overflows into the community."

Remy grumbled, which she took to be agreement.

"What I meant was, your margins are too low because you're too worried about selling to your friends." The ice was building in his tone.

"My margins aren't too low." Were they?

"They are. Lydia bought those same copper bowls for Tink in Denver for over fifty dollars. You had them marked at thirty-five. And don't give me the excuse that this is Sunshine." He pointed at a Mercedes SUV as it drove past. "Folks have money here. Let them spend it."

"I'm not Scrooge." And she was getting by. She'd used some of Marty's life insurance to get the store started, plus some from a family investor. She was saving money by sleeping on Kimmy's couch. "I don't need to fleece people and fill my home with lots of *things*." Expensive things, like dining room sets.

They crossed another street, continuing south. Walking single file. Not talking.

Bright lights adorned houses. Glittering Christmas trees were featured in front windows. Everywhere she looked there was color and life and holiday spirit. It was just inside her that the colors were a bit muted, life less sparkly, her holiday spirit a bit forced. Maybe she'd been working too hard.

"I've hurt your feelings," Everett said softly. "And you don't believe you should charge more because increasing your margins might remind you of the dining room table you wanted."

Her chest constricted. "I never said that."

"But you thought it." Everett increased his pace until they were walking side by side. "It's okay to make a living, a nice living."

Rosalie pressed her lips together.

He touched her arm, stopping her because the contact was so unexpected. "Let me assure you, you'll never get rich running that store. But someday, you might be able to buy a nice dining room set. And when that day comes, you should feel pride, not guilt. And when you use it, it should make you happy, not sad."

That sentiment seemed as out of reach as his heart.

A gust of wind. A patch of ice. They were swept against a six-foot-tall cinder block wall, thick and impenetrable, like the imaginary wall made of the differences between them.

"You and your husband were public servants—a cop and an emergency dispatcher." Everett's voice was soft, gentle, understanding. "You've spent your adult life serving others. Maybe it's time to devote a little more time and energy to yourself."

He was giving her permission to put herself first. No one had ever done that, not even Marty.

"I'm not sure..." She hesitated. "I don't think..."

"Rosalie." Everett touched her hand where her mitten had a hole. "Your dog's sweater is new but you won't even buy a new pair of gloves." He was right.

"I don't live to the excess. I don't have a closet full of clothes. My gloves..." She stared at his hand holding hers. And still, she rebelled against the idea of putting herself first. "My gloves are fine. I'll make do."

The wind gusted again, tugging at her knit cap and her resolve to keep her heart on her side of the imaginary wall.

Everett tucked a shivering Tinkerbell inside his red coat. And then he moved closer, sheltering Rosalie from the mountain gusts. "I understand. Growing up, we made do too. Until the year my dad bought all of life's luxuries—a new car, a big TV, name-brand tennis shoes. And then he left us to pay the bills. After that, Mom was always working. Working at a call center during the day. Scrubbing corporate toilets at night. And still, we had next to nothing." His expression was grim. Not uncaring, just grim. "Nothing in savings either. Which was bad, because when Mom was out of work for three months because of a car accident…" His grim look turned into a grimace. "Living paycheck to paycheck…People like you and me know how dangerous that can be."

"I'll be fine. I've got family to fall back on. And besides, there's a need for my store in Sunshine." Rosalie trembled, hoping she wasn't being overly optimistic. "And I want to provide a service that spreads love and happiness in a small way. Your situation, your job, is completely different from mine."

"Is it? Two years ago, I was doing well. After Lydia was arrested and the government took everything for reparations, no one would hire me." He swallowed, inching closer, seemingly without knowing it. He stared deep into her eyes with a gaze that was warm, not icy. "All my adult life, I had six months' salary in savings, but they took that too and left me with nothing." And then he added, almost under his breath, "Just like when I was a kid."

His comments gave meaning to his career, a reason he chose to be Scrooge.

"You should know," he said, "this job…Sunshine…It's just a stepping-stone."

"You want your life back." She'd bet that included fancy

cars and leather furniture. A life of excess she didn't believe in and wouldn't aspire to.

"You don't approve." He was very close to her now. Close enough to kiss.

But emotionally, they were worlds apart.

"I don't..." Rosalie stared deep into his gray eyes, wondering why she was attracted to this man, wondering if it was their differences that intrigued her. "I'm not interested in making an impression or earning enough to buy creature comforts. And..." She swallowed as a car drove past. "It doesn't matter to me if you're the city manager of Sunshine or of Denver. It doesn't matter to me if you live on the north side or the south side of town. What matters to me is who you are inside and how you treat others."

The imaginary wall between them had come down.

"We weren't talking about..." He drew back by degrees. "We were discussing your business."

"Were we?" Rosalie's cheeks burned with embarrassment but she wasn't going to back down. They'd been discussing their philosophies toward life. They'd found similarities that bridged their differences. They'd made a connection. She knew it.

Beside her, Remy grumbled in apparent agreement.

"I want nothing more than to kiss you right now." Everett's voice was as gruff as Remy's grumble. "But we want different things in life."

"Yes. Although I can't help but believe that common ground motivates us to do what we do. Which makes us not so different after all." To prove her point, she reached for the placket of his jacket and held on. "After all, you're a public servant. That must mean that, deep down, you care about people the same way that I do."

And then Rosalie did something completely out of character. She stretched up on her toes and kissed him.

Chapter Six

The weather outside was frightful.

Rosalie offered warmth, the same way she always did—with unexpected determination.

Yes, Everett had wanted to kiss her. Yes, he knew kissing her wasn't good for his career goals. He was supposed to be the impartial man in town, the executor of hard choices to avoid municipal bankruptcy. He wasn't supposed to feel. And because of Lydia, he'd spent the last eighteen months in an emotionless limbo.

But Rosalie's kiss…It made him feel again. A heart-pounding, breath-stealing feeling that he should drop everything and pay attention to the woman nestled in the crook of his arm.

She ended the kiss on a sigh.

"Rosalie." Her name on his lips was little more than a sigh itself.

She blinked, flinched, and drew the Saint Bernard between them. "You don't approve. Well…I started that," she admitted baldly. "It's all on me." She picked her way carefully along the icy, snowy sidewalk and away from him. "No harm, no foul, no commitments. Don't think you have to ask me to dinner or send me flowers."

Despite common sense telling him to turn the other way, Everett followed her. It was dark, after all, and cold. And she seemed more shaken by their kiss than he'd been.

"I may have stopped traffic in my youth but I don't make a habit of leaping out and kissing random dudes." Her laugh sounded forced.

"I'm not a *random dude*." His comment appeared to go unnoticed.

Inside his jacket, Tink squirmed. He drew his zipper down enough that she could poke her head out.

"Jeez. I'm thirty-four. And a widow." Rosalie laced each word with frustration. "Not the kind of woman to go attacking a man on the street."

"Again, not a random dude on the street, and you didn't attack me." Although it was nice that she'd taken the initiative. And since she wasn't looking at him, he allowed himself a smile.

"If Kimmy ever finds out about this, I'll never hear the end of it. She'll be like, *Rosalie, you always reach out and take what you want.* She'll say that whether I'm reaching for a dinner roll or reaching for you." Rosalie gasped. "Never fear. I'm not going to be reaching for you again."

Everett choked out a laugh.

Rosalie drew up short, turning. "What's so funny?"

He was very careful not to smile. "The fact that it was one kiss and you're having a meltdown. It was a kiss, not a marriage proposal."

She made a frustrated sound and turned down a street. "Are you walking me home?"

"I…" Was he? Everett glanced around. "Do you live on this street?"

"Yes. Don't expect a good-night kiss." For being such a short person, she had a brisk, long stride. "I don't do repeat performances, not when I bombed the first time."

"You didn't bomb."

"Right." She turned up a driveway.

The small bungalow had Christmas lights strung from the eaves and a large wreath hanging from the door. Blanketed in snow, there was a charm to it. But there was something about the house that reminded him of his childhood, of upkeep put off and occupants hopeful that ends would meet.

The front door opened. "Rosalie, dinner is ready. Why do you take that dog for such long walks? We're waiting on you." The woman silhouetted in the doorway gasped. "There's a man behind you."

"I know, Mom. He's—"

"You didn't tell me you were bringing a man home. I'll set another plate." Rosalie's mother turned away from them. "Honey, we have company."

"Mom…" Rosalie's shoulders drooped. She didn't turn. "You do not have to come in."

If he'd been asked to a family dinner in the moments before they'd kissed, he'd have refused. But Rosalie's kiss had breached the security system around his hardened heart. It felt good to laugh, to smile, to enjoy being in a woman's company.

He had tomorrow to regroup and return to the status quo—Scrooge. For tonight, he'd act like a man who'd never been played the fool, one who took everyone at face value.

Everett grinned as he took Rosalie's arm. "I'd love to come to dinner."

"You didn't tell me you were dating Scrooge," Kimmy whispered to Rosalie in the kitchen.

Everett was sitting in the living room next to the Christmas tree with Tinkerbell in his arms and Rosalie's father grilling him as if he were a murder suspect.

"I'm not dating him," Rosalie insisted for what felt like the hundredth time.

I'm just kissing him.

It had been a great kiss too. If only she could keep the memory of that kiss and dump everything that came afterward…except maybe Everett's grin as they'd walked in the door. It was the first time she'd seen a genuine smile on his face. It had transformed him into the man she'd expected him to be when she'd first laid eyes on him.

Aunt Yolanda came into the kitchen. She'd moved into Rosalie's old room last spring after her divorce and planned to stay until she'd regained her financial footing. "What is Scrooge doing in our house?"

"Rosalie's dating him," Kimmy blurted gleefully.

Rosalie hurried to assure Aunt Yolanda this wasn't true.

"You couldn't have warned me?" Mom raced around the kitchen, stirring meat in the frying pan in between filling bowls with condiments. "Why you chose to bring him to the house on Spam taco night…"

"You think he won't like Spam tacos?" Kimmy grinned as she reached for the cluster of garlic on the counter. "I'll add garlic. Garlic makes anything taste better."

"Touch that garlic and you'll be helping me scrub toilets at Prestige Salon." Their mother gave Kimmy the evil eye. She ran her own cleaning service, and when the girls were younger, that particular threat had worked wonders. "These are sriracha tacos. Add more garlic and it'll unbalance the chili."

Kimmy's hand hovered over the garlic just the same.

Rosalie pulled her sister out of garlic range. "We should all just calm down because I'm not dating anyone."

From the dog bed in the corner of the kitchen, Remy grumbled, as if refuting her statement.

"Good." Aunt Yolanda nodded. "Do you know he double-checked my cash box today? I've worked there for over twenty-five years and he doesn't trust me?"

Rosalie decided not to point out Everett's history. With a past like that and a job like his, he wasn't going to trust easily.

"Has anyone seen my phone? I'm expecting a call." In crisis mode over an unexpected guest, Mom flitted about the kitchen, ignoring her sister's complaints. "I don't even have dessert. What will his mother think of me? Spam tacos. No dessert."

"She'd love you," Rosalie reassured her mother, giving her a hug before releasing Mom to swoop around the kitchen some more. "But we're not dating so it's highly unlikely that you'll ever meet her."

"Thank heavens." Aunt Yolanda blew out a breath. "I'd have to rethink my investment in your store, Rosalie. Cash out or something."

Everyone in the kitchen froze.

Rosalie's stomach tumbled to Tinkerbell height. Was this how it was going to be from now on? Her aunt holding her investment over her head?

"Just kidding," Aunt Yolanda mumbled.

"Don't joke about that." Mom darted out of the kitchen on a quest for her phone. "We all pull together in this family."

As if proving Mom's point, Aunt Yolanda followed her out. "Where did you see your phone last?"

Kimmy nudged Rosalie with her hip and whispered, "Everett's staring at you like he's planning his good-night kiss strategy."

Rosalie refused to look. "Stop it." It was bad enough that she'd kissed him but now Kimmy had romance between her teeth and wouldn't let go.

"Let me tell you, Sis." Kimmy's voice dropped even lower, until Rosalie had to strain to hear. "He's thinking hot thoughts right now, despite the fact that Dad is practically asking him for his social security number and date of birth."

"Stop it." Rosalie snatched up a dish towel and swung it in a circle above her head.

"Hot thoughts," Kimmy teased, scooting out of reach.

"Can we eat?" Rosalie demanded. "I need to iron out the details of my Santa Experience after dinner."

"Sit," Mom commanded, charging back into the room, cell phone in hand, Aunt Yolanda still trailing behind her. "Everybody come. Sit. Everett, you take the chair next to Rosalie."

"What is a Santa Experience?" Kimmy asked Rosalie.

"You have experience with Santa, Rosalie?" Everett grinned, carrying Tinkerbell as he approached their kitchen table, which had seen better days. He stared at the scarred surface, and then his gaze sought Rosalie's as if to say, *Do you want to replace this table too?*

Guilty.

But she wouldn't. It was still a sturdy table. Rosalie shook her head slightly and then spoke in a brisk tone. "I'm scheduling an event where people bring their pets for a photo with Santa. I'm calling it the Santa Experience."

Everett sat. Tinkerbell jumped out of his lap and snuggled next to Remington, causing Everett's jaw to drop.

"Pet photos with Santa." Her father passed Everett the warm tortillas. "Our Rosalie is so creative."

"I'm creative." Kimmy frowned. "Everyone raves about my gourmet sandwiches at Emory's Grocery."

Her mother passed Everett the platter of sliced, fried meat. "I hope you like Spam and sriracha sauce. I can always make you something else if you don't." Knowing Mom, if he didn't, she'd race to Emory's Grocery and pick up the ingredients for enchiladas, making Dad promise to keep Everett here until he'd been properly fed.

"I haven't had Spam since college." Everett placed long

slices on his tortilla. "I can't remember why I stopped eating it. It's so good."

Rosalie couldn't tell if Everett was joking or not but she appreciated the effort to make her mother feel at ease.

Aunt Yolanda, on the other hand, appreciated nothing about his presence.

"Everett, you're so nice." Mom sprinkled shredded cheese on her tortilla, visibly beginning to relax. "It's hard to believe..."

Everyone at the table stilled. A smile grew on Aunt Yolanda's face but she was the only one smiling. Rosalie's parents exchanged horrified glances. Mom had just brought up the elephant in the room.

"You find it hard to believe that people call me Scrooge?" Everett doused his taco in sriracha sauce. "Honestly? That's my job description—to save Sunshine's pennies." His tone implied he was fine with the nickname but a muscle in his cheek ticked.

Without thinking, Rosalie patted Everett's knee.

Without thinking... she snatched her hand back.

She couldn't afford not to think. That was how she'd ended up kissing him in the first place.

Chapter Seven

That's it. I'm done." Yolanda blew into the town hall the next afternoon on a flurry of snow.

Everett got up from his desk and went to lean against the doorframe. "You're quitting?"

If he sounded hopeful, Yolanda didn't seem to pick up on it.

"No. I need a new car." She unwound her purple knit scarf from her neck like a spool of twine attached to a rapidly rising kite. "Kevin forgot his speech, and I drove it over to the retirement home. And then my car wouldn't start. Not so much as a *click-click*."

"Dead battery?" Everett asked.

"Dead car." Yolanda threw her scarf at her feet and stared at it in defeat. "Darnell Tucker says he thinks my block is frozen, maybe cracked." She wrapped her arms across her chest in a self-hug. "I invested what little savings I had into Rosalie's store to protect it from my greedy ex." She paused, possibly realizing Everett understood about greedy ex-spouses. "How am I going to pay for a new car?" She lifted her lost gaze to Everett's. "If I ask Rosalie for my money back, she might go under."

It was all Everett could do not to squirm. As part of his cost-cutting plan, he'd been filling out Yolanda's termination paperwork.

He attempted a smile. "I've found Sunshine to be a very walkable city."

"You drive your car to work every day." She sank into her chair and put her head in her hands. "And your apartment is only three blocks down. I really need you to be a compassionate coworker right now, not Scrooge."

Everett hesitated, and then he came to stand by Yolanda's side and gave her shoulder a sympathetic squeeze. "Everything happens for a reason." That was what his mother said every time something bad happened. She'd told him that when he was a kid and they'd been evicted. She'd told him that when Lydia pled guilty. It was a hollow line, something you said when you didn't know what else to say.

"If you're thinking of telling me what doesn't kill me makes me stronger..." Yolanda sniffed, grabbing two tissues from the box on her desk. "I'm not strong enough to hear that yet." Her shoulders shook.

Everett stared at the ceiling, trying to be both supportive and cognizant of a coworker's personal space. "Why don't you take the rest of the day?"

"I can't." Yolanda wiped at her eyes, not that her action stopped the flow of tears. "The tree-lighting ceremony is at six."

"I insist." As a compassionate coworker. "As your boss."

"It's three thirty." She blew her nose. "I can make it."

All that emotion. All her protests. Yolanda claimed she didn't want Scrooge but talking to a caring coworker was sending her into a downward spiral.

"Go home, Yolanda," Everett said in what he was coming to believe was his Scrooge voice—low, gruff, firm. "You can make up your hour tomorrow." Everett stepped back and braced himself for her reaction.

Yolanda's shoulders stopped shaking. Head bowed, she scrubbed her face with a tissue and then blew her nose like a trumpet sounding a charge. Her head came up, revealing eyes sparking for a fight. "You'd send me home on one of the most important nights of the year for us? As if I had nothing to do with the coordination of this event?" Yolanda snatched up her purple scarf and wrapped it around her neck. "What? You think I'll trust you to ring the bell for Haywood?" She laughed, a short bark of sound that echoed through town hall. "Not on your life."

"Okay." Everett nodded, weathering her storm. "Why don't you go outside and make sure everything is going according to *your* plan."

"I will." Yolanda pushed past him, past the nearly empty tin of candy canes, past the full toy drive box. She blew out the door, slamming it behind her. She marched across the snow-spackled road and into the town square without looking back.

That's the way she'll walk out when I lay her off.

Everett's stomach turned. He hadn't realized Yolanda's future was tied up with Rosalie's.

I can't let that influence my decisions.

He glanced toward his desk and the termination paperwork, which sat next to the pet bed, where Tink was curled up, watching him.

The front door banged open, and Bitsy scrambled inside, clinging to a door carried back by the wind. Everett hurried over to help her shut it.

"You're here!" Bitsy clutched his arm. "I need you to come with me right away."

"Why? Is there an emergency?" Everett glanced across the road, gaze searching for prone bodies. "Is anyone hurt?"

"No one's hurt but it's an emergency." Bitsy grabbed his jacket off the rack and thrust it toward his chest. "Grab Tinkerbell and let's go."

Everett didn't budge. "I can't just leave. I'm the only one

here. What if someone needs something for the tree-lighting ceremony?" Unless there was arterial blood spurting, there was nothing the older woman could say to get him out of the office right now.

"If anything happens, they'll call Yolanda the same way they always do." Bitsy gave him an impatient look. "Everett Bollinger. Move it. Rosalie needs you."

There was a line out the door of Sunshine Pets.

A line of customers with pets on leashes, in crates, and in boxes, waiting to come inside.

Rosalie should have been ecstatic. The Santa Experience had struck a chord with Sunshine pet owners.

Just her luck. Santa had called in sick.

She'd enlisted the help of Paul Gregory to play Santa. She'd rented a Santa suit, including a lovely white beard, chest padding, and shiny black boots. And then twenty minutes ago, Paul had called to cancel from the emergency room. His service truck had slid into a ditch and he'd hit his head. He was fine but was being kept at the hospital on concussion watch.

The best-laid plans...

She had fifteen minutes to find Santa.

"I found him," Bitsy said breathlessly as she burst into the shop, dragging Everett behind her. "I found Santa."

"Whoa." Everett dug in his heels, despite little Tinkerbell prancing forward toward Remington. "I thought you said it was an emergency, Bitsy." He gave Rosalie a full-body visual inspection. "You look okay. Are you okay?"

"It is an emergency." Bitsy tried to tug Everett farther inside.

"A serious emergency." Rosalie rushed over to hug Everett, relaxing into the circle of his arms. "Paul canceled. Everyone in my family is at work. I need a Santa Claus."

"I'm Scrooge," Everett said gruffly.

"Not always." Rosalie drew back to look him in the eye, to smile as tenderly as that kiss they'd exchanged. "And not today."

He pressed his lips together.

Unwilling to give up, Rosalie turned him toward the windows. "Do you see that line? That's my line. My new customers. People who love their pets enough to brave the weather for a photo of their fur baby with Santa. And I achieved that line playing by your rules, Everett. Please. Say you'll be my Santa."

He heaved a sigh.

Taking that as assent, Rosalie half led, half dragged him to the back room and the Santa costume, pausing only to hand Tinkerbell's leash to Bitsy. "I know what you're thinking," she said as Everett fingered the full white beard.

"You have no idea," he murmured, staring at the costume.

"You're thinking this is a new low." She rubbed his back, which was broad and strong enough to carry the burdens of others. "You're thinking Scrooge is playing against type."

His gaze swung to hers, eyes narrowed.

Santa Claus isn't coming to town.

"But you're not Scrooge," Rosalie said a bit desperately, pointing at the Santa costume with both hands as if that proved her point. And maybe it did. Scrooge would never don Santa's suit. "What you're not seeing is what a great opportunity this is to prove it."

"You're right about the not-seeing-it part," Everett said.

The clock was ticking. Rosalie needed Everett to move, not hesitate.

"This is just like when you charmed my mother last night." Rosalie laid a hand on his arm. She liked touching him. And the good news was that he hadn't walked out.

"If you want to be understood, you need to show your true colors."

"Only I'll be wearing a fake beard." And a scowl, if his gruff tone was any indication.

"And a bowlful of jelly." Rosalie held up the chest padding and smiled as brightly as she could.

Ar-ar-ar-ooo. From the store proper, Remington sounded like he was nervous.

Tinkerbell barked once.

"Um, Rosalie?" Bitsy called through the closed door.

"*Please.*" Rosalie put all her desperation into that one word. It was either beg or begin to practice her cancellation speech.

Everett sighed. "Okay."

"Really?" She drew back, countering the urge to throw her arms around him. "Can I use your photos on my website?"

"Don't push it, Rosalie." Everett faced her squarely but his gaze landed on her lips. "Out."

She ran out before she succumbed to the impulse to kiss him.

"This was such a fun event." Wendy Adams, the elementary school secretary, had her tortoise in a box on the sales counter. She paid for her purchase, a T-shirt decorated with sea creatures that read, *Skip the straw and save the ocean.*

"Your photo will be ready for pickup tomorrow." Rosalie was sending all photographs to be printed at the pharmacy. She'd probably lie awake tonight wondering if all the files would go through. Next year, she needed to print everything in-store.

Wendy stuck her T-shirt in her hobo bag and pulled her knit cap down on her blond hair. "How in the world did you get Scrooge to play Santa?" She sneaked Everett a look over her shoulder.

"Everett is a charming gentleman," Bitsy said. She'd been a godsend, helping customers find items for their pets while Rosalie worked the register. "Just look at him with little Vivvy."

A blond toddler sat in Everett's lap, cradling a big white bunny. Mims Turner had brought the little cherub in with her rabbit and hovered nearby, grinning.

Rosalie experienced an unexpected wave of pride for Everett. "He makes a perfect Santa." She couldn't stop smiling. Not even when she caught Everett's eye. Her heart was full.

With Everett around, she wasn't alone. He had her back. He may claim to be a number-crunching, detached machine, but she knew that wasn't true. Everett had a heart. He just hadn't been given an opportunity in Sunshine to let others see what Rosalie saw. Until today.

"A man like that..." Bitsy came to stand next to Rosalie. "They don't come along often. A man like that fills the lonely corners of a widow's heart."

Rosalie murmured her agreement, ringing up another customer.

A man like Everett had a heart big enough to accept a cast-off, high-strung dog. He had the strength to talk to Rosalie about sensitive topics, like her dead husband. And for as much as folks complained that he was by the book, no one ever said he did anything shady or underhanded. He must have been crushed when his wife's crime was discovered. Everett was honorable. A great addition to the community.

A wonderful addition to my life.

Love—or its early warning system—pulsed in ever-tightening bands around her chest. Love wasn't supposed to feel constrictive and tense. Love for Marty had been a light-hearted, soaring feeling.

Rosalie glanced at Everett once more. He was leaning

forward to mug for the camera next to a chocolate Labrador's happy face.

He'd said he wasn't staying in Sunshine. He'd said that once the budget issues were resolved he'd move on. He had bigger dreams than she did, bigger desires when it came to material possessions. Was that the source of her tension?

Rosalie stared across the store. Everett sat alone.

It seemed like, almost in the blink of an eye, everyone had left to go to the tree-lighting ceremony. The store was nearly empty. No one else was in line. Everett disappeared into the stock room, presumably to change.

"He's really nice," Bitsy emphasized again. "One of a kind."

"Has my mother been talking to you?" Rosalie shook her head. Love continued to hug her chest as if afraid to let go. She drew a deep breath.

Don't let me fall for a man who isn't planning to stay in Sunshine.

Bitsy studied her closely. "I've been married and widowed three times. I think it's okay to open up your heart to ideas and possibilities. And love."

"You've definitely been talking to my mother." Rosalie rung up the last of her customers.

Tinkerbell trotted over to the supply room door. Remy joined her. They both sat down, waiting. Bitsy rearranged the remaining ornaments on the Christmas tree while Rosalie straightened up endcaps and displays.

A short time later, Everett appeared, his hair askew. He picked up Tinkerbell and snapped on her leash. "Ladies, we need to hurry, or we're going to miss the tree-lighting ceremony."

"Oh, I almost forgot." Bitsy bundled up and gathered her things. "I've got hot chocolate to sell."

Rosalie couldn't move, not even to hand Everett his dog's booties.

"Aren't you coming?" Bitsy turned, pausing at the door.

"We'll be along," Everett told her, a smile building on his handsome face as he looked at Rosalie.

A smile.

The man had been barked at, shed over, and drooled upon. He wasn't Scrooge. He was Santa on vacation—good-natured and joyful. She'd bet he was determined to hide his softer side. But she'd seen it more than once. And now it was on full display.

The tension around Rosalie's chest dissipated into a flurry of heartbeats.

Everett walked toward her, Tinkerbell in his arms. Remy fell into step beside him.

Two sweet dogs and one lovable man.

We could be a family.

Over the store's speakers, the least romantic carol played: "I Want a Hippopotamus for Christmas."

Rosalie didn't care that there weren't flowers, love songs, or candlelight. Nothing could ruin this moment. She was in love, and the world was full of laughter and sunshine. Finally, finally, finally. The something she was missing was here. The world seemed brighter and in sharper focus.

Everett set Tinkerbell down when he was a few feet away from Rosalie. "Your customers were happy?"

"Yes," she breathed, unable to move when more than anything she wanted to step forward and be loved by him.

Everett came and put his arms around her. "And were you happy?" A question spoken in a low, intimate voice.

"Not as happy as I am now," Rosalie said as his lips lowered to hers and she opened her heart to possibilities.

They didn't make the tree-lighting ceremony on time.

They didn't care.

Chapter Eight

Are those the numbers?" Kevin shut his laptop and sat up in his chair.

Despite it being late and no one else being in the office, Everett closed the door behind him. "Yes." He handed Kevin the budget.

Just a few hours ago, the tree-lighting ceremony had been a success—not that there'd been any doubt. The only thing different this year was the bell-ringing by Yolanda after Haywood's proposal.

When the bell had rung, Rosalie had flung her arms around Everett and kissed him. He'd almost walked over and given Haywood fifty dollars. Because in that moment in her arms, he'd forgotten responsibilities and hard choices ahead. There had only been Rosalie and her outpouring of affection.

Kevin stared at Everett, not at the pages. "How'd we do?"

"It's not enough." Everett had run the numbers backward and forward. He'd reduced seasonal employment and scaled down next year's tree-lighting ceremony. "You know what we need to do."

Kevin's expression hardened. "My father never laid anyone off."

"No offense, but..." Everett leaned forward, hoping his words would sink in. "Your father is the main reason the town is in this mess." Him and that warehouse.

"It was a gamble," Kevin said defensively. "A risk taken in good faith." In his eyes, his father could do no wrong.

Will he feel the same way when I lay off Yolanda?

Will Rosalie?

Everett's stomach clenched. "We could still land some federal money." To refurbish the warehouse. "But only if the budget is balanced by January first." A long shot. "I've pitched the warehouse to development companies across the state." And heard crickets in response. "I've reached out to Greeley." The town closest to them. "If we let go of a fireman, a deputy, and someone at town hall"—they both knew the latter was Yolanda—"they're open to being our backup emergency service." If Sunshine's short-staffed emergency-services crew couldn't handle the workload. "But we'll pay a premium." Still, it'd be less than paying salaries and benefits.

Kevin stared at the proposed budget. "There's got to be another way."

"Besides cutting staff and reducing pensions?" Everett shook his head.

"It's Christmas." Kevin raised his gaze to Everett's, blue eyes haunted. "We can't do this to people at Christmas."

"You could find someone famous to buy the town." And when had that ever worked? Never. "That was a joke." Everett sighed. "It's probably not the right time for jokes."

"No, it's not." Kevin handed the budget back. "I can't give you the go-ahead right now. I need a few more days." Kevin was hoping for a Christmas miracle.

Everett was fairly certain that wasn't going to happen. He let the reality of the situation settle between them. "Look, Kevin, I know the last thing you want to do is disappoint people in this town. But…you hired me to be your gunslinger." To take the heat for the tough decisions that needed to be made. "We have to make more cuts. People who lose their jobs will rebound. The town will rebound. By the time the next election rolls around, no one will remember the layoffs."

But Everett wouldn't be around to see it.

No. He'd be working in another town, one with bigger problems and a bigger salary for its town manager. Someplace where he wouldn't walk his dog next to a pretty woman. Someplace where he wouldn't be called Scrooge and think of it as an endearment.

The week after the tree-lighting ceremony was a blur for Rosalie.

There were walks with Everett before and after work. Softly exchanged words and long, slow kisses. Rosalie invited him to her house for dinner. He politely declined, claiming he had a lot of work to do. She invited him for breakfast at the bakery. He politely declined, same reason. She invited him to join her on the dog walk through Sunshine's Christmas Tree Lane. He hedged. Rosalie refused to be discouraged. It was a busy time for him. Love could be patient and so could Rosalie.

"Where's Everett?" Kimmy didn't have a dog but she'd agreed to lead the pack for the evening dog walk with Remy.

"He said he probably wouldn't make it." If not for their twice daily walks, Rosalie would've thought Everett was giving her the brush-off.

She couldn't worry about Everett. There were at least thirty pet owners milling about on Garden Court. It was seven o'clock. Time to organize the group into a line to walk the neighborhood and admire the Christmas displays.

"Okay, everyone stay on the sidewalk and follow the Saint Bernard," Rosalie said when she had some semblance of a line formed.

Yap-yap-yap.

Everyone turned.

"It's Santa!" someone said, inspiring holiday greetings from others for Everett.

He waved, moving to join Rosalie at the end of the line with a small smile.

Rosalie gave Kimmy permission to start before turning to Everett. "Thank you for coming."

There was a furrow in his brow as if he'd had a rough day at work. "Tink needed a walk."

"And you did too, I bet." She linked her arm through his.

Everett slanted her a glance, expression lightening. "And I wanted to see you."

Her heart soared. This is what she'd been waiting for, a sign that she meant something to him. "Most people are here to take in the holiday lights with their fur babies."

"Merry Christmas and all that," Everett said flatly, the crease returning to his brow.

"Merry Christmas and all that," Rosalie repeated. Whatever problem he was facing, she knew he'd find a way to work things through to everyone's satisfaction. Rosalie stretched on her toes to kiss his cheek.

"What was that for?" Everett slowed as they approached the rest of the crowd, who'd bottlenecked to admire a yard with a *Star Wars*–themed holiday display.

"A kiss for luck." Rosalie snuggled closer. "You'll make the right choice. You always do."

He frowned. "The town council approved the parade ending on Sunny Avenue."

"Really? That's wonderful." And just in the nick of time. The parade was in a few days.

Everett walked in silence, accompanied by his frown and his furrow.

"Is there a problem?" Rosalie asked, unable to shake the

belief that they'd be closer if Everett would just open up to her about his concerns and his feelings.

"No. I'm just trying to figure out some work stuff." Everett patted her hand, finding the hole in her mitten.

That simple touch. It reassured. There was more here than heated kisses.

But nothing she said for the rest of the walk seemed to change his mood.

The day of the Christmas parade dawned sunny and bright.

Rosalie's holiday inventory was running low. And like any good retailer, she'd restocked with merchandise for the next holiday—Valentine's Day.

Aunt Yolanda had come by, making noises about needing an early dividend to make car repairs but backing off when Rosalie asked her how much she needed. She'd given Rosalie's new merchandise a frown.

Kimmy showed up to help Rosalie, in case there was a rush after the parade. She'd brought her three-legged kitten, Skippy, and immediately purchased a collar decorated with Valentine hearts and a set of Christmas-themed cat toys.

The Widows Club board entered the store with Mims's adorable granddaughter, Vivvy. Bitsy waved, and then the group drifted over to the live pet display, which Eileen had restocked with roly-poly puppies and a pair of brown furry guinea pigs. Vivvy and Mims were singing "Must Be Santa," flinging lines at each other as if they were in a rap battle.

"I think you and Everett make a cute couple." Kimmy sat on a stool behind the register with Skippy in her lap.

"Are you still blue about Haywood?" It seemed better to change the subject to a man her sister had always been sweet on than to talk about Everett and a future together. He'd kept Rosalie at arm's length all week long.

"Haywood was my childhood crush." Kimmy cuddled Skippy. "And Ariana was his."

"But you dated him—"

"One time," Kimmy said briskly. "Don't make it more than it is. They're engaged. Now about Everett..."

"Don't make it more than it is." Rosalie's heart panged. Nothing seemed right between them, not even their walks.

People were congregating on the sidewalks of Sunny Avenue. The high school band was scheduled to bring up the rear of the parade and perform one last song in front of Rosalie's shop. It was perfect for business but Rosalie couldn't enjoy it.

"I asked Haywood to look for a space for me to open my own sandwich shop." Kimmy stared out the window, gnawing on her lip. "I figured if you could open a store, then I could go out on my own too."

"Oh, Kimmy." Rosalie hugged her sister. "What a fabulous idea."

"You don't think I'll fail?" Kimmy's normal smile was conspicuously absent.

Rosalie was quick to encourage her sister. "I think your gourmet sandwiches are going to be the talk of the town."

"Look, Gammy!" Vivvy pointed out the window. "It's my parade."

"Life is too short." Rosalie hugged Kimmy again. "Don't let the parade pass you by."

Chapter Nine

The Christmas parade was a huge success.

Rerouting the gala to end on Sunny Avenue reduced the amount of congestion on the streets and sidewalks.

Afterward, Everett requested a group of people meet at the town hall. He couldn't put off what had to be done any longer and neither could Kevin.

Sheriff Drew Taylor arrived first. Shortly afterward, the fire chief showed up. And finally, Kevin and Yolanda joined them in the conference room.

Everett left the front office open since many residents had told him they'd be dropping off toys for the toy drive. He took a seat against the wall, intending to let Kevin deliver the bad news.

"First off…" Kevin looked about as comfortable as a chicken trapped in a coop with a fox. "Thank you all for coming. We wanted to use this time to brief you on our progress in balancing the budget in time for federal funding consideration."

Everyone nodded. They all knew about the budget crisis.

"We've come to a point where some hard decisions have to be made." Kevin met the gaze of each person in the room. His smile was the perfect balance of compassion and regret. "We're going to have to cut the budgets for emergency services and—"

"Hang on." Sheriff Taylor's back stiffened. "You want to cut public safety?"

Kevin's expression didn't change. "Yes, and—"

"Is that wise?" the fire chief asked, just as angry as the sheriff. "Shouldn't you be cutting nonessential services?"

Kevin nodded mutely. His gaze came to rest on Yolanda, and he paled.

Silence stretched through the room. Kevin let it linger too long.

Everett stood. "What the mayor is trying to say is that if a miracle doesn't occur by December thirty-first, we will have to lay off someone from the sheriff's office, someone from fire services, and someone from nonessential services here at the town hall."

"You mean me?" Yolanda said in a small voice. She stared at Everett, not Kevin.

"We mean you," Everett said in an equally small voice. "I'm sorry." Despite his best intentions, he'd grown fond of the prickly woman.

Something fell to the floor in the lobby.

Everett stepped out of the conference room, leaving further questions to the mayor.

"I…oh…" Standing next to the Christmas tree, Rosalie picked up the set of toy dishes she'd dropped. "I'm sorry. I didn't mean to eavesdrop." She stared at the dishes and then set them near the overflowing toy drive box.

He'd just let her aunt, her investor, know she might lose her job. She couldn't brush this off the way she brushed off everything else he'd done in town.

Everett moved closer, waiting to hear Rosalie's opinion of him, prepared for the worst.

"So this is what you've been working on?" She stared at the floor. "What you've been stressing over? A plan to fire people?"

"We've been trying *not* to fire people."

It was as if she didn't hear him. "This kind of thing

doesn't happen in Sunshine. We hire our friends and neighbors. We don't let them go, especially not at Christmas." Finally, her gaze came up to meet his. "Your job is done. You're leaving. You came here to do this horrible thing, and now...and now it's over and you're leaving."

"Yes." He could stay another six months per his contract. But if Rosalie stopped talking to him, stopped looking at him like he hung the moon, and stopped kissing him...he'd just as soon leave.

"But you and I..." She gestured back and forth between them. "I've been defending you and your reputation. And all this time..." The blood had drained from her face. "You really are Scrooge."

She whirled and rushed out the door.

"Rosalie, wait." Everett grabbed his coat and followed her, leaving Tinkerbell behind.

Rosalie didn't wait. She walked away with a gait just short of a run. "If my aunt can't find a job, I'll have to cash her out. This changes everything. And you knew. You knew it was coming at me head-on."

"I couldn't tell you." He reached her side, dodging holiday shoppers.

"I ordered specialty products through Easter." She pulled her knit cap around her ears as if she didn't want to hear him. "And I'm a horrible person for thinking about myself when my aunt just lost her job."

"Technically, we have ten days to save her job." Snow and salt crunched beneath his feet as they crossed a street.

"I wish...I wish...I wish I could find the words to express how disappointed I am." Her big brown eyes were shadowed with sadness.

"If I've given you the wrong impression..." Everett couldn't finish that thought. He'd given himself the wrong impression. It was time to come clean. "I'm forty. I'm rebuilding my career. I don't know where I'll be next year."

From down the street, Bitsy wished them a Merry Christmas.

Rosalie returned the greeting. And then she rounded the corner and shifted back into quick-step mode. They had reached the end of the block before she spoke again.

"You never say it to anyone." Rosalie turned and stayed him with a gloved hand on his chest. Her pink skin was apparent through the ever-widening hole in her red mitten. "You never tell people Merry Christmas."

"I'm not feeling very merry," he said in a gruff voice. Truthfully, he hadn't in years. He resisted the urge to draw her into his arms and forget about budgets and layoffs, knowing his touch would be unwelcome.

"Did you ever say Happy Thanksgiving?" Rosalie's hand moved over his heart.

I hope I have a heart when this is over.

"Rosalie..."

"I'm not sure what's been going on between us." She drew back, taking her hand and her warmth with her. "There was...We were..." She raised tear-filled eyes. "I thought I loved you."

Loved. Past tense. If it was...If it had been...His heart seemed to shrivel in his chest.

In the distance, Christmas music played. People's voices and laughter drifted on the air.

"Rosalie..." Everett couldn't seem to string a sentence together. He didn't know how to react. What to say. What to wish for.

When he didn't say anything, she resumed walking, crossing her arms over her chest. "I knew we were different in some ways, but I thought you were the kind of person who'd do anything to protect people and their jobs." She choked on what sounded like a sob. "I was wrong. So don't worry about disappointing me by keeping your feelings to yourself. I don't want to hear them."

Feelings? That was the trouble. When Everett was with Rosalie, he felt too much. He felt happy and hopeful. He felt like he belonged in Sunshine and that could never be the case. He was a hatchet man. People who didn't already hate him were going to hate him as soon as word of the layoffs got out.

"It's okay," Rosalie said softly, walking a few steps ahead. "You may not love me but you gave me something I haven't had since Marty died. I can see my future. I couldn't see it before. Things were in the way. Anger. Grief." She waved her hands as if waving them aside. "The future was all so tenuous and uncertain. And then you bought me a cup of hot chocolate."

Now wasn't the time to admit he hadn't been that generous.

"Rosalie." Panic. It trilled through his veins. He didn't want to lose her. "Rosalie, slow down."

"I can't." She marched ahead. "For the first time in a long time, things are turning around for me. And no matter what happens when I go around that corner toward home..." She stopped suddenly, and her voice turned cold as she faced him. "You won't be with me."

"Rosalie."

"Everett!" Down the block, the front door of Rosalie's childhood home swung open, and her mother leaned out. "We're having tamales tonight. Come inside. You look like you haven't had a good meal since Spam tacos."

The wind gusted, and Everett felt as if he might blow away.

"All your plans. All your numbers." Rosalie backed away. "And you didn't plan for me. You didn't see..."

Rosalie was right. He hadn't figured falling in love in his plans.

"And now…" Rosalie swallowed thickly. "All my plans won't include you."

"Everett is such a jerk." Kimmy sat in the corner of the couch in the apartment they shared above their parents' garage. "Firing Aunt Yolanda? She runs that place. I don't know how you could fall for him."

"Hey, don't judge." Rosalie took a love letter from Marty out of a small cedar chest. She'd found the letter in his bureau after he died. "I didn't question why you fell in love with Skippy."

Kimmy dangled a cat toy over the kitten's belly. "Skippy's never going to mastermind dastardly deeds like Everett did in this town."

"You know it's not like that." Rosalie unfolded the worn paper. It was becoming fragile from being read so frequently. "He was hired to do a job."

On the floor next to her, Remy rolled onto his back with a mild grumble.

"Yeah, well, if you'd been working at the town hall, he'd have fired you."

"Yes."

Kimmy stopped playing with her kitten. "And you're okay with that?"

I am so not okay.

"Don't judge my attempt at adulting." Rosalie smoothed the love letter on her leg. "I'm a business owner trying to see what's good for the town. But you know I hate that he gave Aunt Yolanda the ax." She'd told her aunt she was canceling her spring merchandise orders, which would free up cash in case she was let go. "Am I upset with Everett? Yes."

"That's my girl." Kimmy went back to her cat-toy game. Rosalie turned her attention to Marty's letter.

My darling Rosalie,

If you're reading this, I'm gone. And for that alone, I want to apologize. My job requires me to protect and serve. And if you're reading this, I've had a truly bad day, and I ache for putting you through it.

I can imagine you sitting down and reading this. I can hear your voice in my head, telling me I should have been more careful. I can hear your grief and your anger and your words—you've always been good at tossing words. Kind words. Loving words. And yes, angry words.

It's okay. You can be angry with me. If I'm gone, it's because I was doing something I believe in and because bad stuff sometimes happens to good people. Be angry. It will give you a reason to go on until the anger fades.

I know it may take time, but I want you to remember how much I love you. I want you to remember how important we felt it was to live a life looking outward, helping to spread love and kindness in small and big ways. Take time to grieve, love, but then look around and know that it's okay to reimagine your life. Our jobs take a toll. It's okay to move on, to find another way to touch people's hearts. To live again. To love again, even if you have to fight for it. Even if a good man has to fight for you.

Try new things. Live in new places. Cut that hair you love so much. Take a risk. Reach for a new dream. You won't be alone. I will always have your back.

When you look up at the stars, know that I'm the brightest one shining back on you.

I won't be home tonight but I can keep this one vow, the promise I made you on our wedding day. I will love you to the end of time.

All my love, Marty.

"You shouldn't read that letter so much." Kimmy handed Rosalie a tissue.

"I'm going to read this letter until it disintegrates in my hands." Rosalie wiped her eyes. "And do you know why? Because it reminds me that I loved a good man. And that when I fall in love again, it should only be with another good man. Someone Marty would approve of."

And that man wasn't Everett Bollinger.

"How'd it go?" Everett stood in the doorway to Kevin's office.

Kevin was slumped in his chair with Tink in his lap, his gaze attached to a spot on the wall. "About as well as you'd expect. Rationally, they get it. Emotionally, you and I are the Antichrist."

Everett thrust his hands in his jacket pockets and tried not to remember the look on Rosalie's face when she told him they were through.

"We were so close." Kevin blew out a breath. "You brought the debt down from a couple million to a couple hundred thousand."

"I didn't want it to end like this." Not for Yolanda and the others. Not for the town. Not for Rosalie.

"I know."

"You can blame me." That was what he paid Everett for.

"I know." Kevin swung his head around to look at Everett. "But I won't. The buck stops here."

"If only we could have sold that warehouse." If only they'd had more time. "I can't do anything more for you. Consider this my two weeks' notice."

They both fell silent. Tink stared at Everett as if awaiting a command.

Everett rolled his shoulders, trying to ease the ache that extended throughout his chest, knowing that ache originated in his heart. "If I had the money, I'd have bought the warehouse. Rosalie thought it would make a great set of loft apartments over retail and restaurant space, instead of another small mall."

Kevin sat up. "What a brilliant idea."

"Lofts?" Everett blinked at him.

"No. You. Investing." Kevin put Tink on the floor and reached for a pad of paper. "We contacted developers but we didn't think to organize our own group of investors to—"

"Buy and renovate the warehouse into income-generating space." Everett drew a deep breath as the idea took shape. "We could recruit investors, maybe even offer different levels of financial participation."

"People invest in civic works all the time." Kevin scribbled names on his pad. "We'll need a couple of big investors. But we should let folks buy in at affordable amounts."

"They'll feel good about saving the town and their friends' jobs." Everett picked up his dog and held her close. "But we've only got ten days." Less if you counted the holidays.

Kevin raised his head. "Are you the same guy who worked budget miracles in six months? How hard can forming an investment group be?"

"Hard, not impossible. But hard." Everett latched on to

his boss's enthusiasm. "We'll need a renovation budget and projected rents."

"Luckily, we're on good terms with a Realtor by the name of Haywood, who probably knows a few good contractors."

Everett grinned.

"Well?" Kevin asked. "What are you waiting for? The clock is ticking."

"Right." Everett hurried downstairs with Tinkerbell.

If he could work some Christmas budget magic, he could save a few jobs. And it was a long shot, but maybe he could stay in Sunshine and salvage things with Rosalie. Permanently.

Chapter Ten

The emergency meeting of Sunshine's town council was held on the afternoon of Christmas Eve in the high school gym.

They'd needed a venue large enough to fit everyone who wanted to attend. And everyone wanted to attend. Even Rosalie.

Everett had seen her come in with her family. When the meeting started, he sat next to Yolanda in the front row, holding her hand while Kevin explained how important it was to invest in Sunshine and fielded questions. Yolanda had helped pull things together, both for the warehouse and for a special project of Everett's. They were in this together.

Kevin being Kevin, he wore an expensive suit and his professional smile. If he'd chosen to go into car sales instead of politics, he'd probably have owned a chain of dealerships by now. "Before we make contracts available to those interested in investing, I'd like to turn over the floor to our town manager, Everett Bollinger."

The audience booed.

"Pay no attention to the peanut gallery." Yolanda stood with Everett and gave him a hug. "I've spent over half my life working for this town. You, my dear Ebenezer, are one of the good ones. If my job is saved, I have you to thank. May both of our Christmas wishes come true."

"Thanks for helping me prepare for this." Everett kissed her cheek and whispered, "How about I get up on that stage and do something everyone will remember later?"

"Go slay." Yolanda grinned.

Everett climbed the steps to the stage and took the microphone. He straightened his glasses and surveyed the crowd until he found Rosalie sitting between her mother and her sister. They'd come wearing matching scowls.

"Ladies and gentlemen." Everett tugged down the ends of his ugly Christmas sweater. Yolanda had helped him pick it out. It was purple with a Christmas tree strung with flashing lights. "Before we begin, I'd like to wish everyone a very Merry Christmas."

Rosalie's eyes widened, and the crowd quieted.

"When I was hired to help Kevin and his staff get the budget back in line, I'd never heard of Sunshine, Colorado. I came here..." He'd toyed with glossing over this part but in for a penny..."I came here. Age forty." He ran a hand through his hair. "I earned every one of these gray beauties working in six different cities, doing exactly what you hired me to do here. But all my experience only prepared me for the financial challenges. It didn't prepare me for the challenges of the heart." Everett tapped his chest, sending the star at the top of the tree glittering.

He may have been onstage but he spoke directly to Rosalie. The shadows were back beneath her eyes. He had himself to blame.

"I wasn't prepared for the close-knit community of Sunshine. For the extended families and friends who make up modern-day families." He cleared his throat. He'd considered skipping this next part too. "Most of you know my ex-wife is a convicted felon. Many of you probably know I was the one who uncovered the way she was cooking the books. The day I confronted her...the day I had to turn her in to the police...I thought that was the most heartbreaking day of my life. I loved her. But by abiding by the law, I learned my wife didn't love me as much as she did money. Anyone's money."

The audience shifted, whispering, judging.

Everett didn't care. He still only had eyes for Rosalie. "When I arrived in town, I was still reeling. It was nearly two years later, but I hadn't rediscovered a way to trust my fellow man. So when I showed up in town with my fancy ties and my shiny shoes"—he'd heard people whispering to Yolanda about that—"I didn't care, because I hadn't come here to make friends. Or to find true love."

There was more whispering and perhaps less judging. Nothing pleased a crowd like a teaser. And he'd mentioned the L-word.

"Despite that, a few of you won my respect, like Kevin. And a few of you earned my trust, like Yolanda. And one woman won my jaded, guarded heart." Everett pointed toward that woman. "Rosalie."

The crowd murmur rose to a soft roar. People turned in their seats, looking for the object of his affection.

"She's pretty spectacular," Everett said. "Her store is awesome, and the idea to turn the warehouse into mixed-use space was hers."

This news created a smattering of applause.

"But…" Everett had to raise his voice to be heard, even with the microphone. "But before our love could even get off the ground, we announced the possibility of layoffs."

And they were back to boos.

"Hang with me on this, folks." Everett caught Rosalie's eye. "Because as much as Rosalie and I are different, as much as we've discussed our careers are on different paths, they're not." He lowered his voice, imagining Rosalie was standing next to him, not sitting half a gymnasium away. "We were both raised to make do but lately that feels more like we're just getting by.

Honey, you think I need a big house and a fancy car. I don't. Not as much as I need you. I've put money down on one of the lofts in the warehouse. You think I need the prestige of working for a big city from inside a corporate office? Not as much as I need you, babe. I want to work toward a future with you in Sunshine. And since I've accepted a permanent position as town manager, I'm not going anywhere except on long walks with the woman I love and our two dogs."

Rosalie gave him that warm smile he loved so much. She stood and made her way to the aisle while Everett made his way down the stairs and to her side.

He dropped down on one knee. The crowd was silent now.

"Rosalie." Everett snapped open a blue velvet jewelry box containing a ring Yolanda had helped him pick out. It was big enough to be noticed and small enough to lack ostentation. "I love you. I love the way you saw the good in me and the way you think about the happiness and welfare of others. I love the way you consider pets part of the family. I love that you're brimming with ideas and that you're not shy about telling me what you've come up with. But most of all, I love that you found a place in your heart for me." And by the look of things, despite her words the other night, he still had a place there. "Can you find it in your heart to forgive me?"

"Yes," said her sister, Kimmy, earning a shushing from everyone around them.

Rosalie's warm hands closed around his, closing the ring box. She drew him to his feet. She didn't smile. She didn't speak. She simply stared into his eyes.

Kimmy chuckled.

Nerves had Everett talking. "You know what season it is, don't you, honey?"

"Christmas?" A hint of a smile flashed past her lips before disappearing.

"The season of love and forgiveness." He was in desperate need of both. "I don't want there to be secrets between us. The Widows Club bought you that cup of hot chocolate, not me. But I've regretted not buying it every day since. Can you forgive me? Enough to marry me?"

"Yes," Rosalie said simply, although he'd asked so many questions it wasn't clear what she was agreeing to.

"Yes, you'll marry him?" her father asked before Everett could.

"Or yes, it's the season of love and forgiveness?" her mother asked, hot on her husband's heels.

"She didn't even look at the ring," Kimmy said, laughing. "How can she say yes to anything?"

"I don't need to see the ring." Rosalie hadn't broken Everett's gaze. "Yes. Yes to everything," she said. "As long as my Scrooge says he'll be my Santa too."

"I'll be your anything, love." Everett's arms came around her. His Christmas wish was coming true. "And I'll be your always."

"That's all a girl can ask for." Rosalie kissed him, long and slow.

The meeting went on without them. Two ranchers, Tom Bodine and a man Everett didn't recognize, invested heavily. Enough other residents put up money to make Yolanda's Christmas wish come true.

Later, Kevin announced their financial goals had been met and Sunshine was saved. No layoffs would be made.

All in all, it was a great Christmas. Everett got everything he wanted—love, forgiveness, and a balanced budget.

About the Author

Melinda Curtis is the *USA Today* bestselling author of light-hearted contemporary romance. In addition to her Sunshine Valley series from Forever Romance, she's published independently and with Harlequin Heartwarming, including her book *Dandelion Wishes*, which was made into a TV movie entitled *Love in Harmony Valley*. She lives in Oregon's lush Willamette Valley with her husband—her basketball-playing college sweetheart. While raising three kids, the couple did the soccer thing, the karate thing, the dance thing, the Little League thing, and, of course, the basketball thing. Now when Melinda isn't writing and Mr. Curtis isn't watching college basketball, they do the DIY thing.

You can learn more at:

Website: MelindaCurtis.net
Twitter: @MelCurtisAuthor
Facebook.com/MelindaCurtisAuthor
Instagram: @MelCurtisAuthor
Pinterest.com/MelCurtisAuthor

*For more from Melinda Curtis,
check out the rest of the
Sunshine Valley series!*

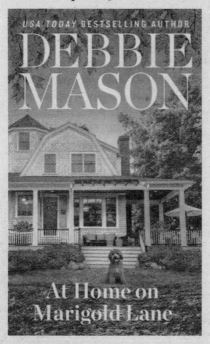

AT HOME ON MARIGOLD LANE
by Debbie Mason

For family and marriage therapist Brianna MacLeod, moving back home to Highland Falls after a disastrous divorce feels downright embarrassing. Bri blames herself for missing the red flags in her relationship and thus worries she's no longer qualified to do the job she loves. But helping others is second nature to Bri, and she soon finds herself counseling her roommate and her neighbor's daughter. Bri just wasn't expecting them to reunite her with her first love . . .

THE BEACHSIDE BED AND BREAKFAST
by Hope Ramsay

Ashley Howland Scott has no time for romance as she grieves the loss of her husband, cares for her young son, and runs Magnolia Harbor's only bed and breakfast. Ashley never imagined she'd notice—let alone have feelings for—another man after her husband was killed in Afghanistan. But slowly, softly, Rev. Micah St. Pierre has become a friend...and now maybe something more. Which is all the more reason to steer clear of him.

RETURN TO CHERRY BLOSSOM WAY
by Jeannie Chin

Han Leung always does the responsible thing, which is why he put aside his dreams of opening his own restaurant to run his family's business in Blue Cedar Falls, North Carolina. But when May Wu re-enters his life, he can no longer ignore his own wants and desires. Garden gnomes are stolen, old haunts are visited, and sparks fly between the pair, just as they always have. Han and May broke up because they wanted vastly different lives, and that hasn't changed—or has it?

THE CHRISTMAS VILLAGE
by Annie Rains
As the competition heats up in the Merriest Lawn decorating contest, Lucy Hannigan can't help feeling like a Scrooge. Her mom had won the contest every year, but Lucy isn't sure she has it in her to deck the halls this first Christmas without her mother. But when Miles Bruno, her ex-fiancé, shows up with tons of tinsel, dozens of decorations, and lots and lots of lights, Lucy begins to wonder if maybe the spirit of the season can finally mend her broken heart.

DREAMING OF A HEART LAKE CHRISTMAS
by Sarah Robinson
To raise enough money to start her own business, Nola Bennett needs to sell "the Castle," her beloved grandmother's historic house, and get back to the city. But Heart Lake's most eligible bachelor, Tanner Dean, rudely objects. He may be the hottest, grumpiest man she's ever met, and Nola has no time to pine over her high school crush. But sizzling attraction flares the more time he spends convincing her the potential buyers are greedy developers. Will Nora finally realize that this is exactly where she belongs?

Discover bonus content and more on
read-forever.com

SUGARPLUM WAY
by Debbie Mason
Aidan's only priority is to be the best single dad ever, and this year he plans to make the holidays magical for his young daughter. But visions of stolen kisses under the mistletoe keep dancing in his head, and when he finds out Julia Landon has written him into her latest novel, he can't help imagining a future together. Little does he know that Julia has been keeping a secret that threatens all their dreams. Luckily, 'tis the season for a little Christmas magic.

A LITTLE BIT OF LUCK
(2-IN-1 EDITION)
by Jill Shalvis
Enjoy a visit to Lucky Harbor in these two dazzling novels! In *It Had to Be You*, a woman's only shot at clearing her tarnished name is with the help of a sexy police detective. Is the chemistry between them a sizzling fling...or the start of something bigger? In *Always on My Mind*, a little white lie pulls two longtime friends into a fake relationship. But pretending to be hot and heavy starts bringing out feelings for each other that are all too real.

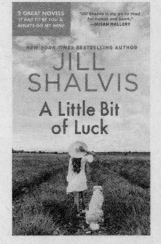